All talk around the wide green-baize covered circular table ceased. The Comanche loomed over the other delegates, his deep brown face solemn with the racial memories of innumerable, wars and slaughters. "The problem is war," Red Eagle told them. "Create a peacekeeping force that will prevent war. No nation need disarm. Whatever goes on within the nation's borders will be of no concern to the peacekeepers. The peacekeepers' sole function will be to prevent attacks — nuclear or conventional — across international borders." The force of Red Eagle's personality greatly multiplied the sheer power of his ideas. Slowly, grudgingly, the conference delegates came to accept the notion that an international peacekeeping force could be created.

It might even work.

BEN BOVA

PEACEKEEPERS

TOR®

A TOM DOHERTY ASSOCIATES BOOK
NEW YORK

PEACEKEEPERS

A TOR Book
Published by Tom Doherty Associates, Inc.
49 West 24 Street
New York, NY 10010

Cover design by Carol Russo

ISBN: 0-812-50238-8   Can. ISBN: 0-812-50241-8

Library of Congress Catalog Card Number: 87-51399

First edition: August 1988
First mass market edition: September 1989

10 9 8 7 6 5 4 3 2 1

To Tom Doherty
A faithful friend is the medicine of life

And they shall beat their swords into plowshares, and their spears into pruninghooks: nation shall not lift up sword against nation, neither shall they learn war any more.

—Isaiah, 2:4

Quis custodiet ipsos custodes?

—Juvenal

How the past perishes is how the future becomes.

—Alfred North Whitehead

PEACEKEEPERS

ORIGINS:
Year 12

THEY'VE appointed me the archivist. My task is to write the official history of the International Peacekeeping Force. I'm doing that, but what happened this morning convinced me that I should also put down this *un*official narrative, these personal recollections, these tales and anecdotes that are the story behind the Peacekeepers.

A true chronicle of something as important as the Peacekeepers doesn't start at one single point. It can't. It's impossible to say, "The history begins *here* and not *there*."

Especially when the account involves so many people, so many events as do the origins of the Peacekeepers. Literally millions of strands of individual lives are woven together under the hand of fate to form an intricate, delicate tapestry. (I like that! "Woven together under the hand of fate." I'll have to work that into the official history somehow.) Anyway, it's literally impossible to select a definite, specific time and place for the origin of the IPF. Easier to pinpoint the fall of the first drop of rain in a summer storm, or the exact moment when a youth becomes a man.

There were many origins for the Peacekeepers, and how I'm going to select a starting point for the official history is a problem that I'll be tussling with for some time to come. But I know where to start this unofficial chronicle: with this morning's events.

VALLEDUPAR: Year 12

THEY assembled in mottled green jungle fatigues with full webbing and helmets, grumbling and muttering as the slanting golden rays of the morning sun filtered through the trees. I watched them from the window of the office that the local commandant had loaned me. They were so young! Twenty-four men and women, hardly out of their teens, each of them bearing replicas of the flags of their nations on the left shoulders of their fatigues. No two flags were alike.

None of the youngsters out there on the parade ground knew it, but the reason for this morning's exercise was me. We were all going to take a little hike into the mountains for the edification of the official IPF archivist.

It was no earlier than they usually assembled for field training, or so I was told. But this morning they all seemed to know that something special was in the air. No one had told them; but like soldiers of every age, they sensed that today would be different.

The master sergeant, face of granite and eyes of flint, snarled them to attention. Twenty-four men and women snapped to. The sergeant inspected them briefly but thoroughly, his normal ferocious scowl even darker than usual. Satisfied that his charges met his uncompromising standards, he saluted to the shavetail lieutenant and reported the squad ready for duty.

The shavetail marched stiffly to the geodesic dome of the administration building, where I stood by my window watching. For long minutes the squad stood in rigid silence while the sun climbed above the lofty shade trees and began broiling the parade ground. The monkeys chattered and jeered at the cadets from the safety of their leafy perches.

A single knock on the flimsy door of the office. I turned as the shavetail opened it and said crisply, "Sir, Director-General Hazard is ready to inspect the squad."

I nodded and reached for my cap with my prosthetic hand. The shavetail stared at it for a moment, realized what he was doing and turned his eyes away. The hand works fine, and I have even grown accustomed to its feel. Marvelous how they were able to link its electronic circuits to what's left of the nerves in my arm.

I had met Hazard twice before, and he greeted me kindly, shaking my hand without the slightest indication that it bothered him. But he seemed preoccupied, his mind elsewhere, his eyes clouded with apprehension. I realized that his thoughts were projecting simultaneously forward into the future and back into the past: to the destination of this day's little trek and to the reason for its existence. I felt sorry for Hazard; this would be a difficult day for the man.

Six of us officers, in our dress uniforms of sky-blue with gold piping, assembled in the administration building's lobby and finally took the plunge into the jungle heat outside. We fell into a natural formation: Hazard and the major in charge of this training base in front, two captains behind them, and the shavetail and I bringing up the rear.

Hazard had grown a beard since I'd last seen him: iron-gray and cut almost as severely as the military crop on his pate. I couldn't help musing that he kept the beard short enough so that everyone could see the diamond-cluster insignia of the IPF director-general on his high choker collar.

He inspected the squad casually; none of the fierce glower of the master sergeant. His bearded face looked fatherly, almost benign. Then he took up a position precisely at the front center of the squad and ordered them to parade rest. I was already sweating, and I saw that the faces of the cadets were glistening.

"Officer candidates of the International Peacekeeping Force," Hazard addressed them. His voice was rough, rasping, like someone who has a bad cold or worse. It made me wonder about the condition of his health. "It is my pleasure to announce that you have been selected for a rare privilege. You members of the first graduating class of the IPF Academy will be allowed, this day, to view the crater where the last nuclear bomb exploded."

Every young man and woman of the squad squirmed unhappily. I could feel them struggling to suppress moans of misery. The crater was a sacred place for old men like Director-General Hazard. To the cadets it meant only a long hard climb in sweltering tropical heat and the distinct possibility of a radiation dose.

You see, an event of crucial importance to the world had taken place near the city of Valledupar about four years earlier, the kind of event that was supremely influential in the development of the Peacekeepers, but will never find its way into the official history. (Except maybe as a brief footnote.) I wasn't there to participate, of course. I was on a ship in the Arabian Sea where I eventually lost my right hand, courtesy of the sovereign governments of India and Pakistan. But I've pieced together the story fairly well and personally visited each site in which it took place—except one. If you'll allow me a little imagination, what happened must have been very much like this . . .

NEUSTRA SEÑORA DE LA
—Misericordia, Year 8

DEATH smells worst in the tropics.

Cole Alexander wrinkled his nose at the stench of decaying bodies. They lay everywhere: men, women, infants. Bloating in the fetid sun, sprawled in the gutted remains of their miserable hovels, swarms of flies black around their bullet wounds, beetles already digging into the rotting flesh.

The merciless sun hung high in the pale sky, steaming moisture from the tropical forest that surrounded the dead village. Alexander felt his own body juices baking out of him, the damp heat soaking him like a chunk of meat thrown into a boiling pot.

Our Lady of Mercy, Alexander thought, hot bile burning in his throat. What a name for the town.

"You see how they slaughter my people." Sebastiano Miguel de Castanada made it a statement, not a question.

Misericordia had been a tiny nothing of a village stuck in the jungle at the base of the mountains, an hour's hard drive up the rutted, twisting road from the city of Valledupar. Now it was a burned-out ruin, the shacks that had once been houses blackened and smashed, the inhabitants machine-gunned down to babies in their mothers' arms.

"Why did they do it?" Alexander asked.

Castanada pointed to where his soldiers had spread a few armloads of trinkets on an aluminum camp table. Other soldiers were still searching the village, stepping over grotesque corpses with staring eyes and silently screaming mouths to hunt for the village's hidden treasures. The soldiers wore crisp khaki uniforms. They all carried automatic rifles slung over their shoulders. But they seemed unconcerned. The dead bodies did not bother them. Neither, thought Alexander, did they seem worried about being attacked.

Castanada led Alexander to the table. It was covered almost completely with slim glass knives, miniature quartz statues, decorated ceramic vases and other dusty artifacts.

"The villagers lived on grave robbing," he said. "The men went up into the mountains, where the old Inca graves must be. When the drug dealers made their headquarters up there, they did not want these villagers bothering them. So three days ago they came down from the mountains and wiped out the village."

Alexander studied Castanada's face. He showed no sign of anger, no hint of fear or remorse or grief. Castanada was a handsome man in his early forties, broad brow, strong jaw, smooth tanned skin. His jet-black hair was brushed straight back; his eyes were the color of his native soil when the peons first turn it over for tilling after the winter rains. But he was turning to fat, his slight body becoming round and heavy, his skin getting that waxy look that comes from overindulgence. He wore an off-white silk suit, light for the summer heat, conservatively cut, precisely tailored, extremely expensive. As befits the man who is not only minister of defense but the eldest son of *el presidente*.

Despite the heat, Cole Alexander wore a rumpled suede jacket over his open-necked olive-green sport shirt, stained with dark pools of perspiration. A broad-brimmed cowboy hat was perched at a slight angle on his head. He was much taller than Castanada, and may have been slightly older than the defense minister or slightly younger. It was difficult to tell from his face. His hair was curly and thick, yet all white. His face looked youthfully handsome, but it was set in a sardonic, nearly cruel jester's smile. A sneer, almost. His cold gray eyes seemed to look out at the world with a mixture of amusement and contempt at the antics of his fellow human beings.

"You've got a serious problem, all right," Alexander said. "But I don't think I can help you with it."

"I quite understand, Señor Alexander," said Castanada, sounding oily and at the same time slightly irritating. "I have already told my father that I would not be surprised if you refused to help us."

"Your father is beset by many problems," Alexander replied, choosing his words carefully. His voice matched his facial expression: not quite harsh yet certainly not gentle, a reedy *norteamericano* tenor with a hint of sharp steel in it.

"I am doing my best to help him, but . . ." Castanada spread his arms in the gesture of a man resigned to struggling against inhuman odds.

Alexander looked around at what was left of the village

as the soldiers continued to search it. The drug dealers had done a thorough job. Not even a dog was left to whimper. The table where they stood was upwind, at least. The smell wasn't so bad here.

"They have created an army of their own, up in those mountains," Castanada said, his voice trembling slightly. "An empire within our borders!"

"Let me try to explain," said Alexander, "why this kind of problem is not in my usual line of operations."

"It is too dangerous for mercenaries, I understand."

Alexander smiled a crooked smile. "You must enjoy fishing in these mountain streams."

Castanada smiled blandly back at him.

"My people work sort of like the Peacekeepers," Alexander said. "We're basically a defensive operation. We protect, we do not attack."

"Please do not fence with words, Señor Alexander. Your . . ." Castanada groped for a word. ". . . Your *organization* is a mercenary force. You fight for pay."

"We fight for pay," Alexander agreed. "But only for those who are under attack. Only for those who can't defend themselves."

"But we *are* under attack! Look around you! The drug dealers have assassinated members of the government! We are at war! A life-and-death struggle!"

"But surely your Army . . ."

"Riddled with corruption." Castanada lowered his voice. "I am ashamed to admit it, but it's true."

"Then you should call in the Peacekeepers."

"We have tried, señor. They are sympathetic but unwilling to help us. They will only intervene if there is an overt attack across an international border. They exist to prevent wars, not to act as police."

Alexander nodded slowly.

"We have nowhere else to turn. I fear for my father's life. For the lives of my wife and children."

"I understand. But it's still not the kind of operation that my people can undertake."

"If it's the money you are concerned about . . ."

Alexander raised one hand. "No, I'm sure we could come to satisfactory terms. It's just not the kind of operation we do."

Castanada turned and took a few paces away from Alexander, his chubby hands clasped behind his back. As if speaking to the empty air, he said, "You know that Jabal Shamar is with them now, up in those mountains."

Alexander muttered, "Shamar."

Turning back to face the *norteamericano*, Castanada added, "According to our intelligence, he has taken charge of their military operations."

"What about the nuclear bombs?"

"It is not certain, but I greatly fear that he has brought them to our soil."

"Shamar," Alexander repeated in a barely audible whisper.

Sí, Señor Yanqui, Castanada said to himself. I do indeed fish in these mountain streams. I know very well how to bait my hook, and how to reel in even the most cunning and elusive fish. He kept his face carefully bland and inexpressive, but he laughed inwardly.

Cole Alexander's smile had disappeared.

Yet even that thread of a beginning had its own beginning, on the final day of what has come to be called (optimistically) the Final War

JERUSALEM:
Year Zero

THE sky was unnaturally black. Not even the high desert sun could burn through the sooty clouds. The streets of the city were empty. Not a car, not a bus, not even a dog moved as the hot winds seared alike the ancient stones of the Western Wall, the domes and minarets of medieval churches and mosques, the steel and glass towers of the modern city.

In the middle of the dark afternoon a limousine, a Rolls-Royce at that, careened through the city's bare streets like a black mouse racing through a maze, losing its way and doubling back again, searching, searching, searching. Finally the limo sniffed out the American embassy and stopped at its barricaded gate.

A man got out: Cole Alexander—dressed in a summer-weight pearl-gray business suit stained dark with sweat and wrinkled as only thirty-six hours of travel can do. His necktie was pulled loose, several shirt buttons undone. His hair was dark brown, almost black, his face set in a breathless expression of anxiety.

He leaned on the buzzer at the gate, ducked back into the limo and took the keys from the ignition, then banged on the buzzer again. He squinted up at the dark sky, then pressed his thumb against the buzzer and left it there until an adenoidal voice finally scratched from the intercom speaker above the buzzer. Alexander spoke loudly and firmly. Within two minutes a Marine guard, his own olive-green uniform almost as sweaty and rumpled as Alexander's suit, dashed out of the building and unlocked the personnel gate.

Alexander and the young Marine sprinted up the driveway and through the main entrance to the building. At a desk set up just inside the entryway, an additional pair of Marines, one of them a sergeant, examined his passport while Alexander explained:

"My parents are here. I've got a private plane at the airport, waiting to evacuate them."

"A private plane?" The sergeant, a tough-looking black, gave Alexander an incredulous stare.

"Money talks, Sergeant," said Alexander. "Even in the middle of a war."

"He's driving a Rolls, Sarge," said the Marine who had opened the gate, with awe in his voice.

The sergeant shook his head. The expression on his face said, You're crazy, man. But he told the other private to escort Alexander to his mother, who was among the civilians being sheltered in the embassy's basement.

Alexander got as far as the metal detector built into the doorway at the end of the lobby. It screeched angrily.

"Oh." Apologetically Alexander hauled a compact .38

automatic from the waistband of his trousers. "Bought it in New York just before I bought the jet. It's registered, all nice and legal."

The sergeant hefted the shiny pistol in his big hand. "You ever fired it?" he asked Alexander.

"Haven't had the time."

"I'll hold it for you here." He placed the gun carefully in a drawer of his desk.

The basement was big and dimly lit; only a few of the overhead fluorescent lights were on, casting almost ghastly bluish light on the people crowded together there. They were mostly women and small children, Alexander saw. Some old men. Cramped together. Sitting on a weird assortment of chairs scavenged from the floors above, huddled on cots, makeshift curtains draped here and there for privacy, staring at the ceiling, whispering to one another, babies crying, old men coughing, worried faces looking blankly at nothing. The basement was jammed with people. Their voices made a constant background murmur of anxiety and tension. The place was hot and stank of sweat and cigarette smoke and cooking oil. And fear.

The waiting room to hell, Cole Alexander thought.

Amanda Alexander was small, a slim little girl with a sweet smile who had grown to a petite white-haired woman who could always charm any man she met. Seeing her in that crowded basement shelter, with the stench of hundreds of bodies pressed too close together, Cole realized with a shock that his mother was *old:* her face was webbed with tiny wrinkles, there were dark lines under her eyes, she seemed haggard and worn-out.

"Don't look so shocked," she said after he had kissed her cheek. "You haven't seen me without makeup for years." Then she smiled and he felt all right again.

"I've come to take you and Dad out of here," Cole said.

"That's not necessary. I'm fine right here."

"I've got a jet sitting at the airport . . ."

His mother seemed genuinely surprised. "How did you do that?"

He shrugged. "Sold the business to Palmerson; he's been after it for a year now. Spent a chunk of it on the plane. Couldn't find a pilot on such short notice so I flew it myself. Now, come on, before somebody steals it."

"Your father's not here," she said. "They sent him to Tel Aviv."

"Goddamned State Department," Cole muttered. "Okay. We'll fly to Tel Aviv and pick him up there. Phone him from here first."

"He can't just *go*," his mother said, "simply because his impetuous son wants him to. He's got a job to do. He's got responsibilities."

"They're throwing nuclear bombs around, Mom! You and Dad have got to get out of here, to where it's safe!"

"They won't bomb Jerusalem. General Shamar has given his word. The Moslems revere the city just as much as the Israelis do."

Alexander forced down his temper. This was his mother he was dealing with. "Mom, they've already nuked Haifa and Damascus. The fallout . . ."

"I'm not leaving, Cole. Your father can't leave, and I won't go without him."

That was when the black Marine sergeant picked his way through the overcrowded basement toward them.

"Mrs. Alexander," he said, so softly that Cole could barely hear him against the background murmurs. " 'Fraid I got very bad news, ma'am. We just got word, Tel Aviv got hit."

Amanda Alexander stared at the sergeant as if she could not understand his words.

"A nuclear strike?" Cole asked, his voice choking.

"Yeah." The sergeant nodded.

"Oh, my Christ."

His mother reached out and touched the Marine

sergeant's arm. "That . . . that doesn't mean that every-one . . . everyone in the city's been . . . killed, does it?"

"No," the black man admitted. "We don't know how bad the damage is or how many casualties. Bound to be plenty, though. Thousands. Tens of thousands, at least."

Cole grasped his mother's wrist. "We're getting out. Now."

"No!" She pulled her arm free with surprising strength. "Your father may be all right. Or he may be hurt. I'm not leaving. Not until I know."

"But that's . . ."

"I'm not leaving, Cole."

So he stayed with her in the basement of the U.S. embassy building in Jerusalem.

It had started as another round of the eternal Middle East wars between Israel and its neighbors. In three days it escalated into a nuclear exchange. By the time four ancient cities had been blown into mushroom clouds, the two great superpowers decided to intervene. For the first time in more than fifty years, the Soviet Union and the United States acted in harmony to end the brief, brutal conflagra-tion that is now called the Final War.

The Americans and Soviets imposed a cease-fire and ringed Syria, Israel and Lebanon with enough troops, ships and planes to make it clear they would brook no resistance. The U.S. Navy moved in force into the Persian Gulf while Russian divisions massed on Iran's northern border. With Damascus and Tehran both reduced to radioactive rubble, with Haifa and Tel Aviv similarly demolished, the fighting stopped.

That was when General Jabal Shamar, supreme com-mander of the Pan-Arab Armed Forces, sent a special squadron of cargo planes to Jerusalem. The lumbering four-engined aircraft circled over the city at an altitude of some three thousand meters, cruising lazily through a sky just starting to turn blue again after three days of darkness.

Men and women cautiously came out into the streets, blinking at the brightening sky and the glinting silvery planes circling gently above. They were obviously not warplanes, not the sleek angry falcons painted in camouflage grays and browns that hurled deadly eggs at the ground. These were fat clumsy cargo carriers, their unpainted aluminum gleaming cheerfully against the clearing sky.

The powder that the planes spewed from their cargo hatches was so radioactive that every crewman in the squadron died within two weeks. So did most of the living creatures in Jerusalem: men, women, children, pets, rats, insects, even trees curled their brown leaves and died. Moslem and Jew alike bled at the pores and died in convulsive agonies. Citizens of the city, refugees who had fled there for safety, tourists trapped by the war, news reporters camping in the hotels, foreigners on duty in Jerusalem—they all died. Two and a half million of them.

After the cease-fire had been declared.

The medical help rushed into the city by the Americans and Europeans saved a pitiful few. Cole Alexander was among those who survived. He was young enough and strong enough to pull through a terrible ordeal of radiation sickness, although it left his hair dead white and triggered a form of leukemia that the doctors said could be "controlled" but never cured. It also left him sterile.

His mother did not survive. Cole watched her die, inch by excruciating inch, over the next seven weeks. She finally gave up the fight when the news came that her husband, Cole's father, had been vaporized in the nuclear bombing of Tel Aviv. The American consulate there had been practically at ground zero.

The Final War led to the Athens Peace Conference, and that's where I suppose I'll have to begin the official history of the Peacekeepers. With the impressive figure of Harold Red Eagle, of course.

ATHENS:
Year 1

H E was a very large man, very grave, and so respected in his own land that not even the ultraconservatives ever had the nerve to make jokes about his name.

Harold Red Eagle was considerably over two meters tall. In his young manhood, when he had made a national reputation for himself as a lineman for the Los Angeles Raiders, he had weighed nearly 130 kilos. Even so, he could chase down the fleetest of running backs. And once Red Eagle got his hands on a ball carrier, the man went *down.* No one broke his tackles.

The Raiders had been known to be a hell-raising team of undisciplined egotists. Red Eagle changed that. He spoke barely a word, and he certainly gave no speeches. He

neither exhorted his teammates to self-sacrifice nor be-
rated them for their macho antics. He merely set an
example, off the field and especially on it, that no man
could ignore or resist. He made the Raiders not only into
champions, but hallowed heroes.

Football was merely a means to an end for Harold Red
Eagle. For an impoverished son of the proud Comanche
people, college football was the key to an education.
Professional football paid for law school and provided the
glory that established him in a lucrative practice in his
native Oklahoma.

When he retired from his athletic career, the governor of
the state appointed him to the bench. (A rather neat pun
there, don't you think?) A few years later he became the
youngest federal judge ever to serve that district. A canny
President nominated him to the U.S. Supreme Court, and
during the Senate confirmation hearings not a word was
spoken against this Amerind, whose massive dignity could
strike even TV talk-show hosts into reverent awe.

Harold Red Eagle was appointed by the next President (a
political opponent of the previous one) to be part of the
American delegation to the Athens Peace Conference. It
was there that the first step toward the International
Peacekeeping Force was made.

The moment was dramatic. Representatives of Israel,
Syria and Iran all demanded reparations for the damage to
their nations. Other Moslem figures warned of the need to
find a homeland for the Palestinian refugees. The Western
Europeans and Americans, terrified of renewed nuclear
war, demanded that the belligerent nations be disarmed
and occupied for an indeterminate time by an international army that would enforce the peace. The Soviets and
Chinese jointly suggested the conference be enlarged to
consider dismantling *every* nation's nuclear arsenal.

Instead of patching together a peace in the Middle East,
the Athens conference was threatening to tear itself asun-

der over the old Cold War issues separating East and West.

That was when Red Eagle rose to his feet.

All talk around the wide green-baize-covered circular table ceased. The Comanche loomed over the other delegates, his deep brown face solemn with the racial memories of innumerable wars and slaughters.

"It is time," he said slowly, "that we end this Cold War. Nothing of peace can be accomplished until we do."

It was as if he had trained a powerful gun on them all. The delegates—politicians and diplomats, for the most part—sat in silent awe as Red Eagle calmly enunciated the plan that he had been shaping in his mind over the many weeks of the conference's fruitless wrangling.

His plan was simple and breathtakingly daring. East and West were at that time both deploying heavily armed satellites in space, each claiming them to be purely defensive in nature. Let a true international peacekeeping force be created, said Red Eagle, to operate both systems of satellites as one and protect *every* nation on Earth against attack by *any* nation.

Further, let this peacekeeping force be empowered to act immediately against any kind of aggression across any international frontier. Give it the weapons and authority to stop wars as soon as they are started.

Impossible! countered the delegates. But over the next several weeks they listened to Red Eagle and a growing host of technical and military experts. Yes, it would be possible to observe military buildups from surveillance satellites in orbit. Yes, defensive technologies could produce highly automated systems that are cheaper and more effective than massive offensive weaponry.

But who would control such an international force? the delegates asked. How could it be prevented from turning into a world dictatorship?

"The problem is war," Red Eagle told them. "Create a peacekeeping force that will prevent war. No nation need disarm, if it does not care to do so. Whatever goes on within a nation's borders will be of no concern to the peacekeepers. The peacekeepers will acquire no nuclear weapons, no weapons of mass destruction of any kind. Their sole function will be to prevent attacks—nuclear or conventional—across international borders."

The force of Red Eagle's personality greatly multiplied the sheer power of his ideas. Slowly, grudgingly, the conference delegates came to accept the notion that an international peacekeeping force could be created. It might even work.

They offered command of the force to Red Eagle, of course. Just as naturally, he politely refused. (The man they did give the command to, unfortunately, was a political compromise, a nonentity who ignored the warning signs and was caught desperately unprepared for the revolt that nearly shattered the IPF. But I'm getting ahead of myself.)

After several months of deliberations the Athens Peace Conference concluded with the signing of the Middle East Treaty. More important, a week later the nations met on the Acropolis, before the ancient splendor of the Parthenon, to sign the document that created the International Peacekeeping Force.

The conference ended on a public note of optimism and private snickers of cynicism. Perhaps this was the way to save the world from nuclear holocaust, the delegates told each other. But none of them truly believed it. It was a gesture, at best. No one expected peace to last in the Middle East. No one expected the newly created IPF to finally end the scourge of war.

But they had tried to take a step in the proper direction. Even the hard-boiled media reporters seemed impressed. Hardly any of them offered a word of criticism or mentioned the fact that General Jabal Shamar, the man responsible for the Jerusalem Genocide, had not yet been apprehended.

I joined the IPF the first day of its existence, I'm proud to say. At first, they put me in an intelligence billet. That experience will serve me well now that I'm an archivist; I have had access to electronic intercepts and other forms of snooping that would have made J. Edgar Hoover tremble with joy. Most of these snippets can't be used in the official history of the IPF, where every source must have its own footnote. But I can use them here. Happily.

MOSCOW, ——— Year 1

THE General Secretary eased his tired body into the gleaming stainless-steel tub. His valet made certain that the old man was safely settled in the steaming water, then touched the button that started the whirlpool action.

The General Secretary leaned back and sighed. It had been a long, difficult meeting. He saw that his valet was sweating heavily, rivers running down his face, dark stains growing on his shirtfront.

"You can remove your shirt, Yuri," he said, over the throbbing and gurgling of the agitated water. "It's all right."

"Thank you, sir," replied Yuri. But he made no move to disrobe.

Always the proprieties, thought the General Secretary. If I asked Yuri to dash out into the snow and into the path of an oncoming tank he would do it without hesitation. But he will never willingly bare his chest in my presence.

The steaming hot water bubbled and frothed, relaxing the tensed muscles of the General Secretary's back and legs. I'm getting old, he thought. The Kremlin ages a man. The responsibilities . . .

He leaned his head back against the soft padding and smiled up at his valet. Yuri looks ten years younger than I. Still has his hair, and it's still as dark as it was twenty years ago. No responsibilities. No worries.

"Yuri, my old friend, what do you think of this International Peacekeeping Force?"

"You signed the treaty in Athens." The valet had to raise his voice to be heard over the whirlpool.

"Yes. It was quite a moment, wasn't it? The Parthenon is one of the most beautiful buildings in the world."

"Too delicate for me. I prefer something more solid, like St. Basil's . . ."

"I don't intend to argue architecture with you! What do you think of this Peacekeeping Force?"

"My son wants to join it."

The General Secretary felt his brows rise. "Little Gregor?"

"He is almost twenty-five, sir," said Yuri with some gentleness. "A lieutenant in the Guards."

Twenty-five, thought the General Secretary. The length of time of a generation.

"Will it be possible for him to join the international force?" asked Yuri. "It won't be a mark against him on his record, will it?"

"Of course not," the General Secretary replied almost absently. "We want loyal Russians in the IPF. It is necessary."

"And we will disband the Red Army?"

The General Secretary felt astonished. "Whatever gave you that idea?"

"From what people say . . . there are so many rumors, and no two of them are the same."

"We have agreed to reduce the size of our armed forces—slowly, according to a fixed timetable. We will also dismantle our nuclear weapons; again, in keeping with a strict schedule. The Americans and Chinese and all the others will do the same. There will be teams of international inspectors."

"Spies," muttered Yuri.

"Our own people will be on the inspection teams," replied the General Secretary. "Our own people will watch the imperialists dismantle their bombs."

"Do you trust them?"

With a slow smile, "Yes, of course. As much as they trust us."

Yuri laughed.

But the General Secretary grew serious again. "My old friend, there have been many changes in the Soviet Union since I dandled your Gregor on my knee."

"Many changes," Yuri agreed.

"We have lived through turbulent times."

"You have been a great leader, sir. The Soviet Union— the Russian people—are richer and stronger because of you."

Accustomed to flattery, the General Secretary asked, "But are they happier?"

"Yes!" Yuri's answer was so swift and certain that the General Secretary knew his valet believed it to be the truth.

He slid down lower in the bubbling water until it was up to his chin. He could feel the knots in his neck and shoulders easing.

Yuri stood by the tub, silent, stoic, as enduring as the

endless steppes and the birch forests. Finally he asked, "Once we have taken apart all our hydrogen bombs . . . what will we do with the pieces?"

The General Secretary smiled lazily. "Why, put them back together again, of course. You don't think that I would leave the nation defenseless, do you?"

I admit to some embellishments in the preceding account, although each word attributed to the two Russians comes straight out of the Security Agency's transcripts. I can't use such dramatic devices in the official history; it's got to be dry, factual, and nonthreatening. Twenty committees will sit in judgment before it will ever see the light of publication. I shudder to think that my name might be on it.

What follows is another (slightly embellished) transcript, this one from a videotape. As I said, being in IPF intelligence was a good experience for me, although, at the time, I fought and argued and fumed through the system until they transferred me to an active unit. Which is how I lost my hand, of course. Young men want glory. They never think about the price.

WASHINGTON, Year 1

I wouldn't trust those Commie sumbitches if Jesus Christ himself came down from heaven and pleaded their case!"

"But that's the beauty of the system: we don't *have* to trust them. We don't have to give up anything unless they do."

The three men sat at one end of a long polished table in a conference room in the Old Executive Building, that rambling pile of Victorian stonework that stands next to the White House. The conference room had old-fashioned luxury built into it: high cofferwork ceiling, oak parquet floor, gracious long windows, the kind of spaciousness that modern office buildings are too efficient to afford.

Senator Zachary, chairman of the Foreign Relations Committee, chewed on his tongue for a moment, a habit he had acquired when his first heart attack ended his smoking. Senator Foxworth, the committee's minority leader, silently wished Zachary would bite the damned tongue off and choke on it.

Aloysius B. Zachary was rake thin, his brittle-looking skin mottled with liver spots, his wispy white hair hanging long and dead down to the collar of his baggy suit. He had been much heavier before each of his heart attacks; lost weight after each one, only to gradually fatten up and have another attack. He was only a month out of the hospital after his latest. A waddling dewlap of grayish skin hung from his chin. For a dozen years now he had chaired the Foreign Relations Committee, wielding as much power over U.S. foreign policy as most Presidents did.

Foxworth knew that only death would remove this ignorant, arrogant, stubborn old fool from his powerful position. His Louisiana political machine would reelect him to the Senate for as long as he lived. As far as Foxworth was concerned, that had already been about one decade too long.

Jim Foxworth was known to be the best poker player on Capitol Hill. His face never betrayed him. He smiled always, especially when he was angry or fearful or making the final arrangements to drive the knife into an opponent's back.

He had the compact build of the health-food athlete: slightly bulging in the middle, but otherwise taut and fit. Tennis and swimming. Horseback riding back home in Wyoming.

The third man in the conference room, seated between the two senators, wore the blue uniform and four stars of an Air Force general. A former fighter pilot, former astronaut, and the first black man to be appointed chief of staff, Charles Madison held degrees in engineering, management and communications. Of all the braid and decorations heaped upon him, though, he treasured most highly the two kills he had made against Nicaraguan MiGs during the Central American War.

"Lemme ask you, General," said Senator Zachary, his dewlap quivering with emotion, "d'y'all trust the Russkies to live up to this treaty they signed?"

"We signed it, too," Foxworth snapped.

"But we ain't *ratified* it, Senator!" Zachary leveled a forefinger at the younger man.

Foxworth turned to General Madison, smiling with his lips only.

"I don't trust the Russians, no, sir," said the general. "And I *certainly* don't trust this international committee that's supposed to protect us against nuclear attack. I don't like the idea of turning our SDI satellites over to them. I don't like it one bit."

Zachary bobbed his head and sneered at Foxworth. "Y'see?"

At that moment the corridor door opened and the ponderous figure of Harold Red Eagle filled the door frame. He wore a business suit of dark blue with a maroon tie knotted precisely.

"Forgive me, gentlemen," Red Eagle said in his deep, slow voice. It was like the rumble of distant thunder, or the suppressed growl of a restless volcano. "I was delayed at the Court. The computer was down for about an hour."

From the size of him, Foxworth thought, he may have broken the computer merely by laying his hamhock paws on it.

Red Eagle pulled a chair out and sat carefully on it, as if testing to see if it could hold his weight. Suddenly the head of the table was where he sat, and the three others turned to face him.

"I understand that you have grave doubts about the

International Peacekeeping Force. I have come here to answer your questions, if I can, and relieve your fears."

"If you can," Zachary said.

Red Eagle turned his sad brown eyes to the senator from Louisiana. "If I can," he acknowledged. Zachary unconsciously edged back a little.

The gist of Red Eagle's argument was simple: The United States need give up none of its defenses. The Strategic Defense satellites were already under NATO control; by allowing the new International Peacekeeping Force to operate them, they lost very little and gained the entire fleet of Soviet SDI satellites, as well.

There would be no disarmament, no dismantling of nuclear weapons, no shrinkage of the armed services that was not matched by the Soviets—gun for gun, bomb for bomb, man for man.

"That still leaves the Russians with three times the conventional forces that we have," said General Madison.

"Yes, it does," admitted Red Eagle. "And three times the burden on their economy."

"If they decide to attack Western Europe . . ."

"The International Peacekeeping Force will stop them."

"That's not possible."

"General," said Red Eagle, gazing at the black man, "it *is* possible. It is even inevitable, if you serve the IPF with all the heart and intelligence that you now devote to the defense of the United States."

"Now, see here," Zachary fumed.

Red Eagle silenced him by raising one enormous hand.

"Gentlemen," he said, "the ways of peace are difficult and strange, especially to men accustomed to war. My people, the Comanche, were a nation of warriors. We drove the Apache into the desert. We defeated the U.S. Army more than once. Yet war ultimately destroyed us. Do not let war destroy your nation."

Foxworth cleared his throat. Otherwise the conference room was quiet.

Red Eagle went on, "The ancient Athenians in all their glory could not conceive of a political loyalty higher than that which they gave to their city. There was no concept of Greece in those days. There was only Athens, or Sparta, or Thebes, Corinth and other city-states, constantly at war with one another. That civilization perished.

"Today you men give your highest political loyalty to your nation. Yet I say to you that unless you have the greatness of soul to see a higher loyalty, a loyalty to planet Earth, to the human race in its greatness and entirety, *this* civilization will soon perish. And there will be none to follow. None! The human race will die."

The three men glanced uneasily at one another.

"A small war has utterly destroyed four of the ancient cities of the Middle East. Seventeen million men, women, and children perished in less than a week. What will the next war bring?"

Zachary, his voice trembling slightly, said, "Nobody wants another war."

"Then support the Peacekeepers who will make wars impossible."

"But how do we know it'll work?" General Madison asked.

"You must make it work."

The general shook his head.

"I understand. There are many, many unknowns. We are striking out into uncharted territory. There is much to fear." Then Red Eagle added, "Including the fact that the pressure to drastically reduce the defense budget will become enormous."

For once in his life, Foxworth let his self-control slip. He threw his head back and guffawed.

General Madison made a sour face, let out a pained sigh and loosened the tie of his blue uniform.

I should point out several things at this point. (Two uses of the same word too close together, I know. Necessary, though.)

First, these events led—rather indirectly, I admit—to the cataclysm at Valledupar. Second, we in IPF intelligence were getting faint but constant hints that a cabal was being formed among some of the line officers. Our warnings to the political appointee who headed the Force went unheeded, alas. Third, the nations of the world had not the slightest intention of giving up war as a means to achieve their goals. Not the slightest.

OTTAWA, Year 2

SHE was a tiny figure, skating alone in the darkness. Dow's Lake was firmly frozen this late in December. Earlier in the evening the ice had been covered with skaters in their holiday finery, the pavilion crammed with couples dancing to the heavy beat of rock music.

But this close to midnight, Kelly skated alone, bundled against the cold with a thickly quilted jacket that made her look almost like one of those ragamuffin toy dolls the stores were selling that year.

The wind keened through the empty night. The only light on the ice came from the nearly full Moon grinning lopsidedly at Kelly as she spun and spiraled in time to the music in her head.

Swan Lake was playing in her stereo earplugs, the same music she had skated to when she failed to make the Olympic team. The music's dark passion, its sense of foreboding, fitted Kelly's mood exactly. She skated alone, without audience, without judges. Without anyone. Her mother had died six months ago, leaving her alone except for a father who had not even bothered to give her his name.

I don't care, she told herself. It's better alone. I don't need any of them.

She was just starting a double axel when the beep from the communicator interrupted the music, startling her so badly that she faltered and went sprawling on her backside.

Sitting spraddle-legged on the ice, Kelly thumbed the communicator at her belt and heard:

"Angel Star, this is Robbie. We've got a crisis. All hands to their stations. Reply at once."

Kelly hated the nickname. Her mother had christened her Stella Angela, but she had grown up to be a feisty, snub-nosed, freckled little redhead, more the neighborhood's tomboy roughneck than an angelic little star. At ten she could beat up any boy in school; at thirteen she had earned a karate black belt. But she could not gain a place on the national skating team. And she could not make friends.

She was stubby, quick with her reflexes and her wits. Her figure was nonexistent, a nearly straight drop from her shoulders to her hips.

And she could not make friends, even after three months of being stationed here in Ottawa.

Picking herself up from the ice, Kelly pulled off her right mitten and yanked the pinhead mike from the communicator, its hair-thin wire whirring faintly.

"Okay, Robert, I'm on my way. Seems like a damned odd night for a crisis, if you ask me."

Robbie's voice was dead serious. "We don't make 'em,

we just stop 'em from blowing up. Get your little butt down here, sweetie, double quick."

Kelly skated to the dark and empty pavilion, grumbling to herself all the way. My twenty-second birthday tomorrow, she groused silently. Think they know? Think they care? But underneath the cynical veneer she hoped desperately that they did know and did care. Especially Robert.

The base was less than a mile from the pavilion, a clump of low buildings on the site of the old experimental farm. Kelly rode her electric bike along the bumpy road, man-tall banks of snow on either side, the towers of Ottawa glistening and winking in the distance, brilliant with their holiday decorations.

Past the wire fence of the perimeter and directly into the big open doors of the main entrance she rode, paying scant attention to the motto engraved above it. Locking the bike in the rack just inside the entrance, she nodded hello to the two guards lounging by the electric heater inside their booth, perfunctorily waved her identification badge at them, then clumped in her winter boots down the ramp toward the underground monitoring center.

If there's a friggin' crisis, she thought, the dumb guards sure don't show it.

In the locker room Kelly stripped off her bulging coat and the boots. She wore the sky-blue uniform of the Peacekeepers beneath it. The silver bars on her shoulders proclaimed her to be a junior lieutenant. A silver stylized T, shaped like an extended, almost mechanical hand, was clipped to her high collar; it identified her as a teleoperator.

Helluva night to make me come in to work, she complained to herself as she changed into her blue-gray duty fatigues. There are plenty of others who could fill in this shift. Why do they always pick on me? And why can't they make this damned cave warm enough to work in?

But then two more operators clumped in, silent and grim-faced. The men nodded to Kelly; she nodded back.

Shivering slightly against the damp chill, Kelly briefly debated bringing her coat with her into the monitoring center, then decided against it. As she pushed the door to the hall open, another three people in fatigues were hurrying past, down the cold concrete corridor toward the center: two women and a man. One of the women was still zipping her cuffs as she rushed by.

Robbie was outwardly cheerful: a six-three Adonis with a smile that could melt tungsten steel. His uniforms, even his fatigues, fitted him like a second skin. He wore the four-pointed star of a captain on his shoulders.

"Sorry to roust you, tonight of all nights," he said, treating her to his smile. "We've got a bit of a mess shaping up, Angel Star."

If anyone else called her anything but her last name, Kelly bristled. But she let handsome Robert get away with his pet name for her.

"What's going on?" she asked.

She saw that all ten monitoring consoles were occupied and working, ten men and women sitting in deeply padded chairs, headsets clamped over their ears, eyes riveted to the banks of display screens curving around them, fingers playing ceaselessly over the keyboards in front of them. Tension sizzled in the air. The room felt hot and crowded, sweaty. Images from the display screens provided the only light, flickering like flames from a fireplace, throwing nervous, jittering shadows against the bare concrete walls.

Several of the pilots were lounging in the chairs off to one side, trying to look relaxed even though they knew they might be called to action at any moment. Robert was in charge of this shift, sitting in the communicator's high chair above and behind the monitors. Standing her tallest, Kelly was virtually at eye level with him.

"What *isn't* going on?" Robbie replied. "You'd think tonight of all nights everybody'd be at home with their families."

He waved a hand toward the screens as the displays on them blinked back and forth, showing scenes from dozens of locations around the world.

"Got a family of mountain climbers trapped on Mt. Burgess up in the Yukon Territory. Satellite picked up their emergency signal." Kelly saw an infrared image of rugged mountainous country over the shoulder of Jan Van der Meer, one of the few monitors she knew by name.

"And some loony terrorists," Robbie went on, pointing to another console down the line, "tried to hijack one of the nuclear submarines being decommissioned by the U.S. Navy in Connecticut."

Kelly saw the submarine tied to a pier from a ground-level view. Military police in polished steel helmets were leading a ragged gaggle of men and women, their faces smeared with camouflage paint, up the gangway and into a waiting police van.

"But the crisis is Eritrea," said Robert.

"Not again," Kelly grumbled. "They've been farting around there for more than a year."

Nodding tightly, Robert touched a button in the armrest of his high chair and pulled the pin mike of his headset down before his lips. "Jan, pick up the Eritrea situation, please."

Van der Meer, a languid, laconic Dutchman whose uniform always seemed too big for him, looked over his shoulder almost shyly and nodded. With his deep-set eyes, hollow cheeks and bony face, he looked like a death's head beckoning. He tapped his keypad with a long slim finger, and his display screens showed ghostly images in infrared, taken from a reconnaissance satellite gliding in orbit over East Africa.

It took Kelly a moment to identify the vague shapes and shadows. Tanks. And behind them, self-propelled artillery pieces. Threading their way in predawn darkness through the mountains along the border of Eritrea.

"They're really going to attack?" Kelly asked, her voice suddenly high and squeaky, like a frightened little girl's.

"If we let them," answered Robbie, quite serious now.

"But they must know we'll throw everything we have at them!"

Robert arched his brows, making his smooth young forehead wrinkle slightly. "I guess they think they can get away with it. Maybe they think we won't be able to react fast enough, or their friends in the African Bloc will prevent Geneva from acting at all. We've never had to stop a real shooting war; not yet."

"Maybe they're bluffing," Kelly heard her voice saying. "Maybe they'll back down . . ."

"Priority One from Geneva!" called Bailey, the black woman working station three. She was an American, from Los Angeles, tall and leggy and graceful enough to make Kelly ache with jealousy over her good looks and smooth cocoa-butter skin. She had almond-shaped eyes, too, dark and exotic. Kelly's eyes were plain dumb brown.

Robert clamped a hand to his earphone. His eyes narrowed, then shifted to lock onto Kelly's.

Nodding and whispering a response, he pushed the mike up and away, then said, "This is it, kid. Everybody up!"

Kelly felt a surge of electricity burn through her: part fear, part excitement. The other pilots stirred, too.

"I'm on my way," she said.

But Robert had already shifted his mike down again and was calling through the station's intercom, "Pilots, man your planes. All pilots, man your planes."

As Kelly dashed through the monitoring center's doors and out into the long central corridor, she thought she heard Robbie wishing her good luck. But she wasn't certain.

Doesn't matter, she told herself, knowing it was a lie.

The technicians backed away as Kelly slid into the cockpit and cast a swift professional glance at the instruments. On the screen in front of her she saw the little plane's snub nose, painted dead black, glinting in the predawn starlight.

She clamped her comm set over her chopped-short red hair and listened to her mission briefing. There was no preflight checkout; the technicians did that and punched it into the flight computer. She swung the opaque canopy down and locked it shut, then took off into the darkness, getting her mission profile briefing from Geneva as she flew.

Dozens of planes were being sent against the aggressors, pilots from every available Peacekeepers' station were in their cockpits, hands on their flight controls. There were the usual delays and mix-ups, but Kelly suddenly felt free and happy, alone at the controls of an agile little flying machine, her every movement answered by a movement of the plane, her nerves melding with the machine's circuitry, the two of them mated more intimately than a man and a woman could ever be.

The plane was as small as it could be made and still do its job. Using the latest in stealth technology, it flew in virtual silence, its quiet Stirling engine turning the six paddle blades of the propeller so gently that they barely made a sound. But the plane was slow, painfully slow. Built of wood and plastic, for the most part, it was designed to avoid detection by radar and infrared heat-seekers, not to outrun any opposition that might find her.

To make it hard to find visually, Kelly was trained to fly close to the ground, hugging the hills and treetops, flirting with sudden downdrafts that could slam the fragile little plane into the ground.

She thought of herself as a hunting owl, cruising silently through the night, seeking her prey. Everything she needed to know—rather, everything that Geneva could tell her—had been fed to her through her radio earphones. Now, as she flew silently through the dark and treacherous mountain passes on the border of Eritrea, she maintained radio silence.

I am an owl, Kelly told herself, a hunting owl. But there were hawks in the air, and the hunter must not allow herself to become the hunted. A modern jet fighter armed with air-to-air missiles or machine cannon that fired thousands of rounds per minute could destroy her within moments of sighting her. And the second or two delay built into her control system bothered her; a couple of seconds could be the difference between life and death.

But they've got to see me first, Kelly told herself. Be silent. Be invisible.

Despite the cold, she was perspiring now. Not from fear; it was the good kind of sweat that comes from a workout, from preparation for the kind of action that your mind and body have trained for over long grueling months.

Virtually all the plane's systems were tied to buttons on the control column's head. With the flick of her thumb Kelly could make the plane loop or roll or angle steeply up into the dark sky. Like a figure skater, she thought. You and me, machine, we'll show them some Olympic style before we're through.

She was picking up aggressor radio transmissions in her earphones now: she could not understand the language, so she flicked the rocker switch on the control board to her left that activated the language computer. It was too slow to be of much help, but it got a few words:

". . . tank column A . . . jump-off line . . . deploy . . ."

With her left hand she tapped out a sequence on the ECM board, just by her elbow, then activated the sequence with the barest touch of a finger on the black button set into the gray control column head.

Thousands of tiny metallic slivers poured out of a hatch just behind the cockpit, scattering into the dark night air like sparkling crystals of snow. But these dipoles, monomolecular thin, floated lightly in the calm predawn air. They would hover and drift for hours, wafting along on any stray air current that happened by, jamming radio communications up and down thousands of megahertz of the frequency scale.

The Law of the Peacekeepers was: Destroy the weapons of war.

One of the prime weapons of modern war was electronic communications. So the first rule of Peacekeeper tactics was: Screw up their comm system and you screw up their attack.

Leaving a long cloud of jamming chaff behind her, Kelly swooped down a rugged tree-covered valley so low that she almost felt leaves brushing the plane's underside. A river glinted in the faint light. Kelly switched her display screen to infrared and, sure enough, there was a column of tanks snaking along the road that hugged the riverbank. Gray ugly bulks with long cannon poking out like erect penises.

Have fun with your radios, fellas, she called to them silently.

If the tanks reached the border and actually crossed into Sudanese territory, they would be guilty of aggression, and small, smart missiles launched from Peacekeeper command-and-control planes would greet them. But until they crossed the border, their crews were not to be endangered.

Second rule of Peacekeeper tactics: You can't counterattack until the aggressor attacks. Show enough force to convince the aggressor that his attack will be stopped, but launch no weapon until aggression actually takes place.

Corollary No. 1: It makes no difference *why* an attack is launched, or by whom. The Peacekeepers' mission is to prevent the attack from succeeding. We are police, not judges.

Kelly had seen what those smart missiles could do. Barely an arm's length in size, their warheads were nonexplosive slugs of spent uranium, so dense that they sliced through a hundred millimeters of armor like a bullet goes through butter.

The Law said to destroy the weapons, not the men. But men operated the weapons. Men carried them or rode inside them.

A tank is a rolling armory, filled with highly flammable fuel and explosive ammunition. Hit it with a hypervelocity slug almost anywhere and it will burst into flame or blow up like a mini volcano. The men inside have no chance to escape. And the missile, small as it is, is directed by a thumbnail-sized computer chip that will guide it to its target with the dogged accuracy of a Mach 10 assassin.

Banking slightly for a better look at the slowly moving column of tanks, Kelly found herself wishing that her chaff fouled their communications so thoroughly that they had to stop short of the border. Otherwise, most of those million-dollar tanks would be destroyed by thousand-dollar missiles. And the men in them would die. Young men foolish enough to believe that their nation had a right to invade its neighbor. Or serious enough to believe that they must obey their orders, no matter what. Young men who looked forward to life, to marriage, to families and honored old age where they would tell their grandchildren stories about their famous battles and noble heroism.

They would die ingloriously, roasted inside their tanks, screaming with their last breath as the flames seared their lungs.

But she had other work to do.

Third rule of Peacekeeper tactics: A mechanized army needs fuel and ammunition. Cut off those supplies and you stop the army just as effectively as if you had killed all its troops.

Kelly's plane was a scout, not a missile platform. It was unarmed. If she was a hunting owl, she hunted for information, not victims. Somewhere in this treacherous maze of deeply scoured river valleys and arid tablelands there were supply dumps, fuel depots, ammunition magazines that provided the blood and sinew of the attacking army. Kelly's task was to find them. Quickly.

If it had been an easy assignment, she would not have gotten it. If the dumps could have been found by satellite reconnaissance, they would already be targeted for attack. But the Eritreans had worked long and patiently for this invasion of their neighbor. They had dug their supply dumps deeply underground, as protection against both the prying satellite eyes of the Peacekeepers and the inevitable pounding of missiles and long-range artillery, once the dumps had been located.

Kelly and her owllike aircraft had to fly through those tortuous valleys hunting, seeking, scanning up and down the spectrum with sensors that could detect heat, light, magnetic fields, even odors. And she had to find the dumps before the sun got high enough to fill those valleys with light. In daylight, her little unarmed craft would be spotted, inevitably. And once found, it would be swiftly and mercilessly destroyed.

All her sensors were alive and scanning now, as Kelly gently, deftly flew the tiny plane down one twisting valley after another. She felt tense, yet strangely at peace. She knew the stakes, and the danger, yet as long as she was at the controls of her agile little craft she was happy. Like being alone out on the ice: nothing in the world mattered except your own actions. There was no audience here, no judges. Kelly felt happy and free. And alone.

But the eastern sky was brightening, and her time was growing short.

The sensors were picking up data now, large clumps of metal buried *here,* unmistakable heat radiations emanating from *there,* molecules of human sweat and machine oil and plastic explosive wafting up from that mound of freshly turned earth. She squirted the data in highly compressed bursts of laser light up to a waiting satellite, hoping that the Eritreans did not have the sophisticated comm equipment needed to detect such transmissions and home in on her plane.

There were many such planes flitting across the honeycomb of valleys, each pilot hoping that the Eritreans did not catch its transmissions, did not find it before it had completed its task and flown safely home.

Small stuff, Kelly realized as she scanned the data her screens displayed. None of the dumps she had found were terribly important. Local depots for the reserves. Where was the big stuff, the major ammo and fuel supplies for the main forces? It couldn't be farther back, deeper inside the country, she reasoned. They must have dug it in somewhere closer to the border.

The sky was bright enough now to make the stars fade, although the ground below her was still cloaked in shadow. Kelly debated asking Geneva for permission to turn around, rather than continue her route deeper into the Eritrean territory.

"Fuck it," she muttered to herself. "By the time they make up their minds it'll be broad daylight out here."

She banked the little plane on its left wingtip and started to retrace her path. Climbing above the crest of the valley, she began a weaving flight path that took her back and forth across the four major valley chains of her assigned territory.

There's got to be a major dump around here somewhere, she insisted to herself. There's got to be.

If there was not, she knew, she was in trouble. If the main supply dump was deeper inside Eritrea and she had missed it because she had failed to carry out her full assignment, she would be risking the lives not only of Eritreans and Sudanese, but Peacekeepers as well. She would be risking her own career, her own future, too.

The plane's sensors faithfully picked up all the small

dumps she had found on her flight in. Even this high up, they were detectable.

But where's the biggie? Kelly worried.

She felt a jolt of panic when she noticed the shadow of her plane racing along the ground ahead of her. The sun was up over the horizon now, and she was high enough to be easily visible to anyone who happened to look up.

Gritting her teeth, she kept stubbornly to her plan, crisscrossing the valleys, back and forth, weaving a path to the frontier. She could see columns of tanks and trucks below her, some of them moving sluggishly forward, others stopped. Long ugly artillery pieces were firing now, sending shells whistling across the border into the Sudan.

The attack had begun.

They've actually started a war, Kelly said to herself, feeling shock and anger flooding through her. Can we stop it? Can we?

Far ahead, she saw columns of smoke rising black and oily into the brightening sky. Men were dying there.

Quickly she flicked her fingers across the display controls. Forward and rear observation scopes: no other aircraft in sight. So far so good, she thought. I haven't been found. Yet.

The infrared scanner showed an anomaly off to her left: a hot spot along the face of a steep rocky slope that plunged down to the riverbed. Kelly banked slightly and watched the sensor displays hopefully.

It was a cave in the face of the deeply scoured hillside. Ages of sudden rainstorms had seamed the slope like rumpled gray corduroy.

"Just a friggin' cave," Kelly muttered, disappointed. Until she noticed that a fairly broad road had been built up in a series of switchbacks from the valley floor to the lip of the cave's entrance. It was a dirt road, rough, dangerous if it rained. But this was the dry season, and a single truck was jouncing up that road at a fairly high rate of speed, spewing a rooster tail of dust from its rear tires.

Kelly coasted her plane lower, below the crest of the hills that formed the valley. Hidden down among the scruffy trees that lined the riverbank was a column of trucks, their motors running, judging from the heat emissions.

Punching her comm keypad furiously, Kelly sang into her microphone, "I've found it! Major supply dump, not more than ten klicks from the frontier!" She squirted the data to the commsat without taking the time to code or compress it.

She knew that the monitors in Geneva—and Ottawa, for that matter—would home in on her transmission. So would the Eritreans, most likely.

It was not Robbie's voice that replied, an agonizing ten seconds later, "It *might* be a supply dump, but how can you be sure?"

"The truck convoy, dammit!" Kelly shouted back, annoyed. "They're starting up the road!"

And they were. The trucks seemed empty. They were going up the steep road to the cavern, where they would be loaded with the fuel and ammunition necessary to continue the battle.

"Even if you are right," came the voice from Geneva—tense, a slight Norse accent in it—"we have no means to get at the dump. It is too well protected."

Kelly said nothing. She knew what would come next.

"Return to your base of operations. Your mission is terminated."

Kelly bit her lip in frustration. Then a warning screech on her instrument panel told her that she was being scanned by a radar beam. Ordinarily that would not have bothered her. But in morning's brightening light, with a few hundred enemy soldiers below her, she knew she was in trouble.

By reflex, she craned her head to look above, then checked the display screens. A couple of contrails way up there. If she tried to climb out of this valley, those two jet fighters would be on her like stooping hawks.

Kelly took a deep breath and weighed her options. Blowing her breath out through puffed cheeks, she said aloud, "Might as well find out for sure if I'm right."

She pushed the throttle forward and angled the little plane directly toward the mouth of the cave.

Tracers sizzled past her forward screen, and her acoustic sensors picked up the sounds of many shots: small-arms fire, for the most part. The troops down there were using her for target practice. They're lousy shots, Kelly told herself. Then she added, Thank God.

Kelly dove at maximum speed, nearly as fast as a modern sports car, through a fusilade of rifle and machine-gun fire, and flew directly at the yawning cavern. It was dark inside, but the plane's sensors immediately displayed the forward view in false-color infrared.

It's their main dump, all right, Kelly told herself. She saw it all as if in freeze-frame, a bare fraction of a second, yet she made out every detail:

Dozens of trucks were already inside the mammoth cave, in the process of being loaded by troops suddenly startled to find an airplane buzzing straight at them. Some men stood frozen with wide-eyed fright, staring directly at her, while others were scattering, ducking under the trucks or racing for the cave's entrance.

The cave was crammed with stacks of fuel drums, cases of ammunition. Be nice to know who they bought all this crap from, Kelly thought. For the briefest flash of an instant she considered trying to pull up and eluding the fighters waiting for her. Maybe the cameras have picked up valuable information on who's supplying this war, she thought.

But she knew that was idle fancy. This mission was

terminated. Not by Geneva, but by the gunners who would shoot the plane to pieces once she tried to make it to the border.

So she did not pull up. She leaned on the throttle, hurtling the plane directly into the cave's mouth and a massive stack of fuel drums. She neither heard nor felt the explosion.

For long seconds Kelly sat in the contoured chair of the cockpit, staring at the darkened screen. Her hands were trembling too badly to even try to unlatch the canopy. A technician lifted it open and stared down at her. Usually the techs were grinning and cracking jokes after a mission. But this one looked solemn.

"You okay?" she asked.

Kelly managed a nod. Sure, she answered silently. For a pilot who's just kamikazed, I'm fine.

Another tech, a swarthy male, appeared on the other side of the cockpit and helped Kelly to her feet. She stepped carefully over the control banks and onto the concrete floor of the Ottawa station's teleoperations chamber. Two other teleoperator cockpits were tightly closed, with teams of technicians huddled over the consoles grouped around them. The fourth cockpit was open and empty.

The captain in charge of the station's teleoperations unit strode from his desk toward Kelly, his face grim. He was a sour-faced, stocky Asian with a vaguely menacing mustache, all formality and spit and polish.

"We lost one RPV due to ground fire," he said in a furious whisper, "and one deliberately destroyed by its operator."

"But I . . ."

"There is no need for you to defend yourself, Lieutenant Kelly. A board of review will examine the tapes of your mission and make its recommendations. Dismissed."

He turned on his polished heel and strode back to his desk.

Anger replaced Kelly's emotional exhaustion. RPV, she fumed to herself. Operator. They're *planes,* dammit. And I'm a pilot!

But she knew it was not so. They were remotely piloted vehicles, just as the captain had said. And expensive enough so that deliberately crashing one was cause for a review board to be convened. Then Kelly remembered that she had also tossed away her prescribed flight plan. The review board would not go gently, she realized.

She dragged herself tiredly down the corridor toward the locker room, longing now for her bunk and the oblivion of sleep.

Halfway there, Robbie popped out of the monitoring center, his smile dazzling.

"Hi there, Angel Star! Good job!"

Kelly forced the corners of her mouth upward a notch. From behind Robbie's tall, broad-shouldered form she saw most of the other monitors pushing through the doors and spilling out into the corridor. It can't be a shift change, she thought. Nobody else has gone in.

Robbie caught the puzzlement on her face.

"It's all over," he said brightly. "The Eritreans called it quits a few minutes ago."

"They stopped the invasion?"

"We beat them back. Clobbered the tanks in their first wave and demolished most of their supply dumps."

The rest of the monitor team headed down the corridor toward the locker room, chattering like schoolkids suddenly let loose.

"Somebody," Robbie added archly, "even knocked out their main ammo dump."

"That was me," Kelly said weakly.

Throwing an arm around her slim shoulders, Robbie laughed. "I know! We saw it on the screens. The explosion shook down half the mountain."

"Must have killed a lot of men," she heard herself say.

"Not as many as a full-fledged war would have taken."

Kelly knew the truth of it, but it was scant comfort.

"They started it," Robbie said more softly. "It's not your fault."

"It's my responsibility. So was the plane."

Robbie broke out his dazzling grin again. "Worried about a review board? Don't be. They'll end up pinning a medal on you."

Somehow Kelly could not visualize that.

"Come on, Angel Star," Robbie said with a one-armed hug, "don't be glum, chum. We're going out to celebrate."

"Now?"

"It's Christmas, isn't it? You didn't see a big sleigh pulled by reindeer while you were flinging around out there, did you?"

Kelly grinned. "No, I don't think so."

With his arm still around her shoulders, Robbie started for the locker room. "I'm throwing a party in my quarters. You're invited."

Kelly let him half drag her to the locker room. Van der Meer and Bailey were already there, pulling on their heavy winter coats.

"Hello there, little sister," Bailey called to her. "Nice job."

The whole group trudged up the sloping corridor and past the guards, who still sat close to the electric heater in their little booth. If they were aware that a war had just been started and stopped within the span of the past hour or so, they gave no indication of it.

"You're quite a flier," Robbie said to her. "You'll have to give me lessons; I'd love to learn how to fly."

Kelly gulped and swallowed, glad that it was too dark for him to see the reddening that burned her face. *I've never flown a real plane, up in the air,* she wanted to confess. *Only simulators and teleoperations.* But she kept silent, too afraid of cracking the crystal beauty of this moment.

The sky was still dark and sprinkled with stars, the air bitingly cold. As she followed along beside Robbie and the others, snow crunching under their boots, Kelly dug her fists in her coat pockets and glanced over her shoulder at the sign carved above the base's entrance:

INTERNATIONAL PEACEKEEPING FORCE
NATION SHALL NOT LIFT UP SWORD AGAINST NATION

We stopped a war, she said to herself. It cost some lives, but we protected the peace. Then she remembered, It might also cost me my job.

"Don't look so down, girl," Bailey assured her. "The review board ain't gonna go hard on you."

"I hope," said Kelly.

"Don't worry about it," Bailey insisted.

Kelly trudged along, heading for the bachelor officers' quarters across the road from the underground nerve center of the base.

Should I tell them? she asked herself. They wouldn't care. Or maybe they'd think I was just trying to call attention to myself.

But she heard herself saying, "You know, this is my birthday. Today. Christmas Day."

"Really?" said Van der Meer.

"Happy birthday, little sister," Bailey said.

Robbie pushed his coat sleeve back and peered at his wristwatch. "Not just yet, Angel Star. Got another few ticks to go . . ."

Then they heard, far off in the distance, the sound of voices singing.

"Your watch must be slow," said Bailey. "The midnight chorale's already started."

"Their clock must be fast," Robbie countered.

The whole group of them stopped in the starry night air and listened to the children's voices, coming as if from another world. Kelly stood between tall Robert and beautiful, warm Bailey and felt as if they were singing especially to her.

> *"Silent night . . .*
> *Holy night . . .*
> *All is calm, all is bright . . ."*

The IPF proved itself that Christmas Eve in East Africa. The world was stunned with surprise. But a hard-line cadre of officers high up in the Peacekeepers' chain of command was still laying its plans for a coup. They knew that if they succeeded, their nations would accept their *fait accompli*. If they failed, their nations would disavow themselves of any knowledge of the cabal. Being military men, they were accustomed to such treatment by the politicians. What the politicians didn't realize was that if the coup were successful, the military officers planned to overpower their political leaders and set up their own version of a world government, with themselves as the chiefs.

If Red Eagle was aware of this plot, he gave no indication of it. He concerned himself with another worry. The matter of the missing nuclear bombs.

COMO, Year 3

Y OU certainly picked a conspicuous way of coming here, Mr. Alexander," said Red Eagle.

Cole Alexander shrugged at the massive Amerind. "The plane? It's my home now. A houseboat with wings. Subsonic, but fast enough to suit me."

"It apparently caused quite a stir when you landed on the lake."

"Hide in plain sight," Alexander said. "Sometimes that's the best way."

Red Eagle held the lace curtains aside and stared out the villa's long window down to the lake below. Alexander's swept-wing jet seaplane was moored down among the powerboats and sailing yachts, like a sleek dark panther among fat little sheep.

Alexander stood slightly behind the Amerind, feeling a bit like a child in the shadow of Red Eagle's huge form. A stray memory of boyhood flitted through his mind, of holding his father's hand as they walked along the Minnetonka lakeside promenade together. Then the surge of sorrow. He would never walk with his father again. Or his mother. He could never walk unprotected in the sunshine again. Too much of a risk of cancer now.

"Hide in plain sight," said Red Eagle, chuckling. The sound was like a freight train rumbling in the distance. "You certainly picked an interesting place for it."

Lake Como was abuzz with pleasure boats churning up the water, hydrofoil ferries speeding past, float planes from the Como Aero Club landing and taking off. A knot of gawkers stood at the club's ramp, admiring the jet seaplane anchored out among the boats. An endless stream of cars and tour buses and motor scooters growled and hissed and honked along the road that twisted around the lake's steep wooded mountains. Even from this high above the water, in this crumbling, dusty old villa, the two men could hear people singing and shouting at each other down along the lakeside where they were fishing or sunbathing.

The city, off in the distance, was a cluster of roofs and towers. The gray-white granite monument to Alessandro Volta rose amidst the greenery of a waterside park.

"It would have been more secure," Red Eagle said, letting the curtain drop, "to meet me on the Swiss side of the lake. I had to go through the border station. My passage will be noted."

Alexander ran a hand through his dead-white hair. "Can you imagine the Swiss letting me land that plane on their side of the lake? It'd take six months just to fill out the forms!"

Red Eagle admitted, "The Italians are somewhat easier

in that respect. Their border police did not even look at my car as we drove through."

"You're worried about security?"

"Yes."

"Why?" Alexander asked. "What's this all about? Why did you ask to see me?"

Red Eagle stepped away from the window. He seemed incongruous in the setting: a huge man of powerful dignity, dressed in a conservatively tailored dark business suit, looking for a safe place to sit in a room filled with delicate rococo furniture. The villa that Alexander had rented was faded with time and neglect. Once the home of a wealthy Milanese factory owner, it now was let for rentals to foreigners who came for Lake Como's scenic beauty. The scenery was there, all right, but it was buried beneath hordes of tourists and Milanese weekenders who fouled the waters and littered the roads and belched filth from their engines into the air.

Red Eagle selected an ornate couch of striped fabric and scrollwork legs. Sitting on it carefully, tentatively, he sank into its overplush cushions.

Alexander pulled up a slim gilt-covered chair to the side away from the window and the sunshine.

"We're okay in here," he said. "My people checked the entire house this morning. No bugs."

Red Eagle nodded slowly. Still, he looked around the room as if he could detect electronic listening devices by sheer force of concentration. It was a large room, with a high ceiling decorated with faded frescoes of plump cherubs and insipid saints floating on pinkish clouds. Dust motes lazed through the sunlight lancing in from the long windows.

"I can close the shutters if you like," Alexander offered.

"No need," said Red Eagle. "It may sound paranoid, but I know that I am watched constantly. Probably someone is listening to this conversation."

"I don't see how."

"Neither do I, but the eavesdroppers are ingenious, and the technology of surveillance is quite advanced."

"What's so secret, anyhow?" Alexander asked.

"I have no secrets," said the Amerind, "but I am concerned about your safety, Mr. Alexander."

"Mine?"

Red Eagle nodded again, just once, a ponderous movement of his head. "You have made no secret of the fact that you are attempting to locate Jabal Shamar."

Alexander's face went taut. "He killed my parents. And a couple of million other people."

"So you want to kill him."

"Damned right," he replied tensely. Then, with an obvious effort to be lighter, "Oh, I'm willing to bring him to the World Court, if I can. But I want him, dead or alive."

"That is a very dangerous pastime."

Alexander made a crooked grin and leaned back in his chair.

"You have given up your career, sold your business, used your money to buy that airplane and a crew . . ."

"And I've hired detectives, spies, informers—anybody who can give me information on Shamar's whereabouts."

"Can you afford to hire a team of mercenary soldiers?"

Alexander's smile vanished like a light snapped off.

Drawing in a deep breath, Red Eagle said, "What I propose to tell you could place you in great danger, greater than you have ever been in before."

The sardonic smile twisted Alexander's lips again. "I lived through Jerusalem. I can deal with risk."

Red Eagle said nothing for a long moment. He merely gazed at Alexander, as if trying to make the final decision on whether to speak or not. At last, he let out another long, painful breath and said:

"Mr. Alexander, the International Peacekeeping Force has impounded all the remaining nuclear weapons of the former belligerents of the Final War. Six of them are unaccounted for."

Frowning, Alexander said, "I don't understand."

"The IPF has checked the inventories very carefully, and double-checked with all the military, technical and political people involved. Apparently when Shamar disappeared, he took six nuclear weapons with him."

"Six nukes?"

"Comparatively small ones, in the one-hundred-kiloton range. Five times more powerful than the bombs that destroyed Hiroshima and Nagasaki, but quite small and compact. Suitcase-sized, according to the technical experts."

"Jesus Christ! Shamar's got six nukes?"

"It is worse than that," Red Eagle said, his voice heavy and deep. "The nuclear powers—the United States, Soviet Russia and the others—have suspended their own nuclear disarmament programs."

"Of course," Alexander said. "They're not going to get rid of their bombs as long as Shamar's running loose with a half dozen of his own."

"Precisely. This is an extremely serious situation, Mr. Alexander. The path to real peace will be blocked as long as those weapons are in Shamar's hands."

"But why come to me? This is a problem for the Peacekeepers."

"No," said Red Eagle, with a ponderous shake of his head. "The International Peacekeeping Force cannot intervene in this problem. The IPF must not even attempt to deal with it."

"Why the hell not?"

Red Eagle placed his huge hands on his massive thighs and lifted his eyes to the faded glories of the ceiling.

"You must understand, Mr. Alexander," he said, looking heavenward, "that the IPF has been created for one reason and one reason only: to prevent nations from attacking one another. The *only* situation in which the IPF can act is when a nation launches an armed attack across an international border. The only duty of the Peacekeepers is to keep the peace—to prevent war."

"But if Shamar's got nuclear weapons, he's going to use them sooner or later."

"Think, Mr. Alexander. Think. Many of the nations of the world do not trust the IPF very much. They fear that the Peacekeepers will turn into a world dictatorship. They refuse to disarm, for fear of leaving themselves defenseless against the IPF. Do you think they will allow IPF personnel to hunt for Shamar inside their own borders? Do you think that they will support the IPF's searching for Shamar in other countries?"

Alexander felt a slight wave of giddiness wash through him as he realized what the Amerind was after. "You want me to get Shamar for you."

Red Eagle lowered his gaze and fixed his deep brown eyes on Alexander. "This is very painful for me, Mr. Alexander. I am a man of the law. I do not approve of vigilantes or assassins."

"But you have to nail Shamar, and damned fast, and you can't use the IPF to do the job."

"That is the truth of it," Red Eagle admitted.

"So you want me to do the job for you."

Red Eagle said, "Through the Peacekeepers, I have access to certain forms of intelligence that are unavailable to you."

Tingling with sudden excitement, Alexander grinned and said, "You've got a deal!"

"He must be brought to justice, if possible," insisted Red Eagle. "I will not be party to an assassination."

Alexander countered, "Listen, you just think of this as an old-time sheriff hiring a deputy—or recruiting a posse."

"Not the most fortunate of analogies for a Comanche," Red Eagle replied dourly.

Laughing, Alexander said, "Yeah, I suppose not. But I'll get him for you. Just like I said, dead or alive."

"And the nuclear weapons. They must be recovered. That is even more important than Shamar himself."

"Of course. Sure." But Alexander thought to himself, More important to you, maybe, but not to me.

Red Eagle got to his feet. It reminded Alexander of a tidal wave rising out of the ocean.

"Mr. Alexander, this has been extremely difficult for me. I thank you for your cooperation."

"We both want Shamar."

"And the six nuclear bombs."

"Yes."

The Amerind headed toward the door, Alexander beside him, almost scampering to keep pace with Red Eagle's stately tread across the elaborately tiled floor.

Then Red Eagle stopped. "You have not asked about payment."

"Payment? For what?"

"You will need an armed force to take Shamar. That will cost money."

Alexander smiled crookedly. "What will those suspicious national governments say if they find that the IPF is hiring mercenaries?"

"We could channel the money through a Swiss bank," suggested Red Eagle.

"Famous last words."

The Amerind frowned slightly. "Then how . . ."

"I'm not broke yet," Alexander said. "If and when I need money I'll let you know. For now, all I want from you is information about Shamar's whereabouts."

"I will get it to you."

"Good."

They shook hands at the door, Alexander's pale white hand engulfed in the Amerind's huge dark paw.

Alexander watched from the shaded shelter of the villa's

front gate as Red Eagle squeezed his bulk into the back seat of a BMW sedan. The car sank on its suspension noticeably.

As the sedan pulled away and into the honking streams of everlasting traffic along the roadway, Alexander almost jumped into the air with glee.

I'm going to get Shamar! I'm going to get the bastard and kill him with my own two hands!

In the back seat of the BMW, Red Eagle was thinking, It is a dangerous thing to sidestep the law. Yet what else can be done?

He looked down at the hand that had shaken Alexander's as if it were already dripping with blood.

Red Eagle knew that we—and others—were watching his every move and listening to as much of his conversation as we could. He told himself that, like Marcus Brutus, he was armed so strong in honesty that it didn't matter. But it did, and what he had to do bothered him immensely. No one was ever able to trace the Meissner assassination to him, but it seemed terribly convenient to have that would-be Hitler killed before he could bring East and West to the brink of war over a reunited Germany.

While the Peacekeepers stopped the Mongolian Crisis from erupting into war before a single shot was fired, we were getting unmistakable signals that the officer's coup was under way. Still the sluggards in Geneva did nothing. And Red Eagle was not officially part of the Peacekeepers; he was mainly concerned during those troubled months with feeding information to Cole Alexander. Discreetly. He thought.

INDONESIA, Year 4

STRETCHED out prone on the damp grass at the edge of the trees, Alexander peered through his binoculars at the village in the clearing. He swept his gaze across the cinder-block huts, then focused beyond them to the six helicopters resting beneath camouflage netting at the village's farther side.

"Those're Shamar's choppers?" he asked the man lying beside him. He kept his voice low, almost a whisper. No telling who might be prowling through these woods.

The man nodded. "One of them is. The others belong to the rebel leaders and some of the government men who are in with them. If the word we picked up from Surabaya is right, Shamar and the rebels will be taking off tonight to rendezvous with the guerrillas over in Vogelkop."

"And the government men go back to Jakarta."

"Right," said the man. "Bloody traitors."

The man's name was McPherson, a lifelong professional soldier. Both he and Alexander wore green-mottled jungle fatigues and floppy Digger hats that broke up the outline of a man's head against the heavy foliage of this sweltering tropical forest. Safer than tin helmets, McPherson claimed. Their plastic armor vests were also jungle green; they felt heavy and hot in the sweltering humidity, no matter what the manufacturer claimed for their lightness and comfort.

It had taken almost a year for Alexander to recruit his mercenary force. It was small, but elite. McPherson had not come easily, nor cheaply. Almost every penny Alexander had inherited he had spent on McPherson and his band of professionals. Their arms and training were first-rate.

What little money he had left Alexander had used to track down the elusive Jabal Shamar. The mass murderer had also turned mercenary, using his skills and cunning in everything from terrorism to rebellion, all around the world from Ankara to Quebec. But he made certain to remain beyond the reach of the Peacekeepers. He never engaged in an attack that the IPF would consider to be aggression.

The thousands he killed died in civil wars, rebellions, guerrilla movements, terrorist demonstrations. But they died just the same, cut down by machine-gun fire or blown to bloody pieces by car bombs. They died and Shamar moved on, devising elaborate schemes of murder for pay.

Shamar had the ultimate insurance policy, of course. Somewhere he had cached six nuclear weapons, six bombs capable of destroying six cities. As long as no one knew where the bombs were, Shamar could range the world and fearful governments would allow him untroubled passage.

Was there a nuclear weapon submerged in a Bangkok canal? Thailand turned a blind eye to Shamar's passage through their territory. Is a nuclear bomb hidden in a slum basement in São Paulo? Why should Brazil risk triggering it by trying to arrest Shamar?

But Alexander hunted him. He recruited McPherson and, through him, a mercenary force whose only task was to find Shamar so that Alexander could execute him.

Now Alexander and McPherson lay on a ridge at the edge of a steaming forest, raucous with birds and monkeys, stinking of tropical rot, crawling with insects. The humid heat pressed on them like a sopping sponge, drenching their fatigues with sweat.

McPherson spoke quietly into a palm-sized radio, ordering the other men to take up positions ringing the village. He was a tall, rawboned New Zealander, ruddy of face, with hair and brows so blond he almost looked albino. He had come to Alexander highly recommended, having seen action in the Katangan Secession, the overthrow of the Díaz government in Chile and the bloody shambles of South Africa.

Alexander had agreed that McPherson would be in tactical command, since he himself had never been in action before.

"You stay close by me, Cole. Check your weapons now."

With sweaty hands Alexander examined the grenades hooked to the web belts across his shoulders, memorizing the different types: concussion, frag, smoke. Then he took the pistol from the holster at his waist. Loaded clip in place, safety off. More clips in the belt pouches. Finally he slid the action of his stubby submachine gun back and forth. Satisfied that it was ready, he slapped a banana-curved magazine into place.

"Now we wait," McPherson said.

"How long?"

"Until dusk. Let them get their dinner fires started."

Alexander felt his guts fluttering. "Suppose they have patrols out around here?"

"They do," McPherson replied with a deprecating little smile. "But they won't find my men. I promise you that."

"Why'd you make me check weapons now if . . ."

McPherson laid a hand on Alexander's shoulder. "Wouldn't do to be caught unready to fight, just in case somebody *does* stumble on us."

"But you said . . ."

"I know what I said, Cole. But it's always best to be prepared for every contingency. Remember that."

Feeling like a student facing a fatherly schoolmaster rather than a mercenary soldier getting ready to attack, Cole nodded and lapsed into silence.

He worried about his exposure to sunlight; solar ultraviolet could trigger skin cancers, or worse. His leukemia was under control as long as he took the pills, but Alexander looked on the sun as an enemy. Shamar's gift to me, he thought angrily. Something else he's taken away from me. But if we nail him here it won't matter. The UV dose will be a small price to pay for killing the son of a bitch.

For hours he scanned the village with his binoculars, turning up the electro-optical gain to its highest, until he could make out the faces of the people. Hard to tell the villagers from the guerrillas, he realized. Except for the tattered camouflage uniforms they wore, there was no real difference among the brown-skinned men. Some of the women were in dirty mottled uniforms, too, with assault rifles slung over their slim shoulders. The village women wore long colorful batik skirts and Western-style loose blouses, all of them shabby and tattered.

This was not a rich village. The paddies out on the other side where the helicopters were hidden seemed pitifully small and scrawny. Even the few water buffalo Alexander spotted looked emaciated.

Why is Shamar here, when he's being paid to organize

the rebel guerrillas in West Irian? Cole wondered. Is he actually here, or is this a ruse—or worse yet, a trap?

And then his heart leaped. He saw Jabal Shamar. The man calmly stepped out of one of the larger cinder-block buildings in the center of the village, squinting at the lowering sun and raising his hand to shield his eyes. It was him, all right! Alexander knew that face, even though he had never met Shamar.

Seeing him live, instead of a picture, brought surprises. Shamar was shockingly young for a general, a youthful forty at most. Practically my age, Alexander realized. He wore desert tan fatigues, unadorned by insignia or any mark of rank. Vigorous, brisk movements. As he spoke he gestured vividly; his hands were never still. Yet he was much smaller than Alexander had expected, a stunted marionette of a man, slim and hard-faced, with a trim dark mustache and a livid white scar that ran from the bottom of his right ear along the jawline almost to the point of his chin.

"The murdering son of a bitch is there," he muttered, passing the binoculars to McPherson.

The Kiwi took them for a moment, then handed them back with nothing more than a grunt of acknowledgement.

The largest building, in the center of the village, was obviously where the meeting was taking place. Alexander clicked on the subminiaturized video camera built into the binoculars as he watched the men gathering around Shamar, bowing to him or shaking his hand. They all seemed so subservient to this mass murderer. The men from Jakarta wore lightweight, light-colored Westernized business suits; bureaucrats through and through, dressed almost identically to their brethren around the world. The guerrillas wore rags and tatters of old army uniforms they had decorated with bright head scarves and armbands.

Alexander videoed it all as he watched, waiting impatiently for sunset.

The shadows lengthened. Spires of smoke began to rise from the roof holes in several of the cinder-block huts inside the village. Alexander could smell vegetables boiling and fresh fish sizzling on the fire.

McPherson checked by radio with his men. No sign of enemy patrols. No hint that they had been detected. Shamar was in council with the rebel leaders and the traitors within the government who were in league with the rebels.

He touched Alexander on the shoulder. Cole jerked as if a hot ember had seared his skin.

"It's time," McPherson said.

Alexander nodded, his lips pressed to a bloodless tight line. "Okay," he said, with a firmness he did not feel. "Let's get it done."

McPherson thumbed his palm-sized radio again. "All units—attack!"

And they were up and running toward the village. It was not walled; it was nothing more than a roughly circular collection of the cinder-block buildings, none of them more than a single story high. Alexander held his submachine gun in both hands, felt the weight of the grenades on his chest, the pistol flopping in its holster at his hip, the bulky electronic binoculars pressing against the small of his back.

On both sides of them other men in jungle green and floppy hats, guns held level, were racing across the clearing between the forest and the outer ring of huts.

McPherson sprinted a few steps ahead of Alexander and dashed in between the two nearest huts. No one else was in sight except his own mercenary soldiers.

But then a burst of gunfire off to his right. Alexander saw McPherson skid to a stop on the dusty bare ground and flatten out along a cinder-block wall. He did the same.

A soldier in a dirt-caked steel helmet popped out of a doorway and squirted a burst of semiautomatic fire at them. McPherson threw himself to the ground and fired back in one motion. The soldier screamed and fell back into the hut.

"Come on!" McPherson yelled. Alexander followed him on legs suddenly gone rubbery as the New Zealander raced to the hut and threw a grenade into the doorway.

It exploded almost immediately. Smoke and screams billowed out the doorway.

"Squirt 'em!" McPherson commanded, already heading for the next hut.

Alexander ducked into the smoky doorway, coughing as he pointed his gun inside the hut. Squinting, he saw a tangle of bodies huddled next to a small table splintered by the grenade's blast. He knew what he was supposed to do: spray the bodies with bullets, make certain no one would stagger out of that hut to shoot them in the back.

His finger froze on the trigger. They're all dead. Have to be.

One of the bodies moaned and writhed in pain. A woman, her colorful skirt smeared with blood.

Alexander doubled over, fighting down the bile that was surging into his mouth. He backed out of the doorway, took a gulp of fresh air, and saw that he was alone.

Gunfire deeper in the village. The *crump* of a grenade. Men's deep voices shouting and cursing. Screams, high-pitched with terror and agony.

He ran down the crooked lane between huts and saw several of the green-clad mercenaries blazing away at the rooftops. Chunks of cinder block flew in all directions, but no one seemed to be up there. Then the black oval shape of a grenade arced against the flaming sunset sky and exploded between the men. Their bodies were flung like rag dolls, smashed against the cinder blocks.

A fragment caught Alexander, nicked his shoulder and spun him halfway around.

He saw three men with assault rifles coming up toward

him. No, two men and a woman. Ragged clothes, but the rifles looked polished and new.

He could not fire at them. He knew he had to kill them or they would kill him. He commanded his finger to squeeze the trigger. He silently raged at his hand to do what it had to do. Yet his finger would not move a millimeter.

The woman shot him, a single round, straight at his chest. Alexander felt a tremendous hammer blow slam him down into the ground. The bloodred sky went dark. The last thing he heard was a man's voice bellowing angrily over the sound of more gunfire. It sounded like McPherson.

He woke to McPherson's voice.

"I expect you to allow me to evacuate my wounded and what's left of my men," the Kiwi was saying.

"You are a professional soldier," replied a harsh, guttural voice in heavily accented English. "You expect all the niceties of polite professional conduct to be extended to you."

Alexander tried to open his eyes. They seemed glued shut.

"You've beaten us," McPherson said, his voice sounding more exasperated than fearful. "What more do you want?"

"Why should I allow you to go? You might come against me again, some other day. Why not kill you all now and be done with it?"

In the silence that followed, Alexander tried to rub the blurriness out of his eyes. His chest flared with pain. Broken rib, he knew. More than one, most likely. The armor vest stopped the bullet, but not its impact.

He focused on the shadowy ceiling, then carefully turned his head toward the voices he had heard.

He was lying on a straw pallet on the floor of a tiny room. The only light came from the doorway from which the voices emanated. The room stank of blood and excrement.

Flies buzzed annoyingly, but Alexander's chest hurt too much to try to wave them away. Two other bodies were stretched out next to him. They both were unmoving, eyes staring—the flies and other insects were crawling over them.

Alexander barely held down his gorge. He looked past them, toward the lighted doorway.

"As you said, I'm a professional soldier," McPherson replied at last. "If you allow us to leave here, I'll give you my word that neither I nor my men will ever hire on against you. Never, no matter who approaches us or what he offers."

Another long silence. Then the other voice—it had to be Shamar's, Alexander reasoned—finally said, "Ah, you English and your honor. Very well, I will allow you to go."

"I'm New Zealand," said McPherson stiffly. "But I thank you anyways."

"All but your employer," said Shamar.

"Hold on now . . ."

"That man will remain here. He is my enemy and I have no intention of allowing him to go free."

He's talking about me! Alexander realized with a pang of shock.

"I can't allow that," said McPherson.

Shamar laughed, a mocking grating sound. "If you wish to stay with him and share his fate, I will accommodate you." His voice suddenly went iron-hard. "You, and what's left of your men."

"That's not fair," McPherson whispered.

Shamar laughed again. "I thought you English had a saying, 'All's fair in love and war.'"

"He's just a silly rich man."

"A stupid rich man," Shamar corrected, "who swallowed the information that my people sold to him. An ignorant Yankee who led you and your men into this trap like a Judas goat leading sheep."

"I still can't . . ."

"You had better take your men and leave while you can." Shamar's voice was flat and cold. The discussion was at an end.

McPherson said, "I'm doing this only for the sake of my men."

"Of course. And don't trouble yourself about this American fool. He isn't worth troubling your conscience over."

Alexander heard McPherson's booted feet clump across the wooden floorboards. A door squeaked open, then banged shut.

It's my fault, he realized. I led McPherson and his men into this mess. I let Shamar bait the trap and I walked right into it. I couldn't even fight, when the chips were down. Worse than a fool. I'm a coward. A gutless coward who can't pull a trigger even to save his own life.

The realization burned him with a searing pain worse than his wound. I'm a coward. A coward.

A lilting Indonesian voice, in tones almost like a flute, asked, "Is it wise to allow the mercenaries to go free?"

Shamar made a coughing, almost barking sound that might have been a single burst of laughter. "No, it is not wise. And they will not leave this village alive."

"But you told him . . ."

"What I told that Englishman I said to make him and his men easier to handle. They will be marched back toward the forest, toward the vans that carried them here from the coast. Before they reach the vans they will be shot. All of them."

Without consciously willing it, Alexander struggled up to a sitting position. The pain made his head swim, but he still heard Shamar's grating voice.

"In a few weeks' time the jungle will have obliterated their bodies. There will be no trace of them."

I can't let him murder Mac and his men. I've killed enough of them. I can't let him slaughter the rest.

Every breath was an agony. Alexander checked his clothes. They had removed everything: vest, webbing, weapons, even his boots. Nothing remained except his fatigues, and the pockets had been thoroughly emptied.

Glancing at the corpses lying next to him, he saw that they had been similarly stripped.

He crawled painfully, slithering along the splintery boards on the side that hurt less, toward the lighted doorway. It took all his willpower not to cry out from the pain. Staying back in the shadows, flat on his stomach and flaming chest, Alexander surveyed the other room.

Shamar was sitting at a warped, swaybacked table, packing wads of paper money into an aluminum case. There was a stack of bills on the table, neatly bundled in bank wrappers. Two of the men from Jakarta, in their lily-white business suits, stood with their backs to Alexander, watching their money disappear into Shamar's case.

Also on the table were some of Alexander's belongings: he recognized his electronic binoculars, his never-used automatic pistol, and the six grenades he had carried into the battle.

There was a guerrilla soldier at the door that led outside, standing nonchalantly with a Kalishnikov assault rifle slung over one shoulder, smoking a crooked brown cigarette, staring at more money than he and his ancestors had ever seen in their combined lifetimes.

Biting his lips to keep from wimpering, Alexander slowly clawed up the wall and inched to his feet. He stood there for a long dizzying moment, swaying, forcing himself to remain conscious and not give in to the soft yielding darkness that tempted him.

Leaning his back against the flimsy wall, listening to Shamar and the Jakarta traitors bantering about money and taxpayers and bank accounts in Singapore, Alexander felt the sweat pouring from every inch of his body. It was not merely the heat, not only the pain that made him perspire.

It was fear. He knew what he had to do. He knew that he had to do it *now*. Ten seconds from now might be too late.

They'll kill me, a voice said inside his head.

Sure, he answered himself. But they're going to kill you anyway. At least you've got to *try*.

Abruptly he pushed himself away from the wall, barged into the lighted room, lurched between the two Indonesians and grabbed for the pistol on the table.

Shamar was faster. His face showed surprise, but his hands moved swiftly and surely. He dropped the wad of money he had been holding, even as the Indonesians staggered away from Alexander and the young guerrilla by the outer doorway dropped his cigarette in shock.

Shamar swept up the pistol in his right hand and with practiced smoothness brought up his left to slide the action back and cock it.

As he did so, Alexander did the only thing he could think of. He grabbed one of the fragmentation grenades and yanked its pin out.

He distinctly heard the pin clatter on the tabletop, and before the sound was gone, the *snick-clack* of the pistol's action.

The two Indonesians started to babble and the guerrilla whipped his rifle from his shoulder.

"No!" Shamar bellowed, holding out his left hand toward the young guerrilla.

He pointed the pistol at Alexander's gut. But he did not fire. Alexander held the grenade tightly in his right hand, woozy with the agony that his effort had caused, sagging back against the cinder-block wall.

"If I let go," he said, his voice thick with pain, "this grenade goes off. We'll all die."

He could see Shamar's eyes, pale blue and calculating.

"It's a three-second fuse," Alexander added. "For house-to-house fighting. You won't have time to pick it up and throw it away."

Shamar eased his tensed body. He even smiled slightly. But the gun stayed pointed at Alexander.

"You are more resourceful than I thought."

"And you," Alexander panted, gasping from the pain of talking, "are just as much a murdering son of a bitch as I thought."

The Indonesians seemed petrified with fear. The youngster had lowered his rifle, but kept his hand on the pistol grip; he could swing the muzzle up and fire in an instant.

"We have a stalemate," Shamar said. The scar along his jaw seemed unusually white, almost pulsating.

"Give the order to bring McPherson and his men back here."

"The mercenaries?"

"Bring them back here," Alexander repeated. "Unharmed."

With a shrug that was half amused, half contemptuous, Shamar reached into a chest pocket of his fatigues and brought out a small black radio, the same miniature size that McPherson had used. He spoke into it in Arabic.

"They will be back here in ten minutes," he said to Alexander.

"Tell 'em to make it faster. My hand's getting sweaty. I might drop this egg."

Shamar spoke into the radio again. Alexander knew that they were waiting for him to pass out, to slump down into unconsciousness from the pain. *He'll try to grab the grenade before it goes off, it's his only chance. I've got to stay awake. Alert. Got to!*

He looked into Shamar's pale blue eyes again. *Watching, waiting, calculating, staring at me like a snake stares at a bird. Odd that they should be so light. Wonder who got into whose harem?*

A wave of dizziness washed over him and Alexander shook his head to clear it. The movement cost him pain, and a surge of nausea in his guts.

He snapped his eyes open when he realized they had been closed. Shamar had tensed slightly, but he smiled and relaxed once again. None of the others in the room had moved a millimeter.

I couldn't have been out long, Alexander said to himself. But it won't take long for him to move.

He stared again at the face of Jabal Shamar, his enemy, the man who had killed his parents and millions of others.

"I was in Jerusalem," Alexander muttered.

Shamar lifted an eyebrow slightly. "And you survived."

"My mother didn't. Neither did my father. He was in Tel Aviv when you nuked it."

"We did not strike first with nuclear weapons."

"No. You struck last. After the cease-fire had been arranged."

"Would you like a chair?" Shamar asked, almost solicitously. He even let the pistol down slightly. Only slightly.

"I'll stay on my feet," replied Alexander.

"For how long?"

"Long enough."

The sound of boots scuffling on the dry ground outside reached Alexander's ears. Someone rapped on the door frame. Shamar said a single word and an older guerrilla, a bandolier of cartridges hanging from his shoulder, stepped into the room.

"Tell him I want McPherson," said Alexander.

Shamar did so.

The big New Zealander took in the situation at a glance. "Mexican standoff, eh?"

"You cannot get out of this village unless I allow it," said Shamar.

Alexander asked McPherson, "Mac, can you fly one of those choppers out there?"

"Sure. So can Alfie or Rodríguez."

"All right." Turning back to Shamar, he said, "Let's go."

"To the helicopters?"

"Right."

"If I refuse?"

Without thinking, Alexander tried to take a deep breath. The pain flared, and he felt his knees turn watery. Bile surged up his throat. He put out his free hand to steady himself against the table.

"Listen to me," he said to Shamar. "If you don't do *exactly* as I say, I'll open my hand and blow all of us to shreds. Understand? Now, move."

Wordlessly Shamar headed for the door. McPherson pushed past him and wrapped an arm around Alexander's shoulders. Tenderly.

"Ribs?" he asked.

"Yeah. Broken, I think."

"Come on, mate. Maybe you ought to give the pineapple to me."

Alexander shook his head. "I'll hold it."

Turning to Shamar, McPherson wordlessly took the pistol from his hand.

Outside it was night. In the dim shadows, Alexander made out only eight men in jungle fatigues, and three of them wore bloodied bandages. Eight out of twenty-nine. It was a shambles, all right, he accused himself.

Slowly they made their way toward the helicopters, a strange procession with Alexander supported by McPherson, Shamar walking beside him, and the two Indonesian government officials two paces in front. The surviving mercenaries trudged on either side. They were completely disarmed; the only weapons in the entire group were the pistol McPherson now held and the grenade Alexander clutched in his cramped, sweaty hand.

But out in the shadows they were escorted by a ghostly convoy of guerrilla men and women, armed and waiting for a chance, a word, a stumble that might allow them to spring. Shamar kept up a steady flow of words, mostly in English, warning them to keep their distance and remain calm.

He doesn't want to die, Alexander realized. He's no more prepared to die than I was to kill.

Yet he sensed the terrifying presence of dozens of guns waiting in the darkness to cut him down. If he felt back in the hut like a bird being hypnotized by a snake, now it was like a small herd of antelope being stalked by a pack of ravenous wolves.

They reached the helicopters. Under McPherson's direction, the mercenaries dismantled the engines on all but one of them. Rodríguez, his white teeth flashing in the darkness, clambered up into the cockpit of the largest chopper and started up its engine. It whined to life, and the big rotor blade began revolving slowly.

Supported by one of the unwounded mercenaries, Alexander made a feeble gesture toward the helicopter.

"Up you go," he said to Shamar.

The man shook his head.

"Into the chopper," Alexander insisted.

"No."

"You'll go or else."

"Or else you'll release the grenade? Go ahead and do it."

In the dim flashing red of the helicopter's safety light, Shamar's face looked coppery, lurid like a devil's lit by the fires of hell. He was no longer sneering, no longer contemptuous.

"You want to take me to your kind of justice, to put me in a jail cell and put me on trial before the world and execute me as a criminal."

"Damned right! Murderer. Genocidal bastard."

Shamar shook his head. "Then kill me here and now. Let the grenade go."

Alexander was trembling with a mixture of rage and fear. "You better get the fuck up that ladder . . ."

"No. And if you try to force me, the guerrillas will open fire and kill you all."

McPherson came out of the shadows to Alexander's side.

"Let him go," he said over the rising thunder of the helicopter's engine.

"I won't! I want him dead!"

"Then kill me," Shamar shouted, his face grim, his voice flat and hard.

"You'll get us all killed," said McPherson.

Alexander said nothing. He could not move, could not speak, could not act.

"Come on, boss. Into the heli. Be glad we're getting away with our lives. That's the important thing."

Gently McPherson coaxed him up the metal ladder and into the helicopter. Shamar stood rooted out on the dusty blowing ground, the flashing red light outlining him against the night.

Over the whining roar of the chopper's engine, Shamar shouted, "We will meet again, Yankee! We will meet again!"

Alexander tried to turn and answer, but McPherson had him wrapped in his strong arms. "Never mind him. He's just putting on a show for the wogs."

He sat Alexander down on the bench at the rear of the chopper's passenger compartment. "Better let me have it now," McPherson said. "Wouldn't want it loose in here."

Alexander felt his strong fingers prying the grenade from his hand.

The other men filed in and slumped onto the remaining seats. McPherson gave a command and the engine roared louder. The helicopter jerked free of the ground and lifted into the darkness.

McPherson went to the hatch, opened it, and tossed the grenade away. Its explosion was barely noticeable. The big New Zealander came back and sat beside Alexander once again.

"I couldn't do it," Alexander said, fighting back sobs. "I couldn't kill the son of a bitch. I had the chance and I couldn't do it."

"You saved us," McPherson pointed out. "That's something."

"I walked you into a trap. I couldn't even fire a shot."

"Some men are not meant for combat. It's just not in their makeup."

"I'm not meant for anything," Alexander groaned. "Useless. A goddamned fucking useless coward."

McPherson was silent for a moment. Then, "Well, at the least you've got enough video in here"—he unhitched the electronic binoculars from his belt—"to blow away the traitors in the Jakarta government."

"Where'd you get that?"

"Took it off the table in the hut back there," said the New Zealander. "Thought the video stuff would look good on global telly."

Despite the pain still flaring in his chest, Alexander laughed. Shakily. "We can expose Shamar's connection with the guerrillas."

"And the blokes who're selling out their own government to him."

"That'll stop him. It'll force him to get out of Indonesia altogether."

"Not a bad day's work, all things considered," said McPherson. "You don't always have to kill a man to defeat him."

Alexander leaned his head back against the padded bench. "I should have killed him. He'll just pop up again somewhere else, cause more trouble. Kill more people."

The New Zealander shook his head. "You're not the killing type, Cole. These men of mine—they can kill. But you can't. It isn't in you."

"I make a helluva mercenary, don't I?"

Mac grinned at him. "Oh, I dunno. You're learning. There's more than one way to skin a rat."

Cole Alexander closed his eyes. The Peacekeepers have the right idea, he realized. Destroy the weapons, not the soldiers. Maybe I can do that, too. Work where the Peacekeepers can't go. Use smarts instead of guns. Maybe it can work like that. It's worth a try.

It's worth a try.

McPherson got up and went forward to check with the pilot. He came back to report that Surabaya was less than an hour away, and a medical team would be waiting for them.

But Alexander was stretched out on the bench, sound asleep, a crooked grin on his grimy, sweaty face.

Cole Alexander recovered from his wounds. The psychic trauma, the injury to his confidence and self-esteem, took longer to heal. Strangely it was his only child who performed the therapeutic process—quite without realizing what she was doing. Transcript of a conversation between them, recorded as they strolled along the grounds of the IPF facility in Ottawa, where he visited his daughter, S. A. Kelly.

Kelly: It's good to see you again, Daddy.

Alexander: You sounded pretty damned miserable on the phone. What's the matter?

Kelly: I shouldn't bother you with it. It's my problem.

Alexander: Listen, kid, I may not be much of a father, but I do care about you, you know.

Kelly: I know.

Alexander: And I don't have much of anything else to do right now. At least let me act like a father, give you some sage advice and all that crap.

Kelly (laughing a little): Oh, I've just got a heart problem.

Alexander (alarmed): Heart?

Kelly: Not medical! Romantic. I fell for a guy, and I thought he fell for me. But now he's getting married to somebody else.

Alexander: The son of a bitch.

Kelly: No, he's not. He's a very fine man. It was my mistake.

Alexander (slowly): We all make mistakes, little lady. I backed off from marrying your mother . . . that was the worst mistake of my life.

Kelly: She really loved you. Her last words were about you.

Alexander (after a long pause): Listen, kid, why don't you chuck this Peacekeeper job and come with me?

Kelly: Leave the IPF?

Alexander: Why not? You've been stuck in the same grade for two years now. They should have promoted you for what you did in Eritrea.

Kelly: The review board . . .

Alexander: Screw the review board! Come with me. I'm doing things that the IPF can't do.

Kelly: What do you mean?

Alexander (lowering his voice): Not here. Come into town with me tonight. We'll have dinner together and I'll lay it all out for you.

Kelly soon did resign from the Peacekeepers to help her father build the tightly knit mercenary force that eventually brought him to the massacred village of Misericordia and his confrontation shortly afterward with Jabal Shamar.

In the meantime, however, the cabal of officers from several nations sprang their coup to take over the International Peacekeeping Force. To understand what happened in orbit, where the main struggle took place, it is instructive to cite two twentieth-century strategic thinkers who strongly disagreed with one another.

Ashton Carter: We should avoid a dependence on satellites for wartime purposes that is out of proportion to our ability to protect them. If we make ourselves dependent upon vulnerable spacecraft for military support, we will have built an Achilles' heel into our forces.

Maxwell W. Hunter II: The key issue then becomes, is our defense capable of defending itself . . .?

As I said, they strongly disagreed with one another. Yet both of them were right.

BATTLE STATION
HUNTER,
Year 5

T‌HE first laser beam caught them unaware, slicing through the station's thin aluminum skin exactly where the main power trunk and air lines fed into the bridge.

A sputtering fizz of sparks, a moment of heart-wrenching darkness, and then the emergency dims came on. The electronics consoles switched to their internal batteries with barely a microsecond's hesitation, but the air fans sighed to a stop and fell silent. The four men and two women on duty in the bridge had about a second to realize they were under attack. Enough time for the breath to catch in your throat, for the sudden terror to hollow out your guts.

The second laser hit was a high-energy pulse deliberately aimed at the bridge's observation port. It cracked the impact-resistant plastic as easily as a hammer smashes an egg; the air pressure inside the bridge blew the port open. The six men and women became six exploding bodies spewing blood. There was not even time enough to scream.

The station was named *Hunter,* although only three of its crew knew why. It was not one of the missile-killing satellites, nor one of the sensor-laden observation birds. It was a command-and-control station, manned by a crew of twenty, orbiting some one thousand kilometers high, just below the densest radiation zone of the inner Van Allen belt. It circled the Earth in about 105 minutes. By deliberate design, the station was not hardened against laser attack. The attackers knew this perfectly well.

Commander Hazard was almost asleep when the bridge was destroyed. He had just finished his daily inspection of the battle station. Satisfied that the youngsters of his crew were reasonably sharp, he had returned to his coffin-sized personal cabin and wormed out of his sweaty fatigues. He was angry with himself.

Two months aboard the station and he still felt the nausea and unease of space adaptation syndrome. It was like the captain of an ocean vessel having seasickness all the time. Hazard fumed inwardly as he stuck another timed-release medication plaster on his neck, slightly behind his left ear. The old one had fallen off. Not that they did much good. His neck was faintly spotted with the rings left by the medication patches. Still, his stomach felt fluttery, his palms slippery with perspiration.

Clinging grimly to a handgrip, he pushed his weightless body from the mirrored sink to the mesh sleep cocoon fastened against the opposite wall of his cubicle. He zipped himself into the bag and slipped the terry-cloth restraint across his forehead. Hazard was a bulky, dour man with iron-gray hair still cropped Academy close, a weather-beaten squarish face built around a thrusting spadelike nose, a thin slash of a mouth that seldom smiled and eyes the color of a stormy sea. Those eyes seemed suspicious of everyone and everything, probing, inquisitory. A closer look showed that they were weary, disappointed with the world and the people in it. Disappointed most of all with himself.

He was just dozing off when the emergency klaxon started hooting. For a disoriented moment he thought he was back in a submarine and something had gone wrong with a dive. He felt his arms pinned by the mesh sleeping bag, as if he had been bound by unknown enemies. He almost panicked as he heard hatches slamming automatically and the terrifying wail of the alarms. The communications unit on the wall added its urgent shrill to the clamor.

The comm unit's piercing whistle snapped him to full awareness. He stopped struggling against the mesh and unzippered it with a single swift motion, slipping out of the head restraint at the same time.

Hazard slapped at the wall comm's switch. "Commander here," he snapped. "Report."

"Varshni, sir. CIC. The bridge is out. Apparently destroyed."

"Destroyed?"

"All life-support functions down. Air pressure zero. No communications," replied the Indian in a rush. His slightly singsong Oxford accent was trembling with fear. "It exploded, sir. They are all dead in there."

Hazard felt the old terror clutching at his heart, the physical weakness, the giddiness of sudden fear. Forcing his voice to remain steady, he commanded, "Full alert status. Ask Mr. Feeney and Miss Yang to meet me at the CIC at once. I'll be down there in sixty seconds or less."

The *Hunter* was one of nine orbiting battle stations that made up the command-and-control function of the newly created International Peacekeeping Force's strategic defense network. In lower orbits, 135 unmanned ABM satellites armed with multimegawatt lasers and hypervelocity missiles crisscrossed the Earth's surface. In theory, these satellites could destroy thousands of ballistic missiles within five minutes of their launch, no matter where on Earth they rose from.

In theory, each battle station controlled fifteen of the ABM satellites, but never the same fifteen for very long. The battle station's higher orbits were deliberately picked so that the unmanned satellites passed through their field of view as they hurried by in their lower orbits. At the insistence of the fearful politicians of a hundred nations, no ABM satellites were under the permanent control of any one particular battle station.

In theory, each battle station patrolled one ninth of the Earth's surface as it circled the globe. The sworn duty of its carefully chosen international crew was to make certain that any missiles launched from that part of the Earth would be swiftly and efficiently destroyed.

In theory.

The IPF was new, its defensive satellite system untried except for computerized simulations and war games. The Peacekeepers had the power and the authority to prevent a nuclear strike from reaching its targets, no matter who launched the attack. Their authority extended completely across the Earth, even to the superpowers themselves.

In theory.

Dressed in fresh fatigues, Hazard pulled aside the privacy curtain of his cubicle and launched himself down the narrow passageway with a push of his meaty hands against the cool metal of the bulkheads. His stomach lurched at the sudden motion and he squeezed his eyes shut for a moment.

The Combat Information Center was buried deep in the middle of the station, protected by four levels of living and working areas plus the station's storage magazines for water, food, air, fuel for the maneuvering thrusters, power generators and other equipment.

Hazard fought down the queasy fluttering of his stomach as he glided along the passageway toward the CIC. At least he did not suffer the claustrophobia that afflicted some of the station's younger crew members. To a man who had spent most of his career aboard nuclear submarines, the station was roomy, almost luxurious.

He had to yank open four airtight hatches along the short way. Each clanged shut automatically behind him.

At last Hazard floated into the dimly lit Combat Information Center. It was a tiny, womblike circular chamber, its walls studded with display screens that glowed a sickly green in the otherwise darkened compartment. No desks or chairs in zero gravity; the CIC's work surfaces were chest-high consoles, most of them covered with keyboards.

Varshni and the Norwegian woman, Stromsen, were on duty. The little Indian, slim and dark, was wide-eyed with anxiety. His face shone with perspiration and his fatigues were dark at the armpits and between his shoulders. In the greenish glow from the display screens he looked positively ill. Stromsen looked tense, her strong jaw clenched, her ice-blue eyes fastened on Hazard, waiting for him to tell her what to do.

"What happened?" Hazard demanded.

"It simply blew out," said Varshni. "I had just spoken with Michaels and D'Argencour when . . . when . . ." His voice choked off.

"The screens went blank." Stromsen pointed to the status displays. "Everything suddenly zeroed out."

She was controlling herself carefully, Hazard saw, every nerve taut to the point of snapping.

"The rest of the station?" Hazard asked.

She gestured again toward the displays. "No other damage."

"Everybody on full alert?"

"Yes, sir."

Lieutenant Feeney ducked through the hatch, his eyes immediately drawn to the row of burning red malfunction lights where the bridge displays should have been.

"Mother of Mercy, what's happened?"

Before anyone could reply, Susan Yang, the chief communications officer, pushed through the hatch and almost bumped into Feeney. She saw the displays and immediately concluded, "We're under attack!"

"That is impossible!" Varshni blurted.

Hazard studied their faces for a swift moment. They all knew what had happened; only Yang had the guts to say it aloud. She seemed cool and in control of herself. Oriental inscrutability? Hazard wondered. He knew she was third-generation Hawaiian. Feeney's pinched, narrow-eyed face failed to hide the fear that they all felt, but the Irishman held himself well and returned Hazard's gaze without a tremor.

The only sound in the CIC was the hum of the electrical equipment and the soft sighing of the air fans. Hazard felt uncomfortably warm with the five of them crowding the cramped little chamber. Perspiration trickled down his ribs. They were all staring at him, waiting for him to tell them what must be done, to bring order out of the numbing fear and uncertainty that swirled around them. Four youngsters from four different nations, each of them wearing the blue-gray fatigues of the IPF with colored patches denoting their technical specialties on their right shoulders and the flag of their national origin on their left shoulders.

Hazard said, "We'll have to control the station from

here. Mr. Feeney, you are now my Number One; Michaels was on duty in the bridge. Mr. Varshni, get a damage-control party to the bridge. Full suits."

"No one's left alive in there," Varshni whispered.

"Yes, but their bodies must be recovered. We owe them that. And their families." He glanced toward Yang. "And we've got to determine what caused the blowout."

Varshni's face twisted unhappily at the thought of the mangled bodies.

"I want a status report from each section of the station," Hazard went on, knowing that activity was the key to maintaining discipline. "Start with . . ."

A beeping sound made all five of them turn toward the communications console. Its orange demand light blinked for attention in time with the angry beeps. Hazard reached for a handgrip to steady himself as he swung toward the comm console. He noted how easily the youngsters handled themselves in zero gee. To him it still took a conscious, gut-wrenching effort.

Stromsen touched the keyboard with a slender finger. A man's unsmiling face appeared on the screen: light brown hair clipped as close as Hazard's gray, lips pressed together in an uncompromising line. He wore the blue-gray of the IPF with a commander's silver comet on his collar.

"This is Buckbee, commander of station *Graham*. I want to speak to Commander Hazard."

Sliding in front of the screen, Hazard grasped the console's edge with both white-knuckled hands. He knew Buckbee only by reputation, a former U.S. Air Force colonel, from the Space Command until it had been disbanded, but before that he had put in a dozen years with SAC.

"This is Hazard."

Buckbee's lips moved slightly in what might have been a smile, but his eyes remained cold. "Hazard, you've just lost your bridge."

"And six lives."

Unmoved, Buckbee continued as if reading from a prepared script, "We offer you a chance to save the lives of the rest of your crew. Surrender the *Hunter* to us."

"Us?"

Buckbee nodded, a small economical movement. "We will bring order and greatness out of this farce called the IPF."

A wave of loathing so intense that it almost made him vomit swept through Hazard. He realized that he had known all along, with a certainty that had not needed conscious verification: his bridge had been destroyed by deliberate attack, not by accident.

"You killed six kids," he said, his voice so low that he barely heard it himself. It was not a whisper but a growl.

"We had to prove that we mean business, Hazard. Now, surrender your station or we'll blow you all to hell. Any further deaths will be on your head, not ours."

Jonathan Wilson Hazard, captain, U.S. Navy (ret.). Marital status: divorced. Two children, Jonathan, Jr., twenty-six; Virginia Elizabeth, twenty. Served twenty-eight years in U.S. Navy, mostly in submarines. Commanded Fleet Ballistic Missile Submarines *Ohio, Corpus Christi* and *Utah.* Later served as technical advisor to Joint Chiefs of Staff and as naval liaison to NATO headquarters in Brussels. Retired from Navy after hostage crisis in Brussels. Joined International Peacekeeping Force and appointed commander of orbital battle station *Hunter.*

"I can't just hand this station over to a face on a screen," Hazard replied, stalling, desperately trying to think his way through the situation. "I don't know what you're up to, what your intentions are, who you really are."

"You're in no position to bargain, Hazard," said Buckbee, his voice flat and hard. "We want control of your station. Either you give it to us or we'll eliminate you completely."

"Who the hell is 'we'?"

"That doesn't matter."

"The hell it doesn't! I want to know who you are and what you're up to."

Buckbee frowned slightly. His eyes shifted away slightly, as if looking to someone standing out of range of the video camera.

"We don't have time to go into that now," he said at last.

Hazard recognized the crack in Buckbee's armor. It was not much, but he pressed it. "Well, you goddamned well better make time, mister. I'm not handing this station over to you or anybody else until I know what in hell is going on."

Turning to Feeney, he ordered, "Sound general quarters. ABM satellites on full automatic. Miss Yang, contact IPF headquarters and give them a full report of our situation."

"We'll destroy your station before those idiots in Geneva can decide what to do!" Buckbee snapped.

"Maybe," said Hazard. "But that'll take time, won't it? And we won't go down easy, I guarantee you. Maybe we'll take you down with us."

Buckbee's face went white with fury. His eyes glared angrily.

"Listen," Hazard said more reasonably, "you can't expect me to just turn this station over to a face on a screen. Six of my people have been killed. I want to know why, and who's behind all this. I won't deal until I know who I'm dealing with and what your intentions are."

Buckbee growled, "You've just signed the death warrant for yourself and your entire crew."

The comm screen went blank.

For a moment Hazard hung weightlessly before the dead screen, struggling to keep the fear inside him from showing. Putting a hand out to the edge of the console to steady himself, he turned slowly to his young officers. Their eyes were riveted on him, waiting for him to tell them what to do, waiting for him to decide between life and death.

Quietly, but with steel in his voice, Hazard commanded, "I said general quarters, Mr. Feeney. Now!"

Feeney flinched as if suddenly awakened from a dream. He pushed himself to the command console, unlatched the red cover over the general-quarters button and banged it eagerly with his fist. The action sent him recoiling upward and he had to put up a hand against the overhead to push himself back down to the deck. The alarm light began blinking red and they could hear its hooting even through the airtight hatches outside the CIC.

"Geneva, Miss Yang," Hazard said sternly over the howl of the alarm. "Feeney, see that the crew is at their battle stations. I want the satellites under our control on full automatic, prepared to shoot down anything that moves if it isn't in our precleared data bank. And Mr. Varshni, has that damage-control party gotten under way yet?"

The two young men rushed toward the hatch, bumping each other in their eagerness to follow their commander's orders. Hazard almost smiled at the Laurel and Hardy aspect of it. Lieutenant Yang pushed herself to the comm console and anchored her softboots on the Velcro strip fastened to the deck there.

"Miss Stromsen, you are the duty officer. I am depending on you to keep me informed of the status of all systems."

"Yessir!"

Keep them busy, Hazard told himself. Make them concentrate on doing their jobs and they won't have time to be frightened.

"Encountering interference, sir," reported Yang, her eyes on the comm displays. "Switching to emergency frequency."

Jamming, thought Hazard.

"Main comm antenna overheating," Stromsen said. She glanced down at her console keyboard, then up at the displays again. "I think they're attacking the antennas with lasers, sir. Main antenna out. Secondaries . . ." she shrugged and gestured toward the baleful red lights strung across her keyboard. "They're all out, sir."

"Set up a laser link," Hazard commanded. "They can't jam that. We've got to let Geneva know what's happening."

"Sir," said Yang, "Geneva will not be within our horizon for another forty-six minutes."

"Try signaling the commsats. Topmost priority."

"Yes, sir."

Got to let Geneva know, Hazard repeated to himself. If anybody can help us, they can. If Buckbee's pals haven't put one of their own people into the comm center down there. Or staged a coup. Or already knocked out the commsats. They've been planning this for a long time. They've got it all timed down to the microsecond.

He remembered the dinner two months earlier, the night before he left to take command of the *Hunter*. I've known about it since then, Hazard said to himself. Known about it but didn't want to believe it. Known about it and done nothing. Buckbee was right. I killed those six kids. I should have seen that the bastards would strike without warning.

It had been in the equatorial city of Belém, where the Brazilians had set up their space launching facility. The IPF was obligated to spread its launches among all its space-capable member nations, so Hazard had been ordered to assemble his crew at Belém for their lift into orbit.

The night before they left, Hazard had been invited to dinner by an old Navy acquaintance who had already put in a three month hitch in orbit with the Peacekeepers and was now on Earthside duty.

His name was Cardillo. Hazard had known him, somewhat distantly, as a fellow submariner, commander of attack boats rather than the missile carriers Hazard himself had captained. Vince Cardillo had a reputation for being a hard nose who ran an efficient boat, if not a particularly happy one. He had never been really close to Hazard: their chemistries were too different. But this specific sweltering evening in a poorly air-conditioned restaurant in downtown Belém, Cardillo acted as if they shared some old fraternal secret between them.

Hazard had worn his IPF summer-weight uniform: pale blue with gold insignia bordered by space black. Cardillo came in casual civilian slacks and a beautifully tailored Italian silk jacket. Through drinks and the first part of the dinner their conversation was light, inconsequential. Mostly reminiscences by two gray-haired submariners about men they had known, women they had chased, sea tales that grew with each retelling. But then:

"Damn shame," Cardillo muttered halfway through his entrée of grilled eel.

The restaurant, one of the hundreds that had sprung up in Belém since the Brazilians had made the city their major spaceport, was on the waterfront. Outside the floor-to-ceiling windows, the muddy Pará River widened into the huge bay that eventually fed into the Atlantic. Hazard had spent his last day on Earth touring around the tropical jungle on a riverboat. The makeshift shanties that stood on stilts along the twisting mud-brown creeks were giving way to industrial parks and cinder-block housing developments. Air-conditioning was transforming the region from rubber plantations to computerized information services. The smell of cement dust blotted out the fragrance of tropical flowers. Bulldozers clattered in raw clearings slashed from the forest where stark steel frameworks of new buildings rose above the jungle growth. Children who had splashed naked in the brown jungle streams were being rounded up and sent to air-conditioned schools.

"What's a shame?" Hazard asked. "Seems to me these people are starting to do all right for the first time in their lives. The space business is making a lot of jobs around here."

Cardillo took a forkful of eel from his plate. It never got to his mouth.

"I don't mean them, Johnny. I mean us. It's a damn shame about us."

Hazard had never liked being called Johnny. His family had addressed him as Jon. His Navy associates knew him as Hazard and nothing else. A few very close friends used J.W.

"What do you mean?" he asked. His own plate was already wiped clean. The fish and its dark spicy sauce had been marvelous. So had the crisp-crusted bread.

"Don't you feel nervous about this whole IPF thing?" Cardillo asked, trying to look earnest. "I mean, I can see Washington deciding to put boomers like your boats in mothballs, and the silo missiles, too. But the attack subs? Decommission our conventional weapons systems? Leave us disarmed?"

Hazard had not been in command of a missile submarine in more than three years. He had been allowed, even encouraged, to resign his commission after the hostage mess in Brussels.

"If you're not in favor of what the American government is doing, then why did you agree to serve in the Peacekeepers?"

Cardillo shrugged and smiled slightly. It was not a pleasant smile. He had a thin, almost triangular face with a low, creased brow tapering down to a pointed chin. His once-dark hair, now peppered with gray, was thick and wavy. He had allowed it to grow down to his collar. His deep brown eyes were always narrowed, crafty, focused so intently he seemed to be trying to penetrate through you. There was no joy in his face, even though he was smiling; no pleasure. It was the smile of a gambler, a con artist, a used-car salesman.

"Well-l," he said slowly, putting his fork back down on the plate and leaning back in his chair, "you know the old saying, 'If you can't beat 'em, join 'em.' "

Hazard nodded, although he felt puzzled. He groped for

Cardillo's meaning. "Yeah, I guess playing space cadet up there will be better than rusting away on the beach."

"Playing?" Cardillo's dark brows rose slightly. "We're not playing, Johnny. We're in this for keeps."

"I didn't mean to imply that I don't take my duty to the IPF seriously," Hazard answered.

For an instant Cardillo seemed stunned with surprise. Then he threw his head back and burst into laughter. "Jesus Christ, Johnny," he gasped. "You're so straight-arrow it's hysterical."

Hazard frowned but said nothing. Cardillo guffawed and banged the table with one hand. Some of the diners glanced their way. They seemed to be mostly Americans or Europeans, a few Asians. Some Brazilians, too, Hazard noticed as he waited for Cardillo's amusement to subside. Probably from the capital or Rio.

"Let me in on the joke," Hazard said at last.

Cardillo wiped at his eyes. Then, leaning forward across the table, his grin fading into an intense, penetrating stare, he whispered slyly, "I already told you, Johnny. If we can't avoid being members of the IPF—if Washington's so fucking weak that we've got to disband practically all our defenses—then what we've got to do is take over the Peacekeepers ourselves."

"Take over the Peacekeepers?" Hazard felt stunned at the thought of it.

"Damn right! Men like you and me, Johnny. It's our duty to our country."

"Our country," Hazard reminded him, "has decided to join the International Peacekeeping Force and has encouraged its military officers to obtain commissions in the IPF."

Cardillo shook his head. "That's our stupid goddamn government, Johnny. Not the country. Not the people who really want to *defend* America instead of selling her out to a bunch of fucking foreigners."

"That government," Hazard reminded him, "won a big majority last November."

Cardillo made a sour face. "Ahh, the people. What the fuck do they know?"

Hazard said nothing.

"I'm telling you, Johnny, the only way to do it is to take over the IPF."

"That's crazy."

"You mean if and when the time comes, you won't go along with us?"

"I mean," Hazard said, forcing his voice to remain calm, "that I took an oath to be loyal to the IPF. So did you."

"Yeah, yeah, sure. And what about the oath we took way back when—the one to preserve and protect the United States of America?"

"The United States of America *wants* us to serve in the Peacekeepers," Hazard insisted.

Cardillo shook his head again mournfully. Not a trace of anger. Not even disappointment. As if he had expected this reaction from Hazard. His expression was that of a salesman who could not convince his stubborn customer of the bargain he was offering.

"Your son doesn't feel the same way you do," Cardillo said.

Hazard immediately clamped down on the rush of emotions that surged through him. Instead of reaching across the table and dragging Cardillo to his feet and punching in his smirking face, Hazard forced a thin smile and kept his fists clenched on his lap.

"Jon Jr. is a grown man. He has the right to make his own decisions."

"He's serving under me, you know." Cardillo's eyes searched Hazard's face intently, probing for weakness.

"Yes," Hazard said tightly. "He told me."

Which was an outright lie.

* * *

"Missiles approaching, sir!"

Stromsen's tense warning snapped Hazard out of his reverie. He riveted his attention to the main CIC display screen. Six angry red dots were worming their way from the periphery of the screen toward the center, which marked the location of the *Hunter*.

"Now we'll see if the ABM satellites are working or not," Hazard muttered.

"Links with the ABM sats are still good, sir," Yang reported from her station, a shoulder's width away from Stromsen. "The integral antennas weren't knocked out when they hit the comm dishes."

Hazard gave her a nod of acknowledgment. The two young women could not have looked more different: Yang was small, wiry, dark, her straight black hair cut like a military helmet; Stromsen was willowy yet broad in the beam and deep in the bosom, as blond as butter.

"Lasers on 124 and 125 autofiring," the Norwegian reported.

Hazard saw the display lights. On the main screen the six red dots flickered orange momentarily, then winked out altogether.

Stromsen pecked at her keyboard. Alphanumerics sprang up on a side screen. "Got them all while they were still in first-stage burn. They'll never reach us." She smiled with relief. "They're tumbling into the atmosphere. Burn-up within seven minutes."

Hazard allowed himself a small grin. "Don't break out the champagne yet. That's just their first salvo. They're testing to see if we actually have control of the lasers."

It's all a question of time, Hazard knew. But how much time? What are they planning? How long before they start slicing us up with laser beams? We don't have the shielding to protect against lasers. The stupid politicians wouldn't allow us to armor these stations. We're like a sitting duck up here.

"What are they trying to accomplish, sir?" asked Yang. "Why are they doing this?"

"They want to take over the whole defense network. They want to seize control of the entire IPF."

"That's impossible!" Stromsen blurted.

"The Russians won't allow them to do that," Yang said. "The Chinese and the other members of the IPF will stop them."

"Maybe," said Hazard. "Maybe." He felt a slight hint of nausea rippling in his stomach. Reaching up, he touched the slippery plastic of the medicine patch behind his ear.

"Do you think they could succeed?" Stromsen asked.

"What's important is, do *they* think they can succeed? There are still thousands of ballistic missiles on Earth. Tens of thousands of hydrogen-bomb warheads. Buckbee and his cohorts apparently believe that if they can take control of a portion of the ABM network, they can threaten a nuclear strike against the nations that won't go along with them."

"But the other nations will strike back and order their people in the IPF not to intercept their strikes," said Yang.

"It will be nuclear war," Stromsen said. "Just as if the IPF never existed."

"Worse," Yang pointed out, "because first there'll be a shoot-out on each one of these battle stations."

"That's madness!" said Stromsen.

"That's what we've got to prevent," Hazard said grimly.

An orange light began to blink on the comm console. Yang snapped her attention to it. "Incoming message from the *Graham,* sir."

Hazard nodded. "Put it on the main screen."

Cardillo's crafty features appeared on the screen. He should have been on duty back on Earth, but instead he was smiling crookedly at Hazard.

"Well, Johnny, I guess by now you've figured out that we mean business."

"And so do we. Give it up, Vince. It's not going to work."

With a small shake of his head Cardillo answered, "It's already working, Johnny boy. Two of the Russian battle stations are with us. So's the *Wood*. The Chinks and Indians are holding out but the European station is going along with us."

Hazard said, "So you've got six of the nine stations."

"So far."

"Then you don't really need *Hunter*. You can leave us alone."

Pursing his lips for a moment, Cardillo replied, "I'm afraid it doesn't work that way, Johnny. We want *Hunter*. We can't afford to have you rolling around like a loose cannon. You're either with us or against us."

"I'm not with you," Hazard said flatly.

Cardillo sighed theatrically. "John, there are twenty other officers and crew on your station . . ."

"Fourteen now," Hazard corrected.

"Don't you think you ought to give them a chance to make a decision about their own lives?"

Despite himself, Hazard broke into a malicious grin. "Am I hearing you straight, Vince? You're asking the commander of a vessel to take a *vote?*"

Grinning back at him, Cardillo admitted, "I guess that was kind of dumb. But you do have their lives in your hands, Johnny."

"We're not knuckling under, Vince. And you've got twenty-some lives aboard the *Graham,* you know. Including your own. Better think about that."

"We already have, Johnny. One of those lives is Jonathan Hazard, Jr. He's right here on the bridge with me. A fine officer, Johnny. You should be proud of him."

A hostage, Hazard realized. They're using Jay-Jay as a hostage.

"Do you want to talk with him?" Cardillo asked.

Hazard nodded.

Cardillo slid out of view and a younger man's face appeared on the screen. Jon Jr. looked tense, strained. This isn't any easier for him than it is for me, Hazard thought. He studied his son's face. Youthful, clear-eyed, a square-jawed honest face. Hazard was startled to realize that he had seen that face before, in his own Academy graduation photo.

"How are you, son?"

"I'm fine, Dad. And you?"

"Are we really on opposite sides of this?"

Jon Jr.'s eyes flicked away for a moment, then turned back to look squarely at his father's. "I'm afraid so, Dad."

"But why?" Hazard felt genuinely bewildered that his son did not see things the way he did.

"The IPF is dangerous," Jon Jr. said. "It's the first step toward a world government. The Third World nations want to bleed the industrialized nations dry. They want to grab all our wealth for themselves. The first step is to disarm us, under the pretense of preventing nuclear war. Then, once we're disarmed, they're going to take over everything—using the IPF as *their* armed forces."

"That's what they've told you," Hazard said.

"That's what I know, Dad. It's true. I know it is."

"And your answer is to take over the IPF and use it as *your* armed force to control the rest of the world, is that it?"

"Better us than them."

Hazard shook his head. "They're using you, son. Cardillo and Buckbee and the rest of those maniacs; you're in with a bunch of would-be-Napoleons."

Jon Jr. smiled pityingly at his father. "I knew you'd say something like that."

Hazard put up a beefy hand. "I don't want to argue with you, son. But I can't go along with you."

"You're going to force us to attack your station."

"I'll fight back."

His son's smile turned vicious. "Like you did in Brussels?"

Hazard felt it like a punch in his gut. He grunted with the pain of it. Wordlessly he reached out and clicked off the comm screen.

Brussels.

They had thought it was just another one of those endless Easter Sunday demonstrations. A peace march. The Greens, the Nuclear Winter freaks, the Neutralists, peaceniks of one stripe or another. Swarms of little old ladies in their Easter frocks, limping old war veterans, kids of all ages. Teenagers, lots of them. In blue jeans and denim jackets. Young women in shorts and tight T-shirts.

The guards in front of NATO's headquarters complex took no particular note of the older youths and women mixed in with the teens. They failed to detect the hard, calculating eyes and the snub-nosed guns and grenades hidden under jackets and sweaters.

Suddenly the peaceful parade dissolved into a mass of screaming wild people. The guards were cut down mercilessly and the cadre of terrorists fought their way into the main building of NATO headquarters. They forced dozens of peaceful marchers to go in with them, as shields and hostages.

Captain J. W. Hazard, U.S.N., was not on duty that Sunday, but he was in his office, nevertheless, attending to some paperwork that he wanted out of the way before the start of business on Monday morning. Unarmed, he was swiftly captured by the terrorists, beaten bloody for the fun of it, and then locked in a toilet. When the terrorists realized that he was the highest-ranking officer in the building, Hazard was dragged out and commanded to open the security vault where the most sensitive NATO documents were stored.

Hazard refused. The terrorists began shooting hostages. After the second murder Hazard opened the vault for them. Top-secret battle plans, maps showing locations of nuclear weapons and hundreds of other documents were taken by the terrorists and never found, even after a French-led strike force retook the building in a bloody battle that killed all but four of the hostages.

Hazard stood before the blank comm screen for a moment, his softbooted feet not quite touching the deck, his mind racing.

They've even figured that angle, he said to himself. They know I caved in at Brussels and they expect me to cave in here. Some son of a bitch has grabbed my psych records and come to the conclusion that I'll react the same way now as I did then. Some son of a bitch. And they got my son to stick the knife in me.

The sound of the hatch clattering open stirred Hazard. Feeney floated through the hatch and grabbed an overhead handgrip.

"The crew's at battle stations, sir," he said, slightly breathless. "Standing by for further orders."

It struck Hazard that only a few minutes had passed since he himself had entered the CIC.

"Very good, Mr. Feeney," he said. "With the bridge out, we're going to have to control the station from here. Feeney, take the con. Miss Stromsen, how much time before we can make direct contact with Geneva?"

"Forty minutes, sir," she sang out, then corrected, "Actually, thirty-nine fifty."

Feeney was worming his softboots against the Velcro strip in front of the propulsion and control console.

"Take her down, Mr. Feeney."

The Irishman's eyes widened with surprise. "Down, sir?"

Hazard made himself smile. "Down. To the altitude of the ABM satellites. Now."

"Yes, sir." Feeney began carefully pecking out commands on the keyboard before him.

"I'm not just reacting like an old submariner," Hazard reassured his young officers. "I want to get us to a lower altitude so we won't be such a good target for so many of their lasers. Shrink our horizon. We're a sitting duck up here."

Yang grinned back at him. "I didn't think you expected to outmaneuver a laser beam, sir."

"No, but we can take ourselves out of range of most of their satellites."

Most, Hazard knew, but not all.

"Miss Stromsen, will you set up a simulation for me? I want to know how many unfriendly satellites can attack us at various altitudes, and what their positions would be compared to our own. I want a solution that tells me where we'll be safest."

"Right away, sir," Stromsen said. "What minimum altitude shall I plug in?"

"Go right down to the deck," Hazard said. "Low enough to boil the paint off."

"The station isn't built for reentry into the atmosphere, sir!"

"I know. But see how low we can get."

The old submariner's instinct: run silent, run deep. So the bastards think I'll fold up, just like I did at Brussels, Hazard fumed inwardly. Two big differences, Cardillo and friends. Two *very* big differences. In Brussels the hostages were civilians, not military men and women. And in Brussels I didn't have any weapons to fight back with.

He knew the micropuffs of thrust from the maneuvering rockets were hardly strong enough to be felt, yet Hazard's stomach lurched and heaved suddenly.

"We have retro burn," Feeney said. "Altitude decreasing."

My damned stomach's more sensitive than his instruments, Hazard grumbled to himself.

"Incoming message from *Graham,* sir," said Yang.

"Ignore it."

"Sir," Yang said, turning slightly toward him, "I've been thinking about the minimum altitude we can achieve. Although the station is not equipped for atmospheric reentry, we do carry the four emergency evacuation spacecraft and they *do* have heat shields."

"Are you suggesting we abandon the station?"

"Oh, no, sir! But perhaps we could move the spacecraft to a position where they would be between us and the atmosphere. Let their heat shields protect us—sort of like riding a surfboard."

Feeney laughed. "Trust a Hawaiian girl to come up with a solution like that!"

"It might be a workable idea," Hazard said. "I'll keep it in mind."

"We're being illuminated by a laser beam," Stromsen said tensely. "Low power—so far."

"They're tracking us."

Hazard ordered, "Yang, take over the simulation problem. Stromsen, give me a wide radar sweep. I want to see if they're moving any of their ABM satellites to counter our maneuver."

"I have been sweeping, sir. No satellite activity yet."

Hazard grunted. Yet. She knows that all they have to do is maneuver a few of their satellites to higher orbits and they'll have us in their sights.

To Yang he called, "Any response from the commsats?"

"No, sir," she replied immediately. "Either their laser receptors are not functioning or the satellites themselves are inoperative."

They couldn't have knocked out the commsats altogether, Hazard told himself. How would they communicate with one another? Cardillo claims the *Wood* and two of the Soviet stations are on their side. And the Europeans. He put a finger to his lips unconsciously, trying to remember Cardillo's exact words. *The Europeans are going along with us.* That's what he said. Maybe they're not actively involved in this. Maybe they're playing a wait-and-see game.

Either way, we're alone. They've got four, maybe five out of the nine battle stations. We can't contact the Chinese or Indians. We don't know which Russian satellite hasn't joined in with them. It'll be more than a half hour before we can contact Geneva, and even then, what the hell can they do?

Alone. Well, it won't be for the first time. Submariners are accustomed to being on their own.

"Sir," Yang reported, "the *Wood* is still trying to reach us. Very urgent, they're saying."

"Tell them I'm not available but you will record their message and personally give it to me." Turning to the Norwegian lieutenant, "Miss Stromsen, I want all crew members in their pressure suits. And levels one and two of the station are to be abandoned. No one above level three except the damage-control team. We're going to take some hits and I want everyone protected as much as possible."

She nodded and glanced at the others. All three of them looked tense, but not afraid. The fear was there, of course, underneath. But they were in control of themselves. Their eyes were clear, their hands steady.

"Should I have the air pumped out of levels one and two—after they're cleared of personnel?"

"No," Hazard said. "Let them outgas when they're hit. Might fool the bastards into thinking they're doing more damage than they really are."

Feeney smiled weakly. "Sounds like the prizefighter who threatened to bleed all over his opponent."

Hazard glared at him. Stromsen took up the headset from her console and began issuing orders into the pin-sized microphone.

"The computer simulation is finished, sir," said Yang.

"Put it on my screen here."

He studied the graphics for a moment, sensing Feeney

peering over his shoulder. Their safest altitude was the lowest, where only six ABM satellites could "see" them. The fifteen laser-armed satellites under their own control would surround them like a cavalry escort.

"There it is, Mr. Feeney. Plug that into your navigation program. That's where we want to be."

"Aye, sir."

The CIC shuddered. The screens dimmed for a moment, then came back to their full brightness.

"We've been hit!" Stromsen called out.

"Where? How bad?"

"Just aft of the main power generator. Outer hull ruptured. Storage area eight—medical, dental and food supplement supplies."

"So they got the Band-Aids and vitamin pills," Yang joked shakily.

"But they're going after the power generator," said Hazard. "Any casualties?"

"No, sir," reported Stromsen. "No personnel stationed there during general quarters."

He grasped Feeney's thin shoulder. "Turn us over, man. Get that generator away from their beams!"

Feeney nodded hurriedly and flicked his stubby fingers across his keyboard. Hazard knew it was all in his imagination, but his stomach rolled sickeningly as the station rotated.

Hanging grimly to a handgrip, he said, "I want each of you to get into your pressure suits, starting with you, Miss Stromsen. Yang, take over her console until she . . ."

The chamber shook again. Another hit.

"Can't we strike back at them?" Stromsen cried.

Hazard asked, "How many satellites are firing at us?"

She glanced at her display screens. "It seems to be only one—so far."

"Hit it."

Her lips curled slightly in a Valkyrie's smile. She tapped

out commands on her console and then leaned on the final button hard enough to lift her boots off the Velcro.

"Got him!" Stromsen exulted. "That's one laser that won't bother us again."

Yang and Feeney were grinning. Hazard asked the communications officer, "Let me hear what the *Graham* has been saying."

It was Buckbee's voice on the tape. "Hazard, you are not to attempt to change your orbital altitude. If you don't return to your original altitude immediately, we will fire on you."

"Well, they know by now that we're not paying attention to them," Hazard said to his three young officers. "If I know them, they're going to take a few minutes to think things over, especially now that we've shown them we're ready to hit back. Stromsen, get into your suit. Feeney, you're next, then Yang. Move!"

It took fifteen minutes before the three of them were back in the CIC inside the bulky space suits, flexing gloved fingers, glancing about from inside the helmets. They all kept their visors up, and Hazard said nothing about it. Difficult enough to work inside the damned suits, he thought. They can snap the visors down fast enough if it comes to that.

The cramped CIC became even more crowded. Despite decades of research and development, the space suits still bulked nearly twice as large as an unsuited person.

Suddenly Hazard felt an overpowering urge to get away from the CIC, away from the tension he saw in their young faces, away from the sweaty odor of fear, away from the responsibility for their lives.

"I'm going for my suit," he said, "and then a fast inspection tour of the station. Think you three can handle things on your own for a few minutes?"

Three heads bobbed inside their helmets. Three voices chorused, "Yes, sir."

"Fire on any satellite that fires at us," he commanded. "Tape all incoming messages. If there's any change in their tune, call me on the intercom."

"Yes, sir."

"Feeney, how long until we reach our final altitude?"

"More than an hour, sir."

"No way to move her faster?"

"I could get outside and push, I suppose."

Hazard grinned at him. "That won't be necessary, Mr. Feeney." Not yet, he added silently.

Squeezing through the hatch into the passageway, Hazard saw that there was one pressure suit hanging on its rack in the locker just outside the CIC hatch. He passed it and went to his personal locker and his own suit. It's good to leave them on their own for a while, he told himself. Build up their confidence. But he knew that he had to get away from them, even if only for a few minutes.

His personal space suit smelled of untainted plastic and fresh rubber, like a new car. As Hazard squirmed into it, its joints felt stiff—or maybe it's me, he thought. The helmet slipped from his gloved hands and went spinning away from him, floating off like a severed head. Hazard retrieved it and pulled it on. Like the youngsters, he kept the visor open.

His first stop was the bridge. Varshni was hovering in the companionway just outside the airtight hatch that sealed off the devastated area. Two other space-suited men were zippering an unrecognizably mangled body into a long black plastic bag. Three other bags floated alongside them, already filled and sealed.

Even inside a pressure suit, the Indian seemed small, frail, like a skinny child. He was huddled next to the body bags, bent over almost into a fetal position. There were tears in his eyes. "These are all we could find. The two others must have been blown out of the station completely."

Hazard put a gloved hand on the shoulder of his suit.

"They were my friends," Varshni said.

"It must have been painless," Hazard heard himself say. It sounded stupid.

"I wish I could believe that."

"There's more damage to inspect, over by the power generator area. Is your team nearly finished here?"

"Another few minutes, I think. We must make certain that all the wiring and air lines have been properly sealed off."

"They can handle that themselves. Come on, you and I will check it out together."

"Yes, sir." Varshni spoke to his crew briefly, then straightened up and tried to smile. "I am ready, sir."

The two men glided up a passageway that led to the outermost level of the station, Hazard wondering what would happen if a laser attack hit the area while they were in it. Takes a second or two to slice the hull open, he thought. Enough time to flip your visor down and grab onto something before the air blowout sucks you out of the station. Still, he slid his visor down and ordered Varshni to do the same. He was only mildly surprised when the Indian replied that he already had.

Wish the station were shielded. Wish they had designed it to withstand attack. Then he grumbled inwardly, Wishes are for losers; winners use what they have. But the thought nagged at him. What genius put the power generator next to the unarmored hull? Damned politicians wouldn't allow shielding; they *wanted* the stations to be vulnerable. A sign of goodwill, as far as they're concerned. They thought nobody would attack an unshielded station because the attacker's station is also unshielded. We're all in this together, try to hurt me and I'll hurt you. A hangover from the old mutual-destruction kind of dogma. Absolute bullshit.

There ought to be some way to protect ourselves from

lasers. They shouldn't put people up here like sacrificial lambs.

Hazard glanced at Varshni, whose face was hidden behind his helmet visor. He thought of his son. Shiela had ten years to poison his mind against me. Ten years. He wanted to hate her for that, but he found that he could not. He had been a poor husband and a worse father. Jon Jr. had every right to loathe his father. But dammit, this is more important than family arguments! Why can't the boy see what's at stake here? Just because he's sore at his father doesn't mean he has to take total leave of his senses.

They approached a hatch where the red warning light was blinking balefully. They checked the hatch behind them, made certain it was airtight, then used the wall-mounted keyboard to start the pumps that would evacuate that section of the passageway, turning it into an elongated air lock.

Finally they could open the farther hatch and glide into the wrecked storage magazine.

Hazard grabbed a handhold. "Better use tethers here," he said.

Varshni had already unwound the tether from his waist and clipped it to a cleat set into the bulkhead.

It was a small magazine, little more than a closet. In the light from their helmet lamps, they saw cartons of pharmaceuticals securely anchored to the shelves with toothed plastic straps. A gash had been torn in the hull, and through it Hazard could see the darkness of space. The laser beam had penetrated into the cartons and shelving, slicing a neat burned-edge slash through everything it touched.

Varshni floated upward toward the rent. It was as smooth as a surgeon's incision and curled back slightly where the air pressure had pushed the thin metal outward in its rush to escape to vacuum.

"No wiring here," Varshni's voice said in Hazard's

helmet earphones. "No plumbing either. We were fortunate."

"They were aiming for the power generator."

The Indian pushed himself back down toward Hazard. His face was hidden behind the visor. "Ah, yes, that is an important target. We were *very* fortunate that they missed."

"They'll try again," Hazard said.

"Yes, of course."

"Commander Hazard!" Yang's voice sounded urgent. "I think you should hear the latest message from *Graham*, sir."

Nodding unconsciously inside his helmet, Hazard said, "Patch it through."

He heard a click, then Buckbee's voice. "Hazard, we've been very patient with you. We're finished playing games. You bring the *Hunter* back to its normal altitude and surrender the station to us or we'll slice you to pieces. You've got five minutes to answer."

The voice shut off so abruptly that Hazard could picture Buckbee slamming his fist against the Off key.

"How long ago did this come through?"

"Transmission terminated thirty seconds ago, sir," said Yang.

Hazard looked down at Varshni's slight form. He knew that Varshni had heard the ultimatum just as he had. He could not see the Indian's face, but the slump of his shoulders told him how Varshni felt.

Yang asked, "Sir, do you want me to set up a link with *Graham?*"

"No," said Hazard.

"I don't think they intend to call again, sir," Yang said. "They expect you to call them."

"Not yet," he said. He turned to the wavering form beside him. "Better straighten up, Mr. Varshni. There's going to be a lot of work for you and your damage-control team to do. We're in for a rough time."

Ordering Varshni back to his team at the ruins of the bridge, Hazard made his way toward the CIC. He spoke into his helmet mike as he pulled himself along the passageways as fast as he could go:

"Mr. Feeney, you are to fire at any satellites that fire on us. And any ABM satellites that begin maneuvering to gain altitude so they can look down on us. Understand?"

"Understood, sir!"

"Miss Stromsen, I believe the fire-control panel is part of your responsibility. You will take your orders from Mr. Feeney."

"Yes, sir."

"Miss Yang, I want that simulation of our position and altitude updated to show exactly which ABM satellites under hostile control are in a position to fire upon us."

"I already have that in the program, sir."

"Good. I want our four lifeboats detached from the station and placed in positions where their heat shields can intercept incoming laser beams."

For the first time, Yang's voice sounded uncertain. "I'm not sure I understand what you mean, sir."

Hazard was sweating and panting with the exertion of hauling himself along the passageway. This suit won't smell new anymore, he thought.

To Yang he explained, "You got me thinking about those heat shields. We can use the lifeboats as armor to absorb or deflect incoming laser beams. Not just shielding, but *active* armor. We can move the boats to protect the most likely areas for laser beams to come from."

"Like the goalie in a soccer game!" Feeney chirped. "Cutting down the angles."

"Exactly."

By the time he reached the CIC they were already

working the problems. Hazard saw that Stromsen had the heaviest work load: all the station systems status displays, fire control for the laser-armed ABM satellites and control of the lifeboats now hovering a few dozen meters away from the station.

"Miss Stromsen, please transfer the fire-control responsibility to Mr. Feeney."

The expression on her strong-jawed face, half hidden inside her helmet, was pure stubborn indignation.

Jabbing a gloved thumb toward the lightning-slash insignia on the shoulder of Feeney's suit, Hazard said, "He *is* a weapons specialist, after all."

Stromsen's lips twitched slightly and she tapped at the keyboard to her left; the fire-control displays disappeared from the screens above it, to spring up on screens in front of Feeney's position.

Hazard nodded as he lifted his own visor. "Okay, now. Feeney, you're the offense. Stromsen, you're the defense. Miss Yang, your job is to keep Miss Stromsen continuously advised as to where the best placement of the lifeboats will be."

Yang nodded, her dark eyes sparkling with the challenge. "Sir, you can't possibly expect us to predict all the possible paths a beam might take and get a lifeboat's heat shield in place soon enough . . ."

"I expect—as Lord Nelson once said—each of you to do your best. Now, get Buckbee or Cardillo or whoever on the horn. I'm ready to talk to them."

It took a few moments for the communications laser to lock onto the distant *Graham,* but when Buckbee's face finally appeared on the screen, he was smiling—almost gloating.

"You've still got a minute and a half, Hazard. I'm glad you've come to your senses before we had to open fire on you."

"I'm only calling to warn you: any satellite that fires on us will be destroyed. Any satellite that maneuvers to put its lasers in a better position to hit us will also be destroyed."

Buckbee's jaw dropped open. His eyes widened.

"I've got fifteen ABM satellites under my control," Hazard continued, "and I'm going to use them."

"You can't threaten us!" Buckbee sputtered. "We'll wipe you out!"

"Maybe. Maybe not. I intend to fight until the very last breath."

"You're crazy, Hazard!"

"Am I? Your game is to take over the whole defense system and threaten a nuclear missile strike against any nation that doesn't go along with you. Well, if your satellites are exhausted or destroyed, you won't be much of a threat to anybody, will you? Try impressing the Chinese with a beat-up network. They've got enough missiles to wipe out Europe and North America, and they'll use them. If you don't have enough left to stop those missiles, then who's threatening whom?"

"You can't . . ."

"Listen!" Hazard snapped. "How many of your satellites will be left by the time you overcome us? How much of a hole will we rip in your plans? Geneva will be able to blow you out of the sky with ground-launched missiles by the time you're finished with us."

"They'd never do such a thing."

"Are you sure?"

Buckbee looked away from Hazard, toward someone off-camera. He moved off, and Cardillo slid into view. He was no longer smiling.

"Nice try, Johnny, but you're bluffing and we both know it. Give up now or we're going to have to wipe you out."

"You can try, Vince. But you won't win."

"If we go, your son goes with us," Cardillo said.

Hazard forced his voice to remain level. "There's nothing I can do about that. He's a grown man. He's made his choice."

Cardillo huffed out a long, impatient sigh. "All right, Johnny. It was nice knowing you."

Hazard grimaced. Another lie, he thought. The man must be categorically unable to speak the truth.

The comm screen blanked.

"Are the lifeboats in place?" he asked.

"As good as we can get them," Yang said, her voice doubtful.

"Not too far from the station," Hazard warned. "I don't want them to show up as separate blips on their radar "

"Yes, sir, we know."

He nodded at them. Good kids, he thought. Ready to fight it out on my say-so. How far will they go before they crack? How much damage can we take before they scream to surrender?

They waited. Not a sound in the womb-shaped chamber, except for the hum of the electrical equipment and the whisper of air circulation. Hazard glided to a position slightly behind the two women. Feeney can handle the counterattack, he said to himself. That's simple enough. It's the defense that's going to win or lose for us.

On the display screens he saw the positions of the station and the hostile ABM satellites. Eleven of them in range. Eleven lines straight as laser beams converged on the station. Small orange blips representing the four lifeboats hovered around the central pulsing yellow dot that represented the station. The orange blips blocked nine of the converging lines. Two others passed between the lifeboat positions and reached the station itself.

"Miss Stromsen," Hazard said softly.

She jerked as if a live electrical wire had touched her flesh.

"Easy now," Hazard said. "All I want to tell you is that you should be prepared to move the lifeboats to intercept any beams that are getting through."

"Yes, sir, I know."

Speaking as soothingly as he could, Hazard went on, "I doubt that they'll fire all eleven lasers at us at once. And as our altitude decreases, there will be fewer and fewer of their satellites in range of us. We have a good chance of getting through this without too much damage."

Stromsen turned her whole space-suited body so that she could look at him from inside her helmet. "It's good of you to say so, sir. I know you're trying to cheer us up, and I'm certain we all appreciate it. But you are taking my attention away from the screens."

Yang giggled, whether out of tension or actual humor at Stromsen's retort, Hazard could not tell.

Feeney sang out, "I've got a satellite climbing on us!"

Before Hazard could speak, Feeney's hands were moving on his console keyboard. "Our beasties are now programmed for automatic, but I'm tapping in a backup manually, just in—ah! Got her! Scratch one enemy."

Smiles all around. But behind his grin, Hazard wondered, Can they gin up decoys? Something that gives the same radar signature as an ABM satellite but really isn't? I don't think so—but I don't know for sure.

"Laser beam . . . two of them," called Stromsen.

Hazard saw the display screen light up. Both beams were hitting the same lifeboat. Then a third beam from the opposite direction lanced out.

The station shuddered momentarily as Stromsen's fingers flew over her keyboard and one of the orange dots shifted slightly to block the third beam.

"Where'd it hit?" he asked the Norwegian as the beams winked off.

"Just aft of the emergency oxygen tanks, sir."

Christ, Hazard thought, if they hit the tanks, enough oxygen will blow out of here to start us spinning like a top.

"Vent the emergency oxygen."

"Vent it, sir?"

"Now!"

Stromsen pecked angrily at the keyboard to her left. "Venting. Sir."

"I don't want that pressurized gas spurting out and acting like a rocket thruster," Hazard explained to her back. "Besides, it's an old submariner's trick to let the attacker think he's caused real damage by jettisoning junk."

If any of them had reservations about getting rid of their emergency oxygen, they kept them quiet.

There was plenty of junk to jettison, over the next quarter of an hour. Laser beams struck the station repeatedly, although Stromsen was able to block most of the beams with the heat-shielded lifeboats. Still, despite the mobile shields, the station was being slashed apart, bit by bit. Chunks of the outer hull ripped away, clouds of air blowing out of the upper level to form a brief fog around the station before dissipating into the vacuum of space. Cartons of supplies, pieces of equipment, even spare space suits went spiraling out, pushed by air pressure as the compartments in which they had been housed were ripped apart by the probing incessant beams of energy.

Feeney struck back at the ABM satellites, but for every one he hit, another maneuvered into range to replace it.

"I'm running low on fuel for the lasers," he reported.

"So must they," said Hazard, trying to sound confident.

"Aye, but they've got a few more than fifteen to play with."

"Stay with it, Mr. Feeney. You're doing fine." Hazard patted the shoulder of the Irishman's bulky suit. Glancing at Stromsen's status displays, he saw rows of red lights glowering like accusing eyes. They're taking the station apart, piece by piece. It's only a matter of time before we're finished.

Aloud, he announced, "I'm going to check with the damage-control party. Call me if anything unusual happens."

Yang quipped, "How do you define 'unusual,' sir?"

Stromsen and Feeney laughed. Hazard wished he could, too. He made a grin for the Chinese-American, thinking, At least their morale hasn't cracked. Not yet.

The damage-control party was working on level three, reconnecting a secondary power line that ran along the overhead through the main passageway. A laser beam had burned through the deck of the second level and severed the line, cutting power to the station's main computer. A shaft of brilliant sunlight lanced down from the outer hull through two levels of the station and onto the deck of level three.

One space-suited figure was dangling upside down halfway through the hole in the overhead, splicing cable carefully with gloved hands, while a second hovered nearby with a small welding torch. Two more were working farther down the passageway, where a larger hole had been burned halfway down the bulkhead.

Through that jagged rip Hazard could see clear out to space and the rim of the Earth, glaring bright with swirls of white clouds.

He recognized Varshni by his small size even before he could see the Indian flag on his shoulder or read the name stenciled on his suit's chest.

"Mr. Varshni, I want you and your crew to leave level three. It's getting too dangerous here."

"But, sir," Varshni protested, "our duty is to repair damage."

"There'll be damage on level four soon enough."

"But the computer requires power."

"It can run on its internal batteries."

"But for how long?"

"Long enough," said Hazard grimly.

Varshni refused to be placated. "I am not risking lives unnecessarily, sir."

"I didn't say you were."

"I am operating on sound principles," the Indian insisted, "exactly as required in the book of regulations."

"I'm not faulting you, man. You and your crew have done a fine job."

The others had stopped their work. They were watching the exchange between their superior and the station commander.

"I have operated on the principle that lightning does not strike twice in the same place. I believe that in old-fashioned naval parlance this is referred to as 'chasing salvos.'"

Hazard stared at the diminutive Indian. Even inside the visored space suit Varshni appeared stiff with anger. Chasing salvos—that's what a little ship does when it's under attack by a bigger ship: run to where the last shells splashed, because it's pretty certain that the next salvo won't hit there. I've insulted his abilities, Hazard realized. And in front of his team. Damned fool!

"Mr. Varshni," Hazard explained slowly, "this battle will be decided, one way or the other, in the next twenty minutes or so. You and your team have done an excellent job of keeping damage to a minimum. Without you, we would have been forced to surrender."

Varshni seemed to relax a little. Hazard could sense his chin rising a notch inside his helmet.

"But the battle is entering a new phase," Hazard went on. "Level three is now vulnerable to direct laser damage. I can't afford to lose you and your team at this critical stage. Moreover, the computer and the rest of the most sensitive equipment are on level four and in the Combat Information Center. Those are the areas that need our protection and those are the areas where I want you to operate. Is that understood?"

A heartbeat's hesitation. Then Varshni said, "Yes, of course, sir. I understand. Thank you for explaining it to me."

"Okay. Now, finish your work here and then get down to level four."

"Yes, sir."

Shaking his head inside his helmet, Hazard turned and pushed himself toward the ladderway that led down to level four and the CIC.

A blinding glare lit the passageway and he heard screams of agony. Blinking against the burning afterimage, Hazard turned to see Varshni's figure almost sliced in half. A dark burn line slashed diagonally across the torso of his space suit. Tiny globules of blood floated out from it. The metal overhead was blackened and curled now. A woman was screaming. She was up by the overhead, thrashing wildly with pain, her backpack sputtering white-hot chunks of metal. The other technician was nowhere to be seen.

Hazard rushed to the Indian while the other two members of the damage control team raced to their partner and sprayed extinguisher foam on her backpack.

Over the woman's screams he heard Varshni's gargling whisper. "It's no use, sir . . . no use . . ."

"You did fine, son." Hazard held the little man in his arms. "You did fine."

He felt the life slip away. Lightning does strike in the same place, Hazard thought. You've chased your last salvo, son.

Both the man and the woman who had been working on the power cable had been wounded by the laser beam. The man's right arm had been sliced off at the elbow, the woman's back badly burned when her life-support pack had exploded. Hazard and the two remaining damage-control men carried them to the sick bay, where the station's one doctor was already working over three other casualties.

The sick bay was on the third level. Hazard realized how vulnerable that was. He made his way down to the CIC, at the heart of the station, knowing that it was protected not only by layers of metal but by human flesh, as well. The station rocked again and Hazard heard the ominous groaning of tortured metal as he pushed weightlessly along the ladderway.

He felt bone-weary as he opened the hatch and floated into the CIC. One look at the haggard faces of his three young officers told him that they were on the edge of defeat as well. Stromsen's status display board was studded with glowering red lights.

"This station is starting to resemble a piece of Swiss cheese," Hazard quipped lamely as he lifted the visor of his helmet.

No one laughed. Or even smiled.

"Varshni bought it," he said, taking up his post between Stromsen and Feeney.

"We heard it," said Yang.

Hazard looked around the CIC. It felt stifling hot, dank with the smell of fear.

"Mr. Feeney," he said, "discontinue all offensive operations."

"Sir?" The Irishman's voice squeaked with surprise.

"Don't fire back at the sons of bitches," Hazard snapped. "Is that clear enough?"

Feeney raised his hands up above his shoulders, like a croupier showing that he was not influencing the roulette wheel.

"Miss Stromsen, when the next laser beam is fired at us, shut down the main power generator. Miss Yang, issue instructions over the intercom that all personnel are to place themselves on level four—except for the sick bay. No one is to use the intercom. That is an order."

Stromsen asked, "The power generator . . . ?"

"We'll run on the backup fuel cells and batteries. They don't make so much heat."

There were more questions in Stromsen's eyes, but she turned back to her consoles silently.

Hazard explained, "We are going to run silent. Buckbee, Cardillo, and company have been pounding the hell out of us for about half an hour. They have inflicted considerable damage. I don't think they know that we've been able to shield ourselves with the lifeboats. They probably think they've hurt us much more than they actually have."

"You want them to think that they've finished us off, then?" asked Feeney.

"That's right. But, Mr. Feeney, let me ask you a hypothetical question . . ."

The chamber shook again and the screens dimmed, then came back to their normal brightness.

Stromsen punched a key on her console. "Main generator off, sir."

Hazard knew it was his imagination, but the screens seemed to become slightly dimmer.

"Miss Yang?" he asked.

"All personnel have been instructed to move down to level four and stay off the intercom."

Hazard nodded, satisfied. Turning back to Feeney, he resumed, "Suppose, Mr. Feeney, that you are in command of *Graham*. How would you know that you've knocked out *Hunter*?"

Feeney absently started to stroke his chin and bumped his fingertips against the rim of his helmet instead. "I suppose . . . if *Hunter* stopped shooting back, and I couldn't detect any radio emissions from her . . ."

"And infrared!" Yang added. "With the power generator out, our infrared signature goes way down."

"We appear to be dead in the water," said Stromsen.

"Right."

"But what does it gain us?" Yang asked.

"Time," answered Stromsen. "In another eight minutes or so we'll be within contact range of Geneva."

Hazard patted the top of her helmet. "Exactly. But more than that. We get them to stop shooting at us. We save the wounded up in the sick bay."

"And ourselves," said Feeney.

"Yes," Hazard admitted. "And ourselves."

For long moments they hung weightlessly, silent, waiting, hoping.

"Sir," said Yang, "a query from *Graham,* asking if we surrender."

"No reply," Hazard ordered. "Maintain complete silence."

The minutes stretched. Hazard glided to Yang's comm console and taped a message for Geneva, swiftly outlining what had happened.

"I want that tape compressed into a couple of milliseconds and burped down to Geneva by the tightest laser beam we have."

Yang nodded. "I suppose the energy surge for a low-power communications laser won't be enough for them to detect."

"Probably not, but it's a chance we'll have to take. Beam it at irregular intervals as long as Geneva is in view."

"Yes, sir."

"Sir!" Feeney called out. "Looks like *Graham*'s detached a lifeboat."

"Trajectory analysis?"

Feeney tapped at his navigation console. "Heading for us," he reported.

Hazard felt his lips pull back in a feral grin. "They're coming over to make sure. Cardillo's an old submariner; he knows all about running silent. They're sending over an armed party to make sure we're finished."

"And to take control of our satellites," Yang suggested.

Hazard brightened. "Right! There's only two ways to control the ABM satellites—either from the station on patrol or from Geneva." He spread his arms happily. "That means they're not in control of Geneva! We've got a good chance to pull their cork!"

But there was no response from Geneva when they beamed their data-compressed message to IPF headquarters. *Hunter* glided past in its unusually low orbit, a tattered wreck desperately calling for help. No answer reached them.

And the lifeboat from *Graham* moved inexorably closer.

The gloom in the CIC was thick enough to choke on as Geneva disappeared over the horizon and the boat from *Graham* came toward them. Hazard watched the boat on one of Stromsen's screens: it was bright and shining in the sunlight, not blackened by scorching laser beams or stained by splashes of human blood.

We could zap it into dust, he thought. One word from me and Feeney could focus half a dozen lasers on it. The men aboard her must be volunteers, willing to risk their necks to make certain that we're finished. He felt a grim admiration for them. Then he wondered, Is Jon, Jr. aboard with them?

"Mr. Feeney, what kind of weapons do you think they're carrying?"

Feeney's brows rose toward his scalp. "Weapons, sir? You mean, like sidearms?"

Hazard nodded.

"Personal weapons are not allowed aboard station, sir. Regulations forbid it."

"And rain makes applesauce. What do you bet they've got pistols, at least. Maybe submachine guns."

"Damned dangerous stuff for a space station," said Feeney.

Hazard smiled tightly at the Irishman. "Are you afraid they'll put a few more holes in our hull?"

Yang saw what he was driving at. "Sir, there are no weapons aboard *Hunter*—unless you want to count kitchen knives."

"They'll be coming aboard with guns, just to make sure," Hazard said. "I want to capture them alive and use them as hostages. That's our last remaining card. If we can't do that, we've got to surrender."

"They'll be in full suits," said Stromsen. "Each on their own individual life-support systems."

"How can we capture them? Or even fight them?" Yang wondered aloud.

Hazard detected no hint of defeat in their voices. The despair of a half hour earlier was gone now. A new excitement had hold of them. He was holding a glimmer of hope for them, and they were reaching for it.

"There can't be more than six of them aboard that boat," Feeney mused.

I wonder if Cardillo has the guts to lead the boarding party in person, Hazard asked himself.

"We don't have any useful weapons," said Yang.

"But we have some tools," Stromsen pointed out. "Maybe . . ."

"What do the lifeboat engines use for propellant?" Hazard asked rhetorically.

"Methane and OF_2," Feeney replied, looking puzzled.

Hazard nodded. "Miss Stromsen, which of our supply magazines are still intact—if any?"

It took them several minutes to understand what he was driving at, but when they finally saw the light, the three young officers went speedily to work. Together with the four unwounded members of the crew, they prepared a welcome for the boarders from *Graham*.

Finally, Hazard watched on Stromsen's display screens as the boat sniffed around the battered station. Strict silence was in force aboard *Hunter*. Even in the CIC, deep at the heart of the battle station, they spoke in tense whispers.

"I hope the bastards like what they see," Hazard muttered.

"They know that we used the lifeboats for shields," said Yang.

"Active armor," Hazard said. "Did you know the idea was invented by the man this station's named after?"

"They're looking for a docking port," Stromsen pointed out.

"Only one left," said Feeney.

They could hang their boat almost anywhere and walk in through the holes they've put in us, Hazard said to himself. But they won't. They'll go by the book and find an intact docking port. They've got to! Everything depends on that.

He felt his palms getting slippery with nervous perspiration as the lifeboat slowly, slowly moved around *Hunter* toward the Earth-facing side, where the only usable port was located. Hazard had seen to it that all the other ports had been disabled.

"They're buying it!" Stromsen's whisper held a note of triumph.

"Sir!" Yang hissed urgently. "A message just came in—laser beam, ultracompressed."

"From where?"

"Computer's decrypting," she replied, her snub-nosed face wrinkled with concentration. "Coming up on my center screen, sir."

Hazard slid over toward her. The words on the screen read:

> From: IPF Regional HQ, Lagos.
> To: Commander, battle station *Hunter*.

Message begins. Coup attempt in Geneva a failure,
thanks in large part to your refusal to surrender your
command. Situation still unclear, however.
Imperative you retain control of *Hunter*, at all costs.
Message ends.

He read it aloud, in a guttural whisper, so that Feeney
and Stromsen understood what was at stake.

"We're not alone," Hazard told them. "They know
what's happening, and help is on the way."

That was stretching the facts, he knew. And he knew *they*
knew. But it was reassuring to think that someone, somewhere, was preparing to help them.

Hazard watched them grinning to one another. In his
mind, though, he kept repeating the phrase "Imperative
you retain control of *Hunter*, at all costs."

At all costs, Hazard said to himself, closing his eyes
wearily, seeing Varshni dying in his arms and the others
maimed. At all costs.

The bastards, Hazard seethed inwardly. The dirty,
power-grabbing, murdering bastards. Once they set foot
inside my station I'll kill them like the poisonous snakes
they are. I'll squash them flat. I'll cut them open just like
they've slashed my kids . . .

He stopped abruptly and forced himself to take a deep
breath. Yeah, sure. Go for personal revenge. That'll make
the world a better place to live in, won't it?

"Sir, are you all right?"

Hazard opened his eyes and saw Stromsen staring at
him. "Yes, I'm fine. Thank you."

"They've docked, sir," whispered the Norwegian.
"They're debarking and coming up passageway C, just as
you planned."

Looking past her to the screens, Hazard saw that there
were six of them, all in space suits, visors down. And
pistols in their gloved hands.

"Nothing bigger than pistols?"

"No, sir. Not that we can see, at least."

Turning to Feeney, "Ready with the aerosols?"

"Yes, sir."

"All crew members evacuated from the area?"

"They're all back on level four, except for the sick bay."

Hazard never took his eyes from the screens. The six space-suited boarders were floating down the passageway that led to the lower levels of the station that were still pressurized and held breathable air. They stopped at the air lock, saw that it was functional. The leader of their group started working the wall unit that controlled the lock.

"Can we hear them?" he asked Yang.

Wordlessly she touched a stud on her keyboard.

". . . use the next section of the passageway as an air lock," someone was saying. "Standard procedure. Then we'll pump the air back into it once we're inside."

"But we stay in the suits until we check out the whole station. That's an order," said another voice.

Buckbee? Hazard's spirits soared. Buckbee will make a nice hostage, he thought. Not as good as Cardillo, but good enough.

Just as he had hoped, the six boarders went through the airtight hatch, closed it behind them, and started the pump that filled the next section of passageway with air once again.

"Something funny here, sir," said one of the space-suited figures.

"Yeah, the air's kind of misty."

"Never saw anything like this before. Christ, it's like Mexico City air."

"Stay in your suits!" It *was* Buckbee's voice, Hazard was certain of it. "Their life-support systems must have been damaged in our bombardment. They're probably all dead."

You wish, Hazard thought. To Feeney, he commanded, "Seal that hatch."

Feeney pecked at a button on his console.

"And the next one."

"Already done, sir."

Hazard waited, watching Stromsen's main screen as the six boarders shuffled weightlessly to the next hatch and found that it would not respond to the control unit on the bulkhead.

"Damn! We'll have to double back and find another route . . ."

"Miss Yang, I am ready to hold converse with our guests," said Hazard.

She flashed a brilliant smile and touched the appropriate keys, then pointed a surprisingly-manicured finger at him. "Sir, you are on the air!"

"Buckbee, this is Hazard."

All six of the boarders froze where they were for an instant, then spun weightlessly in midair, trying to locate the source of the new voice.

"You are trapped in that section of corridor," Hazard said. "The hatches fore and aft of you are sealed shut. The mist in the air that you see is oxygen difluoride from our lifeboat propellant tanks. Very volatile stuff. Don't strike any matches."

"What the hell are you saying, Hazard?"

"You're locked in that passageway, Buckbee. If you try to fire those popguns you're carrying, you'll blow yourselves to pieces."

"And you, too!"

"We're already dead, you prick. Taking you with us is the only joy I'm going to get out of this."

"You're bluffing!"

Hazard snapped, "Then show me how brave you are, Buckbee. Take a shot at the hatch."

The six boarders hovered in the misty passageway like

figures in a surrealistic painting. Seconds ticked by, each one stretching excruciatingly. Hazard felt a pain in his jaws and realized he was clenching his teeth hard enough to chip them.

He took his eyes from the screen momentarily to glance at his three youngsters. They were sweating, just as tense as he was. They knew how long the odds of their gamble were. The passageway was filled with nothing more than aerosol mists from every spray can the crew could locate in the supply magazines.

"What do you want, Hazard?" Buckbee said at last, his voice sullen, like a spoiled little boy who had been denied a cookie.

Hazard let out his breath. Then, as cheerfully as he could manage, "I've got what I want. Six hostages. How much air do your suits carry? Twelve hours?"

"What do you mean?"

"You've got twelve hours to convince Cardillo and the rest of your pals to surrender."

"You're crazy, Hazard."

"I've had a tough day, Buckbee. I don't need your insults. Call me when you're ready to deal."

"You'll be killing your son!"

Hazard had half expected it, but still it hit him like a blow. "Jay, are you there?"

"Yes, I am, Dad."

Hazard strained forward, peering hard at the display screen, trying to determine which one of the space-suited figures was his son.

"Well, this is a helluva fix, isn't it?" he said softly.

"Dad, you don't have to wait twelve hours."

"Shut your mouth!" Buckbee snapped.

"Fuck you," snarled Jon Jr. "I'm not going to get myself killed for nothing."

"I'll shoot you!" Hazard saw Buckbee level his gun at Jon Jr.

"And kill yourself? You haven't got the guts," Jay sneered. Hazard almost smiled. How many times had his son used that tone on him.

Buckbee's hand wavered. He let the gun slip from his gloved fingers. It drifted slowly, weightlessly, away from him.

Hazard swallowed. Hard.

"Dad, in another hour or two the game will be over. Cardillo lied to you. The Russians never came in with us. Half a dozen ships full of troops are lifting off from IPF centers all over the globe."

"Is that the truth, son?"

"Yes, sir, it is. Our only hope was to grab control of your satellites. Once the coup attempt in Geneva flopped, Cardillo knew that if he could control three or four sets of ABM satellites, he could at least force a stalemate. But all he's got is *Graham* and *Wood*. Nobody else."

"You damned little traitor!" Buckbee screeched.

Jon Jr. laughed. "Yeah, you're right. But I'm going to be a *live* traitor. I'm not dying for the likes of you."

Hazard thought swiftly. Jay might defy his father, might argue with him, even revile him, but he had never known the lad to lie to him.

"Buckbee, the game's over," he said slowly. "You'd better get the word to Cardillo before there's more bloodshed."

It took another six hours before it was all sorted out. A shuttle filled with armed troops and an entire replacement crew finally arrived at the battered hulk of *Hunter*. The relieving commander, a stubby compactly built black from New Jersey who had been a U.S. Air Force fighter pilot, made a grim tour of inspection with Hazard.

From inside his space suit he whistled in amazement at the battle damage. "Shee-it, you don't need a new crew, you need a new station!"

"It's still functional," Hazard said quietly, then added

proudly, "And so is my crew, or what's left of them. They ran this station and kept control of the satellites."

"The stuff legends are made of, my man," said the new commander.

Hazard and his crew filed tiredly into the waiting shuttle, thirteen grimy exhausted men and women in the pale blue fatigues of the IPF. Three of them were wrapped in mesh cocoons and attended by medical personnel. Two others were bandaged but ambulatory.

He shook hands with each and every one of them as they stepped from the station's only functional air lock into the shuttle's passenger compartment. Hovering there weightlessly, his creased, craggy face unsmiling, to each of his crew members he said, "Thank you. We couldn't have succeeded without your effort."

The last three through the hatch were Feeney, Stromsen and Yang. The Irishman looked embarrassed as Hazard shook his hand.

"I'm recommending you for promotion. You were damned cool under fire."

"Frozen stiff with fear, you mean."

To Stromsen, "You too, Miss Stromsen. You've earned a promotion."

"Thank you, sir," was all she could say.

"And you, little lady," he said to Yang. "You were outstanding."

She started to say something, then flung her arms around Hazard's neck and squeezed tight. "I was so frightened!" she whispered in his ear. "You kept me from cracking up."

Hazard held her around the waist for a moment. As they disengaged he felt his face turning flame-red. He turned away from the hatch, not wanting to see the expressions of the rest of his crew members.

Buckbee was coming through the air lock. Behind him were his five men. Including Jon Jr.

They passed Hazard in absolute silence, Buckbee's face as cold and angry as an Antarctic storm.

Jon Jr. was the last in line. None of the would-be boarders was in handcuffs, but they all had the hangdog look of prisoners. All except Hazard's son.

He stopped before his father and met the older man's gaze. Jon Jr.'s gray eyes were level with his father's, unswerving, unafraid.

He made a bitter little smile. "I still don't agree with you," he said without preamble. "I don't think the IPF is workable—and it's certainly not in the best interests of the United States."

"But you threw your lot in with us when it counted," Hazard said.

"The hell I did!" Jon Jr. looked genuinely aggrieved. "I just didn't see any sense in dying for a lost cause."

"Really?"

"Cardillo and Buckbee and the rest of them were a bunch of idiots. If I had known how stupid they are, I wouldn't . . ." He stopped himself, grinned ruefully and shrugged his shoulders. "This isn't over, you know. You won the battle, but the war's not ended yet."

"I'll do what I can to get them to lighten your sentence," Hazard said.

"Don't stick your neck out for me! I'm still dead set against you on this."

Hazard smiled wanly at the youngster. "And you're still my son."

Jon Jr. blinked, looked away, then ducked through the hatch and made for a seat in the shuttle.

Hazard formally turned the station over to its new commander, saluted one last time, then went into the shuttle's passenger compartment. He hung there weightlessly a moment as the hatch behind him was swung shut and sealed. Most of the seats were already filled. There was an empty one beside Yang, but after their little scene at the hatch, Hazard was hesitant about sitting next to her. He glided down the aisle and picked a seat that had no one next to it. Not one of his crew. Not Jon Jr.

There's a certain amount of loneliness involved in command, he told himself. It's not wise to get too familiar with people you have to order into battle.

He felt, rather than heard, a thump as the shuttle disengaged from the station's air lock. He sensed the winged hypersonic spaceplane turning and angling its nose for reentry into the atmosphere.

Back to . . . Hazard realized that *home,* for him, was no longer on Earth. For almost all of his adult life, home had been where his command was. Now his home was in space. The time he spent on Earth would be merely waiting time, suspended animation until his new command was ready.

"Sir, may I intrude?"

He looked up and saw Stromsen floating in the aisle by his seat.

"What is it, Miss Stromsen?"

She pulled herself down into the seat next to him but did not bother to latch the safety harness. From a breast pocket in her sweat-stained fatigues she pulled a tiny flat tin. It was marked with a red cross and some printing, hidden by her thumb.

Stromsen opened the tin. "You lost your medication patch," she said. "I thought you might want a fresh one."

She was smiling at him shyly, almost like a daughter might.

Hazard reached up and felt behind his left ear. She was right, the patch was gone.

"I wonder how long ago . . ."

"It's been hours, at least," said Stromsen.

"Never noticed."

Her smile brightened. "Perhaps you don't need it anymore."

He smiled back at her. "Miss Stromsen, I think you're absolutely right. My stomach feels fine. I believe I have finally become adapted to weightlessness."

"It's rather a shame that we're on our way back to Earth. You'll have to adapt all over again the next time out."

Hazard nodded. "Somehow I don't think that's going to be much of a problem for me anymore."

He let his head float back against the seat cushion and closed his eyes, enjoying for the first time the exhilarating sensation of weightlessness.

After such heroics it was inevitable that Hazard would eventually head the IPF, and once he took over, the Peacekeepers began to shape up into a reliable, well-disciplined organization. But neither Hazard nor Red Eagle could track down the missing nuclear weapons until Shamar showed up in South America and Cole Alexander went after him.

VALLEDUPAR, Year 8

$\mathbf{A}$LEXANDER looked up from the lighted map table at the faces of his closest aides.

"That's what Castanada told me. I know it's tricky," he admitted, "and damned dangerous. Trouble is, either we go in and get Shamar up there in the mountains or he takes over the whole damned country."

Four men and two women huddled over the computerized map table. Its lighted display threw eerie shadows up from its screen and across their faces. They sat bunched around the table in the wardroom of the jet seaplane that had served as Alexander's flying home, office and headquarters for more than five years.

Three of the people were a generation younger than Alexander. Barker, the English pilot who wore motorized braces on his lower legs, was Alexander's own age. So was Steiner, the blond logistics specialist. In any other group of mercenaries, one would assume that the willowy Austrian was Alexander's bed partner. The idea had never even been hinted at aboard the seaplane.

The younger woman was the former IPF teleoperator, Kelly, a pert freckled little redhead. She looked almost like a child except when she was in front of a computer. Any computer. Any software. Plain of face and figure, reserved and shy with people, she became a radiant little princess when her fingertips touched an activated computer program.

Sitting next to her, shoulders hunched and leaning on his elbows, was another ex-Peacekeeper, Jonathan Hazard, Jr. The years since the abortive military coup had matured him. The baby fat was gone: his face was lean now, the same spadelike nose and stormy blue-gray eyes that his illustrious father bore. Jay, as he called himself, had the kind of cowboy good looks and quiet charm that made him virtually irresistible to women. Especially when he smiled. But he smiled very little.

Pavel Zhakarov was the youngest of the group, a small, slightly built Russian with dark hair, intensely deep dark eyes, and a ballet dancer's lean ascetic face. He openly admitted to being an agent of the KGB. No one knew where his true loyalties lay; especially Pavel himself. But everyone took great pains to avoid placing him in a situation where his conflicting loyalties could cause disaster.

The seaplane rocked gently at its mooring in the Cesar River, an hour's drive downstream from Valledupar and the handsome hacienda of Sebastiano Miguel de Castanada. From this site Alexander could take off and be out of Colombian airspace in half an hour, if necessary. He always prepared his lines of retreat before starting an operation. Always, since his first experience in Indonesia.

"What's Shamar doing mixed up with Latin American dope dealers?" asked Barker in his languid, almost bored Oxford accent.

"It gives him a firm base of operations," Steiner guessed.

Alexander grinned crookedly. "The way I read it, there's a sort of nasty *quid pro quo* going on between Shamar and the drug guys. The official government can't attack the drug dealers because Shamar's nukes threaten their cities —or even other cities in other countries."

"Like Miami," Pavel muttered.

"Or Leningrad, Red," countered Alexander. He went on, "And Shamar must be getting a hefty cut of the drug money in return."

"But what does he *want?*" Kelly asked. "What's in it for him?"

"As I said," replied Steiner, "a base of operations."

"A whole country," Alexander said.

Jay shook his head. "He can't possibly expect to take over the whole nation."

"Can't he?" Alexander shot back. "How do you think the Castanada family got to be the *el supremos?*"

The American stared blankly at him.

"The way things work down here for the past fifty years or so is this: The drug dealers start operating in the hills and sooner or later take over the whole damned government and make themselves legitimate. Then some other gang starts cooking up cocaine for themselves and selling it outside the official government channels . . ."

Barker objected, "But cocaine and all the other hard drugs have been illegal since . . ."

"Sure they have," snapped Alexander. "That's what makes them so profitable. Why do you think the Castanadas are so pissed at these guys? They're cutting into the Castanada family's personal drug trade!"

"Despicable," Zhakarov hissed.

"Damn right it is."

"And that town they wiped out?" Hazard asked.

"Castanada told me they did it to keep the grave robbers away from the mountains," said Alexander, his smile turning malicious. "Way I see it, though, is this: the villagers grow coca for the Castanada family. The guys in the hills eliminated some competition."

"The whole village?" Steiner's voice was an uncomprehending whisper. "Everyone in it?"

With a grim nod, Alexander answered, "They're a bunch of murdering bastards. We're not going after pushovers."

Her round face wrinkled into a freckled frown, Kelly asked, "Let me get this straight: we're going to help the Castanada family to keep the drug trade to themselves?"

"Nooo," Alexander said with exaggerated patience. "We're going after Shamar and his nukes."

Barker objected, "But if Shamar can threaten to wipe out Bogotá and God knows what else if the government attacks him, why doesn't that threat also apply to *our* attacking him?"

"Because Shamar doesn't know we're working for the Castanadas. As far as he's concerned, this is a personal vendetta between him and me," Alexander said, then added, "Which it sure as hell really is."

"I don't like it," said Zhakarov. "How do we know we can trust Castanada and his family?"

Alexander laughed. "The KGB man worries about trust?"

"That's not fair," said Kelly.

"Nor constructive," added Steiner.

"So he's won both your hearts," Alexander noted. He scratched briefly at his chin. "Okay, I admit that we can't trust the Castanada clan. But we've got to get Shamar."

"And the bombs," Barker insisted.

"And something else, too," Alexander said.

"What?"

"The drug dealers—all of them. The ones in the mountains and the ones in the *capitolio.*"

The others stared at him.

Leaning forward over the lighted table display screen until the shadows across his face loomed like the mask of an eerie devil, Alexander said slowly, "We are going to make it impossible for *anybody*—including the thugs who run the government here—to manufacture cocaine. Ever again."

"How?" asked Jay.

"The nukes," replied Alexander. "We're going to wipe out the fields where they grow the coca plants with the fallout from one of Shamar's nuclear bombs."

"That's insane!"

"Is it?" The light from the tabletop cast a strange glint in Alexander's eyes. "Once we get our hands on those nukes we're going to *use* them. We're going to scrub the world clean of a lot of vermin."

The others stared at him in stunned silence.

I realize that I've jumped slightly ahead of myself once more. I should explain how the woman Kelly and Hazard's son happened to join forces with Alexander's mercenaries. While I'm at it, I might as well tell about Pavel Zhakarov, too.

MOSCOW AND LIBYA, ▬▬ Year 6

PAVEL did not notice them until almost too late.

He had heard of muggers and hooligans in other, more remote outskirts of Moscow, but never near the university, so close to the heart of the city.

Yet there were three young toughs definitely following him as he walked along the river promenade through the darkening evening, his fencing bag slung over one shoulder.

No one else in sight. The towers of the university were brilliantly lit, thousands of students bustling among the many buildings. But here along the riverside all was deserted. Pavel had come for solitude, for a chance to think about the offer he had been given. Was it truly an opportunity to do good for his country? Or was it a scheme by the *apparatchiks* to get him out of the way for a while, perhaps forever?

An offer or a trap? he had been wondering as he strolled in the deepening cold of early evening. An opportunity or an ultimatum?

Then he noticed the three young men in their Western-style leather jackets and zany hairdos. Up to no good, obviously.

Across the river was the Lenin Arena and the big sports palace complex. Hundreds of athletes were rehearsing for the November parades. But here on the riverside promenade, no one except Pavel Mikhailovich Zhakarov and three young hoodlums.

Pavel began walking a little more briskly. Sure enough, the trio behind him quickened their pace.

"Hey there, wait up a minute," one of them called.

There was no sense running. They would overtake him long before he got to an area where there were some people walking about. Of course, he could drop his fencing bag and leave the gear inside to them. It wasn't worth much. But I'll be damned if I give it up to three punks, Pavel said to himself.

So, instead of making a break for it, he turned and smiled at the approaching trio.

They were trying their best to look ferocious: leather jackets covered with metal studs. Wide leather belts and heavy, ornate buckles. Wild hair and faces painted like rock stars. Two of them were big, almost two meters tall and solid muscle from neck to toes. Pavel smiled. Probably solid muscle between the ears, as well. The third one, in the middle, was short and stocky, with an ugly squashed-nose face.

"What are you grinning at, little man?" he asked.

Pavel was not exactly little. True, he was barely 165 centimeters in height, and almost as slim as a girl. His face was delicately handsome, with dark eyes and brows, sculpted cheekbones and a graceful jawline. His hair was dark and naturally curly.

"Pretty man," sneered the big fellow on Pavel's left. The other large oaf giggled.

Pavel said nothing. He simply stood his ground, left hand with its thumb hooked around the shoudler strap of the fencing bag, right hand relaxed at his side. They did not notice that he was up on the balls of his feet, ready to move in any direction circumstances dictated.

"What's in the bag?" the ugly little leader demanded.

Pavel shrugged carelessly. "Junk. It's worthless."

"Yeah?" The leader flicked a knife from the sleeve of his jacket and snapped it open. The slim blade glinted in the light of a distant streetlamp.

"Hand it over."

"Not to the likes of you, my friend," said Pavel.

The other two pulled knives.

"It's worthless junk, I tell you," Pavel insisted. "Not even a balalaika."

"Open up the bag."

"But . . ."

"Open it up or we'll open you up."

Pavel sank to one knee, slung the bag off his shoulder and unzipped it. Opening it wide so that they could see it was fencing gear and nothing more, he grasped one of the sabers and got to his feet.

The two oafs stepped back a pace, but their leader laughed. "It's not sharp, it's for a game. Look."

They grinned and moved toward Pavel.

"I'm warning you," Pavel said, his voice low, as he retreated slowly, "what happens next is something you will regret."

The leader laughed again. "One against three? One toy sword against three real knives." His laughter stopped. "Slice him up!"

Pavel darted to his right, away from the promenade railing, where there was more room for maneuver. The first of the big thugs swung toward him and Pavel made a lightning-fast lunge. His blunted saber, thin and flexible as a whip, slashed at the oaf's hand and sent the knife clattering across the cement of the walkway.

The thug yelped in sudden pain. His companion hesitated a moment, and Pavel gave him the same treatment, ripping skin off his fingers.

The ugly little leader had circled around, trying to get behind Pavel. But Pavel danced backward a few steps and easily parried his lumberingly slow jab, then riposted with a slash at his cheek. He screamed and backed away.

The first one had recovered his knife, only to have Pavel disarm him again and whack him wickedly on the upper arm, shoulder and back: three blows delivered so fast they could not follow them with their eyes. Then it was back to the leader again.

He faced Pavel with blood running from his cut cheek and eyes burning with hatred.

"I'll kill you for this," he snarled.

Pavel extended his arm and pointed the blunted tip of his saber toward his face. "I'll blind you with this," he said, as calmly as a man asking for a pack of cigarettes. "I'll take out your eyes, one by one."

The little hoodlum glanced over at his two accomplices. One of the thugs was sucking on his bleeding knuckles. The other was wringing his painracked arm. The light faded from the ugly one's eyes. He backed away from Pavel. Wordlessly the three of them turned and started walking back the way they had come.

"Jackals!" Pavel called after them.

He retrieved his bag and zipped it up. But he kept the saber out and held it firmly in his right hand as he strode the rest of the way to his dormitory room.

Two days later Pavel was in a luxurious Aeroflot jet airliner, winging southward, away from wintry Moscow and toward the sun and warmth of the Mediterranean.

He still felt uneasy.

"It is a mission of utmost importance," the bureau director had said, "and of the utmost delicacy."

Pavel had sat on the straightbacked chair directly in front of the director's desk. The director himself had called for him, a call that meant either high honor or deepest disaster; all other chores were handled by underlings.

He was a slim, bald man with a neat little goatee almost like that of Lenin in the gilt-framed portrait hanging on the wall behind his desk. But there the resemblance ended. Pavel imagined Lenin as a vigorous, flashing-eyed man of action. The director, with his soft little hands, his manicured nails and tailor-made Hungarian suits, looked more like a dandy than a leader of men. His most vigorous action was shuffling papers.

To the director, Pavel looked like a cat tensed to spring. *A strikingly handsome young man, not quite twenty-three, yet he comes stalking into my office like a cat on the prowl, all his senses alert, his eyes looking everywhere. That is good,* the director thought. *He has been trained well.*

Pavel's life history was displayed on the computer screen atop the director's desk. The screen was turned so that only the director himself could see it. *Only child; mother killed at Chernobyl; father "retired" from his duties as Party chairman of Kursk due to alcoholism. There is nothing in his dossier to indicate romantic entanglements. Best grades in his class, a natural athlete.*

For long moments the director leaned back in his big

leather chair and studied the young man before him. Pavel returned his gaze without flinching. The director smiled inwardly and thought of the eternal game of chess that was his career. *He may be the man we need: not a pawn, exactly. More like a knight. One can sacrifice a knight in a ploy that will advance the game.*

Pavel finally broke the lengthening silence. "Could you explain, sir, what you mean?"

The directly blinked rapidly several times, as if awaking from a daydream.

"Explain? Yes, of course. We can't expect to send you on such an important mission blindfolded, can we?" He laughed thinly.

Pavel made a polite smile. "As you know, sir, I had applied for the International Peacekeeping Force."

The director gestured toward his computer display screen. "Yes, of course. A good choice for you. And you may eventually get it."

"Eventually?"

"After you have completed this mission—successfully." The director leaned back in his chair again and tilted his head back to gaze at the ceiling. "In a way, you know, this mission is somewhat like being with the IPF."

He is trying to stretch my nerves, Pavel realized. *To see how far I can go before I lose my self-control.* Very casually, he inquired, "In what way, may I ask?"

Still staring at the ceiling, "There is a certain Mr. Cole Alexander, an American, although he has not set foot in the United States in more than six years."

Pavel said nothing. He glanced upward, too. The ceiling was nicely plastered, but there was nothing much of interest in it, except for the tiny spiderweb the cleaning women had missed off in the corner by the window draperies.

The director snapped his attention to Pavel. "This

Alexander is a mercenary soldier, the leader of a band of mercenaries."

"Mercenaries?" Despite himself, Pavel could not hide his surprise.

"Yes. Oh, he claims to be hunting for the infamous Jabal Shamar, the man responsible for the Jerusalem Genocide. But he spends most of his time hiring out his services to the rich and powerful, helping them to oppress the people."

Pavel had heard rumors about Shamar.

"Is it true that Shamar took a number of small nuclear weapons with him when he disappeared from Syria?" he asked.

The director's brows rose. "Where did you hear of that?" he snapped.

Pavel made a vague gesture. "Rumor . . . talk here and there."

Tugging nervously at his goatee, the director said, "We have heard such rumors also. Until they are clarified, all nuclear disarmament has been suspended. But your mission does not involve Jabal Shamar and rumored nuclear weapons caches."

"I understand, sir."

"You will join Alexander's band of cutthroats," the director continued. "You will infiltrate their capitalistic organization and reach Alexander himself. And, if necessary, assassinate him."

The airliner landed at Palma, and Pavel rented a tiny, underpowered Volkswagen at the airport. He did not look like the usual tourist: a smallish, athletically slim young man, alone, unsmiling, studying everything around him like a hunting cat, dressed in a black long-sleeved shirt open at the neck and an equally somber pair of slacks, carrying nothing but a soft black travel bag.

Using the map computer in the car's dashboard, he

drove straight across the island of Mallorca, heading for the meeting that agents employed by the Soviet consulate had arranged with a representative of the mercenaries.

Across the flat farmlands he drove, seeing but not bothering to take much note of the fertile beauty of this warm and ancient land: the green farms, the red poppies lining the roads, the terraced hillsides and tenderly cultivated vineyards. But he noticed the steep hairpin turns that scaled the Sierra de Tramunta as he sweated and cursed in a low, angry whisper while the VW's whining little electric engine struggled to get up the grades. A tourist bus whooshed by in the other direction, nearly blowing him over the edge of the narrow road and down the rugged gorge.

When he finally got to the crest of the range, the road flattened out, although it still twisted like a writhing snake. And then he had to inch his way *down* an even steeper, narrower road to the tiny fishing village where he was supposed to meet the mercenaries.

Pavel was drenched with sweat and hollow-gutted with exhaustion by the time he eased the little car out onto the solitary stone pier that jutted into the incredibly blue water of the cove. He turned off the engine and just sat there for a few moments, recuperating from the harrowing drive. The smell of burned insulation hung in the air. Or was it burned brake lining?

He got out on shaky legs and let the warm sunshine start to ease some of the tension out of him. The village looked deserted. Houses boarded up. Even the cantina at the foot of the pier seemed abandoned, its whitewashed cement walls faded and weathered. Not a single boat in the water, although there were several bright-colored dories piled atop one another at the foot of the pier.

He took his black overnight bag from the car and slung it over his shoulder, then paced the pier from one end to the other. He looked at his watch. The time for the meeting had come and gone ten minutes ago.

He heard a faint buzzing sound. At first he thought it was some insect, but within a few moments he realized it was a motor. And it was getting louder.

A black rubber boat came into view from around the mountains that plunged into the sea, a compact little petrol motor pushing it through the water, splashing out a spume of foam every time the blunt bow hit a swell. A single man was in it, his hand on the motor's stick control. He wore a slick yellow poncho with the hood pulled up over his head.

Pavel watched him expertly maneuver the boat into the cove and up to the pier. He looped a line around the cleat set into the floating wooden platform at the end of the pier.

"What's your name, stranger?" the man called in English.

"Pavel."

"That's good. And your last name?"

"Krahsnii." It was a false name, of course, and the lines they had exchanged were code words that identified them to one another.

"Pavel the Red," said the man in the boat, grinning crookedly. "Fine. Come on aboard."

So he understands a bit of Russian, Pavel thought as he trotted down the stone steps onto the bobbing platform and stepped lightly into the rubber boat.

"That's all you've got?" The man pointed at Pavel's bag.

"It's all I need," Pavel said as he sat in the middle of the boat. "For now."

"Want a poncho? The sun's pretty strong here." He lifted another yellow slicker from a metal box at his feet.

Pavel shook his head. "I like the sun."

"You could get skin cancer, you know," he said as he unlooped the line and revved the motor. "Damned ultraviolet—ozone layer's been shot to hell by pollution."

With a grin, Pavel shouted over the motor's noise, "Let me enjoy one day of sunshine, at least. In Moscow we don't see the sun from September to May."

The man grinned back. "Suit yourself, Red."

As they bounced along the waves Pavel thought he was more in danger of drowning than sunstroke. The spray from the bow drenched him thoroughly. His shirt and slacks were soaked within minutes. Pavel sat there as mute as a sainted martyr, enduring it without a word.

I have heard of new agents receiving baptisms of fire, Pavel said to himself. This is more like the baptism of an ancient Christian.

"But I'm not an assassin," Pavel had blurted.

The director had smiled like a patient teacher upon hearing an obvious mistake from a prize pupil.

"You are," he corrected, "whatever we need you to be. You have been trained to perfection in all the martial arts. Your skills are excellent. Is your motivation lacking?"

Pavel suddenly saw an enormous pit yawning before him, black and bottomless.

"I am a faithful son of the Soviet Union and the Russian people," he repeated the rote line.

"That is good," said the director. "And if the Soviet Union and the Russian people require you to assassinate an enemy of the people, what will you do?"

"Strike without mercy," Pavel said automatically.

The director's smile broadened. "Of course."

"But . . ." The young man hesitated. ". . . Why?"

The director sighed heavily. "We are in a time of great upheavals, my young friend. Enormous upheavals, everywhere in the world. Even within the Soviet Union, changes are coming faster than they have since the glorious days of the Revolution."

Pavel had been taught all that in his political indoctrination classes. And the fact that his father was allowed to retire peacefully and seek therapy for his addiction, instead of being sent to some provincial outpost in disgrace, was a more concrete proof of the changes sweeping the Party and the nation.

"The Soviet Union helped to create the IPF and has led the way toward true disarmament," said the director almost wistfully. Then he added, "But this does not mean that we have entirely foresworn the use of force. There are situations where force is the *only* solution."

"And this American represents one of those situations?"

"All that it is necessary for you to know will be explained to you in your detailed mission briefings. For now, let me tell you that this capitalist warmonger Alexander is working some sort of scheme to undermine the regime in Libya. We are the friend and protector of the Libyan regime. We will protect our friend by getting rid of his enemy. Is that clear?"

"Yes, sir."

The man in the poncho cut the motor. The world suddenly became silent; the drenching spray ceased. Pavel unconsciously ran a hand through his soaked hair.

"You don't get seasick, do you?" the man asked.

Shrugging, "I don't know. I've never been closer to the sea than one thousand kilometers."

The man laughed. "Hadn't thought of that."

With the water-slicked yellow poncho on him, there was not much of him that Pavel could see except for his face. Hunched over as he was, it was difficult to tell what his true size was. He seemed rather broad in the shoulder. His face was square, with an almost sad, ironic smile that was nearly crooked enough to be called twisted. His eyes were gray, cold, yet they sparkled with what could only be a bitter kind of amusement. Altogether, his face was not unhandsome, but not truly handsome, either. He seemed big, perhaps close to two meters in height. Not a cowardly type. Yet he kept the poncho over him, claiming to be afraid of solar ultraviolet. A man of contradictions.

"Why are we stopped?" Pavel said. His English was of the American variety, as accentless as the typical Yankee news broadcaster.

"Security," said the man. "Out here we're safe from snoops who want to listen to what we say."

"I might be carrying recording equipment."

The man shrugged. "You might. But you're in *my* boat, and if you're going to work for me, you'll be on my turf for some time to come."

For a moment Pavel was speechless with surprise. "You are . . .?"

"Cole Alexander." He extended his right hand. "Pleased to meet you, Pavel."

Alexander's grip was strong. Pavel said slowly, "I didn't expect you to meet me personally." He was thinking, I could crush his windpipe and push him overboard. The job would be done. But in the bobbing little boat he was not certain of his leverage or his footing.

"You present a problem to me, Pavel," Cole Alexander was saying. "My Russian contacts made it quite clear that your government wants you on my team. Otherwise I'll have *real* trouble with the Russkies. I figure that at the very least you're a spy who's supposed to tell the Kremlin what I'm going to do in Libya. At the most, you've been sent out here to murder me."

Pavel kept his face rigid, trying to hide his emotions.

Alexander grinned his crooked grin again. "If you're an assassin, this would be a good place to give it a try. Think you can take me?"

"You are making a joke."

Alexander shrugged. "You're damned near twenty-five

years younger than I. That's a lot of time; a lot of booze and women. On the other hand, I'm bigger than you. What do you weigh?"

"Sixty-eight kilos."

"I'm about ninety kilos."

"I am faster than you," Pavel said.

"In a footrace, sure. What about your hand speed?"

Pavel cocked his head to one side. It would not be wise to boast.

Alexander dug a hand inside the poncho and came out with a silver coin. "An American half-dollar. Worth about three cents these days."

He motioned Pavel to move back to the bow of the tiny Zodiac, then placed the coin on the midships bench where Pavel had been sitting.

"Hands on knees." Alexander demonstrated as he spoke. "I'll count to three. First one to reach the coin keeps it."

Pavel put his hands on his knees and listened to the American count. This is ridiculous, he thought. A typical American macho contest. It's a wonder he didn't challenge me to a duel with six-shooters.

"Three!"

Pavel felt Alexander's hand atop his the instant his own fingers closed around the coin.

"Damn!" Alexander exclaimed. "You *are* fast. First time anybody's ever taken money off me that way."

Pavel offered the coin back to him, but Alexander laughingly insisted he keep it. Holding it in his palm, watching the sunlight glitter off it, Pavel began to wonder if Alexander had deliberately allowed him to win. He is a very clever man, Pavel thought. Even by losing he makes me respectful of him. No wonder the director fears him so.

"Now then," Alexander resumed, "about my problem. If I don't take you in, I suppose your government will try to blow me out of the water and make it look like an accident. So you're in. But don't think you're getting out until we've finished the job we're on now. And don't think you can get word back to Moscow about what we're doing. You'll be watched *very* carefully."

Pavel nodded, not to show agreement but to show that he understood the situation. What Alexander did not know was that it was not necessary for Pavel to make contact with Moscow or anyone at all. And what Alexander does not know, Pavel thought, could eventually kill him.

"It is an extremely delicate situation," the chief briefing officer had told Pavel.

They had been meeting each day for more than a week, stuffing information and indoctrination into Pavel's aching head. The regular working hours of the day were spent inside the offices and conference rooms of the briefing team. Pavel had to carry on his physical training and normal exercises at night, alone in the gymnasium in the basement of the ministry building. He slept little, and the strain was beginning to make him edgy.

The chief briefing officer was wise enough to recognize Pavel's growing tenseness. She had invited him to dinner at her apartment. It was a large and luxurious flat in one of Moscow's best apartment blocks: a beautiful living room decorated with oriental carpets and precious works of art, a finely equipped kitchen, and a frilly but comfortable bedroom with a large bed covered by a tiger skin.

"It's only imitation," the chief briefing officer had told him when she showed him through the place. "But it keeps me warm and cozy."

Her father was a high Party official, a "Young Turk" when Gorbachev had taken over the Kremlin; one of the older generation desperately clinging to his power now. She was at least ten years Pavel's senior, but she was still attractive in his eyes. Almost his own height, a bit stocky, her bosom seemed to strain at her red blouse. Her face had a slightly oriental cast to it that made her seem exotic in the light of the artificial fire glowing electrically in the artificial fireplace.

Over dinner she explained that, since the Soviet Union was one of the founding members of the International Peacekeeping Force, it was impossible for the USSR to overtly support Libya.

"When Colonel Qaddafi was finally assassinated, everyone thought that Libya would return to being a quiet country that produced oil instead of terrorists."

Pavel sipped his hot borscht and listened, trying to keep his eyes off her red blouse. One of the buttons had come undone and it gapped invitingly.

"But Rayyid is more rabid than Qaddafi ever was, as you know from your briefings. He is not the kind of man we would have chosen for an ally, but the inexorable forces of history have thrown us into the same bed—so to speak. Therefore, any attempt to undermine him must be stopped by us, with force, if necessary."

"But quietly," Pavel added, "so that the world does not know the Soviet Union has supported a madman."

She smiled at him. "Only the madman will know, and feel more dependent on us. And, of course, we will discreetly inform certain others who must be made to realize that the Soviet Union protects its friends—without the kind of stupid publicity that the Americans go in for."

"I can see why it is desirable to crush a band of mercenary soldiers," Pavel said, "but I still don't see why we support a nation that sends terrorists around the world. Wasn't Rayyid responsible for blowing up that Czech airliner last year? Two hundred people were killed!"

The chief briefing officer smiled again at Pavel. "Yes, it is true. And regrettable. But international politics is very complicated. Sometimes it is necessary, as I said, to get into bed with someone you do not love."

Pavel thought of the word *whore,* but did not speak it.

She saw that he was unconvinced. She spent the rest of the night explaining things to him. And he allowed her to, not daring to refuse and—later, when they were both wrapped in the imitation tiger skin—not wanting to refuse.

Alexander started the motor again and the little boat leaped across the waves once more. Just as the sun was starting to dry me out, Pavel thought sourly, squinting into the spray.

They rounded a cliff that tumbled from the wooded ridge line far above straight down into the blue sea. Pavel saw a seaplane tucked into the cove formed by a niche in the line of mountains.

"Home sweet home," shouted Alexander over the drone of the motor.

It was as beautiful a piece of work as anything Pavel had ever seen: the clean graceful lines of a racing yacht wedded to the lean swept-back wings of a jet airplane. Big engine pods bulked where the wings met the plane's body. The T-shaped tail leaned back at a rakish angle. The plane was painted sea-blue, although the underside of the wings were a lighter hue, the color of the sky, Pavel saw as they approached.

A hatch popped open halfway between the wings and tail, and two men tossed out a rope ladder. Alexander maneuvered the Zodiac to the ladder and hooked a line to it. He gestured Pavel into the plane, then clambered up the ladder after him.

"This is where I live," he told Pavel. "This is home, headquarters, and transportation all wrapped up in one." Tapping a forefinger against Pavel's chest, he added, "Let me give you a piece of advice, friend: never stay in one place long enough for the tax collectors to find you!"

Pavel saw that they were in a utilitarian work area, bare

metal walls curving over a scuffed and worn metal flooring. It was tall enough for Alexander to stand erect. He was just under two meters, Pavel estimated. The two other men were deflating the Zodiac and bringing it aboard for stowage.

"My car . . ." he suddenly remembered.

"All taken care of, don't worry," Alexander said as he wormed out of his yellow slicker. He was wearing a turtleneck shirt and jeans. The uniform of a burglar, Pavel thought. His hair was youthfully thick and full, yet dead white. Another contradiction.

Crooking a finger for Pavel to follow him, Alexander strode to the forward hatch and went through. The next cabin almost took Pavel's breath away. It was what he had imagined, as a child, that a plutocrat's yacht would look like. Brass and polished wood. Comfortable cushioned armchairs—with lap belts. Round portholes. Small tables bolted to the deck, which was covered with a thick carpet of royal blue.

"I've got to go forward for a minute and talk to the pilot," said Alexander as Pavel took in all the luxury. "Your bunk is the first hatch on the right, forward of this cabin. You might want to get into some dry clothes before we take off."

Even his "bunk" was a well-appointed private compartment, small as a telephone booth yet comfortable, with a foldout desk and a display screen built into the foot of the bed. I should be able to tap into his computer files, Pavel told himself, given a bit of time.

As he dropped his bag on the bunk and unzipped it, the plane's engines roared to life. The compartment shuddered. Through the porthole Pavel could see that they were turning seaward.

"All personnel, please take seats and strap in. Takeoff in three minutes."

Pavel tucked his bag in the drawer beneath the bunk, lay

down and buckled the safety strap across his middle and was asleep by the time the plane lifted off the water.

It was still daylight when he awoke. Pavel showered and shaved in the coffin-sized bathroom, marveling that he had such facilities all to himself. He dressed in his spare outfit, a loose-fitting maroon shirt and Western jeans, not unlike those Alexander wore. He had only one pair of sneakers: snug and silent.

He went out into the passageway and counted eight sleeping compartments. From his memory of the plane's exterior, he judged that there was another big compartment forward, before the control deck. He went through the open hatch and back into the wardroom where he had last seen Alexander.

The two men who had pulled in the boat were sitting there at a table laden with sandwiches and coffee cups. The young woman sitting with them noticed Pavel.

"Might as well come over and have some chow."

She was small, rather plain-looking, with red hair cut short, almost boyishly. A freckled face with a small stub of a nose. Her face looked somewhat suspicious as Pavel approached; he saw that her brown eyes watched him carefully.

"I'm Kelly," she said, getting up and offering her hand.

"Pavel Krahsnii," he said, making himself smile at her.

"And these two chow hounds are Chris Barker and Nicco Mavroulis."

They mumbled greetings without rising from their seats. Pavel nodded to them.

"Better eat while you can," said Kelly. "Briefing in ten minutes. And in nine minutes these guys will have gone through all the sandwiches."

Pavel took the chair next to Kelly and reached for one of the sandwiches. He noticed that the table was covered with a real cloth spread.

"I haven't the faintest idea of what's going on here," he said. "I've just arrived."

"We know. The boss is worried that you're a spy from the Kremlin. He thinks the best way to prevent you from doing us any damage is to put you to work right away while we keep a close eye on you."

Pavel took a bite of the sandwich, tasting nothing as he assessed the situation. Six eyes were staring at him, none of them friendly.

"The three of you will"—he tried to recall the phrase exactly—"keep a close eye on me?"

"Mostly me," Kelly said. "These guys have plenty of other work to do. The boss doesn't let anybody have much free time."

"The boss is Alexander?"

"You better believe it!" answered Kelly.

Deciding to disarm them with a measured amount of candor, Pavel munched thoughtfully on his sandwich for a few moments more, then said, "The boss is perfectly correct. I am a spy. My government is concerned about your activities and I have been sent to observe what you are doing firsthand."

"I knew it," said Mavroulis. He was dark and hairy, with thick ringlets almost down to his eyebrows and a day's growth of black stubble on his chin. Heavy in the shoulders and chest, like a wrestler. He glared at Pavel.

The other one, Barker, looked English. Light brown hair, almost blond, with calm blue eyes and a faint smile. The kind who could slit your throat while apologizing for it.

"Why does Moscow have any interest in our little operation?" he asked in a high nasal voice. "We don't threaten the superpowers in any way."

Pavel made a small shrug. "Perhaps they fear that you threaten one of our friends."

"Libya," said Kelly. It was a flat statement, toneless.

"Is that where we are going?" Pavel asked.

"We'll find out," she replied, glancing at her wrist, "in eight minutes."

Pavel took another bite of his sandwich.

Kelly forced a smile. "Coffee or tea?" she asked as innocently as a child.

Alexander himself conducted the briefing, which confirmed in Pavel's mind that his band of mercenaries was actually quite small. Perhaps every one of them is aboard this airplane, he thought. Perhaps an accident could wipe them all out of existence.

They cleared the food and cups from the table when Alexander came into the wardroom, each person taking his or her own dirty dishes to a slot set into the aft bulkhead. Pavel followed Kelly and did what she did. By the time he turned around, Alexander had removed the cloth table cover, revealing that the tabletop was actually a large display screen.

"It *is* Libya," said Kelly, studying the map shown on the screen as she sat down again.

"It is Libya," Alexander confirmed.

Pavel sat next to Kelly. He noticed that this time Mavroulis sat on his other side.

"Qumar al-Rayyid is one of the world's leading pains in the ass," said Alexander. He touched a keypad set into the table's edge and a photo of the Libyan strong man appeared in the upper corner of the map, a sun-browned face half hidden by dark glasses and a military cap heavy with gold braid.

"Several of his neighbors, who shall remain nameless"— Alexander glanced at Pavel—"have hired us to get rid of him. Paid good money for it."

"You plan to assassinate him," Pavel said.

Kelly looked surprised, almost shocked. Mavroulis gave a disgusted snort. "The Russians—first thing they think of is murder."

Pavel felt sudden anger flushing his cheeks.

Smiling his crooked smile, Alexander said, "No, my red-faced friend, we are not assassins. We are not even mercenary soldiers, in the old sense. Like the Peacekeepers, we deal in minimum violence."

Out of the corner of his eye Pavel saw Kelly flinch slightly at the word "Peacekeepers." Why? I must find out.

Aloud, he said, "Minimum violence? Such as bombing Tripoli while Rayyid is making a speech there?"

"And killing everybody in the crowd?" Alexander shook his head. "What good would that do? Rayyid would probably be in a blastproof shelter by the time the first bomb fell. And besides, we want to destroy his power, not make a martyr out of him."

"Then what . . . ?" Pavel gestured at the electronic map.

Alexander spelled it out. For more than ten years the Libyan government had been working on a grand project to tap the vast aquifer deep beneath the Sahara and bring the water to the coast, where it would provide irrigation for farming.

"Qaddafi talked about doing it," Alexander said. "Rayyid is making it happen."

Barker arched his brows in a very English way. "What of it? It's entirely an internal Libyan operation. That's no threat to any other nation."

"Isn't it?" Alexander scratched lazily at his jaw. "My sainted old Uncle Max was a dedicated Greenpeacer. Got himself arrested by the Russkies once, trying to save whales from their hunting fleets. He always told me, 'Son, it just ain't smart to tamper with Mother Nature.'"

"You are against the Libyan project for ecological reasons?" Paval could not believe it.

Alexander considered him for a long moment, locking his wintry-gray eyes on Pavel. Finally he answered, "Of course. Why else? If it's not good ecologically, then it's bad politically, as far as I'm concerned."

Pavel said nothing, but he thought to himself, This Alexander is either a liar or a fool.

The aquifer beneath the Sahara had been created more than one hundred thousand years ago, Alexander explained, when glaciers covered Europe and northern Africa was a fertile grassland teeming with game and the earliest bands of human hunting tribes.

"We just don't know what the ecological effects of draining off that water will be," he went on. "Certainly the nations along the Sahel region don't want their underground water sources tampered with. It could wipe them out—cattle and people both."

"The Libyans would use up the underground water in a few decades," Kelly added. "It would be entirely gone: water that took a thousand centuries to accumulate could be used up in less than one generation."

"And when the water is gone?" Barker asked.

"Millions will die," said Mavroulis angrily. "Maybe tens of millions, all across the Sahel, Algeria, Libya itself."

"But while they're using that water," Alexander said, "Libya's economic and political power will grow enormously. Libya will become the leading nation of the region—for a while. Long enough to make her neighbors extremely uncomfortable at the prospect."

"Which is why they've hired us," said Barker.

"Right."

Pavel shook his head. "You are going to kill this man over water. Water that legally he has a right to."

Alexander regarded him with a pitying smile. "You keep talking about killing. We don't kill—we cure."

Puzzled, Pavel asked, "What do you mean?"

Alexander's cold gray eyes shifted away from Pavel. "We're working on a plan that will stop the aquifer project. That's our goal and that's what we're going to do. I have no intention of harming a hair on Rayyid's armpits."

Barker leaned back and said to no one in particular, "The man has the Mediterranean at his doorstep. Why doesn't he buy fusion generators and desalt the seawater? Fusion may be new, but it works well and it would be cheaper than this aquifer scheme. And less damaging ecologically."

Alexander smiled his cynical smile. "That's what *you* would do, Chris. It's what I would do, or Kelly or Nicco or even our Russian friend, here. But Rayyid wants something *big,* something impressive, something that's never been done before."

"He's not looking for the best way to help his people," said Kelly. "He's looking for headlines for himself."

"And power," added Alexander. "Power is always at the root of it."

For the next week Pavel and all the others were kept quite busy. The plane landed in Naples' beautiful harbor, then flew up briefly to Marseille and after that spent two days anchored in an unnamed inlet on the west coast of Corsica.

Pavel began to understand that this plane and the eight men and one woman aboard it were only a part of Alexander's operation. How large a part, he had no inkling. Obviously the man had tentacles that extended far.

None of them left the plane for very long. Alexander stayed aboard constantly. Pavel was allowed to walk the length of the dock in Marseille, but no farther. Kelly watched him from the hatch, and Mavroulis or one of the others was always at the end of the pier. Each night they slept aboard the plane, which always taxied far out from the shore before anchoring. It was like sleeping on a yacht. Pavel enjoyed it, even though he felt somewhat confined.

Now and again the name of Jabal Shamar popped up in conversations. Pavel asked indirect questions, spoke little and listened a lot. Apparently Alexander had a personal hatred for the elusive former leader of the Pan-Arab armies. His parents had been killed in the nuclear exchange of the Final War.

"Is it true that Shamar has his own nuclear bombs?" Pavel asked Mavroulis one afternoon, while they worked side by side loading crates of foodstuffs into the plane's refrigerated cargo bay.

The Greek nodded sourly. "Why do you think Alexander accepted this Libyan job? Shamar might be there, under Rayyid's protection."

"With the bombs?"

Mavroulis grunted as he heaved a crate marked as oranges. "He doesn't care about the bombs. He wants Shamar."

But Moscow must care about the bombs, Pavel thought. Do they *want* Rayyid to have access to nuclear weapons? He wished he could contact the director for clarification.

Wherever he went, the Kelly woman stayed beside him. She was cool, friendly—up to a point—and extremely intelligent. Pavel saw that she could program computers and use other electronic gear with impressive facility.

The second morning at Corsica she approached Pavel in the wardroom shortly after breakfast and asked, "Uh, you want to go for a swim?" She seemed somewhat reluctant, almost troubled, as if someone had forced her to ask him.

Pavel was too surprised to be wary. Kelly provided him with a pair of abbreviated trunks, then ducked into her own compartment to change.

In a bathing suit she revealed what Pavel had guessed earlier: her figure was practically nonexistent. Yet her round, plain face had a kind of prettiness to it. She was not beautiful, by any means. But that did not matter so much. The prospect of pumping information from her in bed began to seem not merely possible, but attractive. Yet, although Kelly smiled at him, her brown eyes were always cautious. Pavel thought there was something very sad in her eyes, something that he should strive to find out.

They used the plane's main cargo hatch as a diving

platform and plunged into the sun-warmed waters. Pavel had swum only in Moscow pools; he was surprised at the lack of chlorine in the water, and its saltiness.

After nearly an hour, they climbed up onto the wing and stretched out on giant towels to let the sun dry them. The sky arching overhead was brilliant blue, cloudless and achingly bright. Pavel squeezed his eyes shut, but still the glow of the fierce Mediterranean sun blazed against his closed eyelids.

"You swim very well," Kelly said. There was real admiration in her voice. The earlier reluctance had washed away.

He opened his eyes and turned toward her.

"Not as well as you," he replied, noticing how the sunlight glinted off the water droplets in her hair. It was a bright Irish red, the kind of coloring that the Vikings had brought with them down the long rivers of Russia to eventually give the country its name.

She was a trained athlete, he found out. Gently leading her on to tell her life story, Pavel learned that she had been a skater but had failed to make Canada's Olympic team.

"The competition must have been very strong in a nation like Canada," he sympathized.

She still seemed saddened by that failure. Then she had joined the International Peacekeeping Force, and had served for almost a year as a teleoperator. She had been involved in stopping the abortive war between Eritrea and the Sudan.

"Why did you leave the Peacekeepers?" he asked.

Kelly's freckled face almost pouted. "I had some trouble with my superiors. Not following orders exactly. Exceeding my mission goals."

"But exceeding one's goals is a good thing!" Pavel felt truly surprised.

"Maybe for you. For me, it just got me in trouble."

"And because of that you were cashiered from the IPF?"

"I wasn't thrown out. I quit."

"Because of that?"

"Not really," she said. "That helped, but it wasn't the real reason."

"Then why?"

She turned her head to look at him, lying beside her. Pavel saw pain and anger in her eyes. And something else, something he could not identify. Suddenly uneasy with her this close to him, he lay back again and closed his eyes against the sun.

"A man," she said. "I thought he was in love with me. I thought I was in love with him."

"Were you?"

"I guess I was," she said, almost in a whisper. "But he wasn't."

"Couldn't you have transferred to another part of the IPF?"

She shrugged her bare shoulders. "Maybe. But Cole Alexander asked me to join his group."

"Alexander offered you better pay?"

He heard Kelly chuckle. "I wish. You don't know him very well yet."

"I don't understand."

"I joined his group because he asked me to. Cole Alexander is my father."

Pavel felt stunned. "Your father? But your name is not . . ." He stopped short, suddenly realizing that he now was treading on very sensitive, dangerous ground.

"He never married my mother," Kelly said matter-of-factly.

"And she . . . ?"

"She loved him 'til the day she died. And so will I."

They left Corsica, after Alexander had a top secret meeting in his private quarters just aft of the flight deck with six men who wore expensive suits and dark glasses. They arrived in six different yachts, and for a few hours the lonely unnamed inlet on the rugged Corsican coast looked like a holiday playground for millionaires.

He serves the rich, Pavel remembered the director's words. *He helps them to oppress the poor.*

The yachts departed and the seaplane took off, landed and refueled at Gibraltar, then flew out over the Atlantic and down the curving bulk of the African coast. Pavel slept poorly that night. The plane flew steadily, with hardly a noticeable vibration. The sound of the engines was muffled to a background purr. But still something in that deepest part of his brain that was always alert kept warning him that he was in danger, that he was surrounded by enemies, and that there was nothing between him and a screaming fall to his death except several miles of thin air.

He breakfasted with Kelly and the others, then was summoned on the plane's intercom to the flight deck. Kelly accompanied him along the passageway that led through the sleeping compartments and her father's private quarters.

"His bedroom is on this side"—she gestured to an unmarked door in the passageway—"and his office is here on the starboard side."

A flight of three steps marked the end of the passageway.

"Flight deck's up there," Kelly said.

"You are not coming?"

"I haven't been invited. He wants to see you. Alone."

She seemed more guarded than ever this morning, as if she regretted having revealed so much about herself. Pavel went up the metal steps and rapped on the door with the back of his knuckles. Nothing happened. He glanced back at Kelly, who motioned for him to open the door and go through. With a shrug, he did.

Strong sunlight poured through the wide windows of the flight deck. Pavel winced and, squinting, saw that the stations for the navigator and electronics operator were unmanned, their chairs empty even though the display screens of their consoles glowed with data. He had expected the noise from the engines to be louder up here, but if it was, it was so marginal that Pavel could discern no real difference from the rest of the plane.

"Come on up here, Red," came Alexander's voice. From the pilot's seat.

Making his way past the unoccupied crew stations, Pavel saw that Alexander was indeed piloting the plane. He was smiling happily in the pilot's seat, wearing aviator's polarized sunglasses tinted a light blue.

"Don't look so surprised, kid," Alexander said, grinning at him. "Flying this beautiful lady is most of the fun of having her. Sit down, make yourself comfortable."

Pavel slid into the copilot's chair.

"Want to try the controls?"

He knew he was wide-eyed with astonishment, despite his efforts to rein in his emotions. All that Pavel could reply was a half-strangled "Yes" and a vigorous bobbing of his head.

"Take 'em!" Alexander removed his hands from the U-shaped control yoke. The plane ploughed along steadily.

Pavel gripped the yoke in front of him and felt the enormous solidity of this huge plane. Alexander began explaining the instruments on the bewildering panels that surrounded Pavel's chair on three sides: altimeter, air speed indicator, radios, throttles, trim tabs, radar display, turn-and-bank indicator, artificial horizon, compass, fuel gauges . . . there were hundreds of displays that could be called up through the plane's flight computer.

"In about ten seconds we have to make a twelve-degree turn southward. That's to our left. Ready?"

"Me?" Pavel heard his voice squeak excitedly.

"You're the man with his hands on the controls, aren't you?"

His mouth suddenly dry, Pavel swallowed once, then nodded. "I am ready."

"Okay . . . now."

Both of them watched the compass as Pavel started to turn the yoke leftward.

"Rudder!" Alexander yelled. "The pedal beneath your left foot. Easy!"

The plane responded smoothly, although Pavel overcontrolled and had to turn slightly back toward the right before the compass heading satisfied Alexander. He was sweating by the time he took his hands off the yoke and let Alexander resume control.

"Not bad for the first time," Alexander said, smiling his sardonic smile. Pavel could not tell if he was being honest or sarcastic.

Alexander flicked his fingers across a few buttons, then let go of the controls.

"Okay, she's on autopilot now until we reach Cape Verde airspace."

Wiping his palms on his jeans, Pavel said, "I have never flown an airplane before."

"Uh-huh." Alexander studied his face for a moment, then asked, "Okay, Red, what have you learned about us so far?"

Pavel searched for the older man's eyes, saw only the blue-tinted glasses. "You mean, what will I report back to Moscow?" he asked, stalling for time to think.

Alexander nodded. His grin was gone. He was completely serious now.

"You are planning to attack Libya, a nation that has friendly ties to the Soviet Union. Your plan involves destroying the Libyan aquifer project, a project that could bring precious water to farmers and herders along the Mediterranean coast—water that legally belongs to Libya, since it now lies under Libyan soil."

"Go on," Alexander said.

"You are conducting this attack for money paid to you by those six men who came aboard this plane in Corsica. One of them I recognized as an Egyptian; two of them were blacks, presumably from Chad and Niger, two neighbors with whom Libya has been at war, off and on, for many years."

"Not bad," Alexander said. "The other three were from Algeria, Tunisia and France."

"France?"

"The Frogs have had their troubles with Libyan terrorists, over the years."

"So they are paying you to get rid of Rayyid."

"Not exactly."

Pavel snorted. "Not exactly? Come, now."

Alexander laughed. "Ah, the righteous defender of the poor."

"Well, is it not so?" Pavel shot back. "Aren't you taking money from the rich? Won't your schemes hurt the poor farmers and herdsmen of Libya?"

Tapping a finger against his lips for a moment, Alexander seemed to be debating how much he should tell. Finally he said, "Chad is a helluva lot poorer than Libya. And the Chadian you saw at our little conference represented several nations of the Sahel area. They're damned worried about Libya draining that aquifer."

"Then let them dig their own irrigation systems."

"With what? They don't have oil money. They don't have *any* money."

"Except a few millions to pay you."

"They're paying me nothing. My money's not coming from the Sahel. And what I *am* getting for this caper is barely enough to pull it off and keep us from starving. I'm not a rich man, Red. This plane and the people in it are my fortune."

Pavel did not believe that for an instant. But he said nothing.

"Besides, my egalitarian friend, Libya is much richer than most of its neighbors."

"That's not true . . ."

"Yes, it is. Check with the World Bank if you doubt it." Alexander's crooked smile returned. "Oh, the *people* of Libya are shit poor. Those farmers and herdsmen you talk about are on the ragged edge of starvation, sure enough. But there's plenty of gold in Tripoli. Rayyid's rolling in money. He could buy fusion desalting plants and string them along his coastline, if he wanted to. Instead, he's using part of his gold to build this monster irrigation project. The rest goes into terrorism."

"So you say."

"Listen, kid"—Alexander pointed a forefinger like a pistol—"a helluva lot of Libyan oil money goes straight to Moscow to buy the guns and explosives that Rayyid terrorist squads use in Paris, Rome, London and Washington."

Pavel leaned back, away from that accusing finger. "So it is all the fault of the Soviet Union, is it?"

"Did I say that?" Alexander put on a look of pained innocence falsely accused. "It's the fault of Qumar al-Rayyid, and we're going to take steps to stop him."

"By destroying his aquifer project."

"Damned right. And letting his own people see that he's been spending their hard-earned money on projects that bring *him* prestige and leave *them* penniless."

"Very clever," Pavel admitted. "You stir up his own people against him, so that when they tear him to pieces you can say that you did not assassinate him."

"What the Libyan people—or, more likely, what the Libyan military do to Rayyid is their problem, not mine. My problem is to see to it that the bastard doesn't drain that aquifer dry and cause an ecological disaster that'll kill millions of people over the next generation."

"I could ruin your plans," Pavel said.

Alexander arched an eyebrow.

"I could escape from you and tell all this to the nearest Soviet consulate. Once they knew that Algeria and France were paying you . . ." Pavel let the sentence dangle.

Alexander grinned at him. "First you have to escape."

Pavel bowed his head in acknowledgement.

"Actually, it wouldn't be too tough for a man of your training," Alexander said, leaning back in his chair. "You're sitting on an ejection seat, you know."

"Really?"

"Just strap yourself into the harness and hit the red button on the end of the armrest and *whoosh!*" Alexander gestured with both hands, "Off you go, through the overhead hatch and into the wild blue yonder. Parachute opens automatically. Flotation gear inflates. Radio beeps a distress call. You'd be picked up before you got your feet wet, almost."

Pavel said nothing. But he glanced at the red button. There was a protective guard over it. With his fingertips he tried it and found that it was not locked; Alexander was telling the truth.

"What's more," the man was saying, "if you're really here to knock me off, now's the time for it. Give me a whack in the head or something, knock me unconscious or kill me outright. I'm sure they taught you how to do that, didn't they?"

His lips were smiling cynically, Pavel saw, but his tone was deadly serious.

"Then slam the throttles and the yoke hard forward, put the plane into a power dive and eject. You go floating off safely and the plane rips off its wings and hits the water at six hundred knots. No survivors, and it looks like an accident. You'd get a Hero of the Soviet Union medal for that, wouldn't you?"

"You are joking," Pavel said.

Alexander went on, "You'd kill me and everybody else on board. Wipe out all of us."

Pavel could not fathom Alexander's motives. Is this a test of some sort? he asked himself. A trap? Or is the man absolutely mad?

"You could knock me out, couldn't you? After all, I'm an old man. Old enough to be your father."

Is he actually challenging me to a fight? Pavel wondered. Here? In the cockpit of this plane?

"She told you I'm her father, didn't she?" Alexander asked.

The sudden shift in subject almost bewildered Pavel. He felt as if he were thrashing around in deep water, unable to catch his breath.

"Kelly's my daughter. She told you that, didn't she?"

There was real concern written on the man's face, Pavel saw. And suddenly he realized that all this talk of assassination and destroying the airplane had been a test, after all.

"Yes, she did tell me," he admitted.

"I think the world of her," Alexander said. "She's the only child I've got. The only one I'll ever have."

"She loves you very much," Pavel said.

"If you kill me here and now, you'd be killing her, too."

"Yes, that is true."

For many long, nerve-twisting moments they sat side by side in silence, staring at each other, trying to determine what was going on behind the masks they held up to one another, while the plane droned on high above the glittering gray ocean.

"When you go into Libya on this mission," Alexander said, "Kelly will be with you. She has a tough assignment, a key assignment."

"And I?"

Alexander took in a deep breath, let it out slowly in a sigh that had real pain in it. "I'm asking you to watch out for her. Protect her. I don't care what your government wants you to do to me. I can take care of myself. But my little girl is going to need protection on this job. I'm asking you to be her protector."

He *is* mad! Pavel thought. Asking me to protect the woman he has assigned to watch me. His own daughter. Absolutely mad . . . or far more clever than even the Kremlin suspects. Yes, devious and extremely clever. He has been watching the two of us together. Now he places her safety in my hands. Extremely clever. And therefore extremely dangerous.

"Hey, look," Alexander exclaimed, pointing past Pavel's shoulder. "The Madeira Islands."

Pavel glanced out the window to his right and saw a large island, green and brown against the steel-gray of the ocean, a rim of whitish clouds building up on its windward side. He could see no other islands, but puffy clouds dotted the ocean and may have been hiding them.

"There's an example of ecological catastrophe turning into something good," Alexander said, as chipper and pleasant as if they had never spoken of death.

Pavel gave up trying to figure out this strange, many-mooded man. He is too subtle for me, he concluded.

"Madeira is the Portuguese word for wood," Alexander was explaining. "The early Spanish and Portuguese explorers working their way down the coast of Africa, looking for a way around to the Indies, they stopped at the islands to cut down trees for lumber and fuel. Masts, too. Cut down so much of it they totally denuded the islands in just about a century."

"A tragedy," Pavel said.

"Yeah. But somebody got the brilliant idea of planting

grapevines where the forests used to be. Now the islands produce one of the world's greatest wines. Madeira was a favorite of Thomas Jefferson's, did you know that?"

Pavel shook his head.

Alexander tilted his head back and began singing in a thin, wavering voice that was slightly off-key: "Have some Madeira my dear, You really have nothing to fear . . ."

His mind whirling, Pavel excused himself and left the flight deck.

For two days the plane stayed anchored in the harbor of São Vicente, in the Cape Verde Islands. Alexander remained aboard, constantly locked in his office, speaking by coded tight beams to contacts over half the world. He must have his own private network of communications satellites, Pavel thought. Then he realized, Of course! He must have free access to commsats owned by half a dozen nations and private capitalist corporations.

The rest of the crew apparently had nothing to do except guard the plane and replenish its stores. Pavel watched closely, but saw no weapons brought aboard.

There was no way for Pavel to make contact with Moscow. He was watched every moment, and each night the plane was moored far from land.

On the second day, though, Alexander insisted that Pavel take Kelly into the town for an afternoon of relaxation.

"Do you both good to get out and away from here for a few hours," he said.

Pavel wondered what Alexander had planned for the afternoon, that he wanted Pavel out of the way—escorted by his watchdog. Or does he want his daughter to have a free afternoon, escorted by *her* watchdog? It was too devious for Pavel to unravel.

Kelly had stayed distant from Pavel since the day they had swum together. But now the two of them took one of the inflatable Zodiac boats to the port and spent an afternoon gawking at the town, like any ordinary couple. They wore inconspicuous cutoff jeans and T-shirts—and generous coverings of sun-block oil over their bare arms and legs.

A big passenger liner was tied to the main pier, and they mingled with the brightly dressed tourists, watching the black-skinned islanders unloading bananas from boats that plied the waters between the Cape Verde Islands and Dakar, nearly a thousand kilometers eastward. Then they climbed the volcanic rocks to the crumbling old Moorish castle that had flown the red and green flag of Portugal for half a millennium.

He stood on the bare hilltop with Kelly beside him and looked back at the harbor, the ships anchored along the modern concrete quay, a rusting hulk half sunk next to a rotting old pier, the seaplane riding the gentle swells out by the breakwater. The equatorial sun was baking its heat into his bones, yet the trade wind was cool and refreshing.

"It's beautiful, isn't it?" Kelly said, smiling out at the view.

Pavel turned his gaze to her. "You are beautiful, too," he said. And he kissed her, wondering just how much he meant by his words, his actions. Kelly clung to him for a moment, then broke away.

Shaking her head slightly, she said, "Don't play games with me, Pavel."

"I'm not playing games."

"Not much."

"Kelly, honestly . . ."

"Let's see the town." She turned away from him, and started down the steep path that led back to the port.

Pavel followed her down the sloping path. They reached the quiet, sun-drenched streets where the stucco fronts of the buildings were painted brilliant hues of blue, yellow, green and white. Children in school uniforms sat up on the roof of a single-story building, intently reading. The outdoor market was noisier, the tang of spices filling the air while women in colorful dresses bargained noisily on both sides of the stalls over freshly caught fish and teeming bins of vegetables. Clouds of flies buzzed over the fish and red meats; Pavel waved at them annoyedly, ineffectively.

Finally he took Kelly by the wrist and led her away from the stalls.

They found a tiny café with a patio that looked out on the municipal square. The food was good, the wine even better. Pavel began to fantasize about spending the rest of the afternoon in a romantic hotel room, but he knew that Kelly would never agree.

Yet she suggested, "Let's go back up the hill and find a quiet spot where we can take a nap."

His thoughts churning, Pavel brought her back to the abandoned Moorish castle. She has almost as many contradictions about her as her father, he said to himself. It's almost as if she is fighting within her own soul.

But another voice in his mind warned, Her loyalty is to her father; always remember that. Your loyalty is to the Soviet Union and its people. Her loyalty is to her father.

They climbed solid stone stairs to the topmost turret, stretched out in the sun and almost immediately fell asleep, more like brother and sister than prospective lovers.

Pavel woke shivering. The sun had dropped toward the horizon, leaving him in the shade of the turret's parapet. It was cold, lying on the stones. Kelly was nowhere in sight.

He sat bolt upright, then quickly got to his feet. Ah, there she is! Kelly was leaning on the weathered stone parapet, off at the other side of the turret, gazing down at the town and the harbor. Pavel felt an immense flood of relief. She had not deserted him. She had not been abducted.

Wondering which reason was the stronger within his own mind, Pavel walked over to her side.

"You were snoring," she said.

"Impossible. I never snore."

"How would you know?"

"Hasn't your father told you that in the Soviet Union, everyone is watched all the time? If I snored, there would be a tape recording of it, and my superiors would have warned me to cease such bourgeois affectations."

Kelly laughed. "Snoring isn't allowed in the USSR?"

"Of course not," Pavel joked, surprised at how happy her laughter made him feel. "We are striving to create the truly modern man. Snoring is definitely not modern."

They laughed and joked their way down the mountain-side and back into the town. The sun was setting, so they walked back to the pier and the Zodiac they had left tied there. Kelly inspected the boat carefully once they had hopped into it, even taking a small electronic beeper from her belt and passing it back and forth over its length twice.

"Don't want to bring any bugs back to the plane with us," she said. "Or bombs."

Pavel sat beside her as she started the motor. "Your father has enemies."

"Yes, he does," she replied. Then, staring hard into his eyes, she asked, "Aren't you one of them?"

He had no answer. They rode back to the seaplane without further words. Pavel felt grateful that the roar of the boat's motor made intimate conversation impossible.

From São Vicente they flew to Dakar, on the bulge of Africa's Senegalese coast. Again, Alexander suggested to Pavel that he take Kelly into the city. But when Kelly said she wanted to go dancing, both men were dubious.

"I don't like the idea of you two out in the wild-life district at night," Alexander said grimly. "Dakar isn't a tourist's city; it's a rough, grungy town at night. It can be dangerous."

Kelly shook her head stubbornly. "We won't go into the red-light district, for God's sake! We'll stay with the country club crowd."

Pavel had a more serious objection. "I don't know how to dance," he confessed.

She grinned at him, her father's sardonic, superior semi-sneer. "I'll have to teach you, then."

So Pavel escorted Kelly on a tour of the city's nightlife, sampling capitalistic delights such as dancing in private clubs that boasted live musicians and dining in posh restaurants, all the while wondering when—if ever—Alexander was going to get his Libyan mission under way.

It was obvious that Alexander wanted Pavel away from the plane for long hours at a time. But under constant observation, nonetheless. Pavel wondered also about his relationship with Kelly. She is Alexander's daughter, he kept telling himself. She is intelligent, charming, lovely in her own way—but she is Alexander's daughter, and her first loyalty is to her father.

Pavel found himself wishing it were not so.

"This is our last night of fun," Kelly said over the din of a torrid Senegalese rock band.

"What?" Pavel had heard her words. With a shock, he realized that he did not want things to change.

Kelly leaned forward over their minuscule table. Two plastic coconut shells half filled with poisonously delicious rum drinks tottered slightly between them. The nightclub was lit by strobing projectors flashing holograms of video stars that sang, played their electronic instruments and even "danced" with the customers. Couples gyrated wildly to the throbbing, drum-heavy music, casting weird shadows across Kelly's snub-nosed face. She was wearing a sleeveless frock, its color impossible to determine in the flashing strobe lights.

"Tomorrow the real work starts," she shouted into Pavel's ear.

He took her by the wrist and led her across the edge of the dance floor, threading through bluish clouds of smoke and past the wildly thrashing couples, even directly through several of the oblivious holos. Once the thickly padded main door of the club closed behind them, the parking lot outside was blessedly quiet. The stars glittered in the breaks between low-scudding gray clouds. The air was damp and heavy with mingled odors of flowers and oil refineries.

"Had enough of the rich capitalist life?" Kelly teased.

"You said our mission begins tomorrow?"

"The real work starts tomorrow, yes," she said. "The exact timing for the mission is still a secret."

"Rayyid will officially open the irrigation system next week," Pavel pointed out. "The news is in all the headlines."

She nodded, began walking slowly toward the rows of parked cars.

"Kelly . . ." Pavel began.

Turning back toward him, her face lit by the garish glow of the nightclub's animated sign, she seemed to be waiting for him to speak the right words.

"A few days ago . . . you said I was one of your father's enemies. That is true."

"I know it."

"But I don't wish to be *your* enemy."

She sighed and shook her head. "Can't be his enemy without being mine, Pavel."

"I have my orders. I am a loyal Soviet citizen. He knew that when he accepted me."

Kelly took a step toward him, "Pavel—I don't make friends easily. I've always been a loner . . ."

"Me, too," he admitted.

She started to say something, changed her mind. Pavel could sense the emotions battling within her.

"Maybe we'd better leave it that way," she said at last. "It might've been good between us, but . . ."

A blow struck between Pavel's shoulder blades like a boulder smashing him. He went down face-first, heard his nose crunch on the asphalt of the parking lot. Kelly screamed.

There was no pain. Not yet. Pavel half rolled over, and a massive black man loomed over him, a thick length of pipe in his upraised hand. Beyond him, Pavel could see two others grabbing at Kelly, twisting her arms painfully and laughing as they tore at her dress.

Without thinking consciously, Pavel blocked the downward swing of the pipe-wielder's arm and kicked his legs out from under him. He went down with a surprised grunt and a thwack as Pavel scrambled to his feet.

Kelly smashed the heel of her shoe into one of her assailant's insteps, wrenched her arm free from him as he yowled in sudden pain, then drove her cupped palm into the nose of the other man holding her. His head snapped back.

Pavel took out the man hopping on one foot with a swift stiff-fingered shot in the throat, then whirled to face the other one. But Kelly smashed lightning-fast chops at his solar plexus, kidney and groin. He hit the asphalt like a dead man.

The big one who had struck Pavel was climbing to his feet. Feeling utter fury boiling within him, Pavel launched a flying dropkick at his head, knocking him to his knees. Pavel landed catlike on the balls of his feet and wrenched the pipe from the man's hand. With every ounce of his strength he swung the pipe into the big man's ribs and felt them give way. Then backhanded across the face and he went down heavily. Then a two-handed swing across his back.

"Stop it! Stop it!" Kelly hissed, grabbing Pavel's shoulder. "Do you want to kill him?"

"Yes!" Pavel snarled. But he stopped. He was trembling with rage, and he knew that it was only in part from the shock of being unprovokedly attacked. They had tried to hurt Kelly.

He turned to the two who had grabbed her, stretched out on the asphalt.

"Subhuman bastards," he muttered.

"Come on," Kelly said, "let's get to the plane."

They took one of the battered ancient taxicabs waiting in line at the club's entrance. As it jounced toward the waterfront, Kelly peered at Pavel's face in the dim light of the occasional streetlamps.

"Your nose is bleeding."

"They tore your dress."

"Is it broken?"

"No, I don't think so. There's a bruise on your shoulder."

"That's nothing. What about your back?"

"It feels numb."

"You're lucky no bones are broken."

"Where did you learn to fight like that?"

"From when I was a kid. Then training at the IPF. My father's people have taught me a few new tricks, too."

Suddenly they were laughing together. Bruised, bleeding, sweating, trembling with delayed reactions of fear and anger—they laughed almost uncontrollably all the way to the waterfront.

"A fine pair of warriors we are," Kelly said as they passed the armed guard at the pier's entrance. "We must look awful."

"But we look better than _they_ do," Pavel reminded her.

It wasn't until they were halfway back to the plane, with cold spray drenching him and throbbing pain starting in his back and face, that Pavel began to ask himself, Were they merely muggers? Or were they sent by someone? Enemies of Alexander's, perhaps? Or could Alexander himself have sent them, as some kind of test of my ability to protect his daughter? The man is devious enough for that.

Alexander was strangely silent as Kelly explained what

had happened. Pavel stood beside her in the softly lit wardroom, his back blazing with pain, his nose still trickling blood, and watched Alexander. No one else was present.

The man listened grimly to his daughter and replied only, "I told you it was a dangerous town."

"When you're right, you're right," Kelly admitted.

"Well . . ." Alexander let out a sigh that was almost a snort. "You're both okay. No permanent damage. That's the important thing."

"Pavel needs treatment for his back."

Turning his steel-gray gaze to Pavel, Alexander said, "Yeah, I guess so. Come with me."

Without another word to his daughter, he led Pavel from the wardroom and down the passageway to his private quarters. His bathroom was as large as Pavel's whole compartment, and wedged between the shower stall and the toilet was a narrow deep tub.

"My one luxury," Alexander muttered. "Whirlpool bath." He touched a button on the tub's control box and steaming hot water started filling it.

Pavel caught a glimpse of himself in the mirror above the sink. His upper lip was caked with blood; his cheek was scuffed raw. His back was so stiff now that he knew he could not raise his arms, even to defend himself.

Alexander placed himself squarely in front of Pavel.

"I asked you to protect my daughter, and you damn near get her raped and murdered."

"I got her . . ." Pavel felt shocked at the accusation.

"Don't you have any goddamned sense? Where the hell did you take her, to some goddamned junk bar or what?"

"It was a private club that *she* selected."

"You're supposed to *protect* her," Alexander snarled. "You're supposed to be on the alert, have some common sense in that thick Russian skull of yours."

Anger flamed through Pavel. "So it's the fault of the

Russian barbarian that muggers and hoodlums infest Dakar!"

"You damned near got her killed!"

And Pavel's anger dissolved as quickly as it had appeared. There was real fear in Alexander's eyes, real anguish in his voice.

"I know," he said, his voice low. "I love her, too."

Alexander's mouth opened, but no words came out. He stood motionless, speechless. Then he gestured toward the rapidly filling tub. Through the steam, Pavel saw that there was a set of three steps built into its side. In silence, Alexander helped him into the tub, turned on the whirlpool action and then left Pavel alone.

It took two days of rest and whirlpool treatments to heal Pavel's back. The hot swirling water eased the pain and swelling to the point where Pavel felt only a twinge when he raised his arms above his head. During those two days he saw Alexander only when he knocked for admission to the bathroom.

Kelly seemed cheerful and friendly, but nothing more. Pavel hoped desperately that her father had not told her of his admission.

On the evening of the third day after the attack Alexander abruptly called for a final mission briefing. Pavel, Kelly, Barker and Mavroulis gathered around the display table in the wardroom. A detailed map of the Libyan aquifer facility glowed in the otherwise unlit compartment, throwing deep shadows across their faces.

Alexander asked each of them to recite their assignments.

Barker spoke about flying from Dakar and landing in the desert, pointing to a spot marked on the map some twenty kilometers from the Libyan facility.

Mavroulis took over. "We meet Hassan and his men here"—he tapped the tabletop display screen—"and proceed to the aquifer facility. We get past the guards and take over the facility."

"Timing?" Alexander asked.

Mavroulis rattled off a series of hours and minutes that meant nothing to Pavel. Obviously they had rehearsed this sequence of actions many times. They all knew exactly what they were supposed to do. All of them, except Pavel.

"Kelly?" her father asked. "Let's hear your story."

"Once we're inside the control building I proceed to the main computer center and reprogram the machine. Reprogramming tapes are in my kit."

Alexander gave her a long, serious look. "You're the key to this whole operation, young lady. Everything we're doing, all the risks we're taking, are so that you can get into their computer."

She nodded, equally serious. "I understand."

Mavroulis then told how they would retreat to the spot where Barker was waiting with their aircraft. Barker said he would fly out of Libyan airspace to a rendezvous with a fighter escort waiting for them in Chad.

Alexander looked at each of them in turn, his lips pressed into a tight, tense line, his gray eyes cold as scalpels. "Okay, sounds like you know your jobs."

"What about me?" Pavel blurted. "I'm going, too, am I not?"

Looking almost surprised, Alexander said, "Sure you're going, Red. Your job is very simple. You're Kelly's protection. Stay with her wherever she goes. If the operation blows up, you're to get her out and back to me. Don't come back without her. *Pahnyeemahyo?*"

His Russian was execrable. "I understand," Pavel answered in letter-perfect English.

Pavel could not overcome the feeling that they were being watched. And followed.

Four would-be tourists: an American woman, an Englishman, a Greek and a Russian. From Alexander's seaplane anchored out in the harbor they went to the waterfront of Dakar in two separate groups of two, Pavel and Kelly first, then Barker and Mavroulis. All dressed in casual slacks and sport shirts, with overnight bags slung across their shoulders. In two separate taxis they went to the airport, where they bought four separate tickets for Casablanca, Tunis, Cairo and Malta.

Each of them started for the gates where their respective planes were waiting. Each of them handed their tickets to strangers who identified themselves as part of Alexander's operation. The strangers boarded the planes while the four of them ducked through an emergency exit (conveniently left unlocked thanks to a small bribe) and into an empty luggage carrier that just happened to be parked there. Barker drove the electrically powered van into a hangar on the far side of the sprawling airport.

A swivel-engined hoverjet sat alone in the echoing hangar. It looked old and hard-used. Paint worn and chipped, except for a fresh-looking smear where the name of the plane's previous owner had been whited over. The only identification on the craft was its registration number, back on the tail. The bulky engine pods, out at the ends of the stubby wings, were black with oil and dirt. Pavel began to wonder if this machine would make it all the way to their base camp in the desert. And back again.

Wordlessly the four of them climbed into it. The plane smelled sourly of oil and tobacco smoke and old human sweat. Barker took the pilot's seat, Kelly the copilot's—to Pavel's surprise. He sat behind them, with Mavroulis beside him, glowering like a dark volcano at Pavel as they strapped on their safety harnesses.

They taxied out onto the ramp, Barker chatting with the traffic controllers in the clipped, professional English of the airways. Pavel watched as they rolled out to a vertical takeoff area marked by wide red and yellow circles. The plane's two turboprop engines tilted slowly backward, their big propeller blades scything the air until they became an invisible blur. The engines roared with full power, shaking the cabin so furiously that Pavel began to worry that the plane might fall apart.

With a lurch, they lifted off the ground and rattled up and away, banking so precariously that when Pavel looked out the window on his side, he was staring straight down at the looming roof of a hangar and the bird nests and droppings that covered it. It looked terrifyingly close.

The plane climbed steadily, though, and soon enough the engines slid back to their horizontal positions and they surged ahead, winging across greenly forested mountains with the sun at their backs.

For days Pavel had searched for a way to warn Moscow, to get out the word of what Alexander was planning to do and how he would do it. But there had been no chance. He was always watched, never alone. And now he rode with three of the mercenaries on their mission of destruction, not entirely sure that he wanted to stop them. That would mean placing Kelly in unbearable danger, possibly getting her killed.

Miserably confused, Pavel sat in the swiveljet and did nothing. There seemed to be nothing he could do.

The landscape changed slowly, subtly, but by the time the long shadows of twilight were reaching across the ground, Pavel was watching low, gently undulating hills of bare rock with patches of pitifully thin grass here and there. Dark circles of water holes appeared every few kilometers; most of them seemed to be wells dug by men rather than natural springs. The grass was worn away around the waterholes, leaving only bare gray dry-looking soil that wafted away in long dusty streamers with each passing gust of wind.

Just at sunset Pavel saw a tiny herd of emaciated cattle

moving slowly toward one of those waterholes. Three stick-thin persons in gray dust-covered robes walked behind them. From this altitude Pavel could not tell if they were men or women.

It was well past sundown when they landed, coming down vertically in a sea of absolute blackness; not a light anywhere except for the stars strewn across the dark bowl of night. But, straining his eyes, Pavel saw briefly a flicker of a campfire down there; it looked very small and lonely. Between Barker's and Kelly's shoulders, Pavel could see a glowing display on the radar panel. Yet he did not feel safe until the plane thumped onto solid ground.

It felt good to stretch his legs again. Pavel tried lifting his arms and stretching his spine, carefully. A twinge, nothing more. He was ready for action.

Barker became their team leader. He strode across the sand to the tiny campfire, and spoke with a trio of men swathed in desert robes and burnooses who were waiting there. Then he beckoned to Pavel and the others.

"Everything's on schedule." Barker pronounced it *shedyule*. "Hassan and his people will rendezvous with us here tomorrow morning."

They spent the next two hours dragging out camouflage nets and radar dispersers to hide the plane from aerial surveillance, then pitching a tan igloo-shaped tent for themselves to sleep in, while the three robed strangers watched in unmoving silence in the flickering light of their fire.

It was surprisingly cold on the desert, although Pavel kept warm by working hard. He did not want his back to stiffen on him. They ate a quick meal from metal-foil packages that heated themselves when their tops were pulled off.

"Sleep now," Barker said. "Big show tomorrow."

Pavel asked, "No one stands guard?"

Barker nodded toward the three bedouins by the fire. "They're our guards."

"You trust them?"

"They're in on this with us."

"I think we should have a guard of our own."

"Now see here . . ."

Mavroulis's voice came out of the dimness like a distant roll of thunder. "For once I agree with the Russian paranoid."

Pavel grinned. "I will stand watch until midnight."

"Hokay," said Mavroulis. "I will take midnight to two."

Kelly offered to take the next two hours and, reluctantly, Barker agreed to the final two.

All four of them crawled into the round tent. Pavel strapped a battery-powered heating pad to his back, then pulled a thermal jacket over it.

"Take this, if you're going to be our guardian," said Barker. He pushed a slim flat pistol into Pavel's hand. "It's a Beretta nine-millimeter automatic. Do you know how to use it?"

Pavel flicked off the safety with his thumb and cocked the pistol.

"For heaven's sake, don't fire the thing unless it's absolutely necessary!" Barker warned.

"Good night," said Pavel, calmly returning the gun to its safe condition.

The others muttered good night and crawled into their sleeping bags. Pavel ached for Kelly to say something more, but soon all he heard was the gentle breathing of his companions. Mavroulis began to snore.

He tucked the pistol into his belt, its weight solid and comforting. It was warm and drowsy inside the tent. And there was utterly nothing to do. Pavel decided to duck outside. At least I can count the stars, he told himself.

A wind had come up. Not enough to stir the desert sand,

but Pavel walked around the tent to the leeward, then sat cross-legged on the ground. He could not see the campfire from this spot, though, and that bothered him somewhat.

But the spectacle of the heavens was so overwhelming that he almost forgot everything else. The stars were incredibly bright in the desert night; so brilliant that he almost felt he could reach out and take them in his fingers. For what seemed like an hour Pavel studied the heavens, as excited as he had been at his first visit to a planetarium.

He renewed his acquaintance with the Great and Little Bears, the Princess, the Hunter. A meteor blazed briefly across the sky, silent and cold despite its fire. The Moon was nowhere in sight. The arching beauty of the Milky Way glowed alluringly, much brighter than he had ever seen it from the streets of Kursk or Moscow. And there was Mars, shining red on the horizon. Russians are there, living and working on another world, Pavel thought with a surge of pride.

Pavel tore his gaze away and looked at the glowing digits of his wristwatch. Hardly half an hour had elapsed. He got to his feet and slowly paced around the tent, hunching his shoulders against the cold wind and pushing his fists deep into the jacket's pockets.

The campfire was down to a few pitiful embers. The men were sleeping beside it, on the bare ground.

There were only two men there!

Pavel tensed. His hands came out of the pockets; his right held the pistol. He cocked it; in the dark night the clicking noise sounded like the heavens cracking asunder.

"Tovarish." It was a whisper.

Slowly Pavel turned his head. A shadowy form stood near the tent behind him. He whirled, the gun leveled at the bedouin's waist.

"Tovarish! I am friend!" the man said in a mixture of Russian and English.

"Who are you?" Pavel whispered.

"A friend. To help you."

"Help me?"

"I was told a Russian would be among the infidels who came to this camp, and he would be a friend to us. I was told to make myself known to the Russian."

In the dim light of the stars Pavel could not make out the man's face, deeply shadowed by the hood of his burnoose.

"Who told you this?"

"Hassan's men. The faithful of God," replied the bedouin. "Hassan himself will be here in the morning. He will remain here while you go to the water machinery. He and the faithful will be waiting for you when you return."

"And then?"

"You will be spared," the man whispered. "Hassan knows who the true friends of God are. You will be spared."

A burning tendril of red-hot fear crawled along Pavel's gut and clutched at his heart.

"And the others?" he asked in an urgent whisper.

"God knows."

"What do you mean?"

"They are infidels, are they not? What does it matter?"

A thousand questions boiled up in Pavel's mind, but he clamped his lips shut so tightly that his teeth hurt. This bedouin is only a messenger, he told himself. He knows very little. And the more questions I ask, the more suspicious he will become.

"Go with God," said the bedouin, tapping his right hand to his chest.

Pavel grunted and nodded, thinking that it was an unlikely alliance: a Moslem fundamentalist and a Soviet atheist.

The bedouin went as silently as a wraith back toward the embers of the campfire. Pavel stayed on his feet, wide awake, and forgot the stars that hung above. Even after Mavroulis came out and took the gun from him, Pavel went inside the tent and stretched out in his sleeping bag but found that he could not keep his eyes closed.

Tense as a hunted mountain lion, eyes burning from lack of sleep, Pavel rolled out of his sleeping bag with the first glint of dawn. He had spent the night debating where his loyalties lay: assassinating Alexander did not mean that he should stand aside and let these desert savages slaughter his companions. He could not let them harm Kelly. Never. Besides, it would make his assignment more difficult if Kelly and the others were killed or even held hostage.

Who is this Hassan? What game is he playing? Is Alexander's plan already known and countered? Are we already in a trap, our necks in nooses?

Kelly and the others gave no sign of apprehension. They shared a quick breakfast of yogurt and honey with the three bedouins, who smilingly assured them that Hassan would soon arrive. Pavel tried to identify which of the three had spoken to him during the night. He could not.

Kelly broke out tubes of dark cream makeup. "We've got to look more like Arabs," she said.

"A red-haired Arab," Mavroulis joked, taking a tube from her.

"I won't be red-haired for long," Kelly shot back, grinning.

Pavel took the tube she handed him.

"You're already a lot darker than you were when you first came to us," she said. "Your skin is almost golden, like toast."

"Tartar blood," Pavel said.

"And those beautiful dark eyes," Kelly added. "You won't need contacts to disguise them."

Pavel felt himself blush.

By the time Hassan and his men arrived, in a pair of armored, wide-tracked personnel carriers, Kelly, Mavroulis and Pavel had daubed their skin as dark as their bedouin companions. Barker had declined to disguise himself.

"I am to remain here with the plane and stay out of the sun," he said with an almost smug air of English self-satisfaction.

Hassan turned out to be a colonel in the Libyan Army. He jumped down from the turret of the leading sand-colored crawler, a handsome energetic man in his late forties, wearing a crisply creased green and gold uniform with his cap cocked at a jaunty angle and a pair of mirrored sunglasses that hid his eyes very effectively.

He looked over the four mercenaries, up and down, as he casually took a flat gold case from his tunic chest pocket and put a slim brown cigar to his lips. Pavel noticed that he sported a pencil-thin mustache.

One of his aides, dressed in sand-colored battle fatigues, leaped forward to light the colonel's cigar. Hassan blew out a thin cloud of smoke, then nodded as if satisfied.

"You will do, I suppose." Without turning his head back to the vehicle, he raised one hand and snapped his fingers. "Uniforms!"

Within five minutes Kelly, Mavroulis and Pavel were decked in the green and gold uniforms of the Libyan Army. Pavel thought them overly gaudy: uniforms meant for show, not for fighting. They did not fit terribly well; Kelly's in particular sagged on her diminutive frame.

Hassan disdained to speak to them, but looked them over like a drill sergeant inspecting a trio of recruits, his lip curled slightly in distaste. Kelly had tucked her dyed hair inside her cap. Otherwise she looked properly boyish.

"That APV will take you to the water facility," Hassan said in British-accented English. "The crew is instructed to wait for you until precisely 1510 hours. Then they will return here, with you or without you. Is that clear?"

Mavroulis said, "The timetable is understood."

Hassan took the cigar from his lips and gestured to the personnel carrier. The three of them climbed up the metal rungs of the ladder and in through the hatch. Two soldiers were already inside, dressed in khaki fatigues and wearing sidearms in well-oiled black holsters, sitting on the thinly padded bench that lined one side of the metal compartment. The three mercenaries sat along the bench on the opposite side. The metal bulkhead felt hot against Pavel's back; almost as good as the heating pad, he thought.

Through the forward hatch in the compartment, Pavel could see two more men in the driver's cab, one of them an officer. With a roar of diesel engines and a bone-shaking rattle, the personnel carrier started off across the desert.

Heat. The armored vehicle was like an oven in the desert morning. Sweat oozed from every pore of Pavel's body. The stink of their bodies became almost nauseating as the APV lurched and swayed. Their uniforms turned dark with perspiration, under the armpits, across the back, everywhere.

"They don't believe in air-conditioning," Kelly said, her voice bleak with misery.

One of the soldiers wordlessly climbed up into the top turret and popped its hatch open. A hot breeze like the blast from a furnace blew in. Mavroulis grunted and swore in Greek under his breath. Pavel wondered if the soldiers understood English.

"Tell me about this aquifer facility. How does it work?" Pavel said to Kelly, more to forget the heat and cover his growing tension than any desire to learn.

Kelly seemed glad of the diversion. She was nervous, too, Pavel realized. She recited facts and figures for the remainder of the jouncing trip across the desert. The only thing that stuck in Pavel's mind was that the great underground aquifer was almost three thousand meters deep; nearly three kilometers below the desert sands.

Could the Libyans actually use up all that water in a single generation? There must be millions of tons of it beneath the Sahara, Pavel realized. Surely Alexander was spouting propaganda. But then he remembered how the vast virgin lands in Siberia had been polluted beyond belief in only a few decades. Exaggerated or not, Alexander was right: sooner or later the aquifer would be drained. Water that had been stored for a hundred thousand years would be sucked away and depleted in the blink of an eye. Kelly believes it, Pavel told himself, and she has no reason to lie to me. She is almost painfully honest.

"There it is!" announced the soldier up in the turret. One by one the three mercenaries climbed up to look.

Pavel saw an immense building made of poured concrete, gray and low against the gray-brown rocks and sand of the desert. Squat towers stood at each corner. Cooling towers for the gigantic pumps housed inside the building, Kelly told him. But they looked like good defensive posts to Pavel, where a few troops could hold off a small army of attackers. All around the building were smaller concrete complexes of pillboxes, missile launchers, and barracks.

The place is a fortress, he realized. And it is defended by Rayyid's best troops.

They drove past an outer fence of electrified wire and along a smooth road flanked by gun emplacements and dozens of similar armored tracked vehicles, all in sandy gray desert camouflage. Pavel heard the thrumming whine of a helicopter. The inner perimeter was a concrete wall lined with troops. They drove past and up to the main gate of the building itself.

The driver stayed behind the wheel, but the officer who had sat next to him, a captain, ducked into the main compartment of the APV and in Arabic directed the two soldiers there to break out automatic rifles for the three mercenaries. Then he led all five uniformed figures out the rear hatch, past several sets of guards, and finally up a narrow concrete stairway to the roof of the main building.

The late morning sun poured down on them like molten lead. Not a breath of breeze, even up on the roof. The guards seemed to cower away from the blazing sunlight and seek shelter in whatever shade they could find. Pavel had never seen a sky so cloudless, the sun so powerful; it turned the heavens into an inverted bowl of hammered brass. He squinted out across the desert, shimmering in the heat haze. Not a tree or a blade of grass as far as the eye could see. Only the distant wavering gleam of a mirage, a cruel illusion of water in this utterly barren wasteland.

Guards lounged in the scant slices of shade offered by the big cooling towers. A pair of helicopters roared by: gunships, Pavel saw, manufactured in Soviet Russia.

We're in the middle of the Libyan Army, he told himself. If anything goes wrong with our operation, we'll never get out alive. Then he recalled that even if they got back to their base camp, Hassan and his zealots were waiting there with sharpened knives.

Mavroulis spoke briefly with the captain, then turned to Kelly and Pavel.

"They've done their task," he said in a low gruff rumble. "We're here. Now it's up to us. They will wait up here until 1500 hours. The APV will wait ten minutes more."

"Then let's get moving," Kelly said firmly.

"One thing," said Mavroulis, patting the rifle slung over his shoulder. "These guns are empty. They don't trust us with live ammunition."

Kelly glanced at Pavel, then said, "Just as well. We're not here to kill anybody."

Pavel thought, Kill or be killed.

They strode out across the roof to a stainless-steel dome, one of many glittering in the high sun.

"According to the plans, this shaft will lead you to the computer center," said Mavroulis.

Kelly nodded. No hint of nervousness now. She was all business and anxious to get started.

"Good luck," said the Greek.

They both glanced around. No guards could see them. Kelly bent over and wormed her lithe body through the gap between the steel dome and the concrete lip on which it was based. Pavel started after her, touched his hand against the metal and flinched with pain.

"Idiot!" Mavroulis growled. "The metal's been sitting in the sun all morning."

Wringing his hand, Pavel ducked through the air space and hesitated a moment to let his eyes adjust to the cool shadows. Kelly was already a dozen rungs down the metal ladder set into the shaft's walls. He hurried after her, the useless rifle slapping against his hip with every move he made.

They reached a horizontal shaft, all cool metal, barely big enough for each of them to crawl through. Mavroulis would never have made it, Pavel thought.

The shaft widened enough for Pavel to slink up beside Kelly.

"These guns are in the way," he whispered. "Let's leave them here and pick them up on our way back."

She nodded and wriggled the rifle off her shoulder. Pavel did the same. Then Kelly took a slim sheet of what looked like microfilm from her tunic pocket. From the other pocket she brought out a miniaturized reader and put it to her eye.

"Okay," she whispered, tucking them back into the tunic, "we're in the main air-conditioning shaft. Two cross-shafts, and then we take the next left fork."

Pavel almost grinned at her darkened face. "I thought the Libyans didn't believe in air-conditioning."

She was totally serious. "This isn't for their people; it's for their computer."

The shaft got narrower and Pavel had to slide back behind Kelly. He realized that no one bigger than himself or Kelly could possibly use these air shafts. They inched along like two moles in a tunnel. Pavel felt blind and helpless.

Finally Kelly stopped and motioned with the wiggle of one finger for Pavel to come forward. He had to climb over her body to bring his face next to hers: not altogether unpleasant, he decided.

Three centimeters in front of their faces was a mesh grille, apparently set high in the wall of a large room filled with humming computer consoles. Several men and women in civilian clothes were sitting at consoles. Two technicians in coveralls had the back of one console off and were installing new circuit boards. All of them looked Asian.

"Minolta J-300s," Kelly muttered, so low Pavel knew she was talking to herself. "C models. Damn! They told us they'd have A models."

"Is that a problem?" he whispered into her ear.

"Maybe. Maybe not."

Kelly wormed a hand down toward her right boot and pulled out a slim rod. Then she did the same with her left boot.

"You, too," she whispered to Pavel.

Sure enough, his boots also carried a pair of concealed rods, about the thickness of normal electrical wire and not more than a dozen centimeters long.

"Okay," she said, "move back."

They inched along in reverse to a spot where a small side shaft branched away from the shaft they were in. Wordlessly Kelly took Pavel's two rods and wormed herself into the shaft. It was barely big enough for her shoulders to squeeze into. Pavel watched her slowly disappear into the tunnel, like a creature being swallowed by a snake, until only her booted feet remained outside.

After several minutes she started wiggling her feet. Pavel grabbed at her ankles and pulled her free.

Kelly was gasping. "Thanks. I got stuck in there. Damned plans said it was wide enough—but just barely."

"Those rods . . ."

"Knockout gas. It's circulating through the air-conditioning vents now. Give it a couple of minutes."

"But won't we . . ."

She shook her head. "It's a nerve gas. Dissipates before it reaches us." Then, with a hard grin, "At least, that's what the specs claim."

They made their way to the grille again and saw that the people tending the computer had slumped over, unconscious. It took a few more minutes to remove the grille, but finally Pavel swung it open and lowered himself gingerly to the floor of the computer room.

He took a deep, testing breath, then reached up to help Kelly down.

"How long will they remain unconscious?" he asked.

Heading straight for the central console, Kelly said, "Until we spray them with the antidote."

She sat at the console, pulled a hand-sized computer from her waistband, and placed it on the desktop beside the keyboard. Unconsciously, Kelly flexed her fingers, like a virtuoso confronting a new piano for the first time.

Pavel looked around at the bodies strewn across the floor, and the single featureless door that apparently was the only way into or out of this computer center—except for the air shaft they had come through.

There were no surveillance cameras. Libyan security was concentrating on preventing anyone from penetrating from the outside; they did not think to observe what was going on inside their fortress. In the Soviet Union such laxness would never be tolerated.

"And what if someone tries to come in here?" he asked.

Without looking up from the display screen in front of her, Kelly said, "That's why you're here: to discourage interruptions."

He grunted.

Kelly's fingers were rapidly tapping across the computer keyboard. "Don't worry, Pavel," she said absently, her mind already absorbed on her task. "According to the information Hassan's people gave us, the routine around here is very strict. The soldiers don't bother the computer technicians. Actually, they're a little afraid of them."

Hassan again. Pavel paced the floor nervously, stepping around the bodies. They seemed dead. Totally unmoving. If they were breathing, it was very hard to detect. He thought about trying the pulse on one of them, but could not bring himself to touch any of the inert bodies. What if they are dead? It's not my fault. What if Hassan's fanatics kill these mercenaries? Kelly and Mavroulis and Barker, waiting for us back at the camp.

That was a different matter. Pavel could not pass that off so easily. Or at all.

"I see your reflection in the screen here every time you waltz by," Kelly complained. "Go find a console and sit. I'll put some TV on the screen for you."

Sighing with impatience and frustration, Pavel took an empty chair at one of the many consoles flanking the central position where Kelly was working. The main screen suddenly lit up with an outdoor scene in some city where the sun blazed down on whitewashed houses and low flat roofs, glittered off towers of glass and steel, danced across waves of the sea far in the background.

"That's Tripoli," Kelly called to him. "You can watch Rayyid and the ceremonies for the opening of the aquifer facility."

Pavel fidgeted in the chair.

"Put on the earphones. I'll pipe you an English-language broadcast."

Slipping on the lightweight headset, Pavel heard a cultivated BBC voice describing the scene he saw on the display screen. The voice droned on as the camera panned across sun-drenched Tripoli and its harbor, then cut to the outdoor stage where Qumar al-Rayyid, the President of Libya and Commander in Chief of its Army, would press the button that would start the water flowing from the aquifer, hundreds of kilometers away, to the symbolic fountain in the center of the main square of Tripoli's government center.

"At precisely 1500 hours," the broadcaster's cultured voice explained, "that fountain will begin to flow with water that was put down into the ground a hundred thousand years ago."

Fifteen hundred hours! The words seared through Pavel's mind. That was when they were supposed to be back on the roof, heading for the tractor that would take them back to the desert camp.

Pavel tore the headset off and wheeled his chair across the concrete floor to Kelly.

"Rayyid's going to start the water flowing at 1500!"

Almost annoyed at his interruption, she shot him a quick glance. "I know."

"But that means the water must begin flowing hours sooner, doesn't it?"

Kelly took her hands from the keypad, flexing her fingers as if they had gotten stiff. "The water's already filling the underground aqueduct," she explained. "They've tested the system, for God's sake. When Rayyid punches the button, the pumps here start up again and begin drawing water. The fountain spurts and everybody in Tripoli cheers —if you don't stop getting in my way."

Pavel pushed his chair back slightly.

"It takes a lot of time and concentration to reprogram their computer," Kelly said, half apologetically. "We don't want them to know there's been any interference. It's got to look like they screwed it up themselves."

Pavel could not stand it any longer. "Hassan is a traitor," he blurted.

With obvious patience, Kelly replied, "We know. When Rayyid's water scheme collapses, Hassan will lead the *coup d'état* that topples him. Then the French sell him fusion-powered desalting systems so that Libya can convert Mediterranean water for irrigation and drinking, and leave the aquifer alone." She turned back to the computer.

"No!" Pavel grabbed her by the shoulders and made her pay attention to him. "Hassan is a traitor to us! His people are religious zealots. They plan to kill you all when we return to the camp."

Kelly's brown eyes showed no trace of fear. Only sudden suspicion. "How do you know?" she whispered.

"I am a Soviet agent, remember?" Pavel answered bitterly. "They assured me that I would be spared."

"Then why are you telling me?"

"Because I don't want you killed! I love you!"

Kelly's head snapped back as if she had been struck in the face. "You . . . what?"

"It's a trap," Pavel insisted. "I don't know what Hassan's game is, but he intends to kill you once we get back to the camp."

"You love me?"

"Yes!"

Kelly grinned at him, half suspicious, half pleased. "We'll have to talk about that later."

"What are we going to do? Hassan . . ."

"First thing we've *got* to do is finish reprogramming this Japanese monster."

"But . . ."

"First things first," Kelly insisted. And she turned back to the keypad.

Pavel watched her for a few moments, then went back to the console where the scenes from Tripoli were showing on the screen. But he could not sit still. He got up, paced the room. It seemed close and stuffy, despite the air-conditioning. He felt sweat beading his lip and brow, trickling down his ribs.

He checked the bodies of the Japanese technicians. They were alive, breathing slowly, regularly. What will happen to them? he wondered. Will they be blamed for the malfunctions Kelly is programming into their computer?

Somehow Pavel found himself at the one door leading out of the computer center. It was solid steel, like the hatch of a weapons bunker, and locked by an electronic combination lock. He could not get out that way even if he wanted to.

Hours dragged by. More and more he watched Kelly, her intent, utterly serious face reflected in the green-glowing display screen, her fingers flicking across the keys. The computer hummed softly as she worked it, and Kelly herself kept up a low-key obbligato of muttered curses and imprecations, alternating with soft crooning sounds, as if she were trying to soothe an infant to sleep.

On the TV screen Pavel saw a huge crowd jamming the square in Tripoli. Color everywhere, from the bright hues of the throng to the long billowing draperies hung from the public buildings, displaying the red, white and black colors of the socialist republic of Libya. There were plenty of deep green banners, too, the color that the desert-dwelling Arabs love most.

The stage where Rayyid would make his appearance was covered against the sun with brightly striped tenting. A slim podium, decorated with gold leaf, stood at its center, with a conspicuous red button atop it. The fountain in the center of the square was a modernist's nightmare of concrete and shining metal, all angles and thrusting arms, like an explosion in a steel yard.

If Kelly understood that their lives were in greater danger with every tick of the clock, she gave no sign of it. She continued to work smoothly, unhurriedly, at the computer console. Pavel glanced at the digital clock set into his console: 1420. Only forty minutes to go.

To go where? he asked himself. There was no answer.

Each change in the red numbers of the clock was an endless agony. To keep himself from going to pieces, Pavel put the headset to his ear once again, and listened to that imperturbable BBC voice while his guts churned and his mind kept shouting for him to do something, to move, to act, somehow to get himself and Kelly to safety.

But he sat, forcing himself to passivity, as Kelly plodded away at her task. He watched as the grandstand filled with dignitaries from thirty nations—including France and some of the others who were paying Alexander—wearing frock coats or dashikis or modern jackets, as their native customs required.

Fourteen-forty. The crowd began to surge and even the BBC announcer's voice took on a keener edge as a military parade, led by six armored cars exactly like the one Pavel and his companions had ridden, made its way down the central area of the square and assembled, rank upon rank, before the stage where Rayyid would speak. The soldiers, each armed with an assault rifle, were more than mere decorations, Pavel knew: they were both a visible symbol of his power and a Praetorian Guard that shielded Rayyid against those who would strike at him.

A cool voice from the back of Pavel's mind reminded him that the Praetorian Guard of Rome often dispatched emperors who displeased them and put new men in their place. Were these troops loyal to Rayyid, or Hassan? Such grasping for power was the sign of a decadent capitalist society, not a true socialist republic. These Libyan barbarians sully the name of socialism, Pavel thought.

At last the crowd roared, the assembled troops snapped to attention, and the dignitaries rose to their feet. Rayyid was making his entrance, preceded by a phalanx of Arabs in rich robes and burnooses, then a squad of military officers in green and gold uniforms.

Finally Rayyid himself appeared, to the tumultuous uproar of the crowd. They shouted his name, their voices blending into one gigantic swell of sound, crashing like waves on a rocky headland:

"Ray-yid, Ray-*yid,* Ray-YEED!"

He acknowledged their cheers with upraised hands. He smiled at his people. He wore the heavily braided uniform of a general, with dark glasses shielding his eyes from the sun's glare. Pavel was shocked to realize how much he looked like Hassan. The two could be brothers.

The crowd silenced as if a regiment of guns had been leveled at them. The dignitaries resumed their seats. Rayyid stepped up to the podium. No microphone was visible, but his amplified voice boomed across the square.

Another BBC voice began translating Rayyid's speech. Pavel looked down at the digital clock: 1454.

Throwing down the headset, he went to Kelly. She was still tapping at the computer keys.

"There's only six minutes!" he urged.

Kelly smiled up at him. "Relax. Don't you want to see what happens in Tripoli?"

"But we've got to get out of here!"

"We will. Lots of time."

"But you're not finished . . ."

"I finished up the main task twenty minutes ago. Now I'm planting bugs in their system that'll take them months to find and debug. I also patched into their comm system and sent a message to my father, via satellite. Let him know what you told me about Hassan."

"And?"

"No return message," she said. "Too risky."

"Too risky? For whom?"

But Kelly looked past him and said, "Hey, Rayyid's going to push the button. Come on, I wouldn't miss this for anything."

The two of them went to the screen displaying the TV broadcast. Rayyid had worked himself into a fine oratorical frenzy; the BBC translator was having a hard time keeping up with him:

". . . and this will prove to the world that Libyan technology and the will of the Libyan people are the equal of any nation on Earth! For we are a powerful nation, feared by our enemies! Let the nations of the world watch with awe as we enter a new era of prosperity! Let our enemies gnash their teeth with envy as the water of life flows—at my command!"

He punched the big red button on the dais with his closed fist and the camera pulled back to the elaborate fountain in the center of the square.

Water spurted from it and the crowd went *Ahh!* The water leaped high into the air, sparkled briefly in the fierce afternoon sun, and then faltered and stopped.

The crowd murmured apprehensively. From somewhere deep in the concrete building where he stood, Pavel could hear the dull thunderous roar of gigantic pumps laboring.

Rayyid waved a hand at the crowd, as if to tell them not to worry, and smacked the red button again.

A dribble of water at the fountain's openings, where streams should have shot twenty meters into the air. Then even that stopped.

Rayyid pounded the button, his face contorted with rage. Nothing.

Pavel heard the pumps whining and screeching now.

"What did you do?" he asked.

"Reversed 'em," she replied sweetly. "They'll burn

themselves out in another couple of minutes. It'll take weeks before they find the instructions in the programming. Drive 'em nuts!" She laughed.

The digital clock said 1501.

"We've got to run," Pavel said.

"Yeah. They'll be battering down that door in another minute or two." She pulled a tiny aerosol can from her belt and quickly sprayed it over the unconscious bodies of the Japanese technicians.

Pavel boosted her up to the ventilator screen, then stood on a chair and hauled himself up into the shaft. It took a few moments to place the screen back in its mounting. Pavel could see the technicians beginning to stir. The lights on the door lock's keyboard were flashing; someone was trying to get into the room.

"Come on," Kelly said. "We've got to make tracks."

They wormed their way through the shafts and at last came out onto the rooftop, blazing hot in the high sun. Mavroulis was there, sweating and wild-eyed with the jitters.

"We've only got three minutes . . ."

Kelly grabbed his arm as they raced down the stairs toward the APV. Its engine was already rumbling, sooty diesel fumes belching from its vertical exhaust pipe.

Soldiers were dashing everywhere. Helicopters crisscrossed the air above. Orders were being shouted. Confusion ruled while the massive building seemed to vibrate as if a mini-earthquake had seized it. Black smoke was pouring from two of the four cooling towers.

They ducked inside the oven-hot vehicle and the driver gunned the engine, slamming them into the metal bulkhead before they could take their places on the padded bench. They lurched toward the gate in a spurt of sand and diesel exhaust. The compartment stank of human sweat and machine oil, and the fumes from the engine.

No one said a word as they approached the gate. The

officer up front with the driver waved a laminated pass at the guards and they shot through, barely slowing in the process. The same at the outer perimeter, and then they were out in the desert, heading back for their camp.

"Do you speak Russian?" Pavel asked Mavroulis.

"No," he said, beetling his dark brows. "Do you speak Greek?"

Casting an eye on the two soldiers on the opposite bench, Pavel asked Mavroulis, "What languages do you speak?"

"English, French, German . . . and Greek."

Pavel understood some French, but he was afraid the Libyan soldiers did, too.

Kelly pulled the pocket computer from her sweat-stained uniform. "This computer has a translator function," she said. "It's slow, but it includes most Indo-European languages."

She tapped the keys and the tiny display screen showed: NO TRANSLATOR BUT WE CAN TALK.

The soldiers watched them tapping on the computer keys, but quickly lost interest. One of them got to his feet and opened the turret hatch. The armored compartment filled with hot sandy desert wind.

Using the computer's tiny display screen, Pavel told Mavroulis that Hassan's camp was a trap. Kelly added that she had sent the information to her father. But they had no way of knowing whether Alexander had received the transmission, or what he could do about it—if anything.

Mavroulis's thick, blunt fingers pecked at the keys: MUST GET BARKER. ONLY HE CAN FLY HOVERJET.

Kelly tapped: HOW???

WE NEED WEAPONS, Pavel typed with one finger.

"Fine," grumbled Mavroulis. "What are you going to do, ask them?" He glanced at the bored soldier lounging opposite them.

NO VIOLENCE, Kelly typed, UNLESS UNAVOIDABLE.

Pavel took a deep breath. This was not a situation that

would be resolved by delicate sensibilities or strategic arguments. This situation called for action.

"It is unavoidable," he muttered.

Kelly began typing something more, but Pavel stood up and stretched his arms as far as possible in the confines of the oven-hot compartment. His back felt all right. It only took a single step to put him in front of the soldier, who now looked up at Pavel.

One lightning-fast chop at the boy's neck and he sagged back against the armor plating, unconscious. The soldier up in the turret did not notice anything. Neither did the two men up front.

Pavel quickly took the pistol from the youngster's holster. It was a nine-millimeter Skoda, manufactured in Czechoslovakia: simple and reliable, though not very accurate at farther than fifty meters. No matter. Pavel was familiar with the gun. He felt better as he hefted it in his right hand.

Mavroulis got to his feet as Pavel reached toward the soldier standing in the turret and tapped him on the back. He ducked down and turned face-to-face with the muzzle of the pistol. Pavel smashed the gun barrel against the soldier's temple. Mavroulis caught him in his arms.

The captain turned to see what the commotion was and Pavel leveled his pistol at him.

"Stop the car," Pavel commanded.

Wide-eyed with surprise, the captain did as he was told. Pavel had him and the driver haul the two unconscious soldiers out onto the sandy track.

"You can't leave them out on the desert!" Kelly objected.

Pavel threw a pair of water cans to them. "They can walk back to the camp. It's only a few kilometers now."

Kelly looked doubtful, but Mavroulis slammed the APV's rear hatch, then hunched forward and took the driver's seat. With a grinding of gears he lurched the vehicle into motion. Pavel climbed up into the turret. Twin twenty-millimeter machine cannon and half a dozen boxes of ammunition. Now they could defend themselves.

But Kelly was still shaking her head when he ducked back into the rear compartment.

"We're hundreds of miles from anyplace safe," she said. "Hassan has at least one armored car like this one, plus who knows what else."

"We can fight," said Pavel.

"Hassan's also got Chris. And the plane. We need them both—unharmed—if we expect to get out of here."

Knowing she was right, Pavel replied merely, "It is better to be armed and prepared to fight than to go like a lamb to the slaughter."

Kelly said nothing.

Late afternoon shadows were lengthening as their vehicle topped a low ridge and Mavroulis shouted over the engine's clattering roar:

"There's the camp."

Kelly jumped up from the bench and wormed into the right-hand seat up front in the cab. Pavel stood at the hatch behind her and Mavroulis, clinging to the baking-hot handgrips on either side.

Half a dozen APVs were parked around the camouflage netting that covered the hoverjet. And several low black tents had been pitched some distance away, swaying in the hot breeze.

"Hassan's gathered a welcoming committee," Mavroulis growled.

"We can't fight our way out of this," said Kelly.

Pavel felt a strange hollowness in his middle. His legs trembled. Fear! Something deep inside him was screaming at him to run away, to dig a hole and hide where none of these enemies could find him. His mouth went dry, his throat raw. He gripped the metal bars on either side of the hatch so hard that his fingernails were cutting painfully into the flesh of his palms.

Mavroulis slowed their vehicle, but kept moving ahead toward the hoverjet. A phalanx of soldiers in sand-tan fatigues fell in on either side of them. Each man was armed with an assault rifle or an armor-piercing rocket launcher.

Pavel climbed up into the turret and swiveled the guns around. A hundred rifles and antitank launchers pointed straight at him.

"You'll get us killed!" Kelly screamed at him.

He looked down at her terrified face. "Better to let them know that we will fight. Better to die like soldiers than as prisoners of these savages."

Mavroulis slammed on the brakes and killed the engine. They were parked twenty meters from the edge of the netting that covered the hoverjet. From his perch in the turret Pavel could see that the plane was undamaged.

For agonizingly long moments no one moved or said a word. The only sounds were the pinging of the diesel's hot metal and the distant flapping of bedouin tents in the desert breeze.

Colonel Hassan stepped out from behind the ranks of his arrayed soldiers. One of the berobed Arabs was at his elbow, pointing up toward the turret.

"You are the Russian?" Hassan called.

"Yes," said Pavel.

Hassan smiled pleasantly from behind his mirrored glasses. Once again Pavel thought that he looked enough like Rayyid to be the man's brother. It is the uniform, he told himself. But still the resemblance was uncanny.

"You may come down and join us now," said Hassan. "You have done your work well. You have nothing to fear from us."

"And the others?" Pavel demanded.

Hassan's smile broadened. He shrugged his epauletted shoulders. "They will be dealt with. My bedouin brothers have prepared a proper ritual for them."

Very slowly Pavel was inching the twin guns toward Hassan. He stalled for time, trying to think of something that could break the stalemate in his own favor.

"The pilot?" he called to Hassan. "The Englishman?"

"He tried to escape. The bedouins had to restrain him—in their own way."

The colonel snapped his fingers and there was a stir from behind the ranks of soldiers. Two Arabs dragged a half-conscious Barker forward and threw him to the ground at Hassan's feet. The Englishman's legs were covered with blood, his face battered and swollen.

"It is traditional to hamstring a prisoner who tried to run away," Hassan said calmly.

Pavel heard a gasping sob from the APV's cab, below him.

"Come now," said Hassan impatiently, "come out of the vehicle and let us treat the other two infidels to their reward."

"No," said Pavel, training the guns a bit closer to the colonel's hateful smile.

The smile vanished. "What do you mean?"

"I mean that my orders are to bring these prisoners to Moscow. My superiors have their own plans for them."

Hassan's face hardened. "I was not informed of that."

"Those are my orders," Pavel insisted.

"And how do you propose to take these prisoners away from here?"

Speaking as the ideas formed themselves in his mind, Pavel replied, "You will provide a pilot to fly this aircraft to Tripoli. I will present the prisoners to the Soviet embassy there. The KGB will know what to do with them."

Hassan snorted. "Impossible! Tripoli is a battlefield now. My brother is fighting for his life against my army contingents."

So they *are* brothers, Pavel said to himself.

"Then fly us to Tunis or Cairo. There are Soviet embassies in both capitals."

Hassan hesitated.

"You may keep the hoverjet as proof that foreign agents tampered with the aquifer system, if you like," Pavel said. With a sudden inspiration he added, "Or destroy it so that no one will be able to link you to the sabotage."

"There must be no trace of these foreigners," Hassan insisted. "No word of this operation must ever leak out."

Pavel made himself laugh. "The only thing that leaks out of the KGB is the blood of capitalist dogs."

"I have no pilot here," Hassan said.

"Call for a helicopter from the aquifer complex," said Pavel, recognizing a stall. "We will remain here."

"You would be more comfortable outside that cramped vehicle."

"We will remain inside." Pavel nudged the guns the final few millimeters so that they were pointing directly at Hassan. "And I suggest that you remain where you are, also."

The colonel paled momentarily, whether from sudden fear or anger, Pavel could not tell. But then he put on his smile again and reached inside his tunic for his gold cigar case. This time he had to light his own cigar; none of the soldiers or bedouins stirred from where they stood.

"Very well," Hassan said at last, exhaling thin gray smoke, "I will send for a helicopter."

He turned to the lieutenant nearest him and spoke swiftly in Arabic.

For nearly fifteen minutes they all waited: Pavel with his fingers on the triggers of the machine cannon; Mavroulis and Kelly sweating down inside the APV cab; Hassan smiling and puffing and chatting with the sycophants around him; the Libyan soldiers grouped around the APV, ready to fire into it at a word from their leader.

Barker lay on the sand, unmoving, his legs crusted with blood, his eyes swollen shut.

The sun sank lower. Shadows lengthened. The desert wind sighed.

And Pavel heard, far in the distance, the faint throbbing sound of a helicopter.

None of us can fly a helicopter, he knew. *Perhaps Barker could, but he is in no condition to try. We will have to let the pilot actually fly us to Tunis and try to make a rendezvous with Alexander there.*

If the pilot is actually going to fly us to Tunis, he added fearfully. *If Hassan has not cooked up some deal of his own to land us in his own territory. Even if he believes my fairy tale about Moscow, he could easily claim that our helicopter crashed in the desert and we were all killed. Moscow will never question him.*

The helicopter materialized in the yellow desert sky, a massive ungainly metal pterodactyl hovering overhead, its engines shrieking, rotors thrumming, blowing up a miniature sandstorm as it settled slowly on its wheels. It was huge, one of the giant heavy cargo lifters built in the Soviet Union. Pavel almost smiled at the irony.

It took several tense minutes for them to get Barker aboard and strap themselves into the bucket seats lined along one wall of the helicopter's barn-sized cargo bay. Hassan watched carefully, puffing his slim cigar, a satisfied little smile on his lips.

We're not going to Tunis, Pavel realized as the ship lifted off the ground. *All I've done is delayed Hassan's fun by a couple of hours.*

But as the helicopter rose into the brazen sky two women in white nurse's uniforms came down from the flight deck and began tending to Barker. Neither of them looked Arabic; one was a blonde.

Then Cole Alexander clambered down the metal ladder

from the flight deck, grinning his crooked sardonic grin at them. Kelly leaped out of her seat and wrapped her arms around her father.

"Ohmygod, am I glad to see you!" she gasped.

"Likewise," Alexander said. "Good work, all of you. 'Specially you, Red. You used your head back there."

Pavel was speechless. Mavroulis leaned his head back and laughed maniacally.

"I knew it!" the Greek roared. "I knew you had a backup for us!"

Detaching himself from Kelly, Alexander squatted cross-legged on the cargo bay's metal flooring. His daughter sat beside him, facing Pavel and Mavroulis.

"I knew Hassan was a double-dealing sumbitch," Alexander said almost apologetically, "but he was the only sumbitch we had to work with. Like my dear Uncle Max used to tell me, 'When they stick you with a lemon, make lemonade.'"

"You expected him to try to kill us?"

"No, he surprised me there. I expected him to take you prisoner and hold you hostage until his fight with Rayyid was settled."

"His brother," Pavel said.

"Yep, they're siblings." Alexander made a sour face at the thought, then went on, "The way I figured it was this: We screw up Rayyid's aquifer project. Hassan and his army people pull their *coup d'état* while the Libyan people are still stunned at Rayyid's flop with the water project. Hassan holds you four as his trump card. If he wins, you go free. If he loses, he can offer you to Rayyid in return for his own life."

Kelly said, "But instead he decided to remove all evidence of sabotage."

"He must be damned confident he'll beat Rayyid," Mavroulis muttered.

"He's probably right," Alexander said.

"But you had a backup plan for us, nevertheless," said the Greek.

Alexander's sardonic smile came out again. He looked down at his daughter, then his gray eyes locked onto Pavel's.

"Wish I'd really been that smart," he admitted. "I did have this old Russkie chopper and a medivac team ready, just in case. And when I got Kelly's message—Pavel's warning, actually—I flew this bird as close to Hassan's camp in the desert as I could."

"Damned good thing you did," Kelly said.

"Yeah, but then I was stuck. I couldn't go flying in there with the four of you surrounded by trigger-happy Moslem fundamentalists. I needed some excuse to come chugging into their camp. Pavel provided the excuse. When Hassan radioed for a chopper to take you guys to Tunis, I got my chance."

"You see?" Mavroulis said, thrusting a blunt finger under Kelly's nose. "I told you to keep quiet and not interfere! I was right!"

Kelly nodded glumly. "You were right, Nicco."

"She wanted to shoot you when you said you were going to turn us over to the KGB," Mavroulis said to Pavel. "I had to hold her down."

"You thought I would really do that?" Pavel's voice was weak with shock. He felt betrayed.

Kelly blushed, even under her dark makeup. "You were damned convincing."

"I had to be."

Alexander interrupted, "Damned good thing you were, Red. Otherwise my little girl here . . ." His voice choked off. He put an arm around Kelly's shoulders and hugged her to him, as if to make absolutely certain that she was with him and safe.

"Hassan was actually going to fly us to Tunis?" Pavel asked.

"Those were the orders he radioed," Alexander said. "Course, they could always be countermanded once you were in the air."

"Pavel," said Kelly, from the protection of her father's embrace, "I'm sorry. You saved our lives, and I didn't trust you. I was wrong, and I'm sorry."

Pavel nodded, his thoughts churning: I had told her that I love her, but that made no difference to her. No difference. She did not believe me.

"Well," said Alexander happily, "all's well that ends well."

"Except for Barker," said Mavroulis.

"He won't be able to walk for some time," Alexander admitted. "But he'll be okay. If I have to donate a few tendons myself, we'll get him back on his feet."

"What about Shamar?" Pavel asked. His voice sounded harsh and hard, even to himself.

The others stared at him, their self-congratulatory smiles fading.

"Hassan claimed Shamar left Libya weeks ago," said Alexander tightly.

"With the bombs?"

Alexander slowly shook his head. "The bombs were not with him. He's got them stashed somewhere, but we don't know where."

"We'll find them," Kelly said.

"We'll find *him*," her father growled.

Pavel looked into their faces. He saw smoldering hatred in Alexander's gunmetal eyes. In Kelly's he saw gratitude, perhaps even affection—but not love.

"I must return to Moscow now," he said. It is better, he told himself. I do not belong among these people.

But Alexander shook his head. "You can't do that, Red.

You haven't accomplished your mission. You're supposed to assassinate me, remember?"

Pavel shook his head. "No jokes, please. I will return . . ."

"The hell you will! You think we went through all this crap just to send you back to shoveling snow?"

"I don't understand . . ."

Alexander took his arm from his daughter and reached out to clasp Pavel's shoulder. "Red, my dear old Uncle Max used to tell me, 'Only a fool does something for just one reason.' You could have fucked up this aquifer mission. You could have made Moscow very happy and gotten three of my best people killed. But you didn't."

Pavel stared at the older man. "You were testing me. My loyalty . . ."

"Damned right," Alexander said, grinning wider than ever. "You did okay, and Moscow isn't gonna be very happy if you go home now."

"I would be considered a failure," Pavel admitted.

"So stay with us! We can use a man with your skills and your smarts."

"But Moscow . . ."

"Moscow wants you to keep an eye on me, right? I'll bet they're just as glad that Rayyid's on his way out. Hassan's the saner of the two. Besides, there's still Shamar and those damned nukes of his."

"You want me to stay?"

Mavroulis grumbled, "For a Russian, you're not so bad."

But Pavel was looking at Kelly. She glanced at her father, then turned to face Pavel.

"We want you to stay," she said, so low it was almost a whisper. "Like I told you back in the computer room—we have a lot to talk about."

Pavel would have preferred that she fling herself into his arms, but he nodded slowly at Kelly and her father. This was better than nothing. Moscow would be suspicious, he knew. I will be playing a very dangerous game; practically a double agent.

Kelly was smiling at him now. From the protection of her father's embrace.

"Very well," Pavel heard himself say. "I will stay."

"Great," said Alexander. "Now that *that's* settled, the next thing we tackle is these poachers in Rwanda. The bastards have nearly wiped out the last remaining free-living gorillas in the world. And Shamar was heading in that direction, according to my information . . ."

So Zhakarov, nicknamed "Red," became a reluctant member of Alexander's little group, his loyalties divided at least three ways among Moscow, Kelly, and a growing admiration for Cole Alexander and his work. Jonathan Hazard, Jr., was not recruited until nearly a year later, and even then it was mostly an unfortunate accident.

I had been a member of the court-martial at the younger Hazard's trial, shortly after the officers' coup had been thwarted by Hazard, Sr. I still had both my hands then. The young man refused every offer of help that his father made. That did not, of course, altogether prevent the older man from helping his son.

J. W. Hazard, Jr., received a much lighter sentence than his fellow conspirators. Cardillo and most of the others went to jail for life. Jay Hazard was merely banished to the Moon for ten years.

MOONBASE, Year 7

Four minutes 'til the nuke goes off!"

The words rasped in Jay's earphones. He knew that the woman was nearly exhausted. Inside his pressure suit he was soaked with sweat and bone-tired himself. The adrenaline had run out hours ago. Now all they were going on was sheer dogged determination.

And the fear of death.

"It's got to be here *someplace.*" Desperation edged her voice. Four minutes and counting.

Long months of training guided Jay's movements. He halted in the midst of the weird machinery, took the last of the antistatic pads from his leg pouch and carefully cleared his helmet visor of the dust that had accumulated there.

Then immediately wished he hadn't.

Six other pressure-suited figures had entered the factory complex. Each of them carried a fléchette gun in his gloved hands.

Jay tried as best as he could to duck behind the lumbering conveyor belt to his right. He motioned for the woman to do the same. She had seen them too, and squatted awkwardly in her suit like a little kid playing hide-and-seek.

No radio now. They would pick up any transmission and home in on it. Actually, Jay realized, all they have to do is keep us here for another three minutes and some, then the nuke will do the rest. They don't care if they go with us. That's their real strength: they're willing to die for their cause.

The woman duck walked to Jay and leaned her helmet against his.

"What do we do now?" she asked. Her voice, carried by conduction through the metal and padding of the helmets, sounded muffled and muted, as if she had a bad cold.

He knew shrugging his shoulders inside the pressure suit would be useless. But he did it anyway. There was nothing else he could think of.

They were hiding in the midst of Moonbase's oxygen factory, out on the broad plain of Mare Nubium, the Sea of Clouds that had seen neither water nor air for more than four billion years. The factory was out in the open vacuum, no walls, covered only by a honeycomb metal meteor screen so thin that it almost seemed to sway in the nonexistent breeze.

Automated tractors hauled stones and powdery soil scooped from the Moon's regolith and dumped their loads onto the conveyor belts, ignoring the human hunters and their prey. Crushers and separators and ovens squeezed and baked precious oxygen from the rocks, then dumped the residue into piles at the far side of the factory, where other automated machinery mined metals and minerals from the tailings. Glass filament piping carried the oxygen to huge cryogenic tanks, giant thermos bottles that kept the gas cold enough to remain liquefied.

The conveyor belts rumbled, the crushers pounded away, in nearly total silence. Jay could *feel* their throbbing through the concrete pad that formed the base of the factory. In the vacuum of the Moon, though, normal sound was only an Earth-born memory.

In all the vast complex there were no human workers. Only robots, which actually performed better in the clean vacuum than they did in the corrosive air needed by their human owners. No humans set foot in the factory, except for the two cowering behind the main conveyor feed—and the six now spreading out to cover all the perimeter of the factory and make certain that Jay and the woman could not escape.

Three minutes thirty seconds.

Jay closed his eyes. Hell of a way to end it. The nuke will wipe out the oxygen factory, and that'll kill Moonbase. We won't go alone, he thought grimly.

It had started innocently.

Jay had reported for work as usual, riding the power ladder from his quarters on level four to the main plaza. It was Tuesday, and sure enough, there was a fresh shipload of tourists hopping and tumbling and laughing self-consciously as they tried to adjust their clumsy Earth stride to the one-sixth gravity of the Moon.

The tourists wore coveralls, as the Moonbase Tourist Office advised. But while Jay's coveralls were a utilitarian gray with Velcro fastenings, the Flatland tourists were brilliant with garish Day-Glo oranges and reds and yellows, stylish metal zipper pulls dangling from cuffs and collars and calves. Just the thing to tangle in a pressure suit, Jay thought sourly as he entered the garage office.

He had expected to spend the day driving a tour bus around Alphonsus, locked away from everyone in his solitary cab while some plastic-smiled guide pointed out the ruins of Ranger 9 and the solar-energy farms with their automated tenders and the robot processors that sucked in regolith soil at one end and deposited new solar cells at the other. The tourists would snap photographs to show the Flatlanders back home and never have to leave the comfort of the bus. Jay would drive the lumbering vehicle back and forth across the crater floor along the well-worn track and never have to speak to anyone.

But the boss had given him a red ticket, instead.

"Special job, Hazard," she had said, in that hard tone that meant she would brook no arguments. "Flatland VIP wants to see Copernicus."

"Christmas on a crutch!" Jay fumed, lapsing back to the euphemism he had used when his father would punish him for profanity. "That's a six-day ride."

"And it's all yours," the boss retorted. "Got number 301 all set for you. See you in six days."

Jay knew better than to complain. He snatched the red ticket from the boss's counter and stomped out into the garage. Actually, he thought, a six-day trip up to Copernicus and back might not be so bad. Away from the tourists and the boss and the rest of the world for nearly a week. Out in the wilderness, where there isn't a blade of grass or a puff of air or even a sound—alone.

Except for some Earthside VIP. A part of Jay's mind wondered who he might be. Somebody I used to know? The thought sent a wash of sudden terror through him. No, it couldn't be. The boss just picked me out of the computer. She knows I like to be left alone. She's trying to do me a favor.

Still, the thought that this VIP might be someone from his former life, someone from his father, even, scared him so much his stomach felt sick.

When he saw who it was, he relaxed—then tensed again. It was a woman, a petite snub-nosed redhead who looked too young, too tiny and almost childlike, to be a Very Important Person. But when Jay got close enough to see her brown eyes clearly, he recognized the kind of no-nonsense drive and determination he had seen in others: his father, his former commanding officer, the grim-faced men who had led him into treason and disgrace and banishment.

She was waiting for him by the bus, in the midst of the noisy, clanging garage. She wore dark maroon coveralls, almost the color of Burgundy wine. No dangling zipper pulls. A small slate-gray duffel bag hung from one shoulder.

"Are you my driver?" she asked Jay.

"I'm the driver."

He was nearly a foot taller than she, and he judged that they were roughly the same age: middle twenties. Jay had not bothered to shave that morning, and he suddenly felt grimy and unkempt in her level stare. She didn't have much of a figure. Her mouth was turned down slightly at the corners.

"Okay, then," she said. "Drive."

He popped the hatch and stood beside it as she climbed the metal steps slowly, uncertain of herself in the low lunar gravity. Jay took the six rungs in one jump and ducked into the shadowy interior of bus 301.

On the outside, 301 looked like any other heavily used tour bus: its bright yellow anodized hull had been dulled by exposure to vacuum and the hard radiation that drenches the lunar surface. There were dents here and there and a crusting of dust along the wide tracks. The crescent and human figure of its stylish Moonbase logo was the only fresh bit of color on its bodywork. Management saw to that.

Inside, though, 301 had been fitted out for a long excursion: the seats removed and a pair of sleeping units installed, each with its own bathroom facilities. The galley was forward, closest to the cab, and the air lock and pressure suits at the rear by the hatch. Jay would have preferred it the other way around, but he had no say in the design of the bus or its interior layout.

Without a word to his passenger, he pushed past her and slid into the driver's seat. With one hand he slipped the comm headset over his thick dark hair, while with his other he tapped the control board keys, checking out the bus's systems displays. He got his route clearance from the transit controllers and started up the engines.

The bus lumbered forward slowly, the thermionic engines purring quietly, efficiently. Jay felt his passenger's presence, standing behind and slightly to one side of him, as he steered along the lighted path through the busy garage and out to the massive air lock.

She slipped into the right-hand seat as he went down the final checklist with the controllers. The inner air-lock hatch closed behind them; Jay thought she tensed slightly at the muted thump when the massive steel doors sealed themselves shut.

Pumps whined to life, their noisy clattering diminishing like a fading train whistle as the air was sucked out of the big steel-walled chamber.

"You're cleared for excursion, 301," he heard in his earphone.

"Three-oh-one, on my way," he muttered.

The controller's voice lightened. "Have fun, Jay. Six nights with a redhead, wow!" He chuckled.

Jay said nothing, but shot a quick sidelong glance at his passenger. She could not hear the controller, thank the gods.

The air lock's outer hatch slid open slowly, revealing the desolate splendor of the Sea of Clouds. It was night, and would be for another sixty hours. But the huge blue globe of Earth hung in the sky, nearly full, shining so brilliantly that there was no true darkness.

Mare Nubium looked like a sea that had been petrified. The rocky soil undulated in waves, almost seemed to be heaving gently, dimpled by craters and little pockmarks and cracks of rilles that snaked across the ground like sea serpents. The horizon was brutally near, like the edge of a cliff, sharp and uncompromising as the end of the world. Beyond it the sky was utterly black.

"I thought we'd be able to see the stars," his passenger said.

"You will," Jay replied.

The ground they traversed was roiled and churned as a battlefield. Treads of giant tractors, bootprints of humans, singed and blackened spots where rockets had landed years ago. Nothing ever changes on the Moon's surface unless people change it, and this close to Moonbase, people and their machines had been moving back and forth for more than a generation.

Jay took 301 out past the old mass driver. The electric catapult was so long that its far end disappeared over the horizon.

"Is that the original mass driver?" his passenger asked.

He answered with a nod.

"I understand it's out of commission. Being repaired or something?"

"Right," he said.

For the next fifteen minutes they drove in silence along the length of the mass driver. They passed a team of pressure-suited technicians gathered around one of the big magnet coils.

"My name's Kelly," his passenger offered.

"It's on the trip sheet," Jay replied. "Kelly, S. A. From Toronto, Canada. First time on the Moon."

"What's your name?"

Jay turned his head toward her. For the love of Godzilla, don't tell me she's a Moon groupie, he said to himself. We're going to be cooped up in this tin can for six days.

"Jay," he snapped.

"The woman at the tourist office told me it was Jonathan."

He twisted uncomfortably in the chair. "Everybody calls me Jay."

"Jonathan, Jr."

Jay looked at her again. *Really* looked at her. "Who the hell are you?"

"I told you. My name's Kelly."

"You're no tourist."

"And you're no bus driver."

"What do you want?"

Kelly studied his face for a moment. It seemed to Jay that she was trying to smile, trying to put him at his ease. Not succeeding.

"I want to know whose side you're on," she said at last.

"Side? What are you talking about? I'm not on anybody's sucking side! Leave me alone!" He kicked in the brake and 301 shuddered to a stop.

"You picked the wrong side once," Kelly said, her voice flat, as if she were reading from a memorized dossier. "The people who sent me here think you might have made the same mistake again."

"I'm taking you back to the base."

She put a hand out toward him. "If you do, I'll have to report our suspicions to the Moonbase security people. You'll lose your job. As a minimum."

"Leave me alone!"

"I would if I could," Kelly said, her voice softening. "But there's a nuclear bomb on its way to Moonbase. It might already be here. Some people think you're in on the deal."

He stared at her. Even here they had followed him. Even here, in the midst of all this emptiness, a quarter-million miles from Earth, even here they were hounding him.

He took a deep breath, then said evenly, "Look. I'm not in on any deal. If you want to tag me with some wild-ass charges, think up something more believable than a nuke, huh? Just let me do my job and live in peace, okay?"

Kelly shook her head. "None of us can live in peace, Jay. A nuclear weapon is going to wipe out Moonbase unless we can find it and the people who are behind it. And damned soon."

"You're crazy!"

"Maybe. But we're not going to Copernicus. We're going to Fra Mauro."

"The hell we are," he growled. "You're going right back to base." He grasped the steering wheel and started to thumb the button that would put the tracks in gear again.

"If I do," Kelly warned, "you won't be just working out a ten-year sentence here at Moonbase. You'll spend the rest of your life in jail."

He glared at her.

Kelly did not glare back. She smiled sadly. "I wouldn't be talking with you if I thought you were part of any terrorist group. But if you refuse to help me, I've got no choice but to turn you over to the people who think you are."

Every muscle in Jay's body was tensed so hard that he ached from toe to scalp.

Kelly leaned toward him slightly. "Look. The nuke is real. These people intend to blow out Moonbase. Help me find the bomb and you can make everybody back Earthside forget about your past mistake."

He felt as helpless as he had when he was a baby and his father would suddenly swoop down on him and toss him terrifyingly high into the air.

"You don't understand," Jay said slowly, miserably. "I don't care if they remember what happened back then or not. All I want is to be away from it all, away from all of them. *All* of them. Forever."

She made a sympathetic sound, almost like a mother cooing at her infant. "It doesn't work that way. They've come here. Maybe not the same people who got you into trouble in the first place, but the same *kind* of people."

His head sank low. He closed his eyes, as if that would make her go away and leave him alone.

"You've got to help me, Jay."

He said nothing; wished he were deaf.

"You've got no choice."

Wordlessly he put the tracks in gear and pushed the accelerator. The lumbering bus shuddered and started forward.

She's right, he told himself. I've got no choice. One mistake haunts you for the rest of your life. They'll never leave me alone, no matter how far I run. Not for the rest of my life.

He realized that the only way out was to end his life, once and for all.

He drove 301 in silence, not even glancing at the young woman sitting beside him. The vehicle plowed along for more than an hour, following the network of tracks worn into the powdery regolith that headed northward across Mare Nubium in the general direction of Copernicus.

But when Jay reached for the radio transmitter control on the dashboard, Kelly's hand quickly intercepted his.

"I've got to get Fra Mauro's coordinates from the data bank."

"I'll punch in the coordinates," she countered.

He pointed to the bus's guidance computer; Kelly typed out the coordinates with smooth, practiced efficiency. Jay noticed that her hands were tiny, her fingers as small as a child's doll.

When the bus turned off the heavily tracked course toward Copernicus and started westward, Jay punched in the autopilot and took his hands from the wheel. He leaned back in his seat and tried to relax. It was like trying to breathe vacuum.

"Are we really going to Fra Mauro?" he asked.

"Close."

"What makes you think the nuke is hidden there?"

"We have our information sources."

"We?" He turned in his seat to look fully at her. "Did my father send you?"

She said, "No. I'm not working for the Peacekeepers. Not directly, anyway."

"Then he *does* have something to do with this!"

"The Peacekeepers have no jurisdiction here. They're only allowed to operate when an attack is launched across an international frontier."

"So they claim."

Kelly ignored his thrust. "Moonbase isn't about to be invaded. It's being threatened by a gang of terrorists. We're trying to stop them."

"Who the hell is this 'we'?"

"Private operation."

He waited for more. When she did not offer it, Jay asked, "And the terrorists?"

"Professionals. Third World fanatics who're against the industrialized nations and against the Peacekeepers."

Jay remembered a group of men and women who were against the Peacekeepers. Feared that the International Peacekeeping Force was a first step toward a world government. Refused to accept the idea of having their nations disarm and trust their defense to a gaggle of foreigners. They had rebelled against the IPF and nearly won. Nearly. Jay had been one of those rebels. His father, now director-general of the IPF, had branded him a traitor.

"Some of the smaller nations," Kelly was saying, "don't like the IPF in general, and hate Moonbase in particular. Lunar ores and space factories are competing with Third World countries. They say that just when they're starting to make a success of industrialization, Moonbase is underselling them."

"So they hire a gang of professionals to nuke Moonbase."

"That's it."

"And where do they get their nuclear device? The IPF's

been pretty damned thorough in dismantling the world's nuclear arsenals."

"Not really," said Kelly. "Disarmament's been more or less at a standstill for the past several years. There's at least half a dozen nukes unaccounted for. Somebody named Jabal Shamar stole them and disappeared."

"And you think one of them's here?"

Nodding, "Or on its way. Shamar sold it for the equivalent of a hundred million dollars. In gold."

Jay whistled with awe. Despite himself, he believed her story. That's just what some of those bastards would do. They don't care who gets killed, as long as it isn't them. The only part that he refused to believe was her insistence that his father had no role in this operation. He knows about it, Jay told himself. He knows exactly where I am. Down to the millimeter.

A flicker of movement caught his eye. Movement meant only one thing on the eons-dead surface of the Moon.

"Another vehicle up there."

Kelly barely moved in her seat, but her body tensed like a gun being cocked.

"Another bus?" she asked.

"Out here? No way."

"Then what . . . ?"

He tapped the camera keyboard and displayed the view on the screen that took up the middle of the dashboard. The vehicle was a smallish tractor, painted bright red, not unlike the automated crawlers that tended the solar energy farms. But the bubble riding atop it was undeniably a life-support module.

"Two-man job," Jay muttered.

"Have they seen us?"

"Probably. Might be from Lunagrad."

"This far south?"

"It's a free territory," Jay said. "They've got just as much right to poke around here as anybody."

"Is it likely?"

"No," he had to admit. "The Russians usually stay close to their own bases. And there's no scientific excursion out here—that I know of."

"Turn around," Kelly said.

"What? I thought you wanted to get to Fra Mauro."

"I do, but I want to get there alive. Turn around!"

She was genuinely frightened, Jay saw. He gripped the wheel and slewed the bus almost ninety degrees, angling roughly northeast.

We can tell them we just took a side trip on our way to Copernicus, Jay said to himself. Then he realized that he had accepted her view of the situation without thinking consciously about it: he had accepted the idea that this crawler was carrying two terrorists who had somehow learned of Kelly's mission and were here to stop her.

Kelly popped out of her seat and went back toward the sleeping compartments. She returned with a pair of binoculars, big and black and bulky. Jay recognized the make and model: electronically boosted optics, capable of counting the pores on your nose at a distance of ten miles.

"They're following us." Her voice was flat, almost calm. Only the slightest hint of an edge in it. "Two men in the cab, both wearing pressure suits with the visors up."

She's been in heavy scenes before, Jay thought. Probably a lot more than I have. In the back of his mind he remembered the only real danger he had ever seen, the battle in orbit that his side had lost. Because of me, Jay heard his mind accuse. We lost because of me.

"They're gaining on us," Kelly announced, the binocs glued to her eyes. "Can't you go faster?"

"This tub isn't built for speed," Jay grumbled, leaning on the throttle. The bus lurched marginally faster.

"There's no place to hide out here," she said.

"It's like the ocean." He thought that his father would know what to do. An old salt like him, with his Annapolis training, would be right at home on this lunar sea.

"You've only got the one air lock?"

Jay nodded. "Emergency hatch here by my side." He nudged the red release catch with his left elbow. "But you've got to be in a suit to use it."

"We'd better suit up, then. And fast."

"Now wait a minute . . ."

She cut him off with a dagger-sharp look. "You say you're not in with them. Okay, I'll believe that. As long as you _behave_ like you're not in with them."

Jay turned away from those blazing eyes and looked out the side window. The red crawler was gaining on them, coming up on their left rear.

Kelly said, "Suits."

She's scared of what they'll do when they overtake us, he thought. Deep inside him, Jay was frightened too. He set the controls back on autopilot and followed the diminutive redhead back toward the air-lock hatch.

It took nearly fifteen minutes to worm into the suits and check out all the seals and systems.

"When we get outside," Kelly said through her open visor, "no radio. If we have to talk, we put our helmets together."

"Tête-à-tête."

She flashed a quick grin at him, thinking it was a pun rather than standard lunar jargon.

They clumped back to the cab, single file, in the bulky suits. The crawler had gained appreciably on them. It was scarcely half a kilometer away. Jay began pecking at the guidance computer's keyboard.

"What are you doing?" Kelly demanded. "We don't have time . . ."

"Instructing this bucket to circle around and head back to base. That way we can pick it up again later. Don't think we're going to _walk_ back to Moonbase, do you?"

"I hadn't thought that far ahead," she admitted.

They made their way back to the air lock and squeezed

inside together. The outer hatch was on the right side of the bus, away from the approaching crawler. His stomach quivering with butterflies, Jay snapped his visor down securely and punched the button that cycled the air lock. He had to override the safety subsystem that prevented the lock from being used while the bus was in motion.

It seemed like an hour. The pumps clattered loud enough to be heard Earthside. Finally the amber light turned to red and the outer hatch popped slightly ajar. Jay swung it open the rest of the way.

The rough landscape was rushing past them at nearly thirty klicks per hour. It looked very hard and solid, totally uninviting.

"You sure you want to do this?" he asked.

"It's better than being killed."

"Maybe."

"You first," she commanded.

Jay obeyed almost by reflex. He waited for a patch of ground that was relatively free of rocks, then jumped from the lip of the air lock. It wasn't until he was soaring through the vacuum in the dreamlike slow motion of lunar gravity that he realized this might all have been her ploy for getting the bus to herself.

He landed on his feet, staggered sideways with the acceleration from the bus and fell to the ground. With instincts honed by almost three years on the Moon, he put out both arms, caught himself before he hit the dusty soil, and pushed himself erect. A few staggering steps and he was safely balanced on his feet.

He had kicked up some dust, but not as much as he had feared. This area's not as dusty as some, Jay thought as he watched the powdery clouds slowly settle around him.

Kelly jumped and tumbled when she landed, skidding sideways down the slight slope of a worn ancient craterlet. Jay dashed after her as 301 trundled off in the opposite direction, on its own, under automatic control.

She was lying on her back and waving frantically at him. God, she's hurt, Jay thought. Or her suit's ripped.

He slipped and slid down the almost glassy slope of the little crater and ended up on the seat of his pants, by her side.

She had turned onto her stomach, lying still. Backpack did not seem damaged. No obvious leaks. He leaned his helmet against hers.

"Are you okay?"

Kelly reached an arm around his neck and yanked hard. "Get *down,* asshole!"

Jay flattened out, feeling his face flame with sudden anger.

"Want those bastards to see us?" she hissed. "Why don't you wave a friggin' flag?"

Jay held on to his swooping temper. For a few moments they lay side by side. Then Kelly wormed her way to the lip of the crater. Jay followed.

Rising only far enough to see across the pockmarked plain, they watched 301 dwindling toward the horizon, with the red crawler still closing the distance between them.

But then the crawler stopped. The pod hatch opened and one of the pressure-suited figures climbed out.

Jay turned his head toward Kelly. "Of all the mother-loving dimwits, you gave yourself diarrhea over nothing. They're surveyors! Look, they're taking out their tools."

"Oh yeah?"

The one man had taken an arm's-length rod from the tool pack on the rear of the crawler. He hiked it up onto his shoulder, then turned and aimed it at the retreating bulk of 301.

The rod flashed sudden flame. A blaze of light streaked across the airless plain and hit 301. The bus exploded. All in total silence.

Jay watched, stunned, as pieces of 301 soared gently

across the landscape. He recognized one fragment as the driver's chair, tumbling slowly end over end and smashing apart when it finally hit the ground.

"Jesus," Jay whispered.

"Some surveyors," Kelly muttered.

How in the name of St. Michael the Archangel are we going to get back to the base? Jay asked himself. If we call for help, those guys will hear us and come over to finish the job.

Kelly was pecking at the radio controls on the left wrist of her suit. Is she going to surrender to them? Not likely, he knew.

She pointed to the frequency setting, then to the side of her helmet, and finally put a finger up in front of her visor. Jay understood her sign language. They're using this freak; listen, don't talk.

They lay side by side at the lip of the little crater, watching and listening. The two terrorists drove their crawler to the gutted wreck of 301 and started inspecting the wreckage. They want to make sure of us, Jay realized.

Leaning his helmet against Kelly's, he whispered, "Maybe we can grab their crawler while they're poking through the debris."

Her voice was muffled, but he could feel the reproach in it. "We wouldn't get fifty meters before they spotted us. They're professionals, Jay. We're lucky they didn't see you dancing around when you jumped from the bus."

His face went red again. And he realized that whispering was stupid, too.

"Then what . . . ?"

"Shh! Lemme hear them."

Jay could not understand the language coming through his earphones, but apparently Kelly could. She repeated it, like a translator:

". . . they could have jumped before the rocket hit

them . . . But that means they knew who we were . . . It makes no difference . . . I can't figure that, must be slang or a joke . . . they're laughing—ah! They're saying we can't get very far on foot. If we call for help they'll home in on our transmission and finish us off."

Jay nodded inside his helmet. That was the crux of the matter.

"Why bother?" Kelly resumed translating. "The oxygen plant will be blasted away in another twelve hours. They'll never get back in time to do anything about it."

Kelly pounded her gloved fist on the glass-smooth rim of rock. "The oxygen factory! That's it!"

She slid down slightly and turned on her side. Jay stayed up at the rim, watching and thinking.

We could send a warning to Moonbase, put them on alert. But then those killers would find us. And that would be that.

So what? he asked himself. You're finished anyway. They're never going to leave you in peace. She told you that. The only way out is death.

He looked out across the desolate expanse of rock. The two terrorists were making their way back to the crawler now, their foreign words sounding musical yet guttural in his earphones, almost like a Wagnerian opera.

It'd be easy enough to open your visor, wise guy, Jay told himself. Just crack the seal and take a nice deep breath of vacuum. Poof! Your troubles are all finished. You wouldn't be the first guy to do it that way.

His gloved hands did not move. I don't want to die, Jay realized. No matter what happens, I sure as hell don't want to die.

Suddenly his earphones shrieked with a wild whining, screeching wail. He clamped his hands uselessly against his helmet, then stabbed at the radio control on his wrist and shut off the skull-splitting noise.

He slid down beside Kelly. She was staring at her wrist controls.

"Jammer," Jay said.

"They're taking no chances," she agreed. "They're going to leave us out here and jam any radio transmission we might send."

"That means they'll be staying with their crawler," he said. "The jammer's only got a limited range—far as the horizon."

"We can walk away from it."

"If they don't see us."

"How long would it take to get back to Moonbase?"

"Too long," Jay answered. "Unless . . ."

"Unless what?"

"Follow me and do what I do. Stay low as possible until we're out of their sight."

They crawled on their hands and knees slowly, carefully, across the small crater and over its farther rim. The powdery top layer of the regolith turned to dust wherever they touched it. Before long the dust was clinging to their suits. Jay could feel it grating in one of his knee joints. That could be dangerous. Worse, it covered the visors, obscuring vision.

Not that there was much to see. Jay watched his gloved hands tracking along the barren regolith. It reminded him of videos about evolution he had seen as a schoolchild: the emergence of life from the sea onto dry land. Never find land drier than this, he knew.

At last he stopped, sat upright, and took a wiper pad from the pouch on his leg. The dust clung stubbornly to his visor, electrostatically charged by the invisible inflow of solar wind particles.

He helped Kelly clear her visor. Cautiously, he rose to his feet. The damned crawler could still be seen, which meant the men in them still had a chance of spotting them.

Back to crawling, like an infant, like a lizard, like a slimy amphibian just learning to walk. We must make a weird sight, Jay thought.

He stopped again and looked back. Only the rooftop of the crawler was in sight. He flicked his suit radio on for the briefest instant; the shriek of the jammer still burned his ears.

Motioning for Kelly to stand, he leaned close to her and said, "They've got a tall antenna. We're still being jammed, but at least we can walk now."

They cleaned their visors again, then headed off almost due east.

After several minutes Kelly tapped Jay's shoulder. He leaned down to touch helmets.

"Isn't Moonbase in that direction?" She pointed roughly southwestward.

Jay snorted at her. "Don't try to navigate by the stars. The Moon's north pole doesn't point toward Polaris."

"Yeah, but . . ."

"I'm following 301's tracks." He pointed to the churned soil. "If we can make it back to the main beat between Moonbase and Copernicus we'll come across an emergency shelter sooner or later. Then we . . ."

He jerked with surprise, then swiftly pulled Kelly down flat onto the ground.

Wordlessly he pointed at the crawler that was slowly making its way toward them. From the direction opposite the crawler they had just left. This one was painted bright orange. It, too, had a life-support module atop it, and a tall whip mast, visible only because of the tiny red light winking at its end.

They sent a team to follow us, Jay realized. They boxed us in: one team from Fra Mauro, the other behind us from Moonbase.

He half dragged Kelly away from the track of 301, angling toward the Copernicus-Moonbase "road" and away from the oncoming crawler. They might not be part of the terrorist gang, Jay thought. Might be a coincidence that they're here. They might even be Moonbase security searching for us. Sure. Might be Santa Claus, too.

For hours they walked, seemingly lost. Not the slightest sign of civilization. Not even a bit of litter. No trace of life. Nothing but rocks and craters and the sudden horizon with the utterly black sky beyond it. And the dust that clung to them, rasped against their suits, blurred their visors.

Suits are good for forty-eight hours, Jay kept telling himself. Oxygen, heat, water enough for forty-eight hours. Radiation protection. They'll even stop a micrometeor without springing a leak. Says so in the instruction manual.

But he wondered.

Time and again they tried their suit radios. Still the wailing scream of the jamming defeated them.

"They must have planted jammers along the whole route," Jay told Kelly.

"That means we'll have to get back to Moonbase itself in"—she peered at the watch on her suit wrist—"six hours."

No way, he knew. Not afoot. But they kept walking. There was nothing else to do. For hours.

Kelly fished a wire from one of her suit pouches and they connected their helmet intercoms, like two kids talking through paper cups and a soaped string.

"It's got a lonely kind of beauty to it," she said. "I never thought of the Moon as beautiful before."

Jay nodded inside his helmet. "I wouldn't call it beautiful. Awesome, yes. It's got grandeur, all right. Like the desert in Arizona."

"Or the tundra up above the Arctic Circle."

"It'll take a long time before people screw up this place. But they'll do it. They're already starting the job, aren't they?"

Kelly was silent for a while, then she asked, "Why'd you put in with the rebels? Against the Peacekeepers."

He expected the old anger seething in his gut. Instead he heard himself answering almost calmly, "I fell for their line. Said the U.S. couldn't trust its defense to a bunch of foreigners. Said Washington had sold us out to the Third World and the Commies."

"I was with the Peacekeepers."

"You were? Then?"

"Before. About three years before."

"So you believe in them."

"They've kept the peace. The nations are disarming. Or they were, before they realized Shamar had made off with his own little arsenal."

"And how do you feel about a hundred little nations bossing the U.S. around?"

"I'm a Canadian," Kelly replied.

"Oh."

They lapsed into silence. Then Kelly spoke up again, "You're lucky you didn't have to go to jail. Most of the other conspirators got long sentences."

"Sure, I'm lucky, all right."

"Your father must have been a big help. He's running the IPF now, you know."

The old anger was strangely muted, but Jay could still feel the resentment smoldering inside him. Or was it shame?

"Big help," he mocked. "Instead of jail he got me banished to the Moon. I can't set foot back on Earth for another seven years, not unless you get me arrested and brought back in handcuffs."

"It's better than being in jail, though, isn't it?"

Jay hesitated. "Yeah, I guess so," he had to admit.

"Your father must've twisted a lot of arms to get you off the hook. Most of 'em got life."

Jay opened his mouth to answer, but he had no reply. He had never considered the proposition before. Dad pleaded with the court to lighten my sentence? He found that difficult to believe. Especially after he had rejected the old man's offers of help. It did not square with all he knew about the stern, uncompromising man who had left his mother so many years ago. Very difficult to believe.

But not impossible.

Jay was still pondering this new thought when he stopped and stared at a tiny red light blinking against the dark sky, just over the horizon. He reached for another cleaning pad and wiped his visor. The light did not move or waver.

"Hey look!" he yelled.

He pointed, then gestured for Kelly to follow him. An emergency shelter. Fresh oxygen and water. His suit was starting to smell bad, Jay realized. He hadn't admitted it to himself until now.

And maybe a radio with enough power to burn through the jamming. Less than three hours left. Won't do us much good to get to the shelter if Moonbase itself gets wiped. Just prolong the agony.

The shelter was a life-support module from the earliest days of lunar exploration, buried under several meters of scooped-up regolith rubble. Safe as a squirrel's nest in winter.

The left leg of Jay's suit was grating ominously as they hurried the last kilometer toward the shelter. The dust was grinding away at that knee joint. He looked over at Kelly. She seemed to be keeping pace with him, loping along in the dreamlike low gravity.

They bounded down the slight slope to the shelter's air-lock entrance. It was too small for both of them to go through at the same time, but they squeezed into it together anyway. Jay heard somebody laughing as the air lock cycled; it was his own voice, cackling like a madman.

"We made it, kid," he said. "We're safe."

"For the time being," she reminded him, as the inner hatch slid open.

"Not even for that," said the man waiting inside. He held a needle-slim fléchette gun in his hand.

There were two of them, both dark of hair and eye, skin the color of desert sand. One was bearded, one not. Both held guns.

The shelter was old and small; its inner walls curved up barely high enough to allow Jay to stand upright. The equipment inside looked ancient, dusty. Even the bunks seemed moldy with age.

They made Kelly and Jay take off their pressure suits. Jay was actually glad to be out of his, yet he felt almost naked and unprotected without it.

"What happens now?" Kelly asked, her voice flat and cold.

"Now we wait," said the bearded one in slightly accented English. "The bomb goes off in little more than two hours. Our superiors will pick us up for transport back to Earth. They will decide what to do with you."

The other was younger, barely out of his teens, Jay saw. He seemed fiercely amused. "There won't be enough room aboard the ship for two prisoners."

Kelly's mouth dropped open. All pretense of cool professionalism disappeared. "You mean you . . . you're going to leave us here? Kill us?"

The bearded one shrugged.

"Oh please don't!" Kelly pleaded. "Please . . . I don't want to die. I'll do anything! Anything!"

She took a step closer to the bearded one. Jay felt his insides churn. *The little bitch. She'll offer them her body to save herself. She doesn't give a tinker's damn about what happens to me.*

But he realized that both men had turned their entire attention to Kelly, who was pleading so loudly and plaintively that it finally got through Jay's skull that this was a ruse.

Is she . . . ?

With one lightning motion Kelly kicked the bearded one in the groin and simultaneously grabbed his right wrist and pushed the gun aside. The gun went off and a slim steel fléchette thudded into the metal wall of the shelter.

With the roar of a jungle savage, Jay launched himself at the younger one, who had turned slightly away from him. He swung back, but not fast enough. Jay snapped his wrist, then knocked him unconscious with a vicious chop against the side of his neck.

He looked over at Kelly, bending over the prostrate body of the bearded one.

"I was worried you wouldn't catch on," she said, grinning.

"I almost didn't."

"Try the radio," she commanded, pointing.

It was useless, Jay saw. They had fired several fléchettes into it.

"Just about two hours now," Kelly said. "How long will it take us to get back to Moonbase?"

"Depends," he replied, "on whether this shelter has a hopper in working condition."

They bound the two unconscious men with electrician's tape, then worked back into their suits. Jay led the way through the air lock and out behind the pile of rubble covering the shelter.

The spidery body of a lunar hopper stood out in the open. It looked like a small metal platform raised off the ground by three skinny bowed legs. An equally insubstantial railing went around three sides of the platform, with a pedestal for controls and displays. Beneath the platform were small spherical tanks and a rocket nozzle mounted on a swivel.

He inspected the hopper swiftly. "Cute. They shot up the oxygen tank. No oxygen, no rocket. Lazy bastards, though. They should have dismantled this go-cart more thoroughly than this."

Explaining as he worked, Jay ducked back inside the shelter and came out with a pair of oxygen bottles from the shelter's emergency supply and a set of tools. It took more than an hour, but finally he got the long green bottles attached firmly enough to the line that fed the rocket's combustion chamber.

At least I *think* it's firmly enough, he told himself.

He helped Kelly up onto the platform and then got up beside her, snapped on the safety tethers that hung from the railing, and plugged his suit radio into the hopper's radio system. Kelly followed his every motion.

"Ready to try it?" he asked.

"Yeah. Sure." Her voice in his earphones sounded doubtful.

He nudged the throttle. For an eternally long moment not a thing happened. Then the platform shuddered and jumped and they were soaring up over the lunar landscape like a howitzer shell.

"It works!" Kelly exulted. Jay noticed that both her gloved fists were gripping the railing hard enough to bend the metal.

"Next stop, Moonbase!" he yelled back at her.

They got high enough to see the lights of the base's solar-energy farm, spread out across the shore of the Mare Nubium, where automated tractors were converting raw regolith soil into solar cells and laying them out in neat hexagonal patterns.

Jay tried to steer toward the lights, but the hopper's internal safety program decided that there was not enough fuel for maneuvering *and* a safe landing. So they glided on, watching the lights of the energy farm slide off to their right.

It was eerie, flying in total silence, without a breeze, without even vibration from the platform they stood upon. Like a dream, coasting effortlessly high above the ground.

Kelly used the hopper's radio to send an emergency call

to Moonbase security. "There's a nuclear bomb planted somewhere in the oxygen factory," she repeated a dozen times. There was no answer from Moonbase.

"Either we're not getting through to them or they're not getting through to us," she said, her voice brittle with apprehension.

"Maybe they think it's a nut call."

He sensed her shaking her head. "They've *got* to check it out. They can't let a warning about a nuclear bomb go without checking on it."

"Nukes are pretty small. The oxygen plant's damned big."

"I know," she answered. "I know. And there isn't much time."

Jay realized that they were flying *toward* the imminent nuclear explosion. Like charging into the mouth of the cannon, he thought.

He heard himself saying, "You were damned good back there. You could have taken both of them by yourself."

"No, that's not likely," she replied absently, her mind obviously elsewhere. "I was counting on your help and you came through."

A long silence. Then Kelly asked, "Will those two have enough air in the shelter to last until their friends pick them up?"

"Probably. I only took the emergency backup bottles. Who the hell cares about them, anyway?"

"No sense killing them."

"Why not? They'd kill us. They're trying to blow up Moonbase and kill everybody, aren't they?"

A longer silence. They were descending now. The ground was slowly, languidly coming closer. And closer.

"Will one nuke really be enough to wipe out the whole base?" Kelly asked.

"Depends on its size. Probably won't vaporize the whole base. But they're smart to put it in the oxygen factory. Like shooting a guy in the heart. The blast will destroy Moonbase's oxygen production. No O_2 for life support, or for export. Oxygen's still the Moon's major export product."

"I know that."

"The bomb will kick up a helluva lot of debris, too. Like a big meteor impacting. The splash will cover the solar-energy farms, I'll bet. Electricity production goes down close to zero."

Kelly muttered something unintelligible.

Jay had to admire the terrorists' planning. "They won't kill many people directly. They'll force Moonbase to shut down. Somebody'll have to evacuate a couple thousand people back to Earth. Neat job."

The ground was coming up faster now. Automatically the hopper's computer fired its little rocket engine and they slowed, then landed with hardly a thump.

"We must be a couple of klicks from the factory," Jay said. "You stay here and keep transmitting a warning. I'll go to the factory and see what's happening there."

"Hell, no!" Kelly snapped. "We're both going to the factory."

"That's stupid . . ."

"Don't get macho on me, Yank, just when I was starting to like you. Besides, you might still be one of the bad guys. I'm not letting you out of my sight."

He grinned at her, knowing that she could not see it through the helmet visor. "You still harbor suspicions about me?"

"Officially, yes."

"And unofficially?" he asked.

"We're wasting time. Let's get moving."

There was less than a half hour remaining by the time they reached the oxygen factory.

"It's *big!*" Kelly said. Their suit radios worked now; they had outrun the jammers.

"There's a thousand places they could tuck a nuke in here."

"Where the hell are the Moonbase security people?"

Jay took a deep breath. Where would I place a nuke, to do the maximum damage? Not out here at the periphery of the factory. Deep inside, where the heavy machinery is. The rock crushers? No. The ovens and electric arc separators.

"Come on," he commanded.

They ducked under conveyor belts, dodged maintenance robots gliding smoothly along the factory's concrete pad with arms extended semi-menacingly at the intruding humans. Past the rock crushers, pounding so thunderously that Jay could feel their raw power vibrating along his bones. Past the shaker screens where the crushed rock and sandy soil were sifted.

Up ahead was the heavy stuff, the steel complex of electrical ovens and the shining domes protecting the lightning-bolt arcs that extracted pure oxygen from the lunar minerals. The area was a maze of pipes. Off at one end of it stood the tall cryogenic tanks where the precious oxygen was stored.

It was dark in there. The meteor screen overhead shut out the Earthlight, and there were only a few lamps scattered here and there. The maintenance robots did not need lights, and humans were discouraged from tinkering with the automated machinery.

"It's got to be somewhere around here," Jay told Kelly.

They separated, each hunting frantically for an object that was out of place, a foreign invading cell in this almost living network of machinery that pulsed like a heart and produced oxygen for its human dependents to breathe.

"Four minutes 'til the nuke goes off!"

The words rasped in Jay's earphones. He knew that Kelly was nearly exhausted. He was himself: soaked with sweat and bone-tired.

"It's got to be here *someplace.*" Desperation edged her voice. Four minutes and counting.

He halted in the midst of the pulsing machinery, took the last of the antistatic pads from his leg pouch, and carefully cleared his helmet visor of the dust that had accumulated there.

Then immediately wished he hadn't.

Six other pressure-suited figures had entered the factory complex. Each of them carried a fléchette gun in his gloved hand.

Jay tried as best as he could to duck behind the lumbering conveyor belt to his right. He motioned for Kelly to do the same. She had seen them too, and squatted awkwardly in her suit like a little kid playing hide-and-seek.

Jay watched the six pressure-suited figures, his mind racing. Less than three minutes left! What the hell can we do? Where's the base security people?

For a wild instant he thought that these six might be Moonbase security personnel. But their suits bore no insignia, no Moonbase logo, no names stenciled on their chests.

Feeling trapped and desperately close to death, Jay suddenly yelled into his helmet microphone, "That's it! It's disarmed. We can relax now."

Kelly scuttled over to him and pressed her helmet against his. "What are you . . ."

He shoved her away and pointed with his other hand. The intruders were gabbling at each other in their own language. Two of them ducked under a conveyor belt and headed straight toward the tall cryogenic storage tanks.

"Come on," Jay whispered urgently at Kelly.

They duck walked on a path parallel to the two terrorists, staying behind the conveyors and thick pipes, detouring around the massive stainless-steel domes of the electric arcs until they came up slightly behind the pair, at the base of the storage tanks.

Jay jabbed a gloved finger, gesturing. Beneath the first of the tanks lay an oblong case, completely without markings of any kind.

One of the terrorists bent over it and popped open a square panel. The other leaned over his shoulder, watching.

"We should have brought the guns from the shelter," Kelly whispered as they huddled together behind a set of smaller tanks.

"Good time to think of it."

Without straightening up, he launched himself across the ten meters separating them from the terrorists. Arms outstretched, he slammed into the two of them and they all smashed against the curving wall of the storage tanks.

Jay had seen men in pressure suits fight each other. Tempers can flare beyond control even in vacuum. Most of the time they were like the short-lived shoving matches between football players encased in their protective padding and helmets. But now and then lunar workers had tried to murder one another.

He knew exactly what to do. Before either of the terrorists could react Jay had twisted the helmet release catch off the nearer one. He panicked and thrashed madly, kicking and fumbling with his gloved hands to seal the helmet again. He must have been screaming, too, but Jay could not hear him.

The second one had time to stagger to his knees, halfway facing Jay. But Kelly slammed into his side, knocking him over against the oblong crate that held the nuclear weapon.

Jay scooped up one of the fallen fléchette guns and fired a trio of darts into the man's chest. The suit lost its stiffness as the air blew out of it, spewing blood through the holes. He turned to see the other terrorist fleeing madly away, legs flailing as he bounced and sailed in the low gravity, hands still fumbling with his helmet seal.

"One minute!" Kelly shouted.

Jay pushed the dead body away and grabbed at the nuke. "It's too heavy for . . ."

"Not on the Moon," he grunted as he jerked the two-meter-long case off the concrete floor and hefted it to his shoulder.

"This way," he said. "Take their guns. Cover me."

They ran, straight up now, five meters at a stride, no hiding. Back the way they had come, toward the rock crushers. If this thing's salvage-fused we're finished, Jay told himself. But the first thing they do when they decommission a weapon is remove the fusing. I hope.

A pressure-suited figure flashed in front of him, then spun and went down, grabbing at its chest. Out of the side of his visor Jay saw two more figures racing to catch up with him. One of them tried to jump over some pipes. Unaccustomed to the lunar gravity, he leaped too hard and smashed into an overhead conveyor belt.

Jay didn't need a watch, his pulse was thundering in his ears, pounding off the seconds. He saw the rock-crushing machines up ahead, felt a sting in one leg, then another in his side.

His suit radio wasn't working. Or maybe he had shut it off back there somewhere, he didn't remember. His vision was blurring, everything was going shadowy. All he could see was the big conveyor belt trundling lunar rocks up to the pounding jaws of the crusher.

Lunar gravity or not, the package on his shoulder weighed a ton. He staggered, he tottered, he reached the conveyor belt at last and with the final microgram of his strength he heaved the bulky package of death onto the rock-strewn belt and watched the crusher's ferocious steel teeth, corroded with dirt and stained by chemicals, crunch hungrily into the obscene oblong package of death.

Jay never knew if the bomb went off. His world turned totally dark and oblivious.

* * *

The first face he saw when he opened his eyes again was his father's.

J. W. Hazard was sitting by the hospital bed, gazing intently at his son. For the first time Jay could remember, his father's grim, weathered face looked softened, concerned. Instead of the hard-bitten, driving man Jay had known, Hazard seemed at a loss, almost bewildered, as he stared down at his son. His eyes seemed misted over. Even his iron-gray hair seemed slightly disheveled, as if he had been running his hands through it.

"You're going to be okay, Jay-Jay," he whispered. "You're going to pull through all right."

Jay's mouth felt as if it were stuffed with cotton. He tried to swallow.

"Wh . . ." He choked slightly, coughed. "What are you doing here, Dad?"

"I came up when they told me what you'd done."

"What did I do?"

"You saved Moonbase, son. They damn near killed you, but you kept the nuke from going off." There was pride in the older man's voice.

"The girl . . . Kelly?"

His father smiled slightly. "She's outside. Want to see her?"

"Sure."

Hazard got to his feet carefully, not entirely certain of himself in the low gravity. We're still on the Moon, Jay realized. His father was in full uniform: sky-blue tunic and trousers with gold piping and the diamond-cluster insignia that identified him as director-general of the International Peacekeeping Force.

Kelly came buzzing into the room on an electric wheelchair, one leg wrapped in a plastic bandage.

"You're hurt," Jay blurted, feeling woolly-headed, stupid.

"They didn't give up after you tossed the nuke into the

crusher," she explained cheerfully. "We had a bit of a firefight."

"This young lady," Hazard said, his gravelly voice resuming some of its normal bellow, "not only held off four fanatics, but managed to patch your suit at the same time, thereby saving your life."

Jay muttered, "Thanks. A lot."

Clasping his hands behind his back and standing spraddle-legged in the middle of the hospital room, Hazard took over the conversation. "The terrorists had launched an attack on the Moonbase security office itself, designed to keep the base security forces tied up while they planted the nuke and waited for it to go off."

"That's why we got no response from base security," Kelly interjected.

"This really was a Peacekeepers' operation," Jay said to her.

"No way! We just called your father when you went into surgery."

"How long have I been out?"

"Three days."

Turning to his father, Jay said, "You must've taken a high-energy express to get here so quick."

Hazard's face reddened slightly. "Well," he blustered, "you're the only son I've got, after all."

"You really care that much about me?"

"I've always cared about you," the older man said.

Kelly was grinning at the two of them.

Abruptly, Hazard turned for the door. "I've got to contact Geneva. Got to get some forensics people up here to look at the remains of that nuke. Maybe we can get some info on where it's been hidden all this time. Might help us find the others that're missing. I'll be back later."

"Okay, Dad. Thanks."

"Thanks?" Hazard shot him a puzzled look.

"For everything."

The old man made a sour face and pushed through the door.

"You're embarrassing him." Kelly laughed and wheeled her chair close to the bed.

"You saved my life," Jay said.

"Not me. You were clinically dead when the medics reached us. They pulled you back."

He licked his dry lips, then, "You know, for a while there, I wasn't certain that I wanted to go on living. But you made me decide. I really owe you a lot for that."

Kelly beamed at him, "Welcome back to life, Jay. Welcome back to the human race."

After my prosthesis I was assigned by the
IPF personnel computers to the intelligence
service once again, this time as deputy
director, with the rank of major. Hazard
himself pinned the ringed-planet insignia on
my collar.

The situation I found was precarious.
Disarmament was stalled because Shamar's
little nuclear arsenal gave the major powers
a lovely excuse to cling to their own
megatonnages of weaponry. The IPF had
stopped several small wars and the largish
affair between India and Pakistan, but no
one truly believed that world peace could be
maintained unless and until the big powers
disarmed themselves seriously. That meant
finding Shamar, a task that the IPF could
not do.

Which is why Red Eagle continued to
deal with Cole Alexander, despite his
growing misgivings. And why I made it my
business to channel every piece of
intelligence about Shamar and his nuclear
weapons to Red Eagle.

WASHINGTON D.C., Year 8

THE night was balmy as Cole Alexander walked the length of the reflecting pool and started up the granite steps of the Lincoln Memorial. He felt a burning anxiety growing within him.

We're close, he told himself. We're almost there. Shamar's almost in our grasp. And afterward . . . He trembled with anticipation.

Taking a deep calming breath of the night air, he inhaled a flowery fragrance. The cherry trees? he wondered. No, more like good old magnolias.

Out there in the darkness, he knew, were Kelly and Pavel. Shadowing him. Protecting him. Alexander grinned sourly. I'm more in danger from muggers around here at this time of night than from Shamar. But his daughter had made up her mind that he must be accompanied by a bodyguard. When Pavel had immediately volunteered, Kelly insisted that she go along, too.

To protect me against the Red? Is she still suspicious of Pavel, or does she just want to be with him? Suspicious, he decided. Strangely, Alexander himself felt confident of Pavel's loyalty. *As long as we don't put him in conflict with his orders from Moscow, the kid will be okay,* he told himself.

The neoclassic Greek temple of the Memorial building was nearly empty this close to midnight; only a few diehard tourists and romantic couples stood scattered around its floor, staring up at the great brooding marble statue of the sixteenth President. Subdued lighting in the ceiling cast moonlight-like shadows across the hollows of Lincoln's craggy cheeks.

Old Honest Abe, said Alexander silently. *Look at that face. You sure as hell saw your share of troubles, didn't you?*

Alexander turned to see Harold Red Eagle climbing the steps slowly, with the ponderous decorum that was his trademark. *Christ, he's almost as wide as the columns holding up the roof,* Alexander thought. *But he's slowed some. He's not just being dignified; he's getting old.*

A bit stiffly, Red Eagle walked straight toward Alexander and extended his massive hand.

"We meet again, Mr. Alexander," he said in a low lion's purr.

Letting the Amerind's hand engulf his own, Alexander realized that Red Eagle's grip was firm but not hard. The big man was a true gentleman: he had the strength to crush bones, yet he withheld that strength. Instead of foolish displays intended to frighten lesser men, Red Eagle husbanded his power and used it only where and when it was necessary.

"It's been nearly six years," Alexander said.

"That long? Yes, I suppose it has."

"You picked a dramatic place to meet."

The Amerind made a small smile. "I felt it best to be discreet. You didn't land your flying boat in the Potomac, did you?"

With a chuckle, Alexander replied, "No, it's up near Baltimore, at the old Martin Marietta seaplane facility. Came down here on the tube train like any ordinary citizen. Took twelve minutes, station to station."

Red Eagle glanced around at the half-dozen others scattered around the shadowy floor. Two of the couples were heading for the stairs. That left only a young Asian family, the mother holding her sleeping child in her arms. She had already placed an incredibly sensitive microphone, the size of a penny, on the marble floor. It would be picked up the following morning before the cleaning crew came into the Memorial.

"I have found, over the years, that there are some conversations that should not be overheard," Red Eagle said.

"Or even remembered," Alexander added.

Red Eagle fixed him with a stare, then admitted, "True enough."

Alexander began pacing slowly. Red Eagle walked beside him, like a dark glacier gliding across the marble floor.

"I guess you know why I need the Peacekeepers' cooperation," Alexander began.

"If you want their help to attack Shamar and the drug manufacturing center in those mountains, I'm afraid that will be impossible."

"I understand that. No, what I need is some intelligence data . . ."

"On where the bombs are located?"

"No, on where the major drug manufacturing centers are. The biggest ones, around the world."

"What makes you think that . . ."

"IPF surveillance satellites can spot them," Alexander

said, feeling some impatience. "You send reconnaissance drones to sniff them out."

"If you are referring to the Peacekeepers' routine aerial patrols, I believe that they may occasionally pick up evidence of illicit drug manufacturing facilities. All such evidence is handed over to the national government in whose territory the facility exists."

"And they file under F, for 'Forget It,'" snapped Alexander.

Glancing around at the little family reading the plaque engraved with the Gettysburg Address, Red Eagle lowered his voice. "May I ask, Mr. Alexander, why you are interested in this information?"

Alexander looked up at the big Amerind and shrugged as nonchalantly as he could. "Since we've gotten involved with this problem in Colombia, I realize how serious the drug traffic is. After we get Shamar for you, I think we'll go after the other big drug centers."

Red Eagle was silent for several moments. He clasped his hands behind his back and paced away from Alexander, across the marble floor and past the seated figure of Lincoln. Alexander thought, They're damned near the same size, the statue and the Injun Chief.

The Asian family left, yawning. Red Eagle and Alexander were left alone with Lincoln's massive marble likeness. And the microphone.

Turning back to Alexander, Red Eagle said slowly, "Mr. Alexander, I am afraid that I don't entirely believe what you've just told me."

Alexander hadn't thought he would. "Really?"

"But we will let it pass, for the moment," he said. "We have need of your services. Your motivations are not my problem, and your future plans are . . ."—he hesitated, then concluded—"something to consider in the future."

He's up to something, and it's big, Alexander realized. He'd never let me get away with the evasions I've just handed him unless he had something much more important at hand.

"You wish to get Shamar," said Red Eagle. "We wish to get the nuclear weapons he possesses. Time grows short. The fuse is burning. Already Shamar has sold off one of his bombs. Last year he came close to destroying Moonbase with it."

"He was stopped by a man who now works for me," Alexander pointed out.

"Hazard's son. Yes, I know."

"You think Shamar's getting desperate?"

Red Eagle shook his head slowly. "I believe he wants us to think he is becoming desperate. He still has five nuclear weapons. One of them is here in Washington . . ."

"What?"

Raising a giant hand in a gesture of calm, Red Eagle said, "It has been found and disarmed. Shamar's people do not know that. They believe it to be still intact and ready to be used."

"Where was it?"

"In a private house on Pennsylvania Avenue, only a few blocks from Capitol Hill. It is still there. Waiting."

"But why . . .?"

"The Russians found another one in Moscow. A third one was discovered in Paris."

Alexander drew in a deep breath to calm the pulse racing through his veins. "I get it. Shamar wants to immobilize the nations that might go after him."

"Precisely so," said Red Eagle. "As far as we know, he still believes each of those bombs to be armed and capable of being detonated when he gives the word."

"So he thinks he can hold France, Russia and the States captive."

"So we believe."

" 'We,' in this case, is who?" Alexander asked.

A look of astonishment came across Red Eagle's normally placid face. "Why, the Peacekeepers, of course. Who else?"

"The Peacekeepers found those bombs and deactivated them?"

Red Eagle replied, "Peacekeeper sensors located the bombs. As you yourself said earlier, Mr. Alexander, we do have surveillance satellites in orbit and drone aircraft patrolling most of the world's land surface."

To himself Alexander silently replied, And you've already plotted out the world's major opium fields and drug manufacturing centers, I'll bet.

"The Peacekeepers shared their information with each national government's top security agency. In Washington, it was the Federal Bureau of Investigation that found and disarmed the nuclear weapon. In Moscow, the KGB."

"And Shamar doesn't know their teeth have been pulled?" Alexander asked.

"We believe not."

"That's three bombs. Where are the other two?"

"One is in Colombia, at the site where Shamar himself is located. We believe he is making plans to place it in Bogotá, the capital."

"Makes sense. And the fifth one?"

"That is where you come into the picture, Mr. Alexander. We need your force to get to the fifth bomb and disarm it—without letting Shamar's people know that you have done so."

"My people? Why me?"

"Because we cannot possibly trust the local government of the nation where the bomb has been hidden."

"Why not? Where is it?"

Red Eagle fell silent again, and stood as still as the brooding statue that loomed above them both.

"Before I tell you that, Mr. Alexander," he said at last, "I would appreciate it if you told me why you want the locations of the major drug manufacturing facilities."

There's no sense beating around the bush, Alexander told himself. Better spit it right out. "I want more than that," he said. "I want Shamar's bombs. All five of them. Intact."

"No, Mr. Alexander. That is not possible."

Ignoring the refusal, Alexander explained, "I've spent six years tracking down Shamar. Now that we're close to getting him, I realize that he's not the only mass murderer walking on God's green earth. The drug dealers are killing millions each year. I'm going to wipe them out, one by one."

Red Eagle's massive head drooped on his shoulders, his chin sinking to his broad chest. His eyes closed, his shoulders sagged. For a moment Alexander thought that the man was undergoing a heart attack or some incredible, unbearable pain.

"The fault is my own," he said slowly, so softly that Alexander barely heard him. "I knew it would come to this."

"I can accomplish what the Peacekeepers can't do and the national governments won't do," Alexander urged. "I can destroy the drug centers . . ."

"And kill how many?"

"They're criminals! Killers!"

"Are the farmers and shepherds downwind of your nuclear attacks also criminals?" Red Eagle asked. "You know what fallout can do, Mr. Alexander. You, of all people, should know."

"The centers are in remote areas . . ."

"Such as Marseille?"

"We'll get that one with different methods."

The huge Amerind seemed on the verge of tears. "The one thing I feared when I first contacted you six years ago was that you would start to enjoy your work too much. I told you then, Mr. Alexander, that I wanted no vigilantes or assassins. I will brook none now."

Trying to hold down the furies burning within him, Alexander countered, "There are others who'll pay me to root out the drug dealers."

"Then you will work against the Peacekeepers, not with them."

"So what?"

Red Eagle stared at him. "I am sorry, Mr. Alexander. Our relationship is at an end."

He began to walk away.

"Not so fast!" Alexander called, scampering to catch up with him. "I've got my people ready to nail Shamar. Nothing's going to change that."

Red Eagle stopped and looked down at Alexander. For a long moment he seemed to peering *through* him, as if his eyes beamed X rays. Alexander stood up to that gaze, his own gray eyes blazing.

It was Alexander who broke the deadlock. "Don't be so damned hasty," he said, trying to make his voice sound light. "I want Shamar, you want the nukes. We can still cooperate on that."

"You have just told me, Mr. Alexander, that you want Shamar *and* the nuclear weapons."

"Getting Shamar is still more important to me than anything else," Alexander said. It was even true, he told himself.

"I don't know that I can trust you anymore."

Grinning crookedly, Alexander countered, "So don't trust me. Just don't get in my way when we go in after Shamar."

"There is still that fifth nuclear bomb," Red Eagle muttered.

"Guess you'll have to find somebody else for that one," said Alexander.

"There *is* nobody else," Red Eagle admitted. "At least, no one who can be called in so quickly."

"Then let us get it for you."

"So that you can steal it and use it for your vigilante justice?"

Puffing out a long, defeated breath, Alexander lied, "No, goddammit. I guess that was a dumb idea, after all."

Red Eagle said nothing for several moments. He knows I'm lying in my teeth, Alexander thought. Question is, can he do anything else or will he have to deal with me?

"Mr. Alexander," the Amerind said at last, "I propose a truce."

"A truce?"

"You disarm the fifth bomb and get Shamar. Then we will discuss ways and means of cooperating in attacking the drug centers."

"You mean it?"

Raising a giant paw, Red Eagle added, "Without nuclear weapons. There are other possibilities. Our researchers have developed nonlethal chemical weapons. And biological agents might be used against the crops themselves . . ." His deep voice trailed off into a faint rumble, leaving the possibilities dangling.

"You've got a deal," Alexander said, extending his hand.

Red Eagle shook it, again taking care not to exert too much strength. But to Alexander it seemed that the Amerind's handclasp somehow lacked the warmth and friendship of their meeting, only minutes earlier.

He doesn't trust me anymore, Alexander said to himself. Maybe he never did. Question is, how far can I trust him, now?

Aloud he asked, "Now this fifth bomb. Just where in hell is it that the local government can't go after it?"

"Barcelona."

Alexander felt puzzled. "Barcelona? In Spain?"

"Yes."

"What's so touchy about the Spanish government that you can't inform Madrid about the bomb?"

Pacing slowly out onto the broad front portico of the

Memorial, to the place where Martin Luther King spoke of his dream, Red Eagle explained:

"Spain is going through another of its traumatic seizures, the kind that has led to civil war in the past. The Basques, the Catalonians, even the Andalusians are demanding complete autonomy from the central government of Madrid. The nation of Spain may cease to exist. It may break up into seven or eight independent entities, each with its own government, its own economy, even its own language."

Alexander nodded understandingly. "But I don't see how a bomb . . ."

"Shamar is extremely clever," Red Eagle went on. "That is what makes him so dangerous. Barcelona is the capital of Catalonia, one of the regions struggling the hardest for autonomy. The city is about to dedicate the first nuclear fusion plant in Spain—a Russian fusion reactor, by the way, financed with loans from French banks."

"You think the bomb is there?"

"It is the obvious place for it, Mr. Alexander. Madrid opposed building the fusion system; the Catalonians claimed it was because the national government wanted to have the first fusion power plant at the capital instead of Barcelona. Imagine what would happen if the plant exploded in a nuclear fireball soon after being turned on. Madrid would blame the Catalonians for the 'accident.' The Catalonians would become enraged at Madrid."

Alexander mused, "And hydrogen fusion power would get a black eye—worse than Three Mile Island and Chernobyl did to the old fission power plants."

"Indeed. To say nothing of destroying much of the city of Barcelona and killing a million or more people."

His face twisting into an almost evil smile, Alexander asked, "When did you say they're turning on the fusion plant?"

"The official dedication is a week from today."

"That doesn't give us much time."

"The bomb will not be set off until the following week."

Alexander's brows shot up. "How do you know that?"

With a heavy sigh, Red Eagle replied, "There will be an international conference in Barcelona during that week. Most of the leaders of the Peacekeepers will be there, including Director-General Hazard and his top aides."

"Jesus Christ!"

"With the proper timing, the bomb could decapitate the IPF."

"*That's* what Shamar is after!"

Red Eagle allowed a slight smile to cross his somber face. "I will be there also, Mr. Alexander. The bomb will also assassinate me, if it goes off."

Red Eagle literally placed his life in Alexander's hands. And Alexander had to postpone his planned strike against Shamar to bring his key people to Barcelona.

BARCELONA, Year 8

DRESSED in a chocolate-brown leather jacket, open-necked sport shirt and neatly creased navy-blue slacks, Jay Hazard watched through the bar's open doorway as the entire city of three million people seemed to be parading by.

The Ramblas was the heart of Barcelona. A broad promenade lined with bars, restaurants, shops and theaters, it extended from the high pillar bearing Christopher Columbus's statue down by the waterfront to the sparkling Fountain of Canaletes, in midtown. On Sundays *everyone* in the city went to church, had a good dinner and a nap, and then went for an afternoon stroll on the Ramblas.

Hazard was not interested in everyone. As he sat by the bar's doorway, nursing a glass of pale yellow Rioja wine, his blue-gray eyes sought only one man's face, a face he had seen only in a three-dimensional holographic picture.

Instead, he saw Kelly, sitting out across the narrow motorway at the sidewalk tables, sipping a tiny cup of the lethal local version of coffee. Hazard had never seen her in a skirt before. Her legs certainly look good enough to show off, he thought, but she had always worn slacks or jeans. Now, however, she was in a tourist's disguise: bright yellow skirt, flowered blouse, and a glitter-decorated sweater to protect her against the springtime chill. She had even put a bright ribbon in her boyishly cropped red hair.

Kelly saw him watching her and smiled at him. Hazard made himself smile back. She seems to like me, he thought. Maybe too much. She's been damned helpful, testifying on my behalf to get me off the Moon, getting me this job with her father's outfit. But I can't let myself get attached to her. Not now. Not yet.

Pavel Zhakarov was out there in the crowd somewhere, too, trying to blend in and look inconspicuous while staying close enough to back them up. Pavel's trained for this kind of thing, Hazard thought, wondering in the back of his mind how far he could trust the Russian.

"He says he's in love with me," Kelly had told him one afternoon as they studied satellite photos of Shamar's base near Valledupar.

"I know," Hazard had replied.

"But I don't love him," she had announced firmly. "Pavel's *nice,* but—I don't love him."

She had glanced up at him as if she expected him to say something, make some declaration. Hazard said not a word. There was nothing for him to say.

He forced his attention back to the job at hand. The man they were looking for was known only as Julio. They had nothing more than the three-dimensional photo by which to identify him. He was a technician at the new fusion power plant, and IPF intelligence claimed that he had helped to place the nuclear bomb there for Shamar's people. In fact, he was to get his final payment for his work this Sunday afternoon, at this particular bar.

According to IPF intelligence.

Hazard sipped at the strong wine. It tasted of iron. He had never been much of a drinker, and had gotten out of the habit entirely during his years at Moonbase.

IPF intelligence, he mused silently. While the bar's loudspeakers hammered out American pop rock and young couples drifted in for a drink and the snacks they called *tapas*, Hazard thought about the Peacekeepers and the career that he had thrown away.

The IPF gives us all the info we need, he thought, but makes us do the dirty work. They can't let themselves get caught interfering with the internal workings of a country, but they can hire us to do it. If that isn't IPF interference, then what the dingdong dell is it?

They're smart, damnably smart. They don't want the nations to know that they're taking over the whole world, but little by little that's just what they're doing. While Cardillo and the others rot in prison, the Peacekeepers are doing just what the rebels said they'd do: building a world government for themselves.

They. My father is one of them. Their leader, in fact. Hazard shook his head as if trying to clear cobwebs from his thoughts. Dad makes a damned good world leader, he admitted to himself. But Augustus was a damned good emperor, too. And look what followed him. Tiberius. Caligula.

His thoughts were stopped dead as Julio sauntered into the bar. No mistaking the face: receding hairline, burn scar on the left cheek.

Holding back the impulse to leap up and grab the technician, Hazard watched as Julio ordered a beer at the bar and then took it to one of the tables toward the rear of the room. He was trying to look casual about it, but he was so tense that his legs seemed unable to bend at the knees.

Hazard could not see that far back into the crowd, so he picked up his glass of wine and pushed through the pack of the crowd. Yes, there he was, with a big German-looking guy, blond and square-jawed. Handing Julio a thick envelope. The payoff, no doubt. Hazard put the wineglass to his lips while he snapped a picture of the two men with the minicamera built into his belt buckle.

As if the German heard the shutter click, his head snapped up and he stared directly at Hazard. As calmly as he could, Jay put his glass down on the bar and made his way toward the washroom.

Inside, he flattened against the tiled wall just next to the door, waiting for the German to come in after him. A minute passed. Jay opened the door and stepped out into the bar again. Julio and the German were gone.

Shinola! Hazard groused to himself, diving into the crowd, shoving his way to the front.

Kelly's table was empty too. She's following them. But which way did they go?

The Ramblas was filled with strolling people: young couples, families with little children, elder men and women enjoying their Sunday afternoon outing.

Jay saw that Kelly's coffee cup was no longer on its saucer. It had been placed at the edge of the table, its tiny handle pointing outward. He started off in the direction the handle pointed, pushing, dodging around knots of people, almost running in his haste to find Kelly and the men she was trailing.

His heart pounding, he spotted her after less than a minute.

Pulling up alongside her, he admitted breathlessly, "The blond guy . . . he saw me and took off."

"The nervous type," Kelly said.

The two men were walking briskly about half a block ahead of them.

"Where's Pavel?"

"He's around somewhere, don't worry," said Kelly. "You ought to get away from me. If they turn around and see us together . . ."

"Yeah. Right."

Just as Hazard started to move away from Kelly, the German did turn around. He pushed Julio in one direction, then started sprinting in the other.

"Follow the blond!" Kelly shouted, taking off after Julio.

Hazard dodged around a family of half a dozen children, the mother pushing still another infant in a carriage, and ran after the German. He was racing up the promenade, knocking over people like a football runner. He barged straight into an elderly couple and sent both the man and the woman sprawling. Hazard ran after him, gaining as he jumped over the fallen bodies.

Suddenly the German whirled, a gun in his hand. Hazard dived for the ground as the pistol boomed twice. People screamed and scattered. Stone chips cut Hazard's face where a bullet smacked into the pavement, inches from his head.

Scrambling to his feet, Hazard saw the German dashing across the narrow street where cars inched along bumper to bumper. He raced after him, cutting in front of an Hispano Electric jammed with teenagers. The driver blared his horn at Hazard and screamed at him. It was in Spanish but her meaning was clear.

Down a narrow alley lined with shops the German ran, Hazard close behind him. This ancient part of the city, the Gothic Quarter, was honeycombed with twisting alleys that had been turned into a sprawling shopping arcade, a kind of bazaar. No cars allowed, only the ubiquitous motor scooters weaved in and out among the pedestrians.

People scattered every which way, shrieking with sudden

fear and anger as the gun-waving German plowed through the throng. The blond turned and took swift aim again. Hazard slammed into a doorway. Two more shots. He heard the flat *crack* of the bullets whizzing past.

Hazard stuck his head out and saw the German running again. The crowd that had been ambling along the alley, window-shopping, made way for him like the Red Sea parting before the Israelites. Hazard ran in the German's wake, gaining on him.

He ducked into a side alley. Hazard ran after him, lungs burning. He skidded to a stop before turning the corner. Perfect spot for him to stop and set up a shot at me.

As Hazard cautiously approached the corner of the old stone building, he heard a motor scooter's raucous snarl. People screaming. A shot, then another. The screech of tires on worn paving stones. All in less than five seconds.

He peered around the corner. The pedestrians were flattened against the shop windows and doorways. A motor scooter was skidding down the alley on its side, striking sparks, its motor racing and wheels still spinning, the young woman who had been driving it tumbling over across the stone pavement, her arms and legs flailing, her leather jacket covered with bright red blood, her long hair crimson with blood, half her face blown away.

The German was down on one knee, aiming at a second scooter roaring straight at him, its young male driver bent over his handlebars, his lips pulled back in a snarl of vengeance.

Hazard watched as the German tried to fire the pistol. It was either empty or jammed. The scooter slammed into him with the sound of a hammer hitting a watermelon. Its driver went flying over the handlebars, hit the pavement with a bone-snapped thud, and rolled head over heels to end up almost touching his murdered girlfriend.

Hazard rushed to the German. He was not dead yet, but in enormous agony. Blood leaked from his mouth. His eyes were glazed with pain and shock. Every bone in his body must be broken, Jay thought.

The crowd began cautiously approaching the dead and dying bodies. Off in the distance Hazard heard the wail of a police siren. He backed away, edging through the thickening crowd, unable to understand their murmuring Catalan, and made his way back toward the Ramblas. His legs were shaking, vomit was surging inside him, burning his throat.

He stopped at one of the small fountains built into the corner of a building and doused his face with cold water. Leaning against the stone wall, he forced himself to take deep lungfuls of air. By the time he got back to the hotel where he, Kelly and Pavel were staying, he had himself under some semblance of control. Barely.

He and Pavel shared one room, Kelly had the adjoining one. Spacious, high-ceilinged rooms with sturdy furniture that had seen decades of wear. Their windows overlooked the noisy, bustling Ramblas.

Opening the door, Hazard saw the unconscious form of Julio sprawled on his bed. Pavel was sitting on the edge of the bed, Kelly over at the desk, pecking away at the keyboard to her lap computer.

They both looked up as he entered.

Kelly leaped to her feet and ran to Hazard. "You're hurt!"

"Just scratches."

She threw her arms around his neck. "I heard shots. I was so worried . . ."

Gently Hazard disengaged her arms. The look on Pavel's face was awful: he was trying to hide his jealousy and failing miserably.

"You got him," Hazard said to the Russian.

Pavel blinked and squared his shoulders. "Yes, we got him. And the information we wanted." He lifted an empty hypodermic syringe from the bedside table.

"What about the other one?" Kelly asked.

Hazard explained what had happened.

"Is he dead?" asked Pavel.

"Probably. I couldn't hang around and wait for the police to arrive. Somebody might have told them I'd been chasing him."

Kelly went to the door that connected to her room. "I've got a first-aid kit in my bag."

Frowning at her urgency, Pavel said, "He might have told us more about Shamar's plans."

"He's not going to talk to anybody for a while," Hazard countered.

In the quiet moonlit night, the power plant looked strangely small and simple to Hazard. No smokestacks, of course. But no cooling towers, either. No huge dome of a containment building. Just a small windowless flat-topped concrete structure with an even smaller one-story office building attached at one side, down at the end of the long pier.

They're going to generate a thousand megawatts from something that small? Hazard asked himself. Intellectually, he knew that inside that modest building a tiny man-made star had been created, fed by nothing more than heavy hydrogen. No moving parts. No spinning turbines or armatures or massive machinery that looks so impressive. The more advanced the technology, Hazard thought, the simpler and smaller the hardware.

The three of them were sitting in a rented Honda-Ford sedan, dressed in black turtlenecks and slacks, wearing noiseless black sneakers. Hazard was behind the wheel, Pavel beside him, and Kelly in the back with the drugged Julio sleeping peacefully.

"Security's a snap," Kelly had told them, once she had analyzed Julio's truth-serum ramblings back at the hotel. Looking at the fusion power plant buildings from their parking spot along the waterfront, Hazard had to agree with her. A chain link fence was all the physical security he could see. Of course, there were all sorts of electronic safeguards as well, but Kelly assured them that she could get past them with no trouble.

They don't expect to be attacked, Hazard realized. There've been no demonstrations against fusion power. The Peacekeepers have given everybody the illusion that war and terrorism are a thing of the past. They're not worried about security.

His mind drifted back to the final briefing they had undergone, in Cole Alexander's jet seaplane, moored in the harbor of Gibralter.

"I want that nuke," Alexander had told them. Insisted on it, despite their misgivings. Kelly had argued against it. So had Pavel and even Barker.

"Damned dangerous to bring that thing aboard this plane," the pilot had grumbled. "Foolish thing to do."

Alexander gave him a parody of a smile. "Safe as a church, Chris. Why, in the bad old days a B-1 bomber would carry thousands of megatons worth of bombs. No sweat."

"I flew a NATO bomber back then," the crippled Englishman retorted, "and I *always* sweated."

"The bomb comes to me," Alexander repeated, tapping the glass top of the map table for emphasis. "That's the deal. We'll land in Barcelona harbor just before dawn and take it and you guys"—he waved a finger at Kelly, Hazard and Pavel—"back to Valledupar."

"I don't like it," Hazard said.

"I don't care if you like it or not," Alexander snapped.

"But why do you want it?" Kelly asked. "Why not deliver it to the IPF?"

Alexander's smile twisted slightly wider. "Shamar's got a nuke, doesn't he? I want to be able to deal with him on equal terms."

Sitting in the car, sizing up the fusion power plant,

Hazard realized that Pavel had said nothing during the discussion about the nuclear weapon. Not a word. It wasn't that he had nothing to say, or that he didn't care. Hazard knew the Russian better than that. He's got his orders from Moscow, Jay told himself. Whatever his personal opinions about this might be, he'll do what Moscow has told him to do.

"All right," Kelly said from the shadows of the car's rear seat. "It's time to get moving."

"You sure he's going to be okay?" Hazard jerked a thumb at Julio. The man was utterly limp, head laid back against the seat cushions, mouth gaping open. He was breathing deeply, evenly.

"Nothing will wake him for at least four more hours," Pavel assured him.

They left the car and walked to the gate blocking the entrance to the pier. Kelly fiddled with a palm-sized black box and the lock flickered its tiny red lights, then clicked open.

"Pretty easy," Hazard muttered.

"Opening the lock is no problem," Kelly explained. "Opening it without its sending an alarm to the central security program—*that's* the tough part."

The three of them sprinted down the length of the pier. This was the most vulnerable part of their mission: out in the open, under the bright moon, with no place to hide. Despite all the electronic gadgetry, if some security guard should happen to look in their direction they would be instantly spotted.

But the building was windowless and no one patrolled outside. They got to the shadow of its wall, panting slightly from the run. Hazard leaned against the concrete. It felt warm. From the day's sunlight, he told himself. It's not radioactive.

The city's lights were glittering as far as the eye could see, far outnumbering the stars shining in the pale sky. The waters of the harbor lapped gently and sparkled in the bright moonlight. A romantic spot, Hazard thought briefly. If he and Kelly were here alone, under other circumstances . . .

"Up to the roof," Kelly whispered.

Pavel led the way. Up to the roof to a skylight and down a snaking nylon rope. In swift succession they touched down on the floor. The fusion reactor was a small dome of stainless steel, barely taller than Hazard himself. But he knew that within that dome were several layers of the toughest, densest alloys that human ingenuity could create, with pipes that carried liquid sodium, deuterium, and other strange fluids. And at the core of it all a minuscule star glowed fiercely, radiating hot neutrons that could fry a man to cinders in less time than it would take him to fall to the floor.

There were other, bulkier shapes of machines in the area. Power converters and electrical conditioning equipment, dimly seen in the reduced night lighting of the ceiling panels, high overhead. The building was just one large enclosure, almost filled with machinery except for the walkways intended for human and robotic maintenance personnel. The place hummed with power. The fusion generator was working, converting heavy hydrogen to electrical energy, cleanly, cheaply, with almost the same efficiency as the Sun itself.

Water in, energy out, Hazard thought. But still a part of him was frightened to be this close to the raging plasma glowering at the heart of the fusion reactor. The area was warm with throbbing hidden energies, the air seemed to crackle with electricity.

Don't be an idiot! he told himself. There's not enough material in the reactor to make an explosion. He knew that. But still his insides trembled.

Like three cat burglars, they glided silently along the walkways until they reached the long metal-clad channel of the power converter. It was rectangular in shape, painted bright blue.

"Should be wedged in under here," Kelly whispered, dropping to her knees for a better look.

Pavel knelt beside her. "Is that it?"

A metal box the size of a very large suitcase. It had been painted the same shade of blue as the generator channel, but Hazard recognized the shape.

"That's it," he hissed.

He and Pavel flattened themselves on the floor and tugged the case loose while Kelly stood guard over them. Then she used the electronics gear she carried to open the locks.

Hazard swung the lid back and played his penlight across the panel. "Bingo," he said.

"First thing we do is deactivate it," Kelly said.

It took nearly half an hour, but finally she said, "Okay. It's on safe now. Won't go off even if you chomp it up in an ore grinder." She grinned at Hazard.

He smiled back at her.

Then he heard himself say, "There's one more thing we've got to do."

"What?"

"Remove the fissionable material."

Kelly's eyes glinted with sudden terror in the shadowy lighting. Even Pavel looked shocked.

"I'm not turning this device over to your father or anybody else," Hazard said, "in a condition where it could be used."

Pavel nodded vigorously. "I agree."

They both turned to Kelly.

She hesitated, biting her lip. Finally she said, "It's too dangerous. You're talking about plutonium. The risks . . ."

He cupped her chin in his hand. "I have to do it, Kelly. Nobody should have a live nuclear bomb to play with. Not even your father."

"I know," she whispered bleakly.

"Then I'll have to take the fissionable material out of it."

"But it's so dangerous."

"Not if you know how. I've worked with warheads before. The plutonium's always protected by plenty of shielding." As he spoke, Hazard realized that *this* is what had been making him jumpy, earlier. Not the fusion plant. He had known, in his subconscious, that he was going to try to disarm the bomb. He had been carrying the tools for the task ever since they had left the seaplane at Gibralter.

"What do we do?" Pavel asked.

"Get out of my way," Hazard replied. "This is a one-man job."

"There's nothing . . .?"

"Go back to the doors that connect with the office building and make sure nobody disturbs me." Silently he added, And that'll keep you far enough away so that if I do spill the plutonium, you'll have a chance to get away. Plutonium is not only fiercely radioactive; it is a deadly chemical poison as well.

Kelly was almost gasping with fear. "I won't leave you!" she insisted. "I can watch the doors from here. I won't leave you alone!"

But Pavel took her gently by the arm and raised her to her feet. "Do as he says," the Russian whispered.

Hazard nodded to him. He understands the risks.

"Go with Pavel," he said to her. "I'll call you when I'm finished here."

The Russian had to drag her away. Kelly stared after Hazard as she was hauled to a safe distance.

It was actually almost easy. Almost. Hazard had to turn the heavy suitcase over, carefully unscrew six bolts and then lift the thick lead-lined oblong that held the plutonium. It was about a third of the volume of the entire case; the rest of the device was electronic fusing and safeguard systems.

The bomb was not booby-trapped. He pulled up the handle that folded flush against the case's top. The lead-lined case slid out smoothly. Still, Hazard's hands were slippery with sweat, and perspiration stung his eyes.

Damned thing feels awfully light, he thought. If I didn't know better, I'd swear it was empty.

He took the hand-sized radiation meter from his pocket and ran it across the oblong box. Hot, but not dangerously so, he told himself. Not if I don't hold on to it for hours on end.

Getting to his feet, Hazard waved Kelly and Pavel back to him.

"Guard patrol's due in another thirty . . ." Kelly saw the look on his face. "What's wrong?"

Lifting the steel case by its handle, Hazard told them, "This thing is lined with lead, so it's heavier than it looks. But it feels a lot lighter than it ought to be."

"You shouldn't be holding it," Kelly said.

Pavel picked up on Hazard's meaning. "Lighter than it should be? You mean that it might be empty?"

Hazard nodded wordlessly.

"Empty? No plutonium in it?" Kelly asked.

"It should be heavier."

"We must check it," said Pavel.

"Before we get back to the plane," Hazard added.

Kelly glanced at her wristwatch. "Rendezvous in one hour and forty-eight minutes."

"We're going to miss the rendezvous," Hazard said. "There's an American consulate here in Barcelona. Should have X-ray equipment."

"There is also a Soviet consulate," said Pavel.

Kelly planted her fists on her hips. "And while you guys are re-inventing the Cold War, tell me what good an X-ray machine will be with a lead-lined box."

So they hauled the oversized suitcase up to the roof,

Pavel clambering up the dangling nylon rope first. Kelly followed the bomb and Hazard went up last, with the box hanging from a length of rope attached to his waist and the radiation meter in his pocket clicking away.

They drove along the docks to the pier where the fishing boats came in and found the wholesalers already at work in the predawn darkness. The place was a madhouse of furiously busy people, with the bustle and smell of cranes swinging cargo nets loaded with fish, men and women shouting prices at each other, diesel trucks waiting with their motors clattering and fumes fouling the air.

Kelly found a friendly dealer who let her weigh the case on a scale used for weighing fish. Then she went to the phonebooth at the end of the pier and plugged her portable computer into its access port. A few taps on her keyboard and she came back to Hazard and Pavel at the car with a worried frown on her face.

"You're right, Jay," she said as she got into the car. "The case is almost exactly ten kilograms lighter than it should be if it were loaded with fissionable material."

Hazard clenched both hands on the steering wheel. "Then there's no plutonium in it. The bomb's a fake."

"Or someone else has already disarmed it," Pavel suggested.

"It's a fake," Hazard insisted. "Shamar has the plutonium back at his base."

"The plutonium from all of the bombs?" Kelly wondered.

Hazard revved the car to life and started through the predawn darkness to their rendezvous point.

"Your father's going to piss himself when he finds this out," Hazard said.

Kelly said, "Maybe we should bring Sleeping Beauty here along with us, to see how much he knows about this."

"Julio won't know a damned thing," Hazard shot back.

"He's just the guy who stashed the bomb in the power plant, a guy who took a wad of money to do his employer dirt. He didn't even know it was a nuke."

Pavel said nothing. But his mind was racing with the possibilities that this new twist had opened up. None of the possibilities looked good to him. Not one of them.

Two days later, one of our ferret satellites picked up this series of electromagnetic vibrations as it cruised slightly to the south and west of Moscow. The voices were identified by computerized voiceprint matching.

Pavel Zhakarov: There is no plutonium in the bomb. We conclude that Shamar has the plutonium with him, and all the bombs that have been discovered so far are duds.

Gregor Volynov (KGB operations director): So we have heard through the IPF. The bomb in Moscow is likewise empty.

Zhakarov: The operation against Shamar becomes even more important, then.

Volynov: Yes. And more difficult.

Zhakarov: I am confident that we can make a success of it.

Volynov: Good. Once it is finished, Alexander will be too dangerous to be permitted to continue.

Zhakarov (after a pause of nine seconds): You wish me to eliminate him?

Volynov: You are ordered to do so, comrade. At the earliest possible moment.

VALLEDUPAR, Year 8

THE jet seaplane was moored once again in the Cesar River, but this time at a spot well above the city of Valledupar, in a branch of the river that cut through thick tropical growth as it curved around the base of the steep granite mountains.

While Chris Barker worried loudly about ripping out the hull against the shallow rocky river bottom, Alexander urged him to nose the seaplane as close to shore as possible. Once anchored, the whole crew spent the rest of the day covering the broad wings and graceful fuselage with foliage to hide it from prying eyes.

That evening after dinner they convened in the wardroom. To an outsider, it might have looked like half a dozen men and women taking their ease in casual conversation. To Alexander, the dynamics of who sat where were not only interesting, but important.

Barker picked the lounge chair closest to the forward bulkhead and the flight deck, the braces on his lower legs bulging beneath his slacks. Alma Steiner, the logistics expert, wore a faded gray jumpsuit cinched at the waist with an old U.S. Army belt, tight enough to show off her neatly curved figure. She sat close to Alexander himself. Jay Hazard took a seat near the map table; Kelly automatically picked the seat beside his. Pavel was off in the corner by the rear bulkhead, looking alone and unhappy.

"It's been confirmed," Alexander said without preamble. "Each one of those goddamned bombs is empty. Duds, all of 'em."

"But why?" Barker asked. "Why go to the risk . . .?"

"Shamar's smart," Alexander interrupted with a grim smile. "He gets local crazies to plant fake bombs in Washington, Moscow, Paris and Barcelona, then he makes sure that the IPF finds out about it. We spin our wheels trying to neutralize the bombs and find out what he's up to . . ."

"While he remains here in these mountains, constructing new bombs from the plutonium," Steiner concluded.

"Is that possible?" asked Barker.

"It isn't too difficult," Kelly replied. "It's mainly an electronics job, and he should have access to plenty of people who can do the work."

"College kids have made nuclear bombs," Hazard pointed out. "They just didn't have the fissionable material to make them go boom."

"Shamar does," Alexander said.

"Enough to make five one-hundred-kiloton bombs," Kelly murmured.

"Which makes the task of nailing him even more important," said Alexander.

Steiner took a deep breath, something she did quite well, as far as Alexander was concerned. "The mercenary troops will arrive over the next four days. Two separate groups, each of them coming in two contingents, for a total of seventy-eight men."

Alexander added, "They'll disperse their camps along the river. Cold camps, no fires, so they run the minimum risk of being detected."

"Don't you think Shamar has the river under surveillance?" Hazard asked, his handsome face looking slightly worried.

"And spies in the city?"

With a shrug, Alexander replied, "We do the best we can."

Pavel finally spoke up. "We strike in four days, then?"

"Six," corrected Alexander. "Got to give the mercs a couple days to get settled and learn the tactical plan." With a sardonic smile, he added, "You can tell Moscow we'll hit Shamar six days from now."

Pavel did not smile back.

The meeting broke up. The three youngsters headed for their bunks. Alexander watched his daughter; she lingered near Hazard and ignored Pavel, who watched them with dark liquid eyes. Young love, Alexander said to himself. What a pain.

Barker got to his feet and headed forward, muttering about an engine overall that was long overdue.

"After this job is finished," Alexander said, starting forward toward his own quarters.

When he got to the door to his quarters, the passageway was empty of everyone else except Steiner. She was at her own door, but she looked over her shoulder at Alexander and smiled charmingly.

"Want a drink?" he stage-whispered.

She nodded eagerly.

Motioning her to him, Alexander opened the door and stepped into his bedroom. Unlike the built-in bunks of the smaller sleeping compartments, his quarters contained a real double bed, a couch, and even a low bookcase that covered the entire forward bulkhead. The shelves were encased in glass; all except one section that was fronted by a polished teak door.

A plastic worktable, its top painted to resemble teak, extended the length of the inner wall, from the door to the rear bulkhead of the room. It was covered with photographs and strange artifacts.

"Satellites can't see much of Shamar's base," Alexander said, gesturing to the photos. "Too much foliage. Locals call it Montesol; say it's an old Inca city. They claim it's haunted."

Steiner picked up an exquisite quartz carving of a panther, no more than six inches long, but beautifully detailed. "Did this come from there?"

"All this junk did," Alexander said. "The carvings, the silver medallions, the glass knives and all."

"*Someone* is not afraid of ghosts," she murmured, fingering the smooth back of the panther.

"Oh, I think the old grave robbers spread the story about the place being haunted to keep everybody else away."

"Someone should tell the university about this. The anthropologists would be ecstatic over a lost Inca city."

Alexander gave her a crooked grin. "Shamar wouldn't be too happy with them."

"Yes. Of course."

"First we clean out the rats. Then we can tell the anthropologists about Montesol."

He pulled down the teak door of the cabinet to form a miniature desktop. Inside was a small bar, complete with a row of tumblers fitted snugly into wooden racks.

Steiner sat on the couch while Hazard poured two

brandies. She was a tall woman, almost Alexander's own height, with long legs and a lithe figure that her faded fatigues accented rather than concealed. Her face was strong, a good jaw and clear blue eyes. Hair the color of straw, always tied up neatly. A young Brunhilde, visiting in the twenty-first century.

"Don't have snifters," he said almost apologetically.

"I'm surprised that you have alcohol of any kind aboard," she said, accepting the heavy tumbler with its inch of amber liquor.

"Rank hath its privileges," he said, tossing off the drink in one gulp as he stood before the couch.

Steiner's smile saddened slightly. "You didn't give me time to offer a toast."

Raising one finger of his free hand, Alexander replied, "Easily fixed." He turned back to the bar and poured himself another.

Sitting down next to her, he asked, "What should we drink to?"

"Success to our mission."

His lips twisted into a grin. "Confusion to our enemies."

They touched glasses and sipped.

"You know," Steiner said, looking into his eyes, "I almost feel like one of those people you see in the war videos. The night before a mission."

"Eat, drink and be merry," Alexander quoted, "for tomorrow we die."

"Yes. That sort of thing."

Her eyes were incredibly blue, Alexander noticed. And staring straight at him. "Are you trying to get into my pants?" He forced a laugh.

Steiner did not laugh. "I think making love would be a better release for you than getting drunk, don't you?"

Pursing his lips as if deep in thought, Alexander answered, "Well . . . there's no hangover the next morning."

"Not for the man."

"Not for you either, Alma. I'm sterile."

She made a little sigh. "Ahh. I suspected as much. From the radiation."

"Yeah. It's killing me slowly."

"But you are not impotent?"

Alexander made a bleak smile. "No, not impotent. Just—not interested, I'm afraid."

"Not interested?" Steiner put on a girlish pout. On her strong features it looked almost comical.

"It's got nothing to do with you, Alma," he said, looking away from her, staring into his glass. "It's my problem. Maybe after we get Shamar . . ." He drifted to silence.

She took a long swallow of her brandy. "I suppose it would make things difficult if members of the crew began —fraternizing with each other."

Alexander made a bleak smile. "Some companies have rules against that sort of thing."

"Yes." Steiner finished her drink swiftly and got to her feet. "You'd better speak to your daughter, then. If you don't want a romantic mess on your hands."

"Yeah, I know." He stood up beside her. There were fires smoldering in her eyes now. Fires of anger, barely suppressed. Hell hath no fury, Alexander realized.

Aloud, he said, "Look, I'm sorry . . ."

Steiner turned from him and put her glass down on the bar. "As you said, it's your problem."

"Yeah."

She went to the door, then turned. With a slow, warming smile she said softly, "Maybe after we get Shamar your problem will be solved, eh?"

Alexander went to her and kissed her on her lips, briefly, chastely, almost as a brother would. "Maybe then," he said, his voice choking slightly.

She nodded, opened the door and left.

He stood there for several minutes, damning himself for not feeling anything.

Alexander watched the trees that hung out over the water as he held the tiller of the little inflatable Zodiac. He stayed under their shade as much as possible, not satisfied that his bulky bush jacket and wide-brimmed hat gave him sufficient protection from the sun.

The morning was broiling hot. The rising sun baked moisture from the thick forest on each side of the river; wisps of steam rose up through the trees to waft away on the soft breeze.

Kelly sat up in the prow of the dark gray rubber boat, an Indian shawl over her head, more to hide her red hair from prying eyes than to keep the solar ultraviolet off her. She wore a simple native blouse and skirt, both of them loose enough to hide a small arsenal. If anyone saw them, they would look like a well-to-do planter and his daughter out for a trip to Valledupar. Or so Alexander hoped.

With a twist of his wrist Alexander turned the throttle down low. The engine's roar muted and the Zodiac's bow settled into the water.

"Why'd you slow down?" Kelly asked. "I was enjoying the spray."

"Time for us to have a talk," said Alexander.

She nodded knowingly. "So that's why you brought me along with you."

"I want to talk with you," he said.

"Father-daughter kind of talk?"

"You bet."

Kelly sniffed, "That means you want to talk to me, not *with* me."

"I'll listen too."

"Really?"

"Yeah. What's going on with you, kid?"

She made a sad little smile. "Nothing very much."

"Come over here." He tapped the bench alongside him. "I don't want to holler the length of the damned boat."

Kelly made her way down the rocking boat, across the midships bench, to sit beside her father.

"Now what's happening, little lady?"

Leaning her head against his shoulder, Kelly replied, "Like I said, nothing much."

"Looks like a romantic triangle to me."

Kelly nodded.

"Pavel's gawking at you like a little lost calf, and you seem to be mooning the same way over Jay."

"True enough," she admitted miserably.

"So?"

"So I fall for tall rugged guys. First Robbie, now Jay."

"Must be a father fixation," Alexander joked.

Kelly did not laugh. "I love Jay. I know Pavel thinks he's in love with me, but I love Jay."

"And Jay?"

"He's so hurt and mixed up he doesn't know what he's doing." Her words came in a rush, filled with pain and despair. "He's afraid of letting down his defenses, afraid of letting anybody get close to him."

He's not the only one, Alexander told himself.

"Pavel's nice," Kelly went on. "I mean, I like him and he's sweet and terribly romantic but there's just no *chemistry* there. I don't have the vibes with him that I get from Jay. He's so lonely and scared, really, when you get right down to it. So far from home and so mixed up."

"Pavel?"

"No," she said, "Jay."

Alexander slid an arm around his daughter's slim shoulders. "So you love Jay but he doesn't love you, while Pavel loves you but you don't love him. Is that it?"

"That's it." Kelly's voice was small, almost childlike. Alexander wondered what in hell he was supposed to do about this. You've never been much of a father, he thought.

You were never around when she was growing up. Now's your big chance to make up for all that neglect. Come up with some fatherly wisdom that'll set everything straight and make her smile.

But not a thing came into his head.

He heard himself say, "Sooner or later Pavel's either going to be called back to Moscow or he's going to try to nail me."

Kelly pulled free of his arm. "You don't think he's still . . ."

"He's still on the KGB payroll, kid. We've been helping him to play them along, but once this Shamar business is finished, he's going to have to make his decision: us or them."

"If he chooses *them,*" Kelly murmured, "you think they'll order him to assassinate you?"

With a nod, Alexander replied, "Especially if I get the plutonium Shamar's holding."

"But if he chooses us, then Moscow will send somebody to kill him!"

Alexander made his crooked smile. "Not necessarily. I might be able to work out a deal—maybe."

Kelly fell silent and leaned back against her father once more. The boat purred quietly along the river, to the accompaniment of raucous shrieks and chattering from the colorful birds that lived among the thickly leafed trees. The sun climbed higher and the heat became like a steam bath that turned solid flesh to streams of perspiration, a scalding towel that muffled the face so that it became difficult even to breathe.

"What you're saying," Kelly spoke at last, "is that if I'm nice to Pavel he'll decide in our favor, instead of trying to kill you."

Alexander shook his head, making the wide brim of his hat wobble. "What I'm saying, little lady, is that I can deal with Pavel one way or the other. He'll decide what he wants to do based mainly on you. But I don't want you to make up to him when you really are in love with Jay. That'd be worse than stupid—it'd be immoral."

She actually laughed. "You? Old-fashioned morality from you?"

"And why not?" Alexander suddenly felt distinctly uncomfortable. "Have I been such an immoral monster all these years?"

"Not exactly. But you sure haven't been a perfect model of Christian virtues either."

"Who the hell has? One of St. Peter's first miracles was to strike some poor sucker dead."

"No!"

"And his wife."

"I don't believe you!"

"Look it up. Acts of the Apostles."

Kelly laughed, and Alexander enjoyed the sight and sound of it. But she sobered quickly.

"If only there was some way I could reach Jay and make him stop being afraid of letting somebody love him."

Choosing his words carefully, Alexander said, "I presume you have offered him the delights of your flesh."

Without a hint of hostility she replied, "He's too straight-arrow for that. He doesn't think people who work together ought to get themselves into romantic entanglements."

Alexander grinned his widest grin. "Well that's easily fixed! After this Shamar business is over, I'll fire the bastard."

"You do, and I'll quit!"

"Suits me."

"Really?" She seemed surprised, almost shocked.

Alexander said, "Damned right. What I've got to do next is something you won't want to be mixed up with anyway. Red Eagle calls it vigilante justice."

"You're going to be a one-man crusade, is that it?"

"It won't be just one man," Alexander countered. "There are plenty of people willing to fight against the drug trade. And terrorism. Plenty. And others who are willing to pay the bills, too."

"But the Peacekeepers will be against you."

"I doubt it." The river was widening now. Other boats were chuffing along on ancient diesel engines. "They won't be *for* me, of course. Ol' Red Eagle will fuss and fume, but the IPF won't actively oppose what I do."

Kelly looked altogether unconvinced.

Alexander nosed the little dark gray Zodiac through the growing river traffic, always remaining as much under the shade of the trees on the bank as possible. Abruptly the foliage ended and stark cinder-block and concrete buildings rose along the river's edge. Docks poked their fingers out into the water. Construction cranes swung high overhead. The city of Valledupar was growing.

"This is what the fight is all about," Alexander said to his daughter over the noise of machinery and motors. "The country's getting rich on narcotics. The Castanada family wants to keep control of the trade."

"And you want to end it altogether."

"That," he said firmly, "is exactly what I'm going to do."

Alexander found the pier he was looking for, a busy commercial wharf where work gangs were unloading boats laden with tropical fruits from upriver. He tied his inflatable boat to a stanchion set into the new-looking concrete. An unmarked four-door sedan was waiting for them at the end of the pier, its rooftop photovoltaic cells glittering in the sun.

Kelly shivered slightly as they ducked into the air-conditioned interior and the driver wordlessly started the engine and headed out into the city. He was a thickset unsmiling man, swarthy and grim, with a black Pancho Villa mustache that drooped over his heavy lips. Through a tangle of crowded narrow streets they drove, the driver blatting his horn at the people milling around the sidewalk stalls.

"Must be market day," Alexander muttered.

The driver said nothing.

"Where are we going?" asked Kelly.

"Final meeting with Castanada. He's supposed to fork over the cash for the mercs."

She caught the note of skepticism in his voice. "You don't think he . . ."

"Remember how the good burghers of Hamelin paid off the Pied Piper? They offered him a thousand guilders *before* he drove out the rats."

"And once he'd done the job . . ."

Alexander made a crooked grin. " 'Besides, our losses have made us thrifty,' " he quoted. " 'A thousand guilders? Come, take fifty!' "

Despite herself, Kelly giggled.

"We get the money for the mercs *now,"* her father said. "Those guys don't work for promises; they want to see cash. Our own payment can come later. Castanada can keep our money in his Swiss account for another week; earn more interest on it."

The car left the narrow streets and headed into the broader avenues that climbed up the hills that overlooked the city. Wide green lawns and large whitewashed houses with graceful colonnaded facades and red tile roofs were spaced generously along the quiet, treelined thoroughfare.

"This is definitely the high-rent district," Alexander said.

"The Castanadas must live here," Kelly guessed.

"Nope. The whole family lives down in the presidential palace, where the army surrounds 'em. I don't know what the hell we're doing up here."

He leaned forward and tapped the driver on the shoulder. "Where are we going?"

The driver grunted.

"Dónde vamos?" Kelly asked.

Raising a heavy, blunt-fingered hand, the driver pointed, *"Allí."*

The street ended in a cul-de-sac with a little park of carefully clipped bushes and a few tall trees. A second car was sitting along the curve: a long gray limousine with mirrored windows.

"I don't like this," Kelly whispered.

Alexander looked at the driver, who turned off the ignition, folded his arms across his chest, and sat stoically unmoving. A rear door of the limousine opened and a slightly built man wearing a dapper double-breasted suit got out. His gray hair was brushed sleekly back and his mustache was neatly trimmed.

"It's okay," said Alexander, with relief in his voice. "I know him; he's one of Castanada's flunkies."

Both of them got out of their car and walked over to the limousine.

"Señor . . ." Alexander groped for the name. "Rodríguez?"

"Ah, good morning, Señor Alexander!" Rodríguez smiled broadly, obviously pleased that his name had been remembered.

"It's good to see you again."

"And you, my dear sir. But please tell me, who is this charming young lady with you?"

"An assistant of mine," Alexander said curtly. No one outside the immediate "family" of his organization knew of Kelly's relation to him.

"Ah," said Rodríguez, his smile starting to look a bit forced. "I see."

Alexander said, "I believe you have a package for me."

"Sí, sí. A rather heavy one, in fact. It is here in the car."

He opened the limousine's door and ducked inside it. Alexander had just enough time to wonder why the chauffeur wasn't doing his usual job of opening doors. Rodríguez wasn't the kind of man who allowed a servant to sit inside the limo while he . . .

"Look out!" Kelly yelled.

Six men with snub-nosed submachine guns sprang out of the bushes. A roar of motorcycles made Alexander whirl; another half dozen on bikes were coming up the street, blocking them off.

The heavy-set driver of their car pushed his way out from behind the wheel, yanking a pistol from his shoulder holster. Kelly was already on one knee, an automatic in one hand while she slid a second one across the asphalt toward her father.

A burst of gunfire slammed the driver back against the sedan, his chest spouting blood. Kelly fired back, then ducked behind the car. Alexander froze where he stood crouched beside the limousine. Machine-gun fire raked the limo, making it jounce on its springs as the slugs hit it. Something smashed into Alexander's head and he pitched face-first onto the asphalt paving. He heard more gunfire and a scream. He tried to push himself up, but everything turned black and silent.

When he came to, Rodríguez was bending over him, wild-eyed, babbling about the money being stolen. The limo was riddled with bullet scars, but its armor and bulletproof glass had saved Rodríguez and his chauffeur. Not so the other driver. He lay dead in a pool of his own blood.

And Kelly was gone.

If we had known that Shamar was going to strike at Alexander before he could get his own attack started, we would have certainly warned the man. But we did not know. Even with the intelligence-gathering services of the International Peacekeeping Force, we did not know what Shamar had planned. Cynics claim that we set Alexander up; some even lay the blame for what happened next at Red Eagle's doorstep. But I was there at Geneva. I was serving with IPF intelligence at the time. We did not know. How could we?

And we certainly had no part in what came afterward.

MONTESOL, — Year 8

AS he lay prone in the high grass, studying the ancient stone city that clustered in the hollow just below the mountain's crest through electronically boosted binoculars, Jay Hazard sensed that he was no longer alone.

The morning air was crisply cool this high above the forest. The Cesar River was nothing more than a glinting gray ribbon snaking through the thick greenery that stretched as far as the eye could see. Up here the trees were smaller, sparser, and tall fronds of grass waved in the moaning mountain wind.

Somewhere in the grass a man was crawling toward him. Jay could feel it in the back of his neck.

Damned fool! he raged at himself. Dashing off like a one-man army without taking more than a handgun and canteen of water. What are you going to accomplish except getting yourself killed?

He went absolutely still. Except for his left hand, which snaked down to the holster at his hip and slowly pulled the heavy blue-black automatic pistol.

He lay the electro-optical binoculars on the ground before him and cocked the gun as quietly as he could, pulling the action back carefully and holding it as it slid forward again so that it did not make too much noise.

Slowly, ever so slowly, he turned over onto his back so that he could see who was approaching. The city and the men in it would have to wait. Kelly was there; Shamar had made the ancient ruin his headquarters. But whoever was sneaking up on him had a more immediate priority.

He lay there in the grass, gun cocked and ready, wishing he had a silencer for it. Or a knife. The morning sun was hot despite the altitude. His shirt was already soaked with sweat from the long climb up here.

"Jay, is that you?" A whisper carried by the wind.

He said nothing.

"It's me, Pavel. I'm going to stand up so you can see me. Don't shoot."

Sure enough, the small slim Russian rose amidst the waving fronds of grass. Jay felt the breath he had been holding back puff out of his lungs.

Half annoyed, half relieved, he waved Pavel to him. The young Russian bent forward and crawled to his side, staggering under a backpack almost the size of his own torso. He flopped on the grass next to Jay with a grunt.

"What the hell are you doing here?" Jay growled.

"Same as you: trying to find Kelly."

"Who gave you permission to try a stunt like this?"

"Same as you: nobody."

Jay looked into the Russian's dark eyes, thinking, He's

here, nothing you can do about it. And you're going to need all the help you can get.

"How's Alexander?"

"Still under sedation. Steiner says he has a concussion, probably from a ricocheting bullet."

"And the mercs?"

Pavel started to struggle the pack off his shoulders. "It will still be two days before they arrive, even with our emergency call."

"We can't wait two days."

"I agree. We must get Kelly out of there *now.*"

Jay felt his jaw tighten. "Moscow order you to come and rescue her?"

"Moscow knows nothing of this," Pavel snapped.

"Then why are you here?"

"I could ask you the same question."

"She saved my life," Jay said immediately. "When I thought it was over, when I was exiled at Moonbase, Kelly had faith in me. She brought me back to Earth, back to life."

"So you love her." Pavel's voice trembled slightly.

"Love her? No! I *owe* her."

Shaking his head, the Russian said, "But she loves you."

"That's crazy!"

"She does."

His voice was so low, his face suddenly so miserable, that Jay finally recognized what he had not understood before. "And you love her."

"Yes." The faintest of whispers.

Jay made a coughing noise that might have been a laugh. Not even he could tell for sure. "Fine mess."

"You're certain she's there?" Pavel cocked his head slightly in the direction of the ancient city.

"Haven't seen her, but that's Shamar's base of operations, all right. Must be a couple hundred men there. Women, too."

"He sent a message to Alexander, after you left."

"Message?"

"Last night. By radio, over the civilian band frequency."

"What the hell did he say?"

"That Kelly was alive and unhurt and that he would exchange her for Alexander himself."

Jay felt a surge of emotions blaze along his veins. "So that's his game. He wants Alexander."

"Shamar will kill Alexander if he gets his hands on him."

"He'll kill Kelly if Alexander doesn't agree."

"That is why we must get her out of there," Pavel said.

"Right." Jay rolled back onto his stomach, then asked, "What answer did you make to Shamar?"

"Barker took the message. He told them that Alexander was under sedation and would be unable to reply for twenty-four hours."

"And what'd Shamar say?"

"He said that in exactly twenty-four hours Kelly would be killed, unless Alexander agreed to surrender himself."

"How long . . . ?"

"Seven hours ago. That is when I decided to come up here after you."

Jay's thoughts were tumbling wildly through his mind. "Kelly . . . did they let Kelly speak?"

"No."

"Then how do we know she's still alive?"

"We only have Shamar's word for it."

"Those bastards could do anything to her," Jay said.

"We must act quickly."

"Yeah. But there's a couple hundred of them and only two of us."

Pavel took the binoculars that lay before them and focused them on the stone structures in the hollow. It was an ancient city that must have been magnificent in its day. But now it was abandoned, crumbling with age, half tumbled down. Massive stone statues had toppled over and rested on their sides. On some of the buildings entire walls were gone, leaving their interiors gaping. Grass and shrubs had invaded those broken buildings, making them look as if they were rotting, covering them with a green slimy decay. Pavel observed that the stones were not blackened by fire; earthquakes must have done the damage.

The city had been built around a large central plaza paved with gray stones. Now it was weed-grown and cracked, but it served as a helicopter landing pad. A chopper stood off at one end of the square, covered with a camouflage net. At the head of the square was an impressive temple raised on a tiered platform. A steep flight of stairs led to its colonnaded front entrance; most of the massive pillars were still standing, but much of the roof was gone. Several other old buildings were still intact, their roofs whole, although sprouting grass and flowers and even a few small trees here and there. Ideal camouflage, Pavel realized. Even satellite sensors would detect nothing much except natural vegetation.

Focusing tighter, he could see dozens of men in the plaza, most of them in military fatigues, assault rifles slung over their shoulders. Some Kalishnikovs, he noted, but mostly American Colts and Springfields.

Some of the ancient buildings had new additions of corrugated metal and even cinder block. Always the roofs were covered with dirt and greenery. Men in jeans and T-shirts lounged around the largest one. Pavel saw another man in a white laboratory smock come out of a door, followed by three others—one of them a woman.

"Their processing factory is here," he muttered.

"Yeah," Jay replied. "But where're they keeping Kelly?"

All through the morning, as the sun climbed higher into a pale blue sky dotted with wisps of cirrus clouds, they took turns studying the city through the binoculars.

Slowly, by a process of elimination, they tried to determine where Shamar might be holding Kelly. Not in the factory, of course. Across the square was a smaller building where all the windows had been boarded up and a half-dozen armed guards lounged by the only door.

"Could that be it?" Pavel asked.

Jay brushed an insect away from his face. "My guess is that's the bomb-storage depot. And the building next to it, where the truck is parked, is probably their electronics facility."

Pointing to the temple at the head of the plaza, Pavel said, "She must be in there. None of the other buildings are guarded. Most of them are half destroyed."

Jay nodded agreement. "Plenty of guys with guns hanging around that entrance, too. How do we get in?"

"Through the back. It's only a few dozen meters from the trees to the rear of the platform. Can you climb the stones?"

"I guess, if I have to."

Pavel reached into the pack lying beside him and pulled out a coil of rope. "This will be helpful."

"Only if there's a door back there. Or a window."

They circled around the hollow, staying low, using the grass for cover, until they could train the binoculars on the rear of the temple.

Jay saw a dark oblong shape, focused the binocs on it. It wavered in the heat haze, then snapped into clear sight: a window, about ten feet above the floor of the stone platform. Unbarred. Unguarded.

Passing the glasses to Pavel, he murmured, "That's the way in."

The Russian nodded. "Let's go."

It was late afternoon by the time they reached the edge of the woods behind the temple. What had looked like a short distance to the stone base of the platform now seemed like a mile of terribly exposed open territory.

Both men were studded with tools and weapons from the pack Pavel had brought: ropes, grenades, knives, electron ics gear, pistols on their hips. Both men held machine pistols in their hands, long black ammo clips jutting from their grips.

"Come on," Jay whispered. "Hurry it up."

Pavel looked up from his kneeling position. He had spread a satchel full of antipersonnel mines along the ground at the edge of the trees, tiny gray plastic discs that could blow a man's feet off or shred his legs from ten meters' distance.

"This will cover our retreat," he whispered harshly. "It is necessary."

Jay knew he was right. The Russian had a lot more training in this kind of thing than he did, Jay knew. His own background consisted of a one-week course in guerrilla warfare, part of the mandatory training the Peacekeepers insisted upon. Not much. Would it be enough?

Finally Pavel was ready. Jay tossed the rope up to the twenty-foot-high tier of the platform. The electrochemical bonding agents in the grapnel at the end of the rope took hold of the ancient stone surface. Jay tested the rope with a hard pull, then started scrambling up the face of the stones. Pavel looked around one wary time, then followed him up the rope.

There were four tiers to the platform, and then they were at the base of the temple wall. Once more Jay flung the rope upward, this time into the dark cavity of the window. They scrambled up the rope and disappeared inside the ancient temple, the site of countless human sacrifices in centuries long past.

Down at the base of the platform a hidden stone door swung outward and four armed men dressed in ragged fatigues calmly walked out to the edge of the woods and began picking up the small gray disc-shaped antipersonnel mines that Pavel had so carefully scattered there to cover their retreat.

Gunfire broke out from inside the temple, booming,

echoing weirdly. The four men looked up briefly. One of them pointed a finger to his head and made a circular motion.

"*Los gringos hay muy loco, no?*"

His companions grinned. Then they returned to their task.

That scene was a re-creation, of course. A bit of dramatic license. We know some details of the ancient city and its temple from questioning the grave robbers who had been methodically looting Montesol until the drug manufacturers chose it as their headquarters. We assume that young Hazard and the Russian Zhakarov made the best use of the resources available to them. More than that we cannot say.

MONTESOL, ━━━
━━ Year 8

ALEXANDER stood on shaky legs as four men in dirty fatigues searched him. They pulled his arms out from his sides and roughly pawed his chest and midsection, his legs and groin, both arms. They even yanked off the bandage wrapped around his head, revealing a nasty wound along his left temple, a gash crusted with dried blood and oozing slightly with medication.

Jabal Shamar sat on a canvas camp chair some ten feet away, smoking a cigarette, watching Alexander intently with eyes that looked only faintly amused. Shamar wore a one-piece jumpsuit of mottled jungle greens, the shirt unbuttoned halfway down his hairy chest to reveal an oblong black box hanging by a silver chain about his neck. A silver-plated pistol was tucked into his black leather belt, invitingly.

The room was deep inside the Incan temple, solid-stone walls, floor polished smooth even after centuries of neglect. No windows. Only one door. Yet natural light seemed to be filtering through from some sort of hidden access up in the stone ceiling. Alexander tried to look up and see where the sunlight was coming from, but his head throbbed so hard that it made him woozy with pain.

"You must excuse the primitive way in which my men are searching you," Shamar said in his slightly guttural English. "We lack modern facilities such as X-ray machines and metal detectors."

The four years since he had last seen Shamar had not been kind to the man. His hair was almost entirely gray now, the scar along his jaw seemed more pronounced, harsher, almost as white as the cigarette that dangled from his thin lips. He was leaner, too, his face sculpted with hollowed planes and jutting cheekbones. Four years of running and hiding have taken its toll, Alexander told himself.

His head was pounding, his stomach doing nervous rollovers. Every nerve in his body was stretched taut. He had been forced to pull a gun on Alma Steiner before she would back away and allow him to leave the plane.

"You're mad," the blond Austrian had whispered, staring at the pistol Alexander held in his wavering hand.

"Maybe so," he admitted. "But I'll kill you if you don't get the fuck out of my way."

"He'll murder you!" she screamed. "He's probably already murdered Kelly."

Alexander tottered toward the helicopter Shamar had sent in response to his call. "Maybe so," he shouted over his shoulder. "But I've got to go. I've got no choice."

Alma understood, although she could not agree. Her tears were as much rage and frustration as mourning for a man she could have loved.

The helicopter crew had searched him before letting him come aboard, but now Shamar's personal guards were searching him again. Very thoroughly. But will it be thoroughly enough? Alexander asked himself. Unbidden, a shadow of a smile touched his lips. Standing there, even on legs rubbery from his concussion, Alexander loomed over the diminutive Shamar on his camp chair.

Finally they removed his boots and tossed them across the bare little room, where they had thrown the miniature radio transmitter and electrostatic stun wand he had carried inside his belt.

He stood on the cool stone floor, barefoot, beltless, wearing only a pair of light denim jeans and a long-sleeved sport shirt.

The four men backed away, leaving Alexander to stare down at the seated Shamar, radiating hatred.

"She is your daughter, isn't she?" Shamar asked.

Alexander nodded. "Where is she? I want to see her. If you've harmed her . . ." He suddenly stopped, realizing the words were totally empty. There was not a thing he could do to save Kelly from whatever harm Shamar wanted to inflict on her.

Taking the slim cigarette from his lips, Shamar asked calmly, "Have you learned to kill? The last time we met, you could have killed me, but failed to do so."

"That was four years ago."

"Yes, but some men lack the ability to take a human life. I myself have never killed a man in combat; not face-to-face."

"You just order others to kill for you."

"As you do," Shamar countered. "We are very much alike."

Alexander swayed on his feet, a wave of nausea and

dizziness washing over him. "Can I have a chair? They told me I've got a concussion . . ."

Shamar's eyes narrowed suspiciously. "You can sit on the floor. At my feet."

Alexander did so. Shamar seemed pleased to be able to look down at the American.

"So now what happens?" Alexander asked.

"Now you die."

"Not before I see my daughter."

"You will see her, I guarantee that."

The way he said it sent a chill along Alexander's spine. He tensed, his hands clenched into fists.

Lighting a fresh cigarette from the butt of the one he had been smoking, Shamar said, "Please do not think that you can leap up and disarm me. I know how your mind works, Cole Alexander. Remove all such romantic notions from your thoughts."

Alexander said nothing.

Fingering the slim oblong black box hanging around his neck, Shamar said, "Do you know what this is? I will tell you. It is a radio trigger for the nuclear bombs that my technicians have assembled. It is tuned to my heartbeat. If by some strange chance you should kill me, it will set off the bombs. Everyone here will die. Everyone."

"Including Hazard and Zhakarov," Alexander muttered.

"Hazard?" Shamar's slim brows rose in surprise.

"The son of the IPF's director-general."

Shamar let a thin jet of blue-gray smoke stream from his lips. "I did not realize he was Hazard's son."

"Was?" Alexander felt startled.

"They are both dead," said Shamar. "Brave men, to try to rescue the woman. But foolish, also. They fought to the death. They killed more than a dozen of the drug merchant's hired men. They nearly fought their way to the very room where your daughter is being kept."

"Both dead." Alexander bowed his head. "Both of them."

"They would not surrender. Even after they had been wounded repeatedly, they fought on. I would have treated them mercifully."

"Sure you would."

"I am a soldier," snapped Shamar, "not a cutthroat."

"Go tell it in Jerusalem."

"What I do I do for a cause! You may not believe in my cause, but I do. Millions do!"

"You're nothing but a bloodthirsty murdering son of a bitch." Alexander started to clamber to his feet. The four men behind him stirred, gripped their guns.

But Shamar merely smiled and tapped the tiny box on his chest. "Be careful, Cole Alexander. If my heart should stop, this entire mountaintop explodes."

Alexander sagged back to the floor, his head thundering. Shamar smiled at him pityingly.

Finally Alexander asked, "Aren't you being a little too dramatic about this? Triggering the bombs to your heartbeat? You've got a couple hundred people here protecting you and you know I'm no killer."

With a sardonic laugh Shamar tapped the electronic medallion and replied, "This is not because of you, Cole Alexander! I have no need of such elaborate precautions as far as you are concerned." His face grew more serious. "But I know that you have recruited a small army of mercenaries. Professional soldiers. *They* could cause much trouble. Therefore this little challenge for them. Once they know that I am willing to blow up the entire top of this mountain, I doubt that they will even try to attack. They fight for money, and they will see no reason to march into guaranteed death. I am willing to die; they are not."

Alexander had to admit to himself that Shamar was entirely right. Once the mercenaries realized the nukes were rigged with a dead-man's switch, they'd pack up their gear and go home. Hell, he told himself, once they realize I won't be around to pay them they'll call the whole operation off.

"You see, Cole Alexander," said Shamar, "I am a dedicated, *professional* soldier. A true military man, willing to sacrifice my life to my cause. You are an amateur; you are driven by emotion, not logic. And you value your life too highly to be truly effective."

Alexander made no reply.

"You have bungled everything," Shamar went on. "All your efforts have led to your defeat and humiliation."

"Seems to me you've gone to a lot of trouble over my bungling efforts," Alexander retorted.

"Oh, you have been troublesome. I grant you that. But today I will remove your slight irritation and go forward with my plans."

"To what end?" Alexander asked, his voice hoarse, choked. "Just what in hell are you trying to obtain?"

"Power, of course. That is the only goal worth pursuing. Power. Without power a man is nothing. But *with* power, ahh." Shamar's smile widened to show his perfect teeth. "With power comes wealth, and respect. A man of power can go where he wishes and do what he wants."

"And your cause?" Alexander asked dryly.

"What is more vital to my cause than power, real power? The power to bend nations to my will. The power to exterminate the Peacekeepers."

Alexander made himself laugh. "With five little nukes?"

"Five nuclear weapons are quite enough—for a start," replied Shamar. "Three of them will level Geneva." His smile faded, his voice became harsher. "I had hoped that the Peacekeepers would believe they had located my weapons in Washington and those other cities, but your prying fools canceled that plan." He took a deep pull on his cigarette. The acrid smell made Alexander realize that it contained more than tobacco.

"However," Shamar went on, "three small planes piloted by three zealots will obliterate Geneva soon enough. The two other major Peacekeeper facilities, in Colombo and Ottawa, will receive one nuclear kiss each."

"That won't eliminate the IPF," Alexander said.

"Of course it will! They will be blown off the face of the Earth. Think of how many nations will welcome that moment. Think how many will flock to me, to form a new coalition of true *power*." Shamar clenched his fist and held it up before his face. The scar along his jaw seemed to glow. "There will be no Peacekeepers to stop us."

"Then the world will go back to the way it was, with every nation building all the weapons it can."

"Yes. Including nuclear weapons. And I will lead the nations of the southern hemisphere—my own lands of the desert, together with most of Latin America and Africa. We will bring the industrialized nations of the north to their knees!" Shamar's eyes glittered with the vision of it.

"Or blow up the world trying."

"What of it? I am ready to die. Are you?"

"Not before I see my daughter," Alexander said.

"Ah yes, your daughter." The gleaming light in his eyes disappeared like a lamp being switched off.

"You promised that she'd be released if I came to you. I want to see her before you let her go."

Shamar gestured to his men, and Alexander was hauled roughly to his feet.

"This way." Shamar ducked through the low stone doorway. The guards hustled Alexander through after him, into a narrow dark passageway. It was difficult to see, but Alexander felt a dampness, a slimy dank chill seeping from the stones. Like an old-fashioned dungeon, he thought. The passageway sloped upward, climbing.

"I actually had intended to seize you, not the young woman," Shamar said. "If I had sent my own men they would have done the job correctly. But these drug gangs—" Alexander could sense the man shrugging. "They are nothing but common thugs. They botched it."

"Well, I'm here now," he said to the shadowy form walking ahead of him.

"Yes, that is true. For more than four years you have troubled me, Cole Alexander. You are a fanatic, just as I am. And therefore very persistent and annoying. Today I will eliminate you. Tonight I will sleep more soundly than I have in four years."

"I'm flattered to think I've kept you awake."

Shamar did not reply. They strode along the narrow passageway. Alexander felt the grip of the guards on his upper arms, half helping him along, half pushing him along.

"This coalition of southern hemisphere nations," he called to Shamar's back. "Won't they be at the mercy of the industrialized nations once the Peacekeepers are gone? After all, it's the nations of the north that have nuclear weapons."

Again he could sense Shamar's reaction: a self-satisfied little smile. "Cole Alexander, once the Peacekeepers are gone, how long do you think it will take Brazil or Argentina or even my own native Iraq to build nuclear weapons? We have the capability. Once the restraints of the Peacekeepers have been lifted, we will build bombs within a few months."

And the world goes back to the edge of Armageddon, Alexander said to himself.

He heard voices up ahead, arguing loudly in Spanish. They were speaking much too fast for Alexander to catch more than a few words: it was an argument about money. Something to do with a shipment of "goods"—narcotics, he guessed.

But one of the voices sounded vaguely familiar. Alexander tried to identify it as they marched along the passageway.

Light spilled out from a room up ahead. The voices were coming from there. Shamar passed without even glancing inside; the arguments among the drug dealers were of no interest to him.

But Alexander looked as the guards half dragged him past the open doorway set into the massive stones. It was Sebastiano Miguel de Castanada, son of the *presidente*, minister of defense, his face red with anger, his impeccably tailored white suit rumpled and stained with perspiration, bellowing at a sallow, skinny, ragged little man who sat behind a table snarling back at Castanada. On the table between them were piles of money, neatly stacked and wrapped with dirty elastic bands. In that one glance into the room Alexander recognized that one pile was American currency, another French francs. There were at least a dozen stacks on the table. The American seemed to be the highest.

Alexander's heart sank. The breath sagged out of him. So Castanada's in with them! It's been a trap all along. This entire operation has been nothing more than an elaborate snare to catch me. The Castanada family has been working with Shamar and these drug merchants all along. There's been no war between them; they're on the same side. Shamar used Castanada to lure me up here. The only fight between them is over how big a cut of the money Castanada's entitled to!

And I walked into it. Like a fucking lamb going to the slaughter. I got Hazard and the Russian kid killed. And Kelly—what have they done to Kelly?

He wanted to cry. He wanted to scream. If his arms had been free he might have tried to kill himself.

It's my fault. It's all my own stupid, blind, arrogant fault. As they hustled him along the dark endless passageway, Alexander knew that he had been beaten and nothing awaited him but death.

If I can get Kelly out of this, that's all I can hope for. To get her away from here. To see her safe. That's the most I can do. That's _all_ I can do.

The little procession finally stopped. Alexander peered into the darkness and saw that they were at a tightly bolted wooden door.

"Your daughter is in here." Shamar's voice was strangely tight, low.

The guards released their grip on Alexander's arms. One of them unbolted the door and swung it open. The room inside was small, but lit by a narrow slit of a window. Late afternoon sunlight slanted in, blood red.

Kelly lay on the floor, unmoving.

We know about Shamar's plan to attack Geneva and the other IPF centers from interrogations of suspects arrested in Bogotá and elsewhere in the wake of the Valledupar fiasco. The dead-man's switch that Shamar wore around his neck was actually constructed by a Pakistani electronics technician who was picked up in London on a narcotics charge. We got the story on Alexander from Alma Steiner and Barker, the crippled pilot. It took months to sort out all the details, of course. More than a year, as a matter of fact. We are still not certain of exactly every point, and there is considerable pressure from several sources not to investigate it further. I pursue whatever leads I can lay my hand on, for reasons of personal curiosity and professional pride. The complete story will never get into the official IPF history. But I can tell it here as completely and honestly as I can, if you will continue to grant me a modicum of artistic license.

MONTESOL,
Year 8

SHE lay on the stone floor in that awkward grotesque sprawl of death, beyond dignity, beyond shame, beyond help.

Alexander sagged to his knees, bile burning in his throat. Alongside Kelly's body lay Jay Hazard and Pavel, riddled with bullets, crusted with blood. Their eyes stared sightlessly at the stone ceiling of the sunlit chamber. Buzzing flies and other insects crawled over them.

Someone had closed Kelly's eyes. Most of her clothing was torn off. Welts made by men's strong fingers purpled her thighs, her arms, her face.

She's so little! Alexander sobbed to himself. So tiny and frail. My baby . . . my baby.

"I wanted you to see this," Shamar said. Alexander heard him as if from a long distance away. His voice echoed hollowly, like someone calling from far down a narrow stone tunnel. "This is your fault, Cole Alexander, not mine."

Alexander turned his head slightly. "My fault?"

"If you had not pursued me, if you had not made yourself dangerous to me, this would never have happened. *You* killed these people. You caused your daughter's death."

Alexander said nothing. He remained on his knees beside Kelly's crumpled body, as if there was no strength left in him.

"And now you must die," said Shamar.

Running a hand through his white hair, Alexander muttered, "Go ahead. You've killed everyone I care for. Killing me will be a relief."

Shamar turned and spoke to the guards at the open doorway. One of them nodded and left. The other remained at the door, his face as cold and immobile as the stones of the walls.

"The natives of these hills make a poison that they use in hunting. It comes from the same plant that produces the cocaine."

"I know," said Alexander. "It kills you quickly, while the cocaine can take years to do it."

With a grim smile, Shamar said, "It is painless, I am told."

"That's what I've been told, too."

Alexander brushed at his hair again. This time he reached back for the slim glass blade taped to his spine just below the collar of his shirt. Yanking it free, he lunged with every ounce of strength left in him at his surprised enemy.

Shamar's eyes went wide and his arm automatically went up to block Alexander's feeble blow. But Alexander slashed with the glass knife and opened a cut in the meaty part of the man's forearm, through the sleeve of his fatigues.

With his other hand Shamar slapped Alexander a stinging blow on the side of the face that sent him toppling to the floor. The knife dropped and shattered against the stones into dozens of fragments of green glittering glass.

His head reeling, ears ringing, Alexander looked up to see the guard leveling his rifle at him. Shamar held his left arm up, peering at the bleeding scratch.

"That was stupid, Cole Alexander. You are no fighter. Even when you work up the passion to try to kill, you botch the job."

Alexander slowly, painfully sat up and clutched his knees with both arms. "Botched it, did I? How long does it take for the natives' poison to work?"

Shamar stared at him, mouth agape.

"I told you I knew about it. It's painless. A nerve poison. Starts at the area of the wound and works its way through the nervous system, from what the professors at the university told me."

"You're mad!"

Alexander laughed at him. "You've got about a minute to live, friend. Maybe less."

"But—the bombs!" Shamar's voice was a terrified rat's squeak. He clutched at the oblong black box hanging on the chain around his neck. Clutched at it with his unwounded arm.

"You made a couple of serious mistakes," Alexander said, his smile twisting viciously. "You were so fucking convinced I'm a gutless coward that you didn't think I'd try to kill you, even after you showed me what you did to my daughter."

"The bombs will explode if I die! You will be killing yourself!" Shamar pawed at Alexander's shirtfront with one hand, trying to lift him to his feet. But his own legs collapsed and he was suddenly on the floor, too, eye-to-eye with Alexander.

"And you also thought," Alexander went on, ignoring his frenzied bleating, "that you and your kind are the only ones willing to die for their cause. You depended on that little piece of ego-inflation too much, pal. There are plenty of men like me who'd gladly die to rid the world of the likes of you."

"You've killed us all!" Shamar whimpered. He was choking now, gasping for air. He ripped the electronic medallion from his chest and stared at it with fear-crazed eyes.

"So you're afraid to die, after all," Alexander said calmly. His smile was a terrible thing to see.

"You . . . madman . . ."

"Think of this as an environmental action. I'm cleaning up a source of pollution."

A few hundred meters away a radio receiver lost the signal that had been steadily beamed to it for more than forty-eight hours. The simple electronic switch attached to the receiver clicked, and the equally simple trigger controlling five nuclear weapons fired. Hemispherical shells of plutonium were slammed together. In less than a microsecond they achieved criticality and underwent five simultaneous chain reactions. The incredible power of the strong nuclear force was liberated in an explosion that shook seismographs as far away as Boston and Buenos Aires.

The explosion took off the entire top of the mountain. The ancient Incan city was simply vaporized. It was a particularly dirty mushroom cloud: millions of tons of radioactive rock and soil were lifted into the stratosphere and wafted across the mountainous forests where the natives eked out their meager incomes by cultivating the particular species of coca bush from which cocaine is derived.

With the help of the Peacekeepers most of those poor families were evacuated and saved from the fallout. Their crops did not fare so well. The area is still a desert today, and will be for many years to come. The farmers were resettled in safer areas, under careful supervision. Satellite sensors watch for the signature of *Erythroxylon coca,* and IPF inspectors make frequent tours of areas where it might be grown—as well as parts of the world where the opium poppy grows.

Cole Alexander's final act accomplished his goal: the Peacekeepers now actively pursue international narcotics dealers and have the reluctant approval of the world's national governments to strike at the source of the drug trade: the fields where the plants are grown. Satellites search for them; genetically specific biological agents sprayed from IPF planes destroy them.

The Castanada government, deprived of its prime source of cash income, collapsed within months. President Alfonso Jorje de Castanada suffered a fatal heart attack just after he was thrown out of office. His

friends say the loss of his son at Montesol
left him bereft and led to his demise; his
enemies say it was the loss of political
power and privilege; cynics say it was the
loss of money from the drug trade that
stopped his heart.

All that happened four years ago. Which
brings us to the morning trek up from the
steaming jungle base of the International
Peacekeeping Force to the glassy crater of
what was once Montesol.

MONTESOL CRATER, — Year 12

I have never been to the Moon, but the crater makes me think of what that airless, waterless ball of rock must look like.

It was a scene of utter desolation. There was nothing before us except bare stone glazed and glittering under the bright cloudless sky. The wind rushed by, keening softly almost like a mourner's dirge, without a tree or a shrub or even a blade of grass to be moved by it. There was absolutely nothing on what was left of this mountaintop except the hard lifeless rock, still so radioactive four years after the explosion that our time here was limited to one hour.

Thirty-one of us, panting with exertion and altitude, the

officers' uniforms and cadets' fatigues equally darkened with great pools of sweat, stood at the lip of the glass-smooth crater and stared at whatever private demons haunted us.

I thought of my lost hand and felt bitterly glad that the Indians and Pakistanis had not attacked our little Peace-keeping task force with nuclear weapons. I had my life, my family, my new work as archivist. The prosthetic hand had become almost natural to me. And new models with improved sensitivity were being developed.

Then I looked across the lip of the crater at Director-General Hazard. The old man stood motionless, his back stiff and shoulders squared away. The bright sun was forcing him to squint as he stared into the crater, but the cool mountain wind could not ruffle his short-cropped iron-gray hair.

A man can sense when someone is staring at him, and I stared hard at Hazard. He did not look up. He did not move. His son had died here, and he stood alone amongst the thirty of us, squinting against the sunlight and the pain.

I heard a foreign sound carried by the softly wailing breeze. A mechanical sound. A motor purring from some distance away. Looking up, I saw a dark speck against the clean blue sky. It quickly grew to recognizable size: a small helicopter, painted in the sky-blue and gold of the IPF.

The cadets and other officers turned their eyes skyward. All except Hazard, who still stared blindly into the crater.

The helicopter circled us at a respectful altitude, then came down and settled onto the bare slope that had once born thick tropical growth. Its whining rotor kicked up dust as it touched the ground lightly and then sank on its shock struts. The rotor slowed until once again the only sound we could hear was the keening mountain wind.

When the rotor stopped altogether, the oval hatch of the helicopter opened and a huge man stepped stiffly onto the dusty ground.

Red Eagle. He walked slowly toward us; age had not diminished him, but it had taken its toll of his agility. He wore a fringed tan leather jacket and faded jeans. His feet were shod in a modern variation of moccasins. I almost smiled, despite the somber tone of the occasion. Red Eagle was going native in his latter years. I wondered what he wore beneath his judge's robes in Washington.

The major at Hazard's elbow leaned slightly toward the director-general and whispered briefly into his ear. Hazard stirred, almost seemed to shake himself, as if trying to throw off an evil dream. He took a deep breath and resolutely turned his back on the crater to march forward and extend his hand to Red Eagle.

They spoke together for a few moments, and then Hazard waved the cadets to gather around the giant Amerind.

"I don't really have to tell you who our guest is," Hazard said in his rasping voice. "It is a great honor for me to introduce to you the Honorable Harold Red Eagle, Justice of the United States Supreme Court and spiritual founder of the International Peacekeeping Force."

If Red Eagle thought Hazard's introduction too fulsome, or not fulsome enough, he gave no indication. He shook hands gravely with each of the cadets and officers, including me. He noticed my prosthesis, of course, and looked deeply into my eyes as he engulfed it in his huge hand. He said not a word, except to murmur my name, yet those eyes of his told me of all the sorrow and understanding that a truly great man can offer to one of his fellow sufferers.

Once he had met each individual among us, Red Eagle raised his voice to address us all. It was as if the wind had stopped; his deep, majestic voice was all that we could hear.

"Ladies and gentlemen, I did not mean to intrude on your exercise, but I could not resist the temptation of joining you here, at this special place.

"You are the first class to be graduated from the Peace-keeping Academy. The future safety of the world and all its people will be in your young, strong hands—a heavy responsibility, I know. In my own lifetime I have carried a share of that responsibility. I gladly pass the burden on to you."

He glanced at their young faces, the variations in skin tone, in eye and hair color, in shape and bone structure. He saw the flags that each cadet wore on his or her shoulder.

"As Peacekeepers you have only one goal: to protect the peace. No matter what race or nationality you may be, no matter your religion or your politics, your task as a Peacekeeper is to do whatever must be done to preserve and protect world peace. Whatever must be done."

Red Eagle seemed to look past them for a brief moment, toward the crater. Was he seeing Alexander's face smiling sardonically at him?

He returned his attention to the young cadets grouped before him.

"You have come from many different nations, from many different parts of this globe. I ask you now, each and all of you, to stop thinking of yourselves as Koreans, or Brazilians, or Poles, or Ugandans. I ask you to think of yourselves as human beings, as members of the great family of humankind, as Peacekeepers dedicated to protecting our world and our people—all of them. Each of them.

"The age of nationalism has passed. Nations still exist, I know, as they will continue to exist for many generations to come. But the *idea* of nationalism is fading. Inside many nations, local ethnic or religious or geographic minorities want autonomy. And modern technology is erasing the very meaning of national borders. The world's economy is an integrated, global interrelationship. The vast funds once spent on armaments are beginning to help the less-developed nations to feed and educate and house their poor. We are expanding into space, and bringing new treasures of knowledge and energy to Earth.

"We are a global family. We will grow and thrive—if we can remain at peace with one another. Yours is the task of preserving and protecting the peace. You must make certain that the devastation that took place on this mountaintop is never repeated—*never*—anywhere in the world."

Red Eagle raised both arms and gestured toward the barren crater. The cadets slowly turned and gazed at it with new eyes.

"Think of this lifeless devastation as the site of *your* home, your village or town or city. That is your responsibility: to make certain that such inhuman destruction will not take the lives of those you hold dearest."

I could feel the emotional response from the cadets. Red Eagle was electrifying them, like a shaman of old preparing his clan for battle.

"I ask you once again, therefore, to stop thinking of yourselves as representatives of a single nation and begin to look upon yourselves as members of the great and unified human race."

There was a long moment of utter silence. Not even the breeze made a sound. Then one of the women cadets reached up to the flag of her shoulder patch and tugged at one corner of it. It yielded slowly, reluctantly; it had been firmly sewn into place. But with determination that gritted her teeth, she ripped it free.

One by one, and then all of them together, the cadets removed the emblems of their nations until the entire class of them wore nothing but their identifications as Peacekeepers.

REFLECTIONS,
Year 12

T HE last nuclear weapons on Earth were destroyed earlier this year. The Peacekeepers have established close ties with the world's scientific organizations and we keep particularly careful eyes on any work that might lead to weapons of mass destruction—nuclear, chemical, or biological. The system is far from foolproof, but it seems to be working.

The scourge of war is receding into history, like other diseases that have been conquered by advancing knowledge and social consciousness.

Would all this have happened without Red Eagle? Would it have happened without Hazard or Cole Alexander's dogged hunt for Jabal Shamar? Yes, I believe it would have, sooner or later. Perhaps it would have taken another nuclear war. Perhaps hundreds of millions would have had to perish before the nations accepted the fact that war had to be stopped altogether. There are no inevitabilities to history. There are no indispensable men.

But it happened the way I have told it. The world's attention has shifted away from the problems of war, now that the Peacekeepers have proved that war can be stopped. The irony is that the stronger the Peacekeepers become, the less likely they are to be needed.

The problems facing the world today are the ancient enemies of humanity: poverty, hunger and ignorance. And at least one fairly new one: narcotics. Alexander was right in the sense that the narcotics trade is a global problem that cannot be solved by individual nations. The Peacekeepers are helping to orchestrate a global solution—while naysayers point trembling fingers and warn that the IPF is turning into a world dictatorship.

But that's another story. Perhaps someday I will write it, too. For now, I must start the official history of the International Peacekeeping Force. It will be factual, enormously detailed, and quite dull. But once it is finished I can turn to the *real* stories of the men and women who work to make a reality of the prophecy of Isaiah, the motto of the International Peacekeeping Force:

NATION SHALL NOT LIFT UP SWORD AGAINST NATION

BEN BOVA

☐	53217-1	THE ASTRAL MIRROR	$2.95
☐	53218-X		Canada $3.50
☐	53202-3	BATTLE STATION	$3.50
☐	53203-1		Canada $4.50
☐	53212-0	ESCAPE PLUS	$2.95
☐	53213-9		Canada $3.50
☐	53215-5	ORION	$3.50
☐	53216-3		Canada $3.95
☐	53161-2	VENGEANCE OF ORION	$3.95
☐	53162-0		Canada $4.95
☐	53210-4	OUT OF THE SUN	$2.95
☐	53211-2		Canada $3.50
☐	53205-8	PRIVATEERS	$3.95
☐	53204-X		Canada $4.95
☐	53219-8	PROMETHEANS	$2.95
☐	53220-1		Canada $3.75
☐	53208-2	TEST OF FIRE	$2.95
☐	53209-0		Canada $3.50
☐	53206-6	VOYAGERS II: THE ALIEN WITHIN	$3.50
☐	53207-4		Canada $4.50
☐	53225-2	THE MULTIPLE MAN	$2.95
☐	53226-0		Canada $3.95
☐	53245-7	COLONY	$3.95
☐	53246-5		Canada $4.95
☐	53243-0	THE KINSMAN SAGA	$4.95
☐	53244-9		Canada $5.95
☐	53231-7	THE STARCROSSED	$2.95
☐	53232-5		Canada $3.95
☐	53227-9	WINDS OF ALTAIR	$3.95
☐	53228-7		Canada $4.95

THE BEST IN SCIENCE FICTION

☐	54989-9	STARFIRE by Paul Preuss	$3.95
☐	54990-2		Canada $4.95
☐	54281-9	DIVINE ENDURANCE by Gwyneth Jones	$3.95
☐	54282-7		Canada $4.95
☐	55696-8	THE LANGUAGES OF PAO by Jack Vance	$3.95
☐	55697-6		Canada $4.95
☐	54892-2	THE THIRTEENTH MAJESTRAL by Hayford Peirce	$3.95
☐	54893-0		Canada $4.95
☐	55425-6	THE CRYSTAL EMPIRE by L. Neil Smith	$4.50
☐	55426-4		Canada $5.50
☐	53133-7	THE EDGE OF TOMORROW by Isaac Asimov	$3.95
☐	53134-5		Canada $4.95
☐	55800-6	FIRECHILD by Jack Williamson	$3.95
☐	55801-4		Canada $4.95
☐	54592-3	TERRY'S UNIVERSE ed. by Beth Meacham	$3.50
☐	54593-1		Canada $4.50
☐	53355-0	ENDER'S GAME by Orson Scott Card	$3.95
☐	53356-9		Canada $4.95
☐	55413-2	HERITAGE OF FLIGHT by Susan Shwartz	$3.95
☐	55414-0		Canada $4.95

Buy them at your local bookstore or use this handy coupon:
Clip and mail this page with your order.

Publishers Book and Audio Mailing Service
P.O. Box 120159, Staten Island, NY 10312-0004

Please send me the book(s) I have checked above. I am enclosing $_____
(please add $1.25 for the first book, and $.25 for each additional book to
cover postage and handling. Send check or money order only—no CODs.)

Name _____

Address _____

City _____ State/Zip _____

Please allow six weeks for delivery. Prices subject to change without notice.

THE TOR DOUBLES

Two complete short science fiction novels in one volume!

- ☐ 53362-3 A MEETING WITH MEDUSA by Arthur C. Clarke and $2.95
  55967-3 GREEN MARS by Kim Stanley Robinson   Canada $3.95

- ☐ 55971-1 HARDFOUGHT by Greg Bear and $2.95
  55951-7 CASCADE POINT by Timothy Zahn   Canada $3.95

- ☐ 55952-5 BORN WITH THE DEAD by Robert Silverberg and $2.95
  55953-3 THE SALIVA TREE by Brian W. Aldiss   Canada $3.95

- ☐ 55956-8 TANGO CHARLIE AND FOXTROT ROMEO $2.95
  55957-6 by John Varley and   Canada $3.95
  THE STAR PIT by Samuel R. Delany

- ☐ 55958-4 NO TRUCE WITH KINGS by Poul Anderson and $2.95
  55954-1 SHIP OF SHADOWS by Fritz Leiber   Canada $3.95

- ☐ 55963-0 ENEMY MINE by Barry B. Longyear and $2.95
  54302-5 ANOTHER ORPHAN by John Kessel   Canada $3.95

- ☐ 54554-0 SCREWTOP by Vonda N. McIntyre and $2.95
  55959-2 THE GIRL WHO WAS PLUGGED IN   Canada $3.95
  by James Tiptree, Jr.

THE BEST IN FANTASY

☐ 53954-0 SPIRAL OF FIRE by Deborah Turner Harris $3.95
  53955-9 Canada $4.95

☐ 53401-8 NEMESIS by Louise Cooper (U.S. only) $3.95

☐ 53382-8 SHADOW GAMES by Glen Cook $3.95
  53381-X Canada $4.95

☐ 53815-5 CASTING FORTUNE by John M. Ford $3.95
  53826-1 Canada $4.95

☐ 53351-8 HART'S HOPE by Orson Scott Card $3.95
  53352-6 Canada $4.95

☐ 53397-6 MIRAGE by Louise Cooper (U.S. only) $3.95

☐ 53671-1 THE DOOR INTO FIRE by Diane Duane $2.95
  53672-X Canada $3.50

☐ 54902-3 A GATHERING OF GARGOYLES by Meredith Ann Pierce $2.95
  54903-1 Canada $3.50

☐ 55614-3 JINIAN STAR-EYE by Sheri S. Tepper $2.95
  55615-1 Canada $3.75

Buy them at your local bookstore or use this handy coupon:
Clip and mail this page with your order.

Publishers Book and Audio Mailing Service
P.O. Box 120159, Staten Island, NY 10312-0004

Please send me the book(s) I have checked above. I am enclosing $_____
(please add $1.25 for the first book, and $.25 for each additional book to
cover postage and handling. Send check or money order only—no CODs.)

Name _____

Address _____

City _____ State/Zip _____

Please allow six weeks for delivery. Prices subject to change without notice.